GIDEON FALLS THE PENTOCULUS

Jeff Lemire
Andrea Sorrentino

with colors by:
Dave Stewart

lettering and design by:
Steve Wands

and edited by:
Will Dennis

GIDEON
FALLS

LAYOUT & PRODUCTION BY RYAN BREWER

IMAGE COMICS, INC. • **Robert Kirkman**: Chief Operating Officer • **Erik Larsen**: Chief Financial Officer • **Todd McFarlane**: President • **Marc Silvestri**: Chief Executive Officer • **Jim Valentino**: Vice President • **Eric Stephenson**: Publisher / Chief Creative Officer • **Jeff Boison**: Director of Publishing Planning & Book Trade Sales • **Chris Ross**: Director of Digital Services • **Jeff Stang**: Director of Direct Market Sales • **Kat Salazar**: Director of PR & Marketing • **Drew Gill**: Cover Editor • **Heather Doornink**: Production Director • **Nicole Lapalme**: Controller • **IMAGECOMICS.COM**

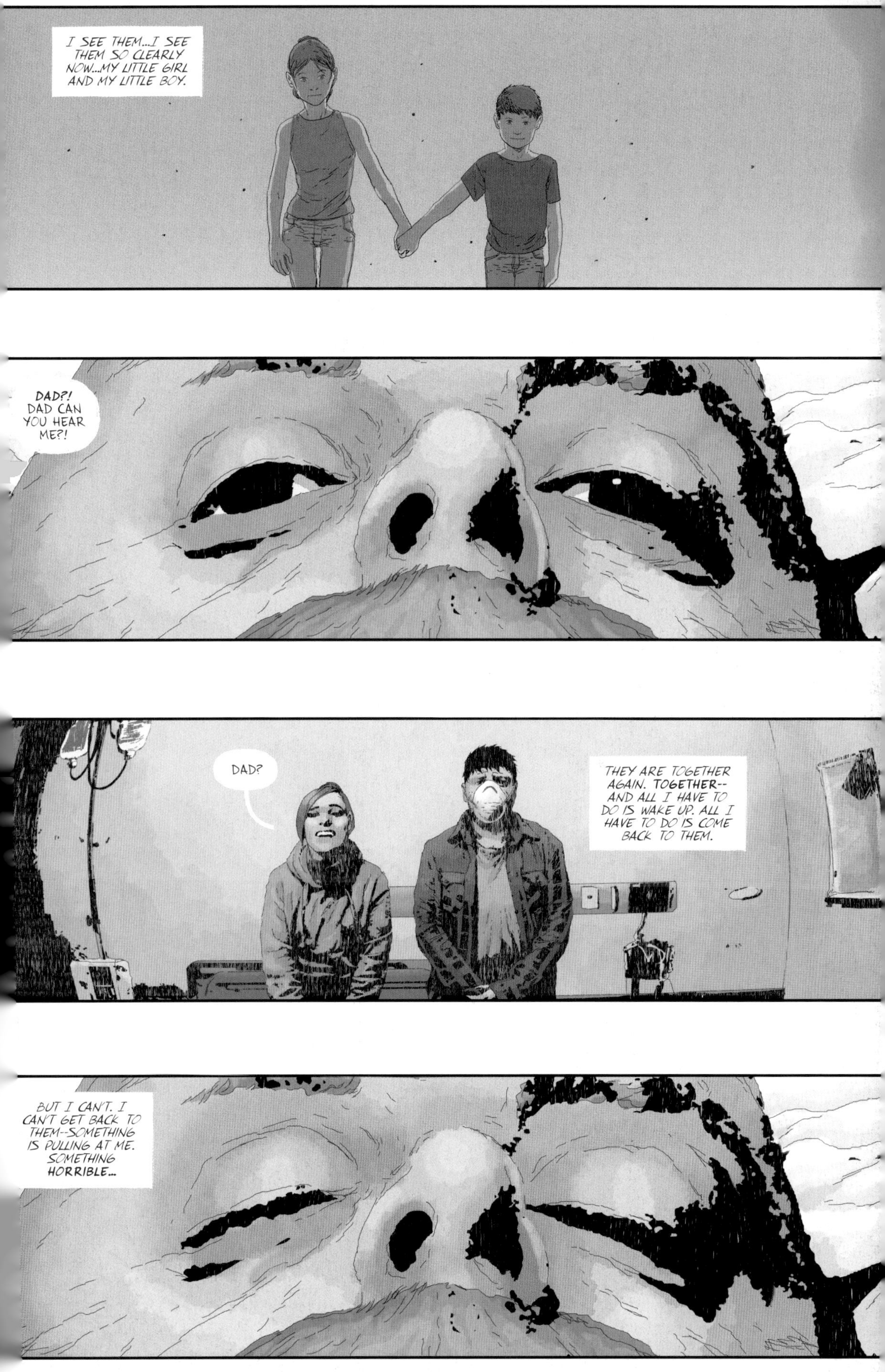
I SEE THEM...I SEE THEM SO CLEARLY NOW...MY LITTLE GIRL AND MY LITTLE BOY.
DAD?! DAD CAN YOU HEAR ME?!
DAD?
THEY ARE TOGETHER AGAIN. TOGETHER-- AND ALL I HAVE TO DO IS WAKE UP. ALL I HAVE TO DO IS COME BACK TO THEM.
BUT I CAN'T. I CAN'T GET BACK TO THEM--SOMETHING IS PULLING AT ME. SOMETHING HORRIBLE...

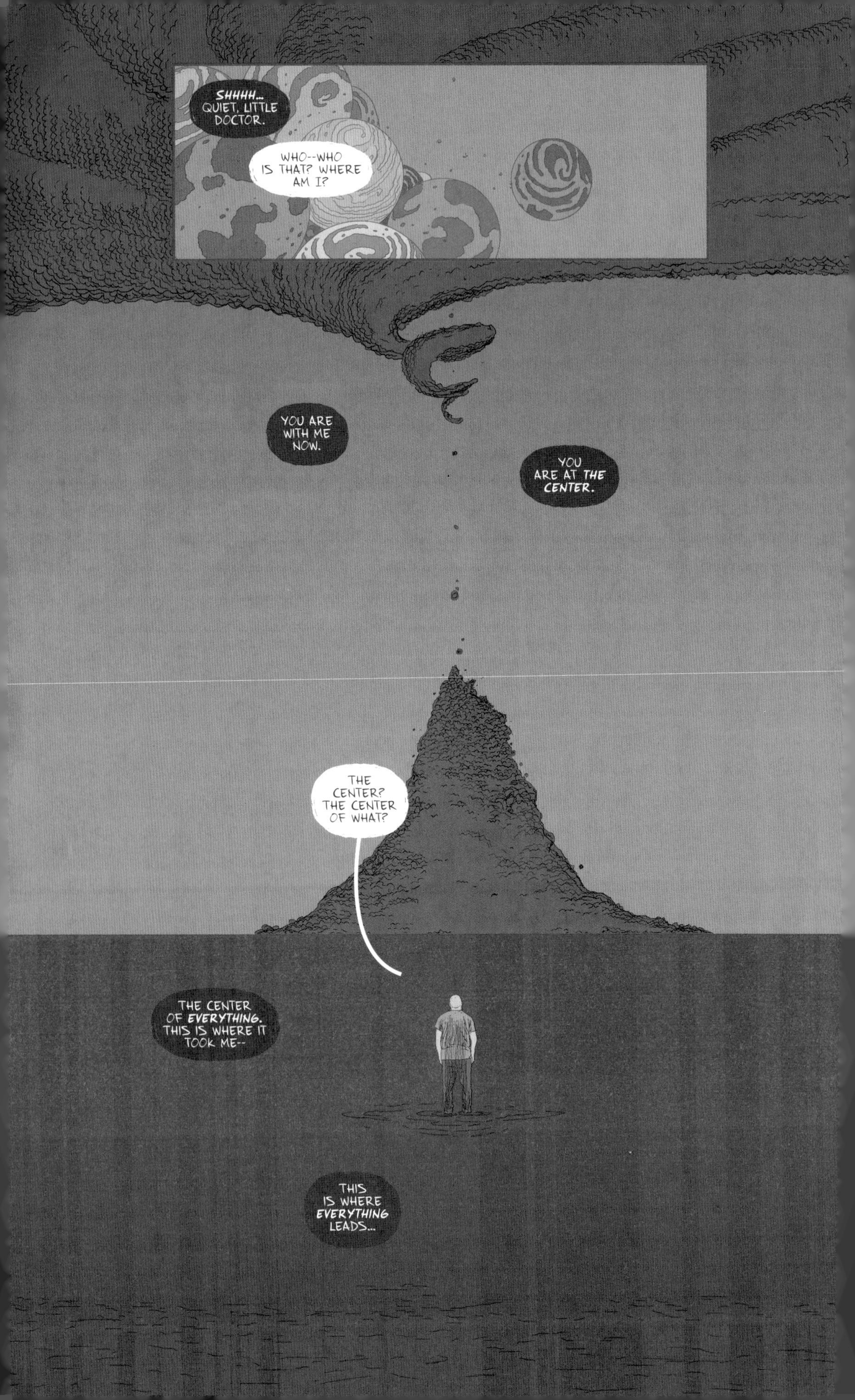
SHHHH... QUIET, LITTLE DOCTOR.
WHO--WHO IS THAT? WHERE AM I?
YOU ARE WITH ME NOW.
YOU ARE AT THE CENTER.
THE CENTER? THE CENTER OF WHAT?
THE CENTER OF EVERYTHING. THIS IS WHERE IT TOOK ME--
THIS IS WHERE EVERYTHING LEADS...

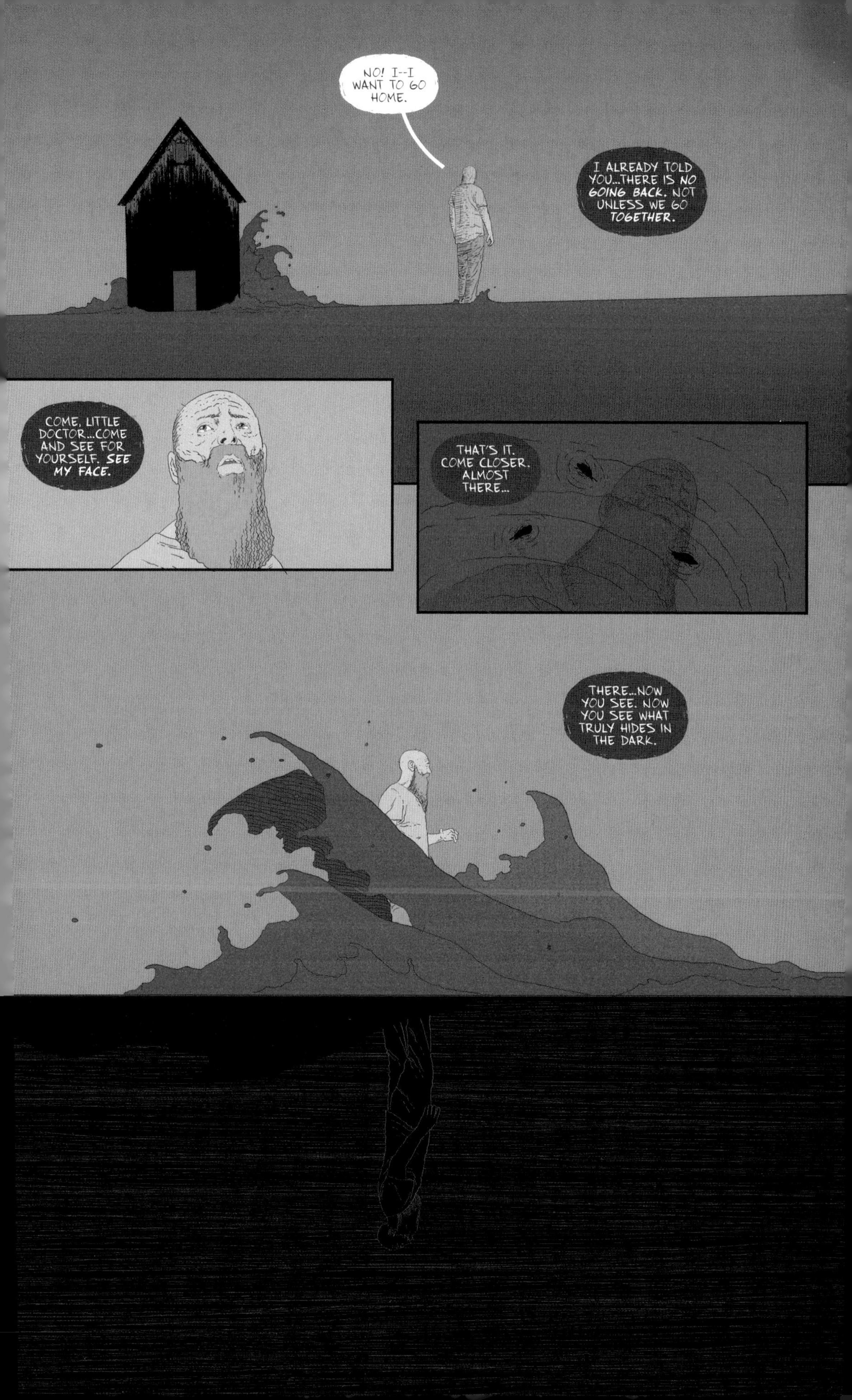
NO! I--I WANT TO GO HOME.
I ALREADY TOLD YOU...THERE IS NO GOING BACK. NOT UNLESS WE GO TOGETHER.
COME, LITTLE DOCTOR...COME AND SEE FOR YOURSELF. SEE MY FACE.
THAT'S IT. COME CLOSER. ALMOST THERE...
THERE...NOW YOU SEE. NOW YOU SEE WHAT TRULY HIDES IN THE DARK.

YOU SEE...
YOU SEE ME NOW.

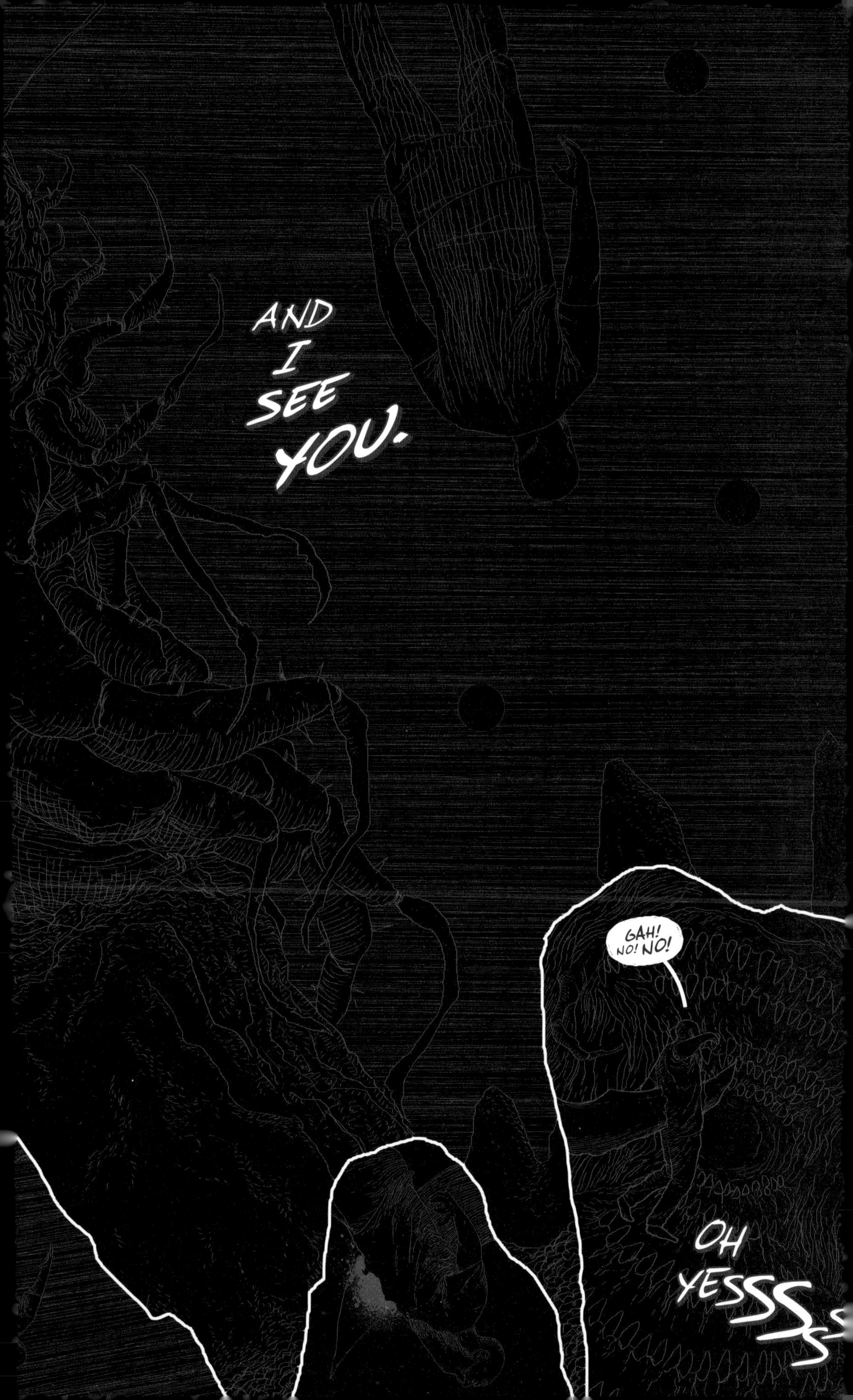
AND I SEE YOU.
GAH! NO! NO!
OH YESSSSS

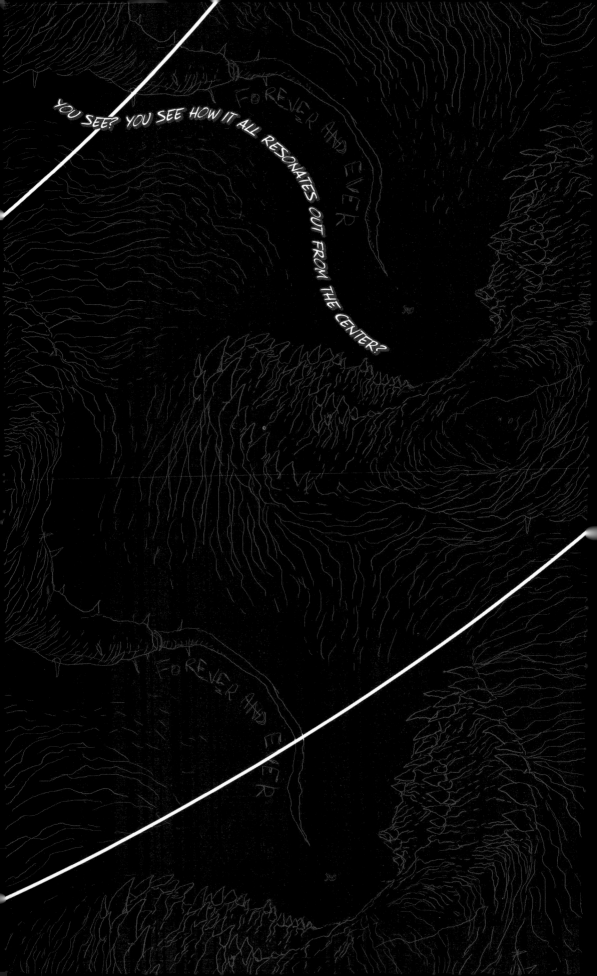

YOU SEE? YOU SEE HOW IT ALL RESONATES OUT FROM THE CENTER?

FOREVER AND EVER

FOREVER AND EVER

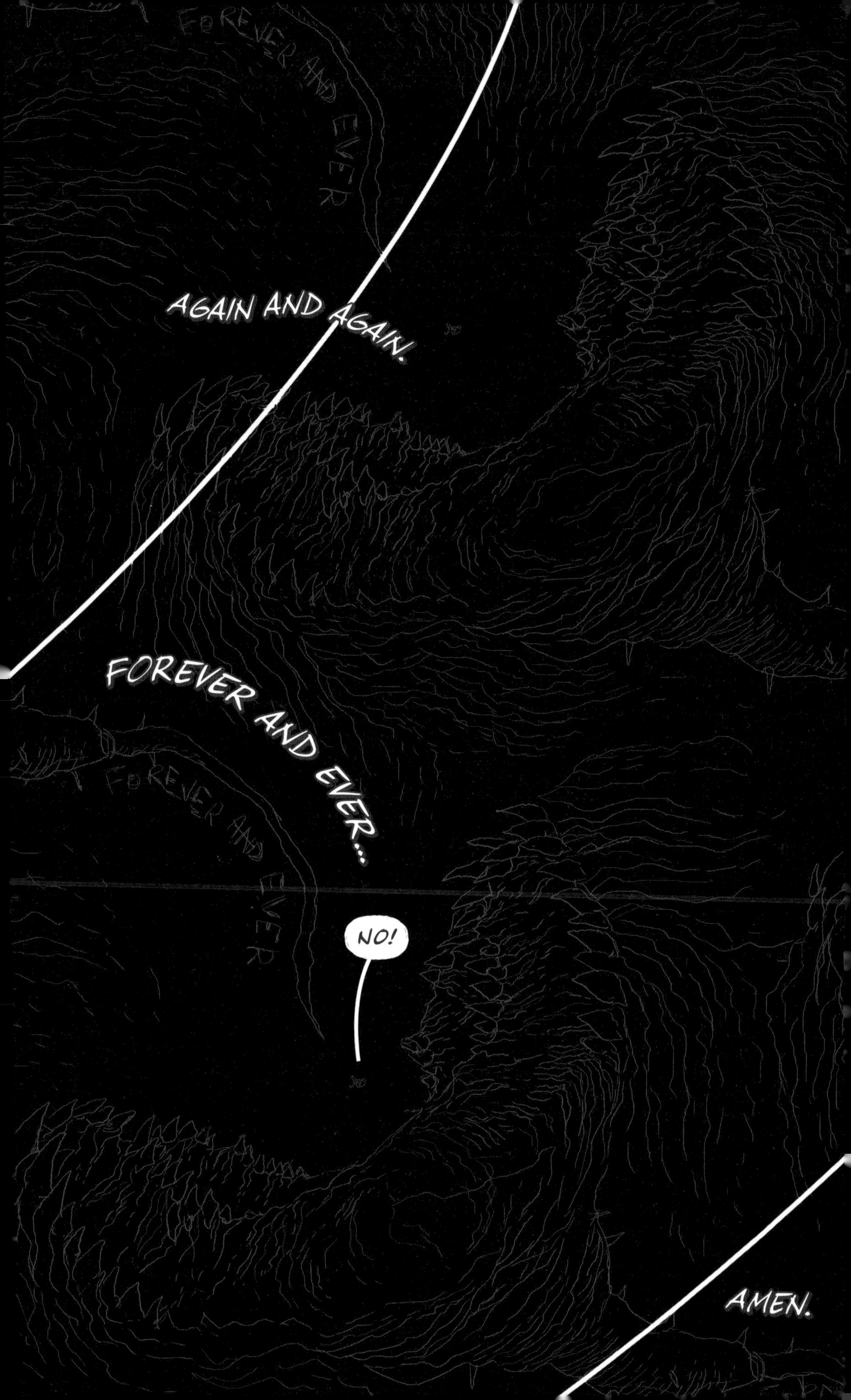
AGAIN AND AGAIN.
FOREVER AND EVER...
NO!
AMEN.

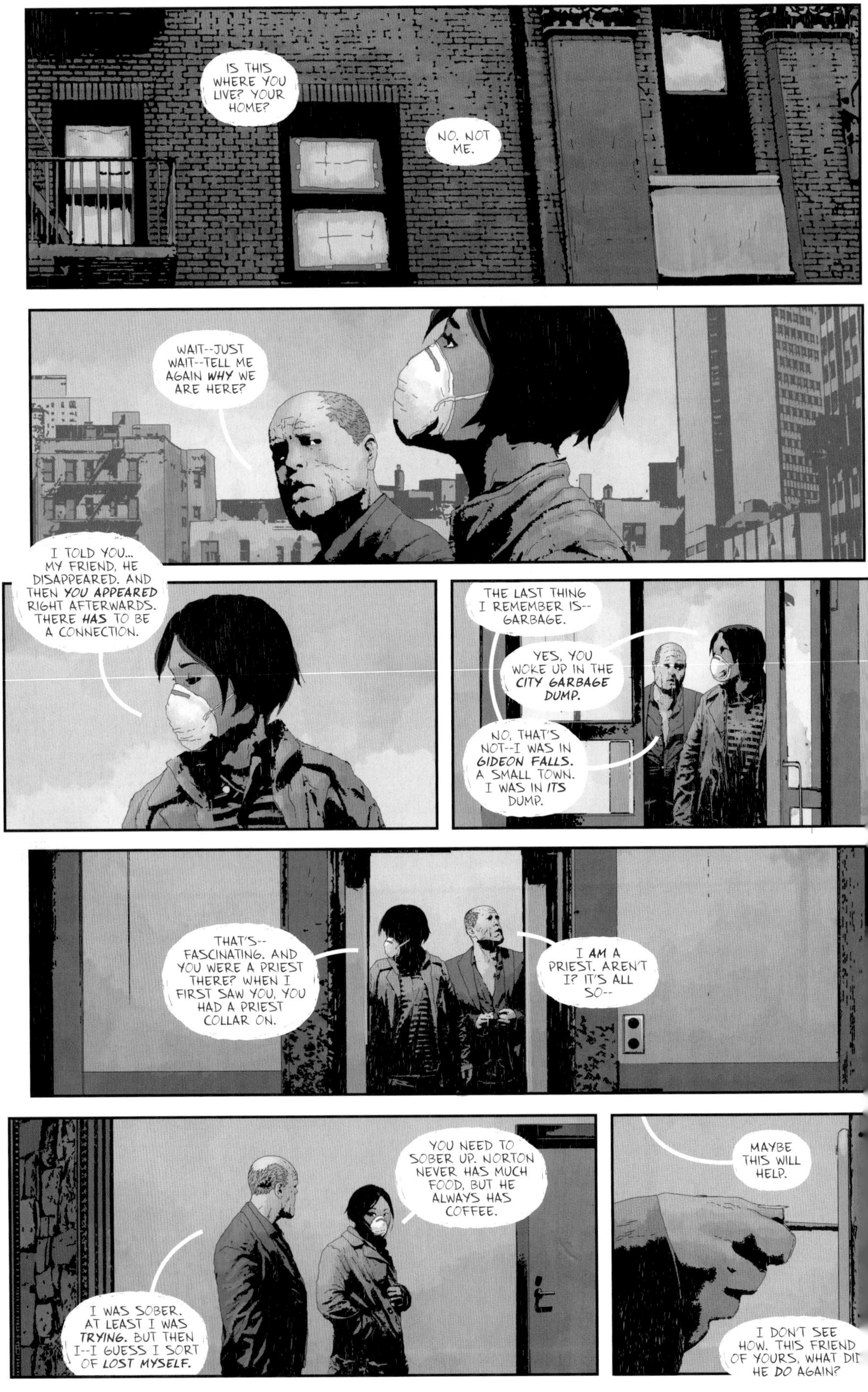
IS THIS WHERE YOU LIVE? YOUR HOME?
NO. NOT ME.
WAIT--JUST WAIT--TELL ME AGAIN WHY WE ARE HERE?
I TOLD YOU... MY FRIEND, HE DISAPPEARED. AND THEN YOU APPEARED RIGHT AFTERWARDS. THERE HAS TO BE A CONNECTION.
THE LAST THING I REMEMBER IS--GARBAGE.
YES, YOU WOKE UP IN THE CITY GARBAGE DUMP.
NO, THAT'S NOT--I WAS IN GIDEON FALLS. A SMALL TOWN. I WAS IN ITS DUMP.
THAT'S--FASCINATING. AND YOU WERE A PRIEST THERE? WHEN I FIRST SAW YOU, YOU HAD A PRIEST COLLAR ON.
I AM A PRIEST. AREN'T I? IT'S ALL SO--
YOU NEED TO SOBER UP. NORTON NEVER HAS MUCH FOOD, BUT HE ALWAYS HAS COFFEE.
I WAS SOBER. AT LEAST I WAS TRYING. BUT THEN I--I GUESS I SORT OF LOST MYSELF.
MAYBE THIS WILL HELP.
I DON'T SEE HOW. THIS FRIEND OF YOURS, WHAT DI
HE DO AGAIN?

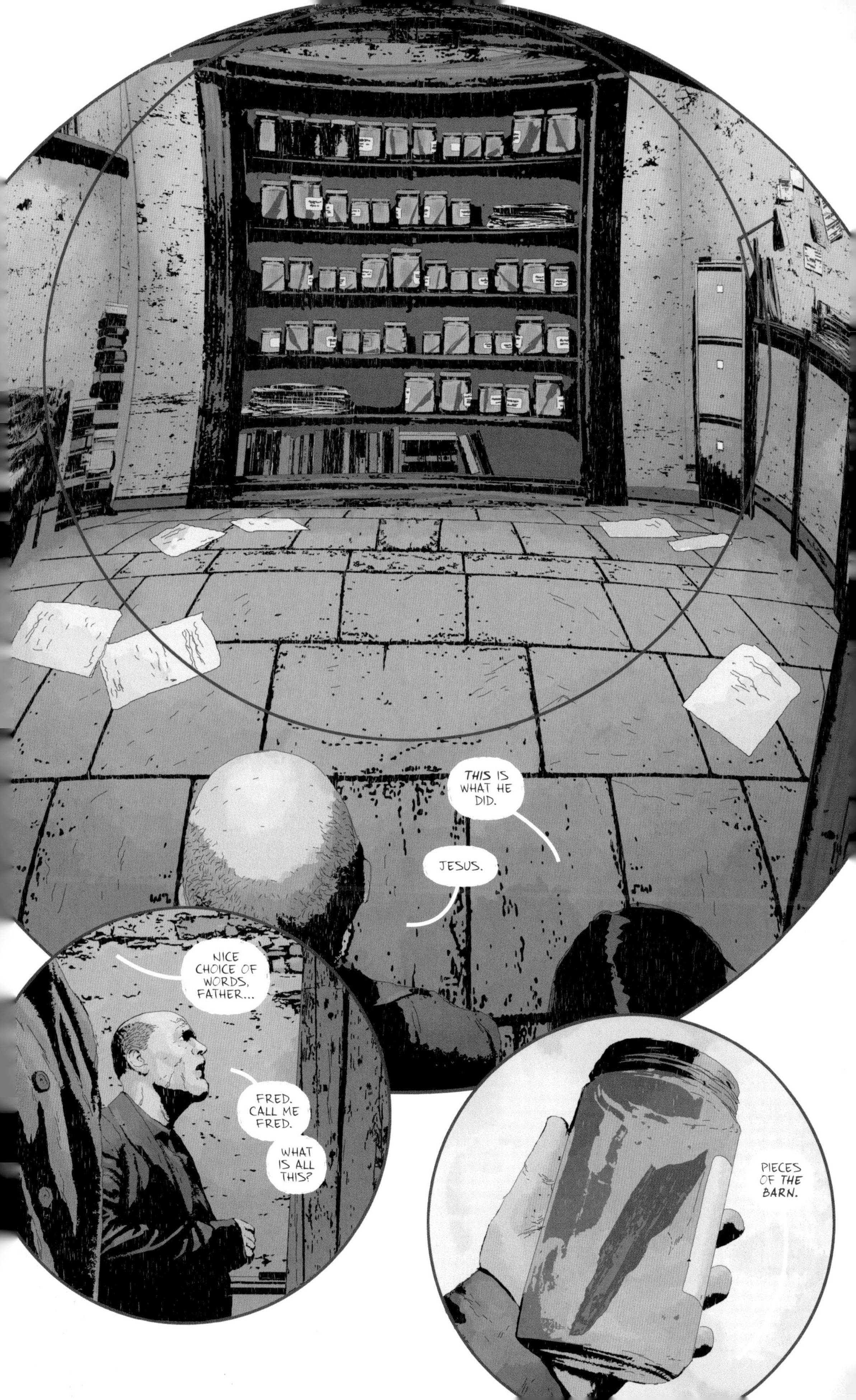
THIS IS WHAT HE DID.
JESUS.
NICE CHOICE OF WORDS, FATHER...
FRED. CALL ME FRED.
WHAT IS ALL THIS?
PIECES OF THE BARN.

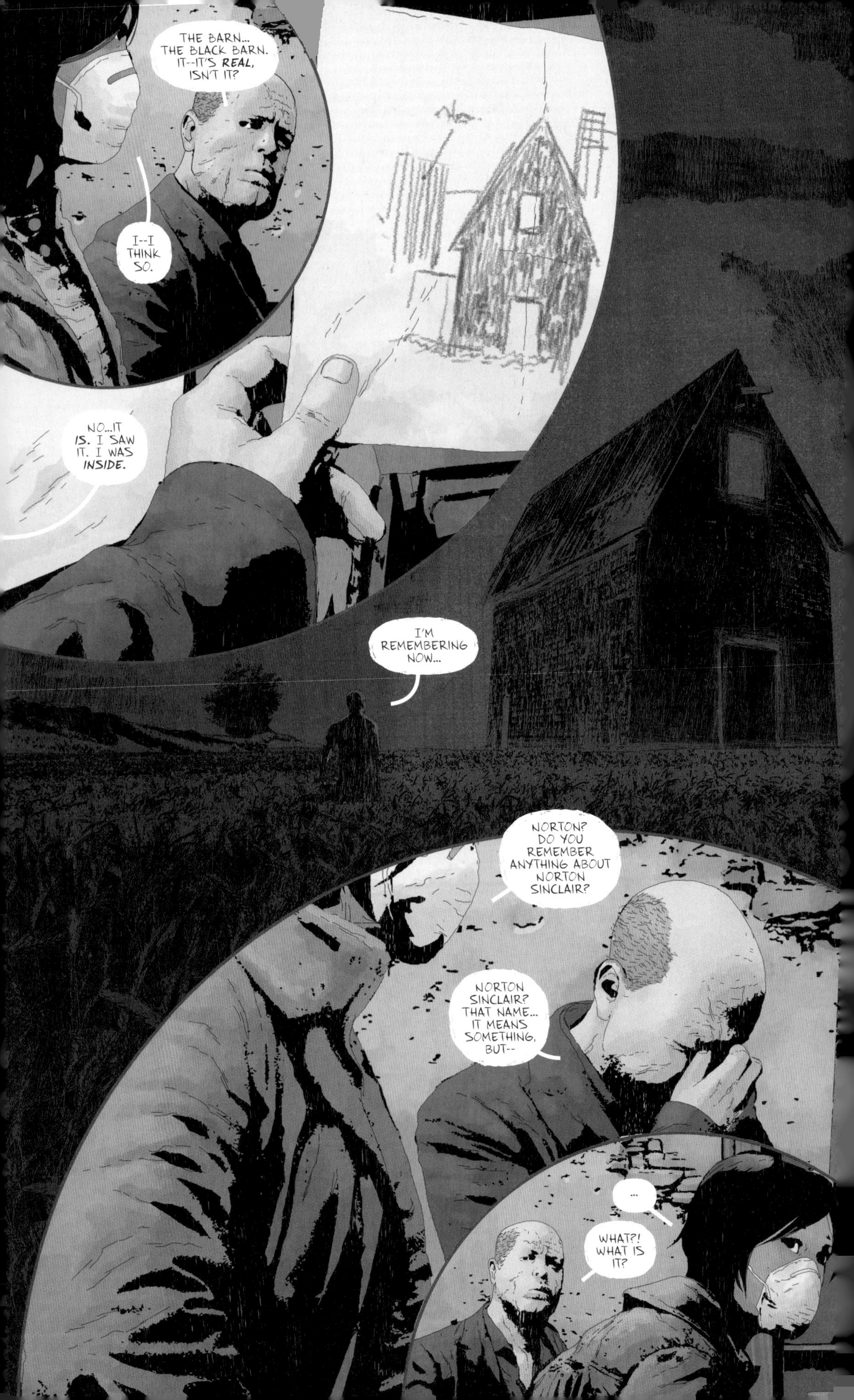
THE BARN... THE BLACK BARN. IT--IT'S **REAL**, ISN'T IT?
I--I THINK SO.
NO...IT **IS.** I SAW IT. I WAS **INSIDE.**
I'M REMEMBERING NOW...
NORTON? DO YOU REMEMBER ANYTHING ABOUT NORTON SINCLAIR?
NORTON SINCLAIR? THAT NAME... IT MEANS SOMETHING, BUT--
...
WHAT?! WHAT IS IT?

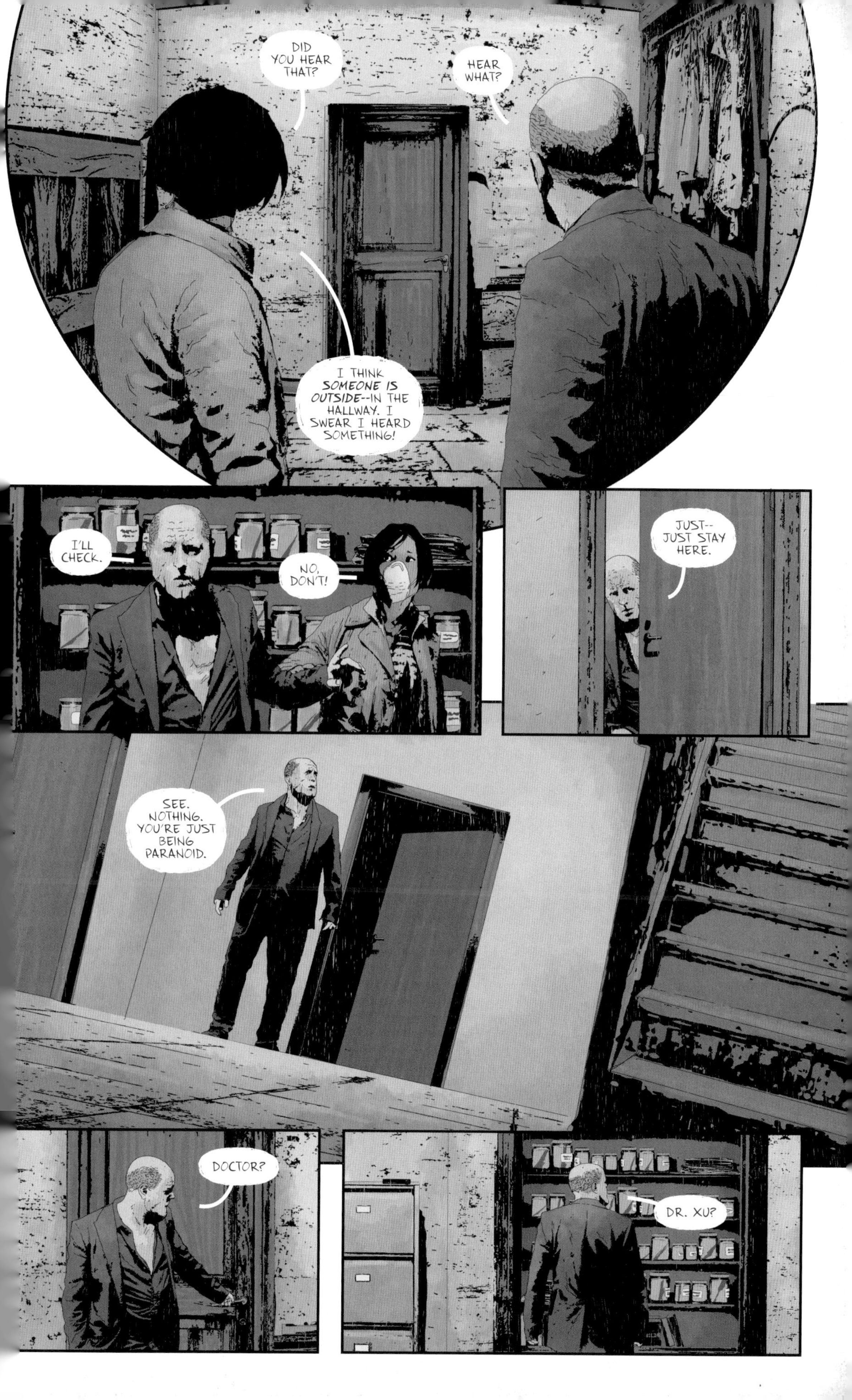
DID YOU HEAR THAT?
HEAR WHAT?
I THINK SOMEONE IS OUTSIDE--IN THE HALLWAY. I SWEAR I HEARD SOMETHING!
I'LL CHECK.
NO, DON'T!
JUST-- JUST STAY HERE.
SEE. NOTHING. YOU'RE JUST BEING PARANOID.
DOCTOR?
DR. XU?

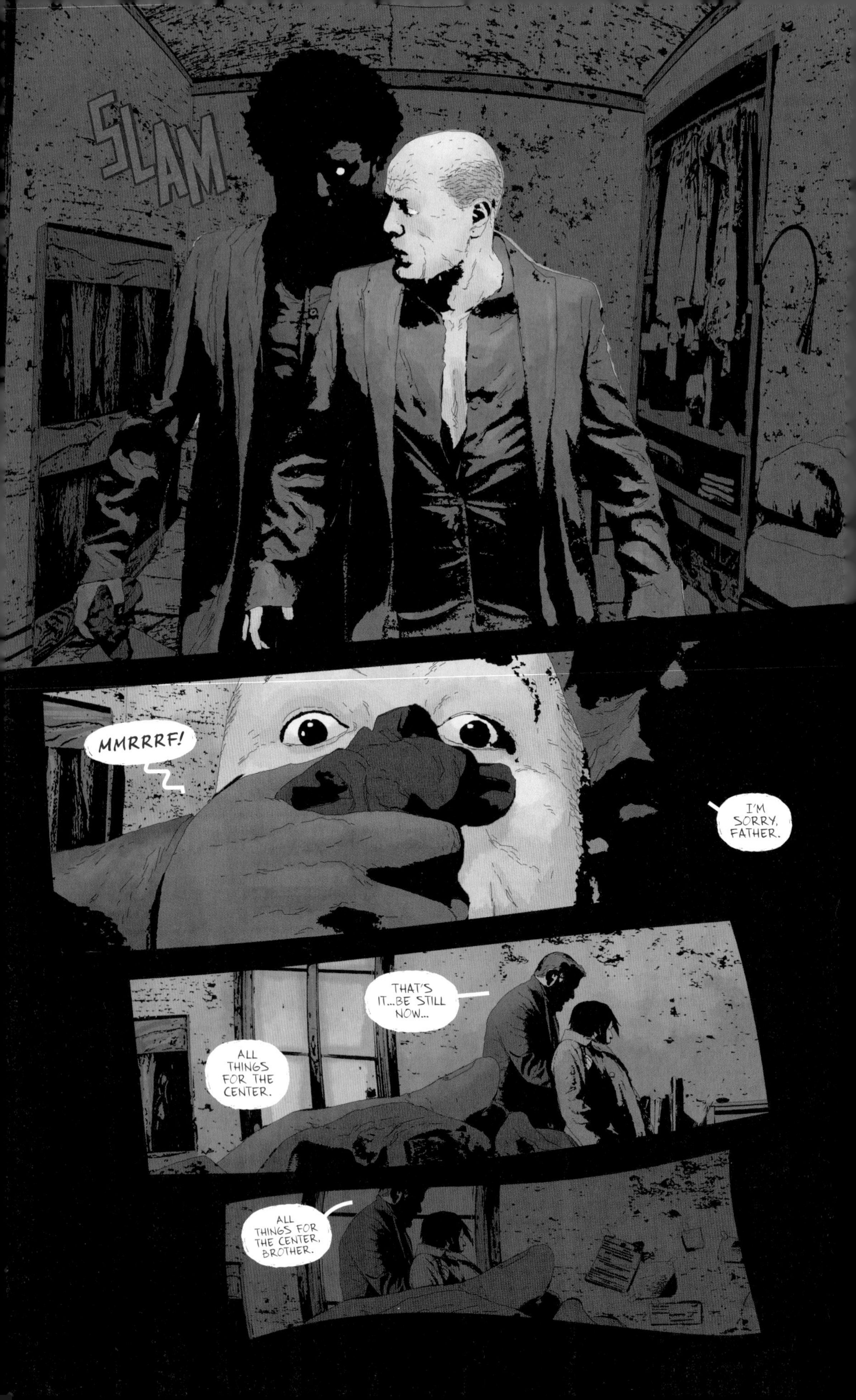
SLAM
MMRRRF!
I'M SORRY, FATHER.
THAT'S IT...BE STILL NOW...
ALL THINGS FOR THE CENTER.
ALL THINGS FOR THE CENTER, BROTHER.

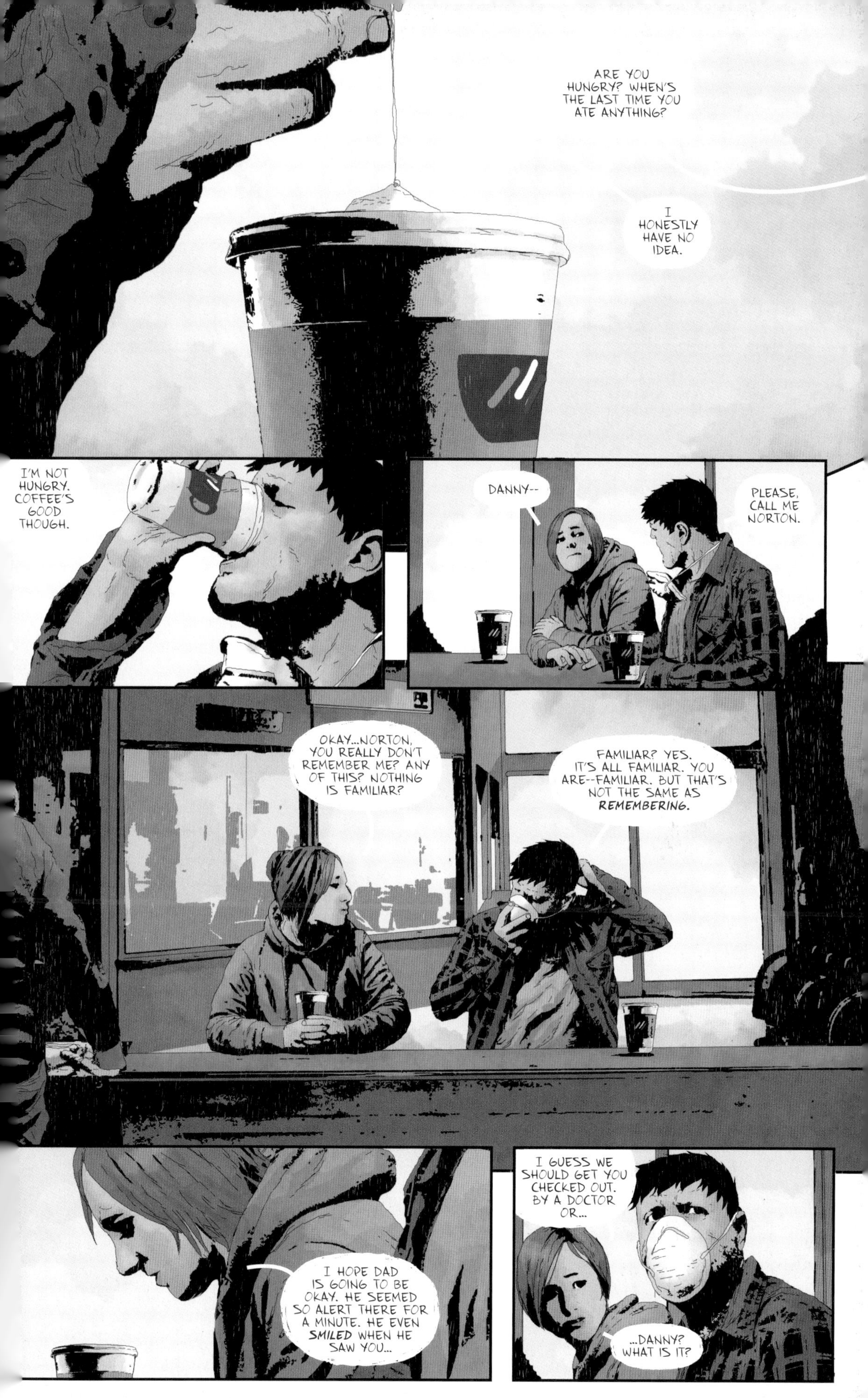
ARE YOU HUNGRY? WHEN'S THE LAST TIME YOU ATE ANYTHING?
I HONESTLY HAVE NO IDEA.
I'M NOT HUNGRY. COFFEE'S GOOD THOUGH.
DANNY--
PLEASE, CALL ME NORTON.
OKAY...NORTON, YOU REALLY DON'T REMEMBER ME? ANY OF THIS? NOTHING IS FAMILIAR?
FAMILIAR? YES. IT'S ALL FAMILIAR. YOU ARE--FAMILIAR. BUT THAT'S NOT THE SAME AS **REMEMBERING.**
I HOPE DAD IS GOING TO BE OKAY. HE SEEMED SO ALERT THERE FOR A MINUTE. HE EVEN **SMILED** WHEN HE SAW YOU...
I GUESS WE SHOULD GET YOU CHECKED OUT. BY A DOCTOR OR...
...DANNY? WHAT IS IT?

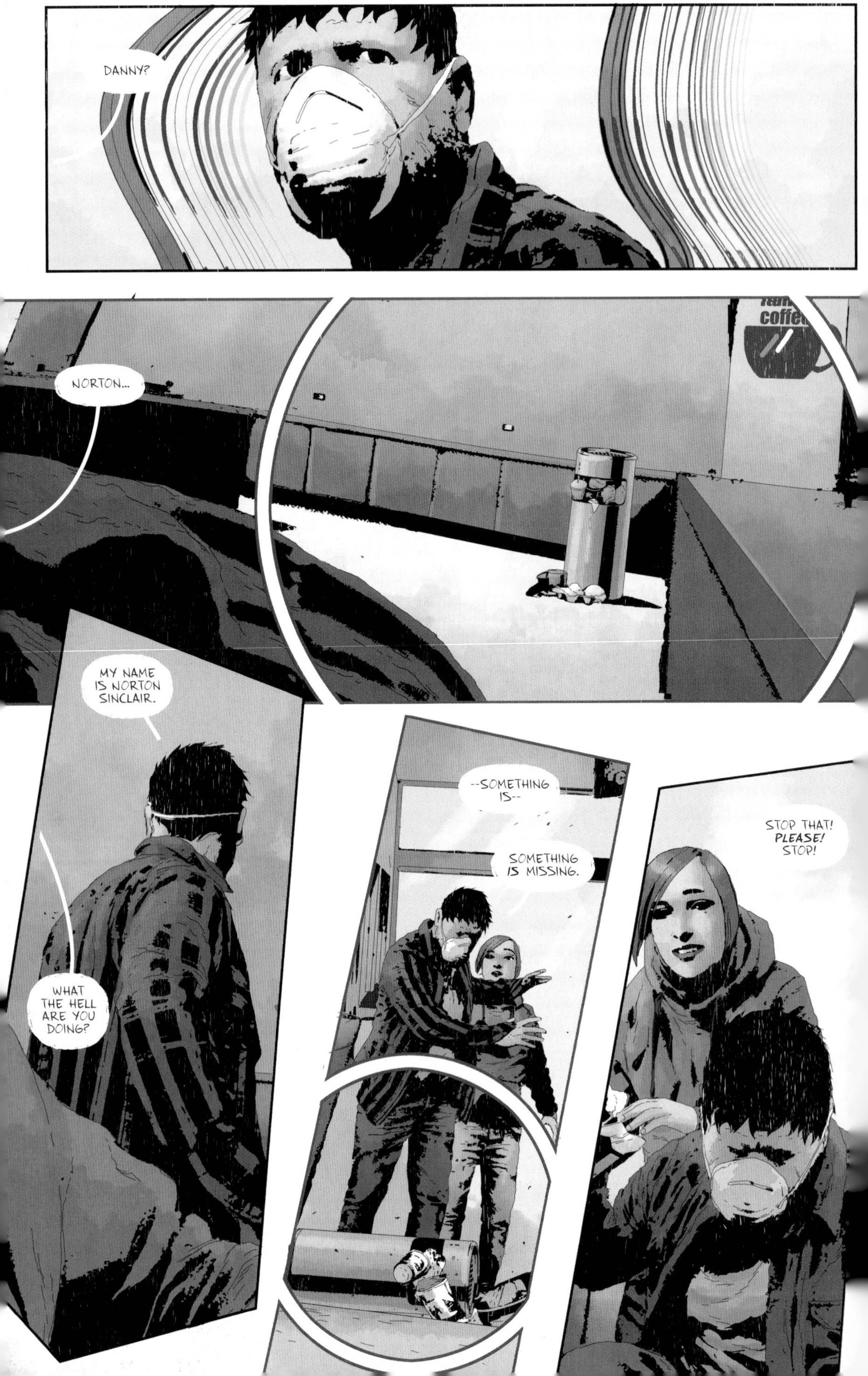
DANNY?
NORTON...
MY NAME IS NORTON SINCLAIR.
WHAT THE HELL ARE YOU DOING?
--SOMETHING IS--
SOMETHING **IS** MISSING.
STOP THAT! **PLEASE!** STOP!
coffee

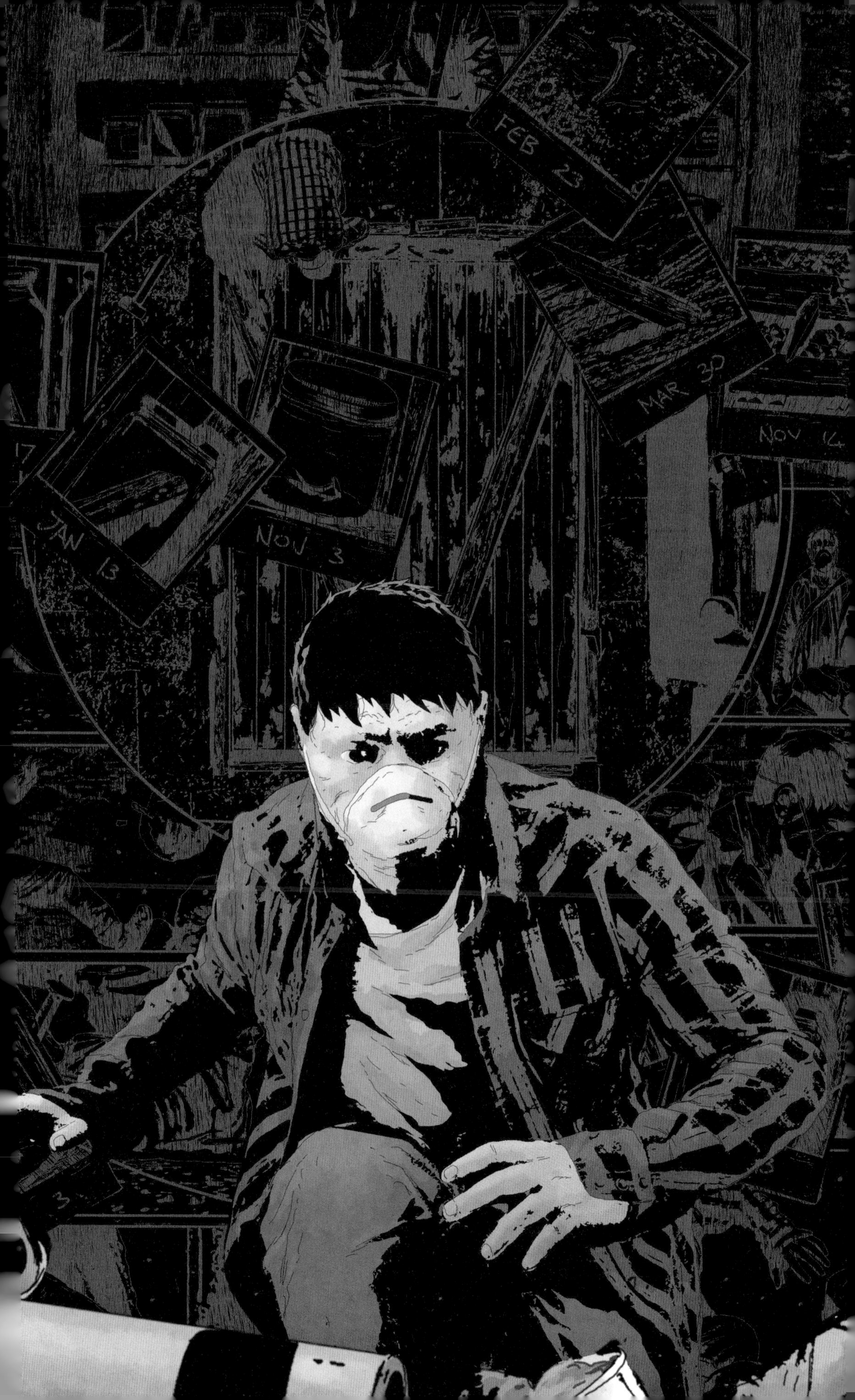
FEB 23
MAR 30
NOV 14
JAN 13
NOV 3

DANNY!

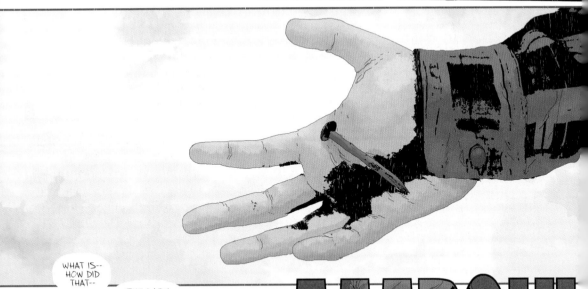

WHAT IS-- HOW DID THAT--

THE BARN. I WAS *BUILDING* THE BLACK BARN. ANGIE AND I--IT'S *CLOSE* NOW.

AAARGH!

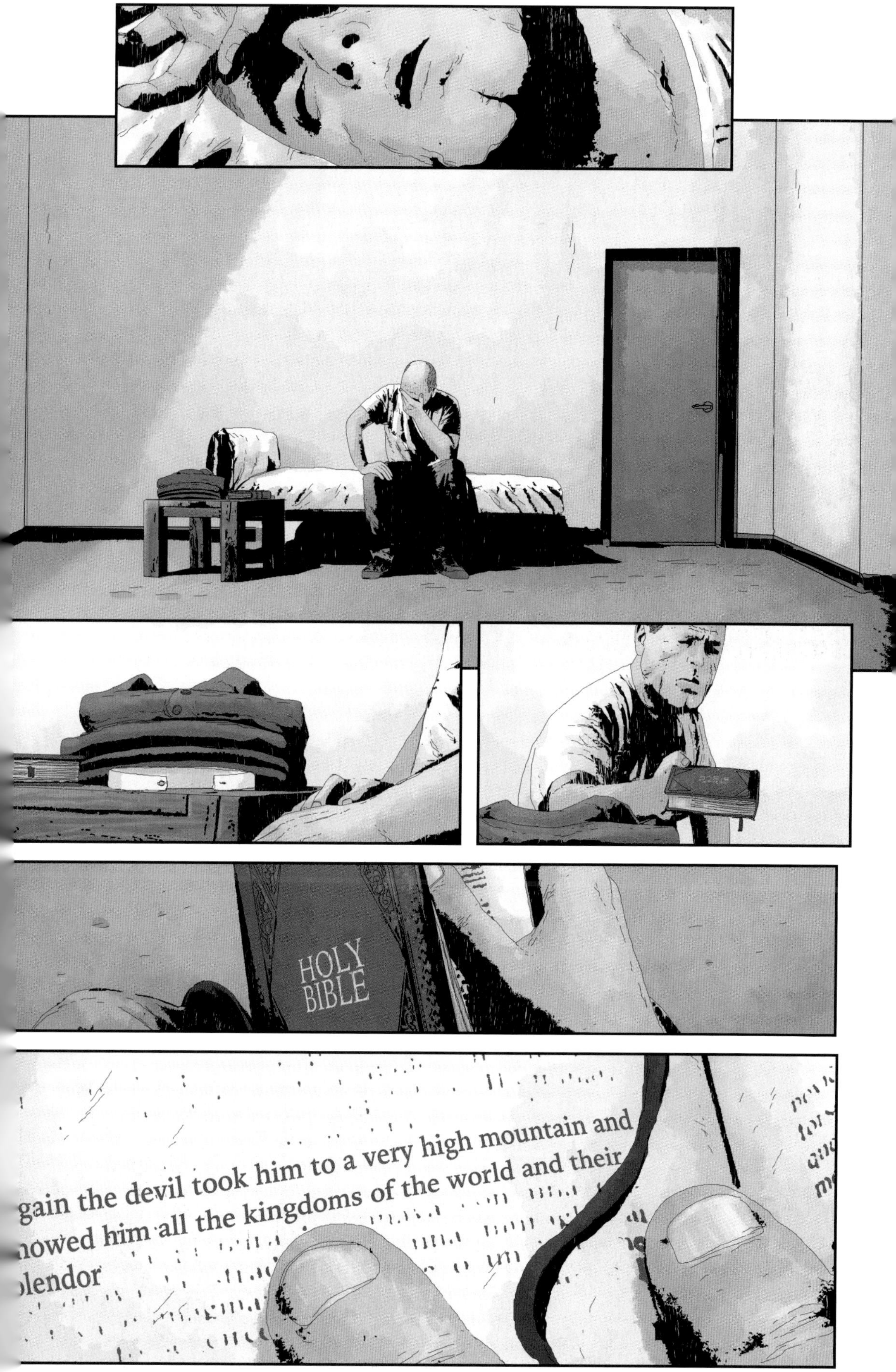
HOLY
BIBLE
gain the devil took him to a very high mountain and
nowed him all the kingdoms of the world and their
plendor

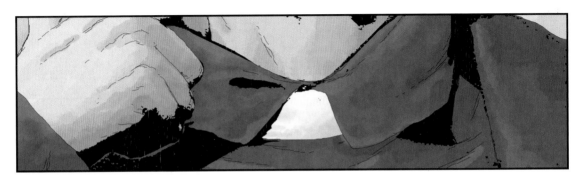

HELLO?

DR. XU?

DR. XU!
WAKE UP!

--NNGH?

WHAT
IS--

SHIT!

SLOW
DOWN--WE'RE
OKAY.

WHERE
THE HELL
ARE WE?

I HAVE
NO IDEA.

AH!
THERE YOU
ARE! BOTH
AWAKE I
SEE...

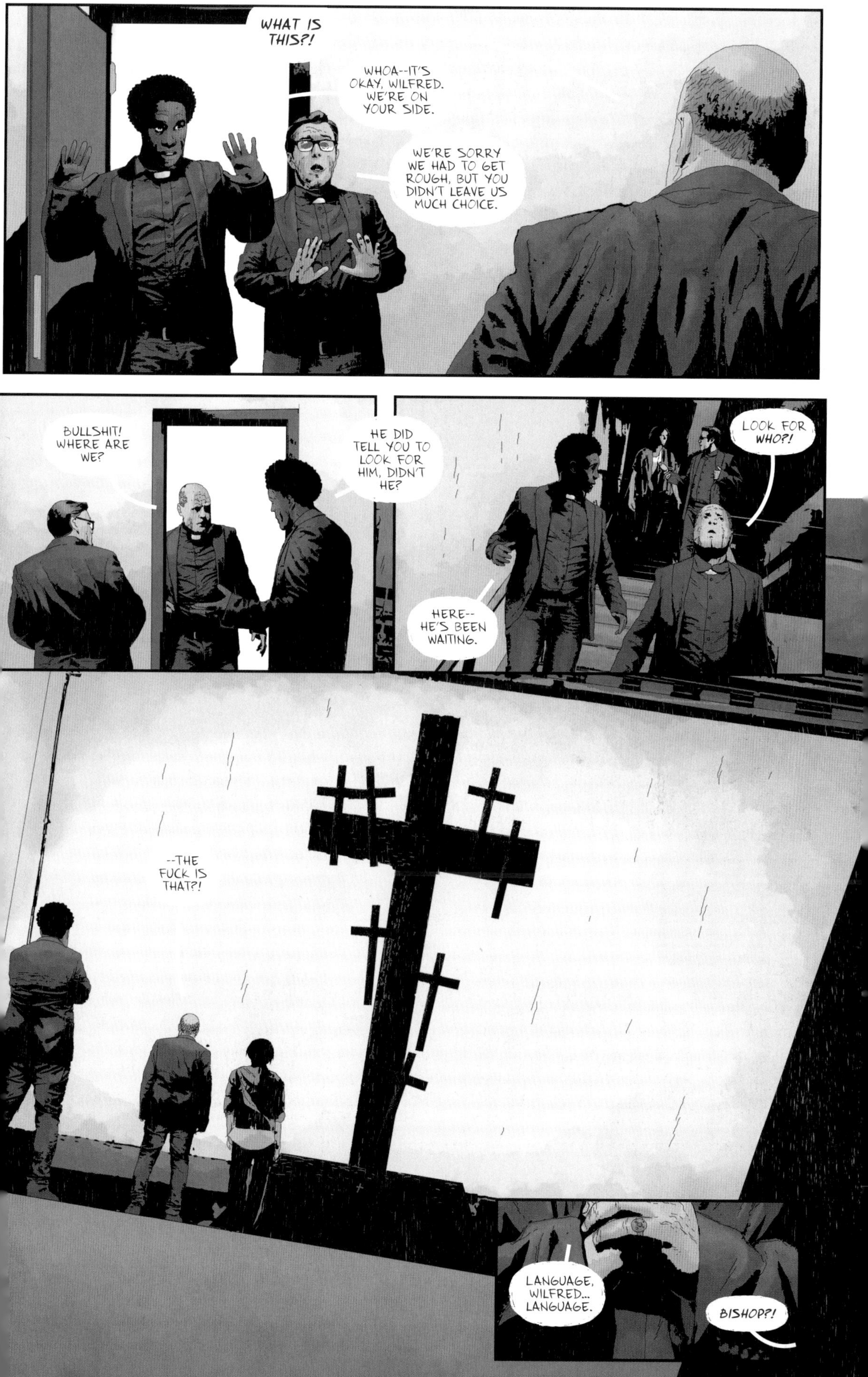
WHAT IS THIS?!
WHOA--IT'S OKAY, WILFRED. WE'RE ON YOUR SIDE.
WE'RE SORRY WE HAD TO GET ROUGH, BUT YOU DIDN'T LEAVE US MUCH CHOICE.
BULLSHIT! WHERE ARE WE?
HE DID TELL YOU TO LOOK FOR HIM, DIDN'T HE?
LOOK FOR WHO?!
HERE-- HE'S BEEN WAITING.
--THE FUCK IS THAT?!
LANGUAGE, WILFRED... LANGUAGE.
BISHOP?!

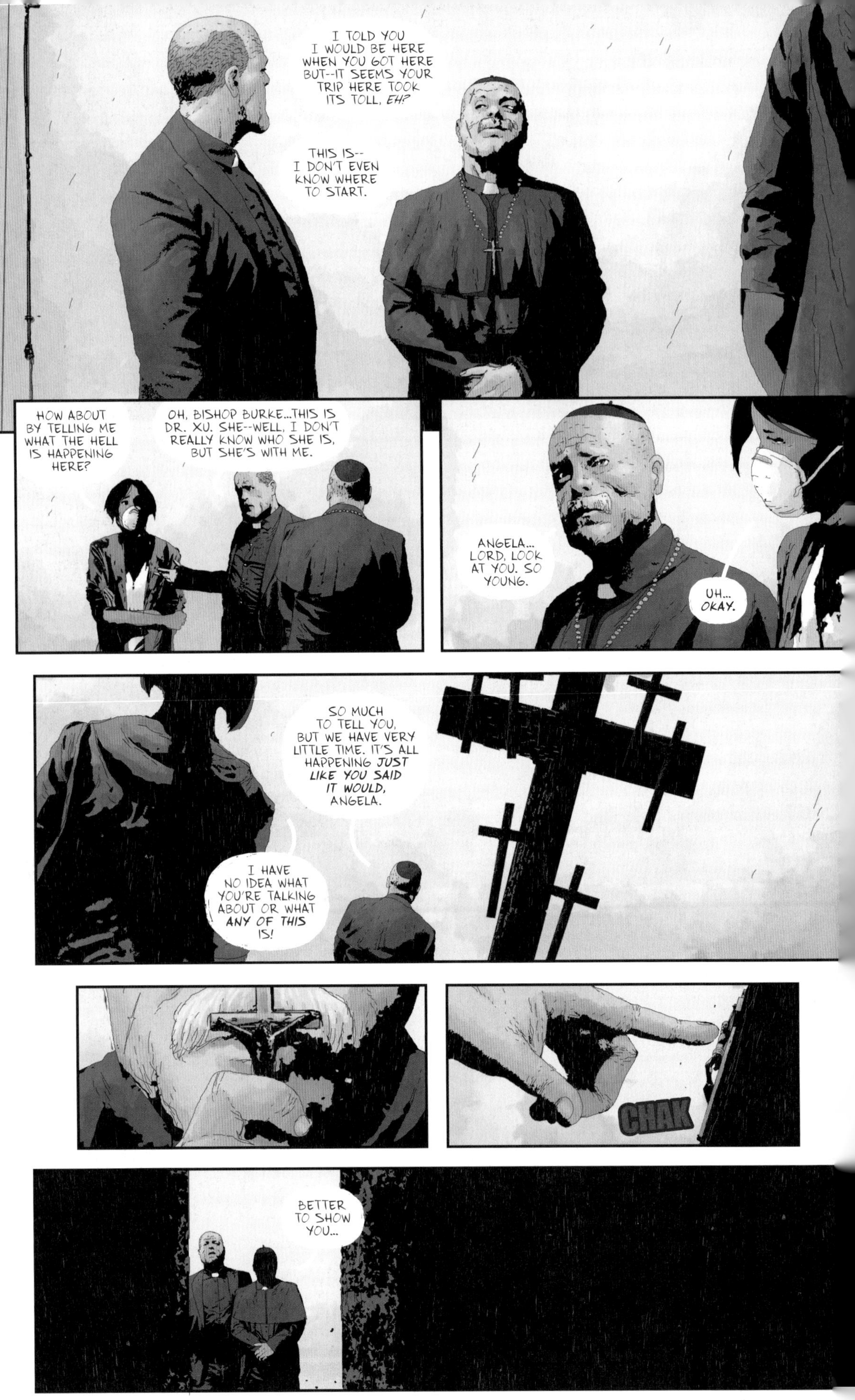
I TOLD YOU I WOULD BE HERE WHEN YOU GOT HERE BUT--IT SEEMS YOUR TRIP HERE TOOK ITS TOLL, *EH?*
THIS IS-- I DON'T EVEN KNOW WHERE TO START.
HOW ABOUT BY TELLING ME WHAT THE HELL IS HAPPENING HERE?
OH, BISHOP BURKE...THIS IS DR. XU. SHE--WELL, I DON'T REALLY KNOW WHO SHE IS, BUT SHE'S WITH ME.
ANGELA... LORD, LOOK AT YOU. SO YOUNG.
UH... OKAY.
SO MUCH TO TELL YOU, BUT WE HAVE VERY LITTLE TIME. IT'S ALL HAPPENING **JUST LIKE YOU SAID** IT WOULD, ANGELA.
I HAVE NO IDEA WHAT YOU'RE TALKING ABOUT OR WHAT **ANY OF THIS** IS!
CHAK
BETTER TO SHOW YOU...

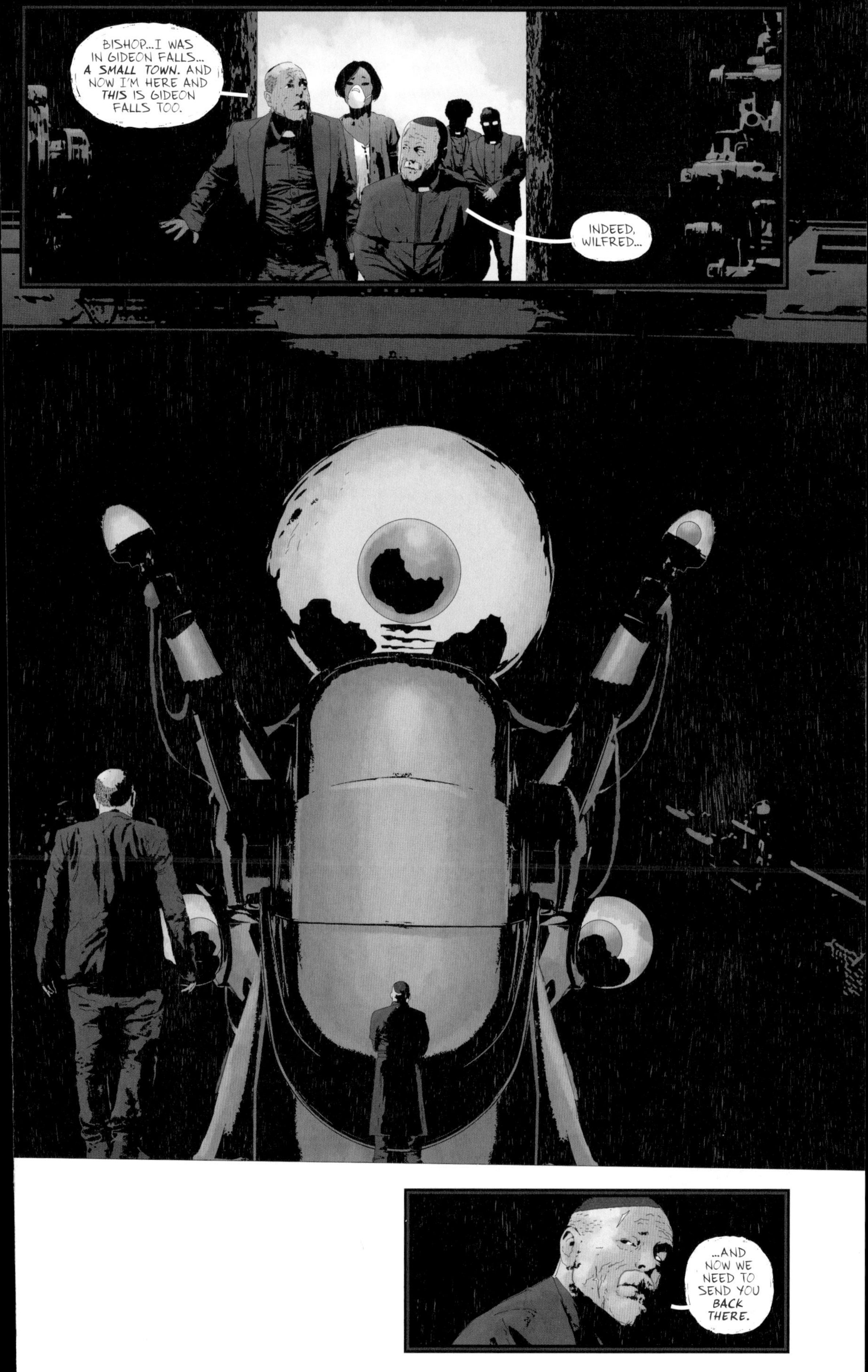
BISHOP...I WAS IN GIDEON FALLS... **A SMALL TOWN.** AND NOW I'M HERE AND **THIS** IS GIDEON FALLS TOO.
INDEED, WILFRED...
...AND NOW WE NEED TO SEND YOU **BACK THERE.**

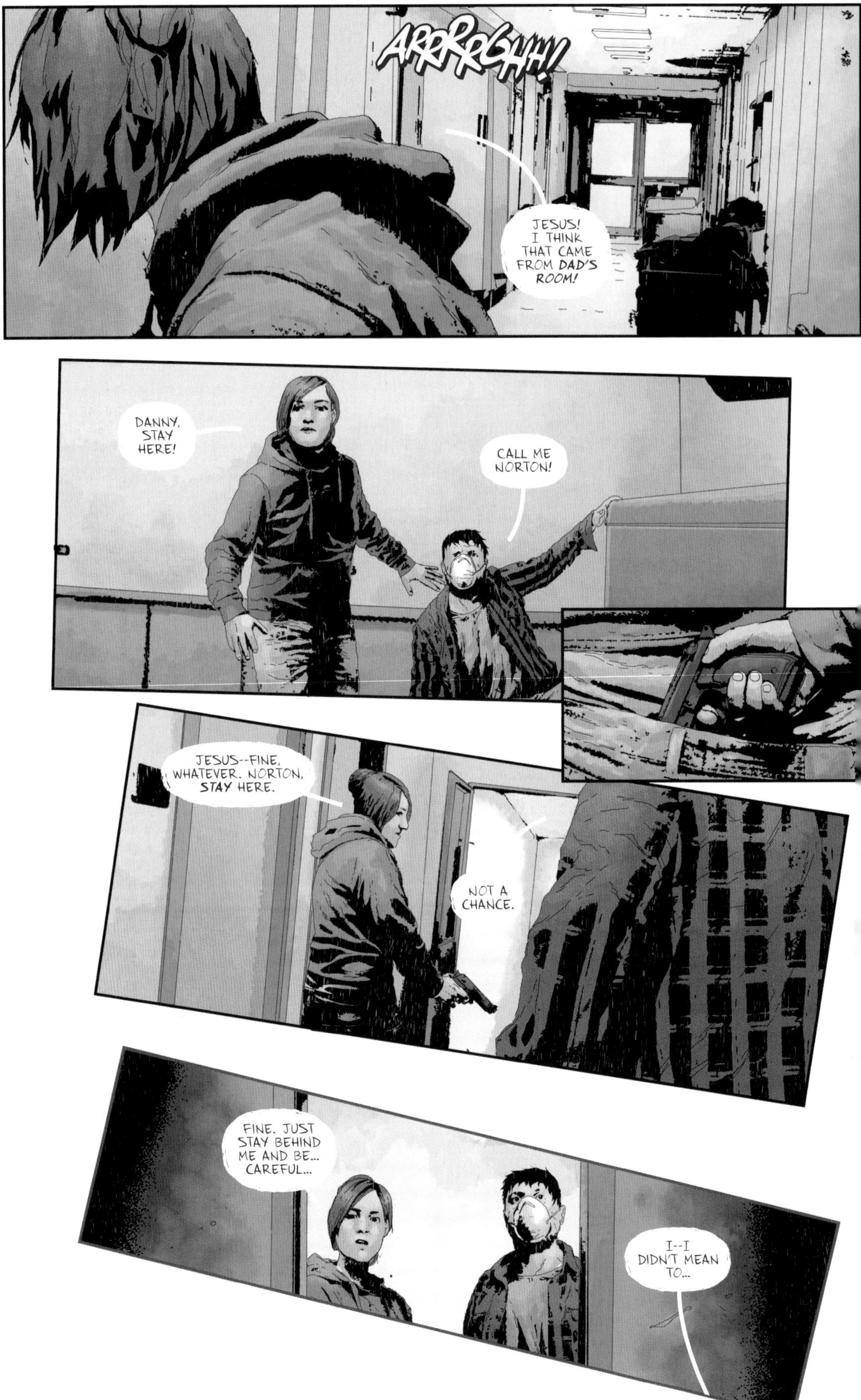
ARRRRGHH!
JESUS! I THINK THAT CAME FROM DAD'S ROOM!
DANNY, STAY HERE!
CALL ME NORTON!
JESUS--FINE, WHATEVER. NORTON, STAY HERE.
NOT A CHANCE.
FINE. JUST STAY BEHIND ME AND BE... CAREFUL...
I--I DIDN'T MEAN TO...

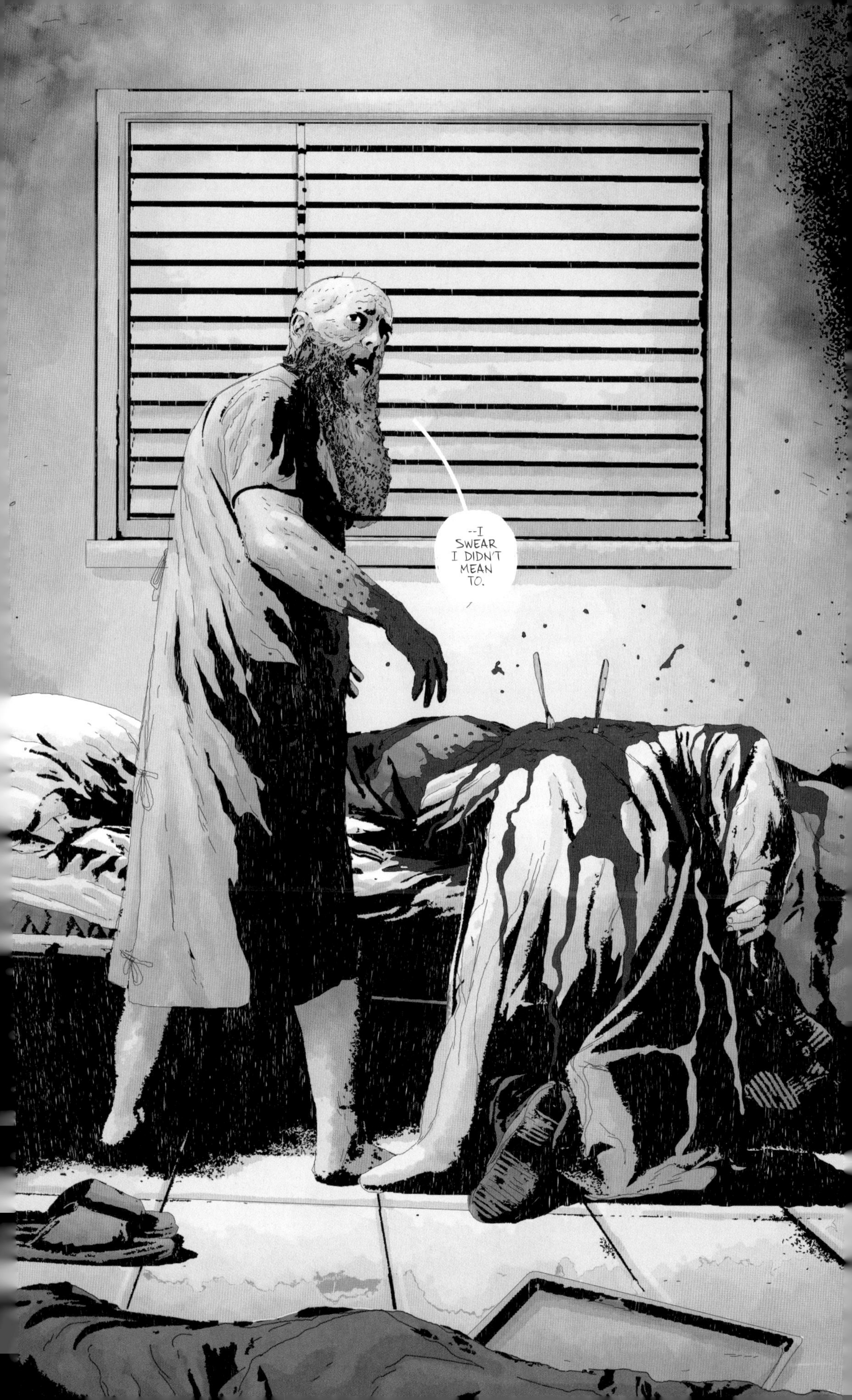
--I SWEAR I DIDN'T MEAN TO.

Eighteen

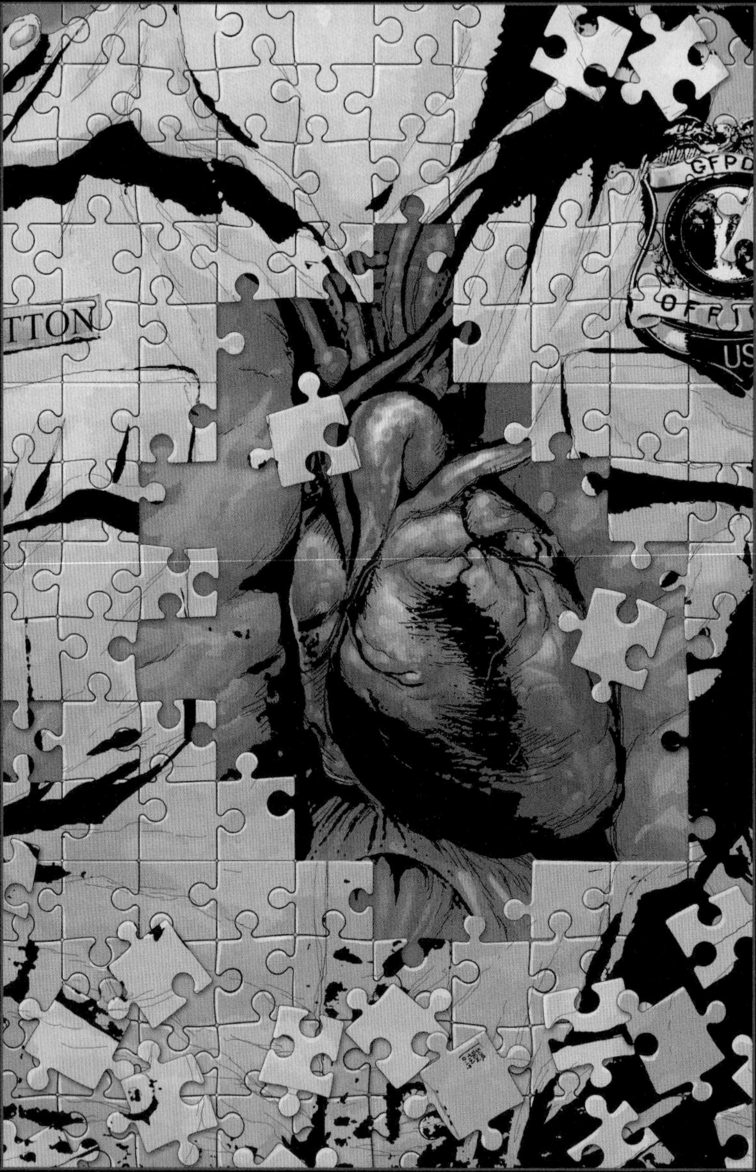
TTON
GFPD
OFFI
US

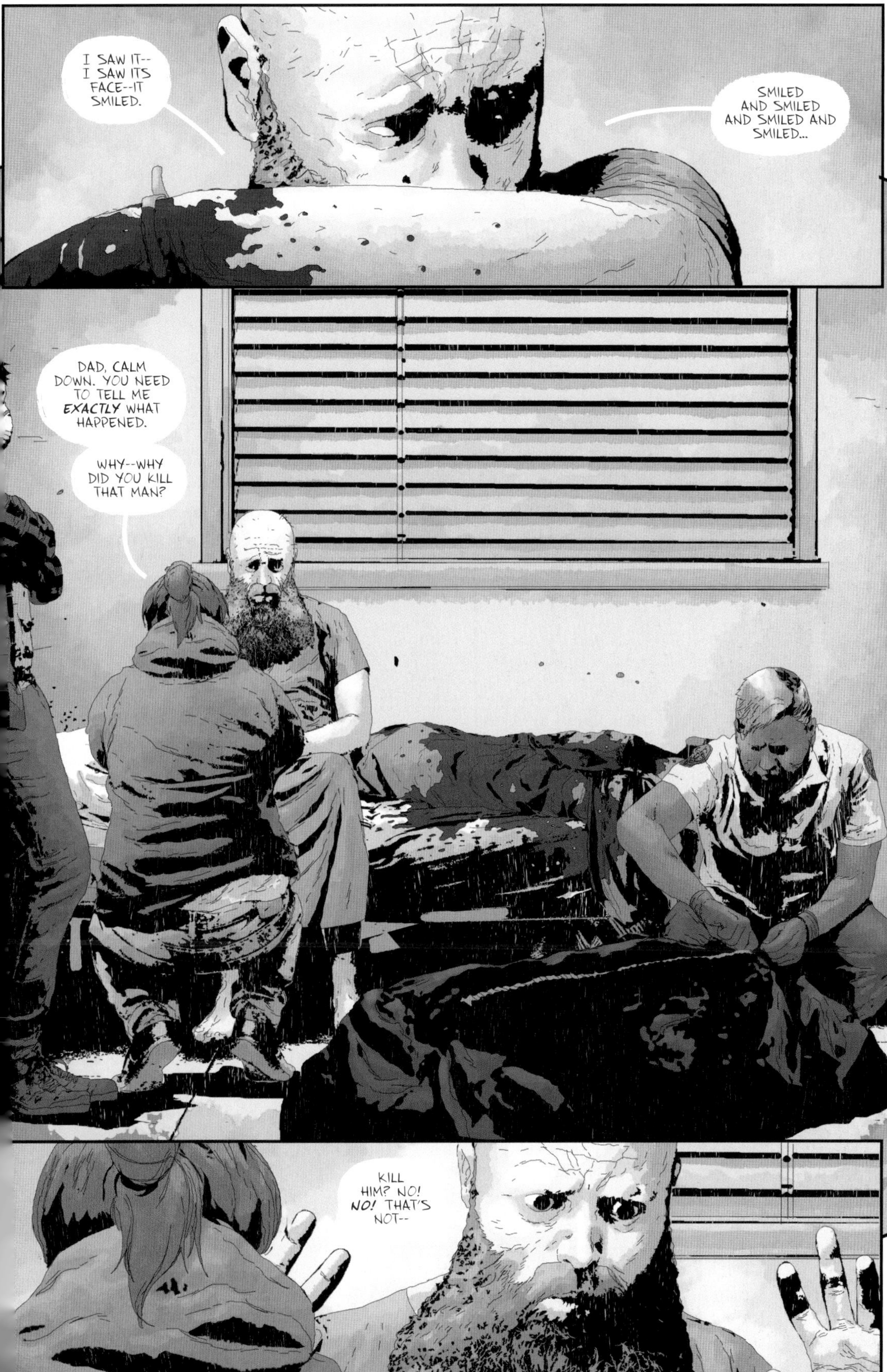
I SAW IT--
I SAW ITS FACE--IT SMILED.
SMILED AND SMILED AND SMILED AND SMILED...
DAD, CALM DOWN. YOU NEED TO TELL ME **EXACTLY** WHAT HAPPENED.
WHY--WHY DID YOU KILL THAT MAN?
KILL HIM? NO! **NO!** THAT'S NOT--

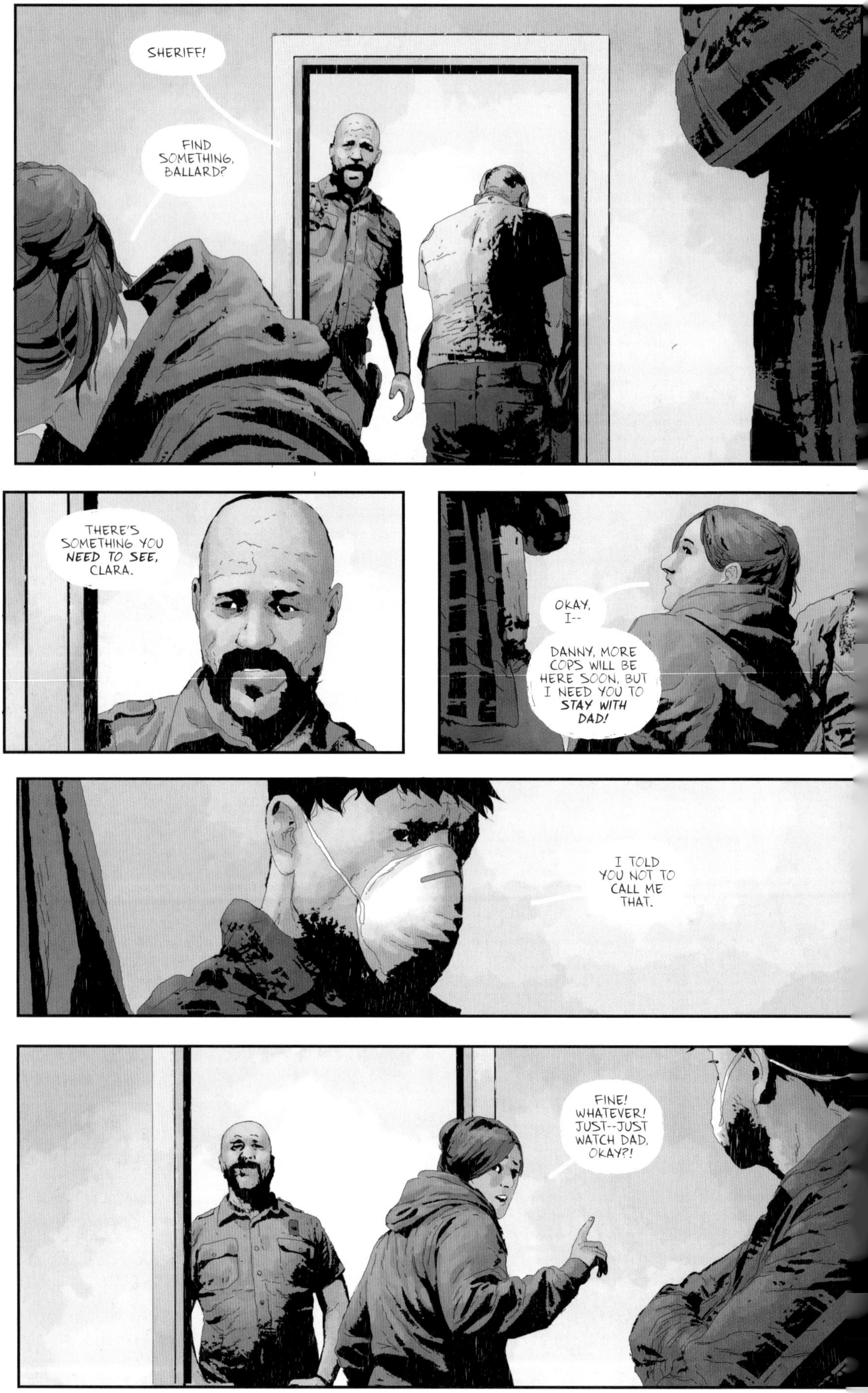
SHERIFF!
FIND SOMETHING, BALLARD?
THERE'S SOMETHING YOU NEED TO SEE, CLARA.
OKAY, I--
DANNY, MORE COPS WILL BE HERE SOON, BUT I NEED YOU TO STAY WITH DAD!
I TOLD YOU NOT TO CALL ME THAT.
FINE! WHATEVER! JUST--JUST WATCH DAD, OKAY?!

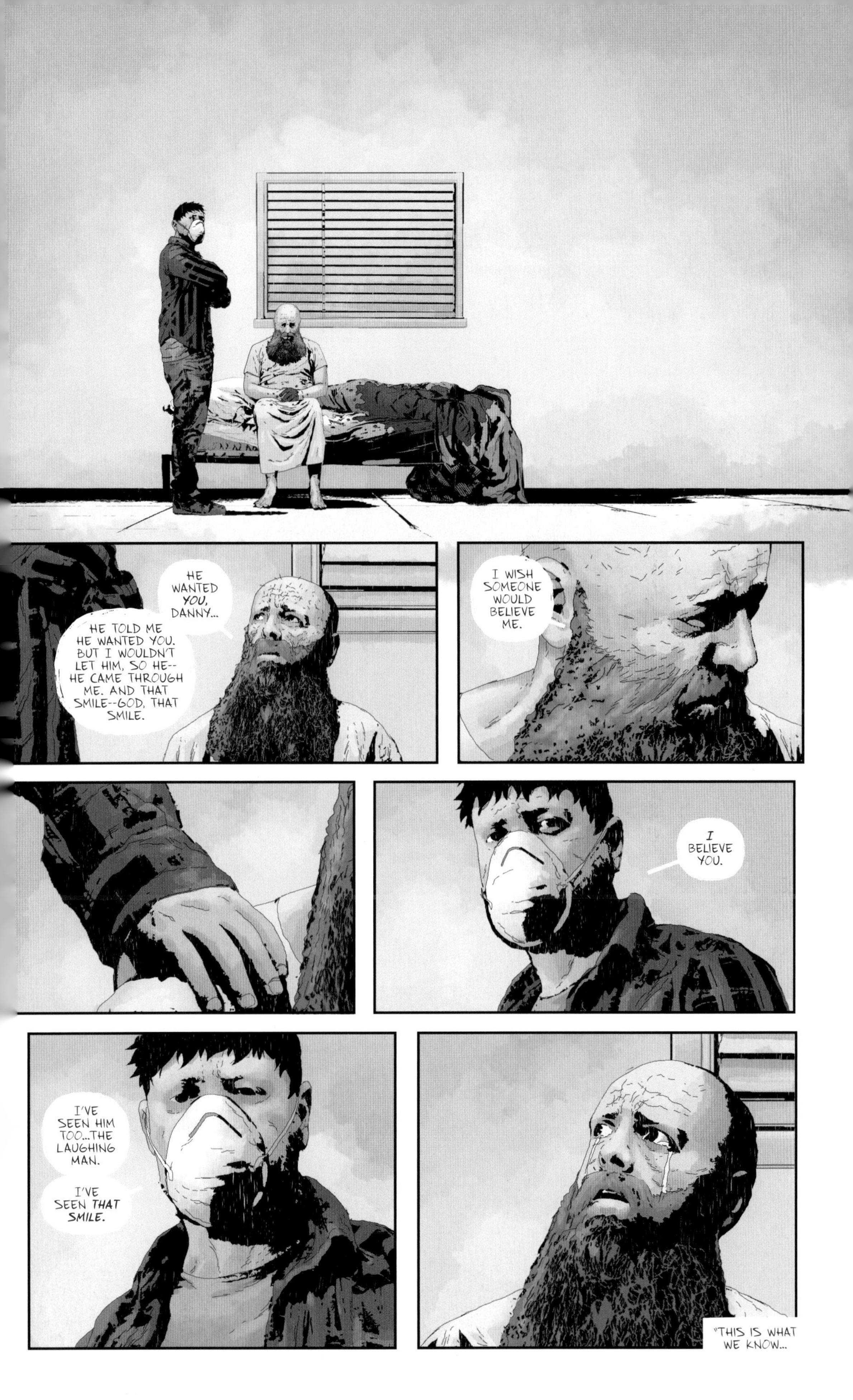
HE WANTED YOU, DANNY...
HE TOLD ME HE WANTED YOU. BUT I WOULDN'T LET HIM, SO HE--HE CAME THROUGH ME. AND THAT SMILE--GOD, THAT SMILE.
I WISH SOMEONE WOULD BELIEVE ME.
I BELIEVE YOU.
I'VE SEEN HIM TOO...THE LAUGHING MAN.
I'VE SEEN THAT SMILE.
"THIS IS WHAT WE KNOW...

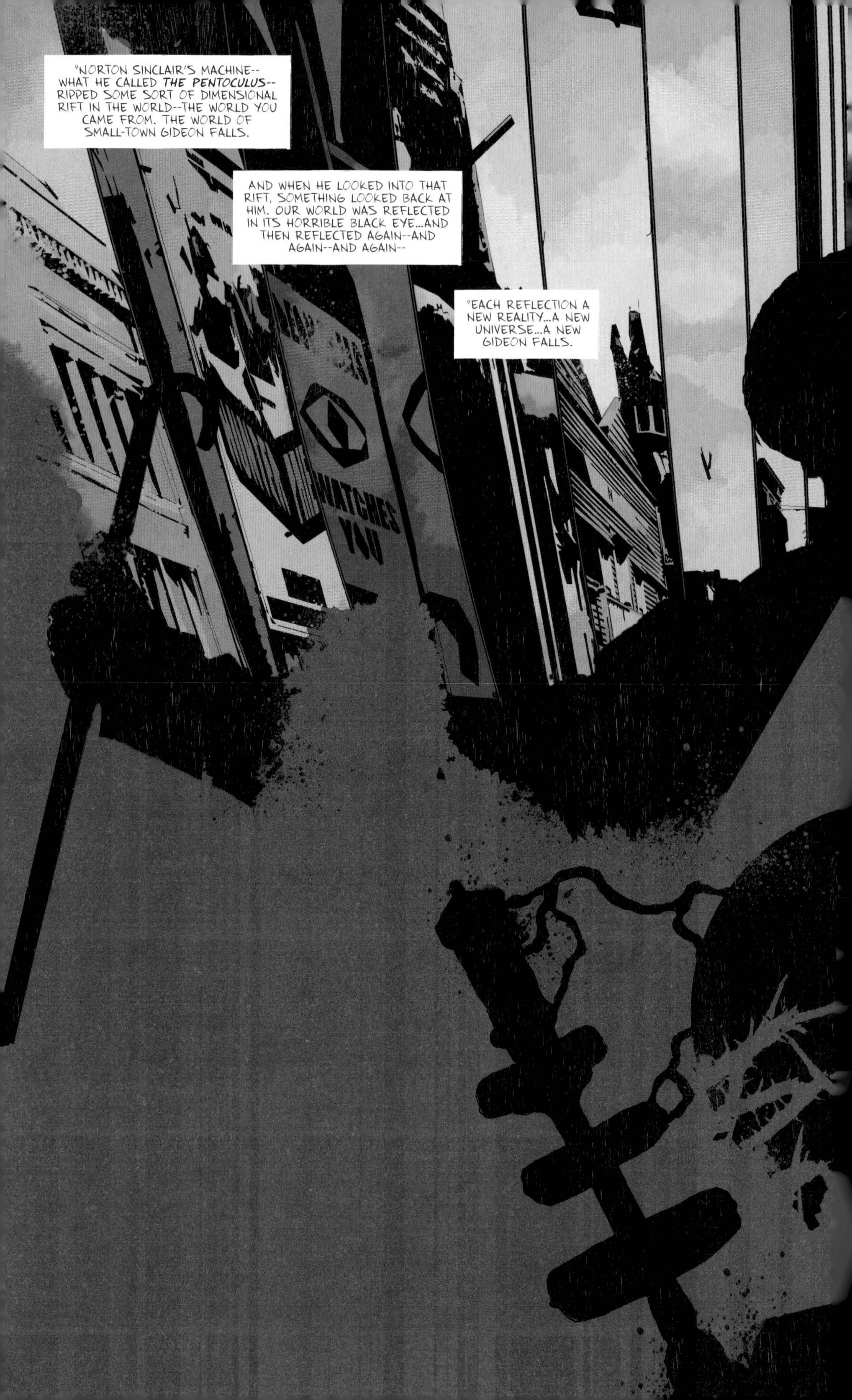
"NORTON SINCLAIR'S MACHINE--WHAT HE CALLED *THE PENTOCULUS*--RIPPED SOME SORT OF DIMENSIONAL RIFT IN THE WORLD--THE WORLD YOU CAME FROM. THE WORLD OF SMALL-TOWN GIDEON FALLS.
AND WHEN HE LOOKED INTO THAT RIFT, SOMETHING LOOKED BACK AT HIM. OUR WORLD WAS REFLECTED IN ITS HORRIBLE BLACK EYE...AND THEN REFLECTED AGAIN--AND AGAIN--AND AGAIN--
"EACH REFLECTION A NEW REALITY...A NEW UNIVERSE...A NEW GIDEON FALLS.
WATCHES YOU

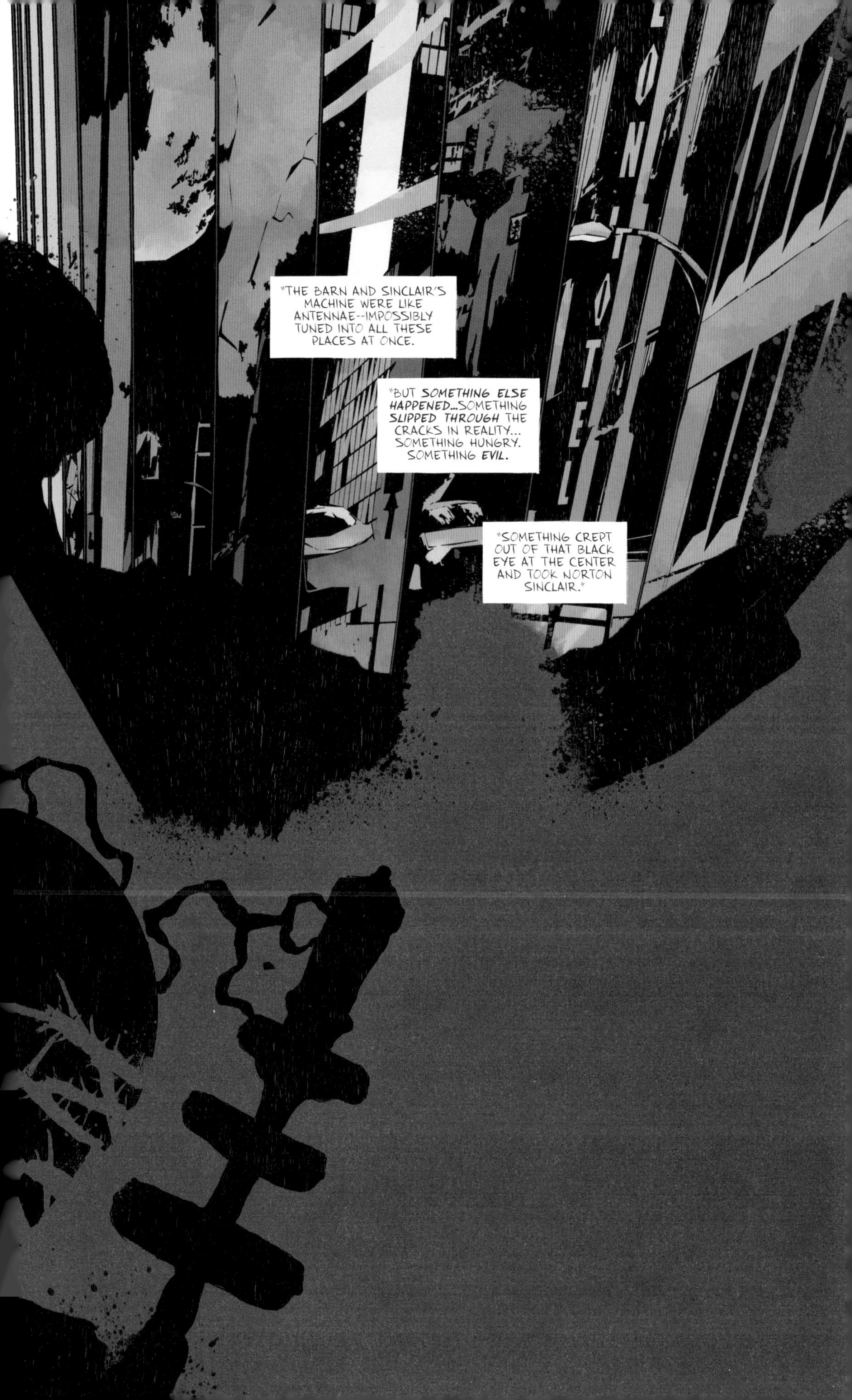
"THE BARN AND SINCLAIR'S MACHINE WERE LIKE ANTENNAE--IMPOSSIBLY TUNED INTO ALL THESE PLACES AT ONCE.
"BUT SOMETHING ELSE HAPPENED...SOMETHING SLIPPED THROUGH THE CRACKS IN REALITY... SOMETHING HUNGRY. SOMETHING EVIL.
"SOMETHING CREPT OUT OF THAT BLACK EYE AT THE CENTER AND TOOK NORTON SINCLAIR."

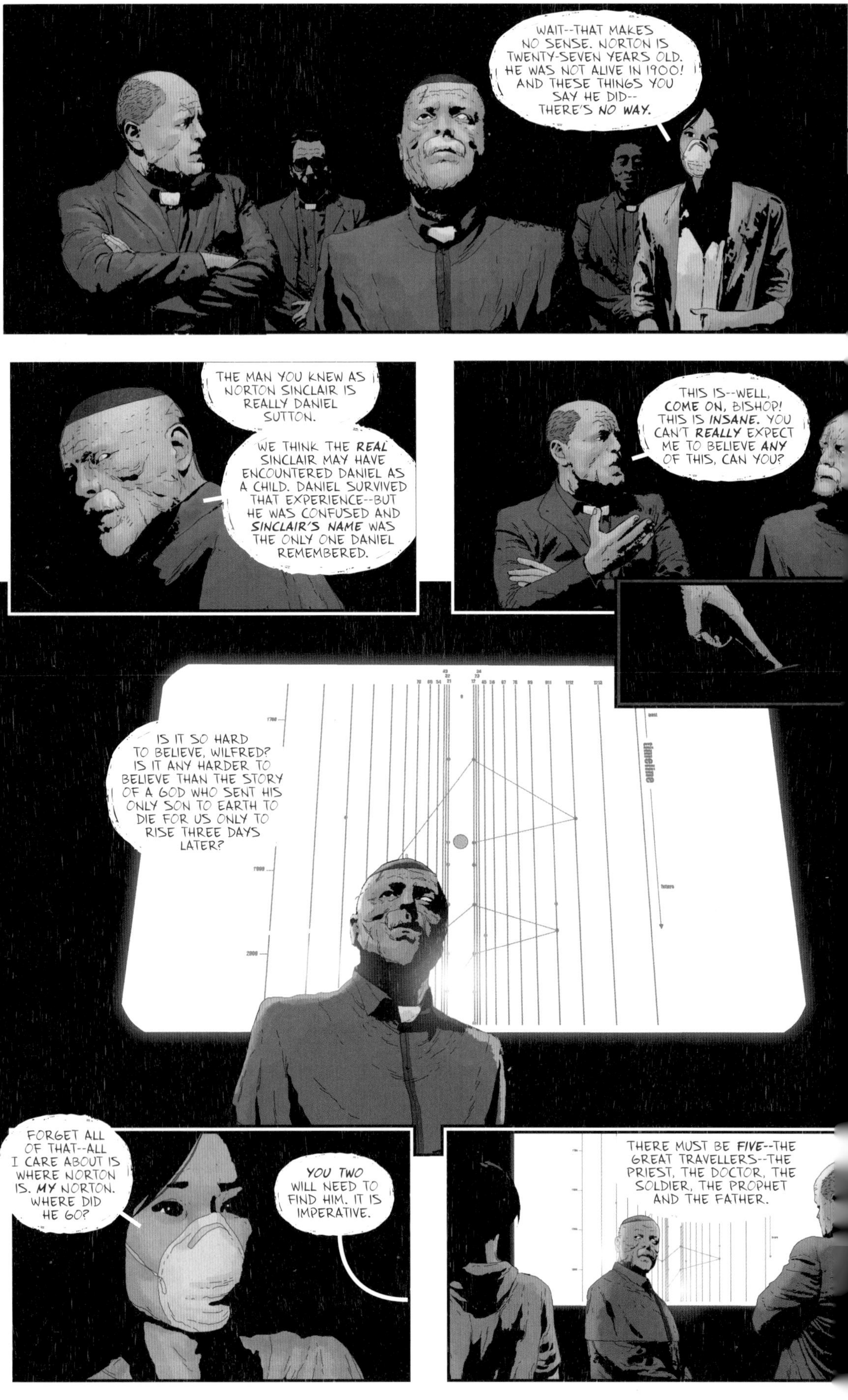
WAIT--THAT MAKES NO SENSE. NORTON IS TWENTY-SEVEN YEARS OLD. HE WAS NOT ALIVE IN 1900! AND THESE THINGS YOU SAY HE DID-- THERE'S NO WAY.
THE MAN YOU KNEW AS NORTON SINCLAIR IS REALLY DANIEL SUTTON.
WE THINK THE REAL SINCLAIR MAY HAVE ENCOUNTERED DANIEL AS A CHILD. DANIEL SURVIVED THAT EXPERIENCE--BUT HE WAS CONFUSED AND SINCLAIR'S NAME WAS THE ONLY ONE DANIEL REMEMBERED.
THIS IS--WELL, COME ON, BISHOP! THIS IS INSANE. YOU CAN'T REALLY EXPECT ME TO BELIEVE ANY OF THIS, CAN YOU?
timeline
IS IT SO HARD TO BELIEVE, WILFRED? IS IT ANY HARDER TO BELIEVE THAN THE STORY OF A GOD WHO SENT HIS ONLY SON TO EARTH TO DIE FOR US ONLY TO RISE THREE DAYS LATER?
FORGET ALL OF THAT--ALL I CARE ABOUT IS WHERE NORTON IS. MY NORTON. WHERE DID HE GO?
YOU TWO WILL NEED TO FIND HIM. IT IS IMPERATIVE.
THERE MUST BE FIVE--THE GREAT TRAVELLERS--THE PRIEST, THE DOCTOR, THE SOLDIER, THE PROPHET AND THE FATHER.

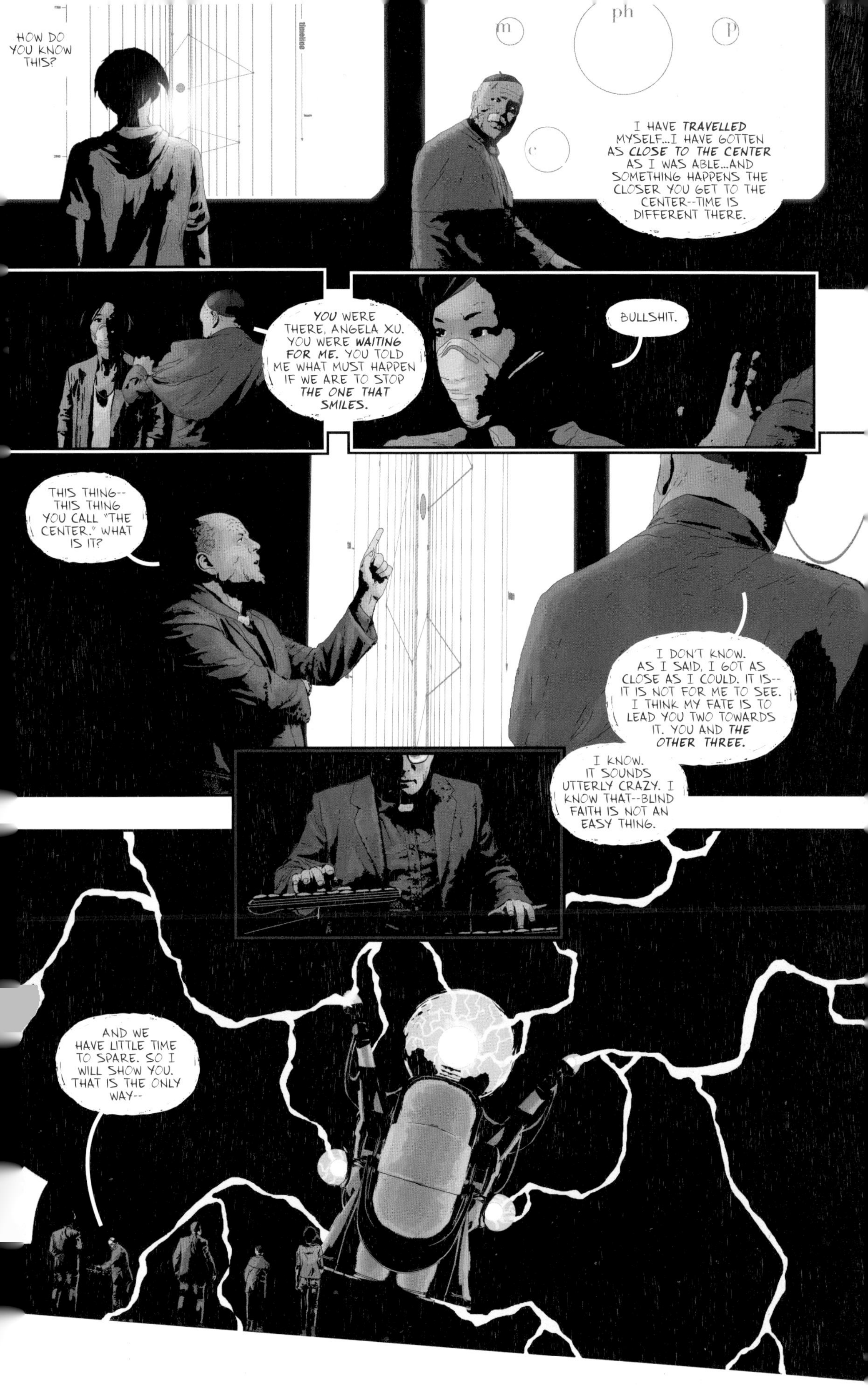
HOW DO YOU KNOW THIS?
I HAVE TRAVELLED MYSELF...I HAVE GOTTEN AS CLOSE TO THE CENTER AS I WAS ABLE...AND SOMETHING HAPPENS THE CLOSER YOU GET TO THE CENTER--TIME IS DIFFERENT THERE.
YOU WERE THERE, ANGELA XU. YOU WERE WAITING FOR ME. YOU TOLD ME WHAT MUST HAPPEN IF WE ARE TO STOP THE ONE THAT SMILES.
BULLSHIT.
THIS THING--THIS THING YOU CALL "THE CENTER." WHAT IS IT?
I DON'T KNOW. AS I SAID, I GOT AS CLOSE AS I COULD. IT IS--IT IS NOT FOR ME TO SEE. I THINK MY FATE IS TO LEAD YOU TWO TOWARDS IT. YOU AND THE OTHER THREE.
I KNOW. IT SOUNDS UTTERLY CRAZY. I KNOW THAT--BLIND FAITH IS NOT AN EASY THING.
AND WE HAVE LITTLE TIME TO SPARE. SO I WILL SHOW YOU. THAT IS THE ONLY WAY--

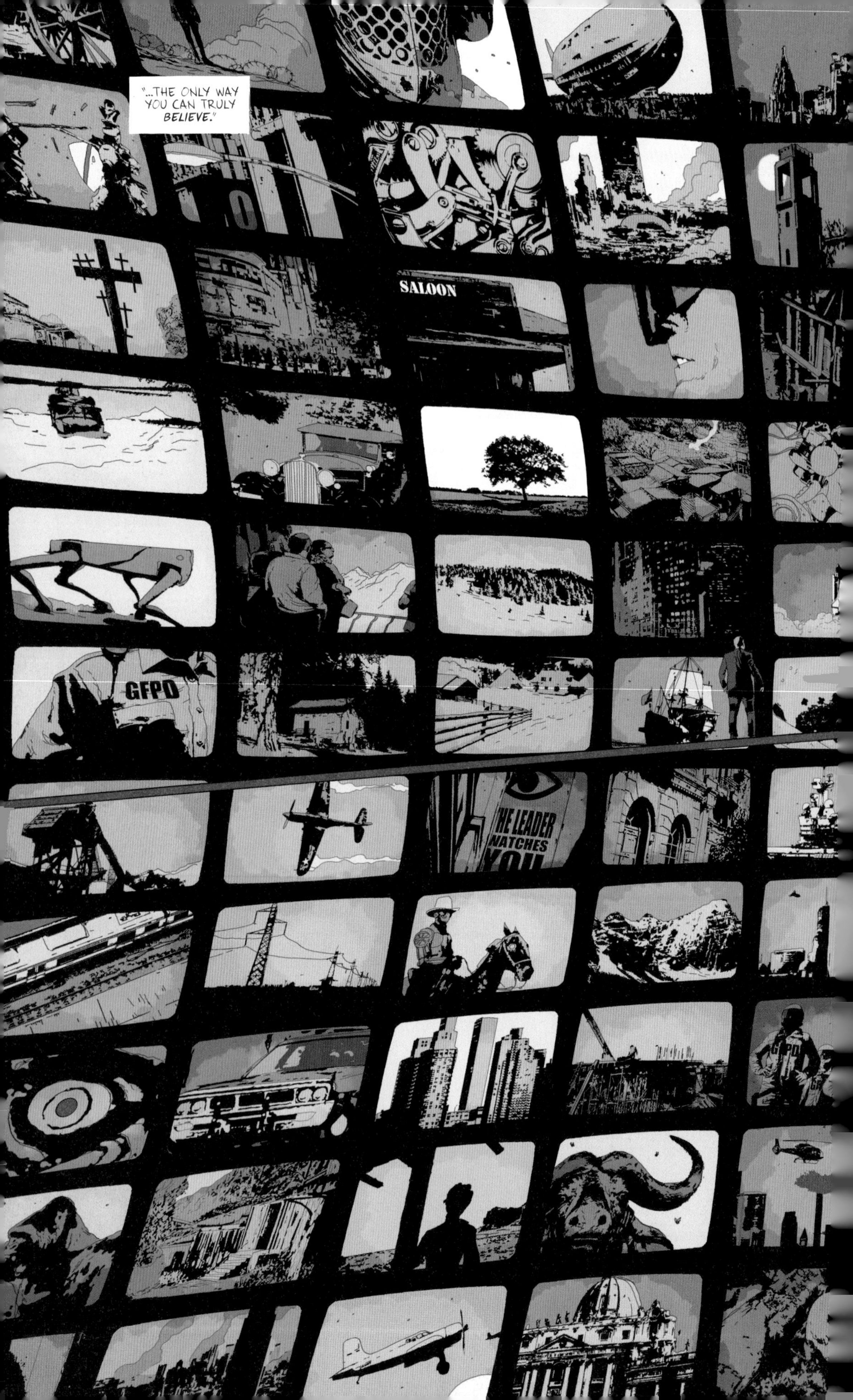
"...THE ONLY WAY YOU CAN TRULY BELIEVE."
SALOON
GFPD
THE LEADER WATCHES YOU

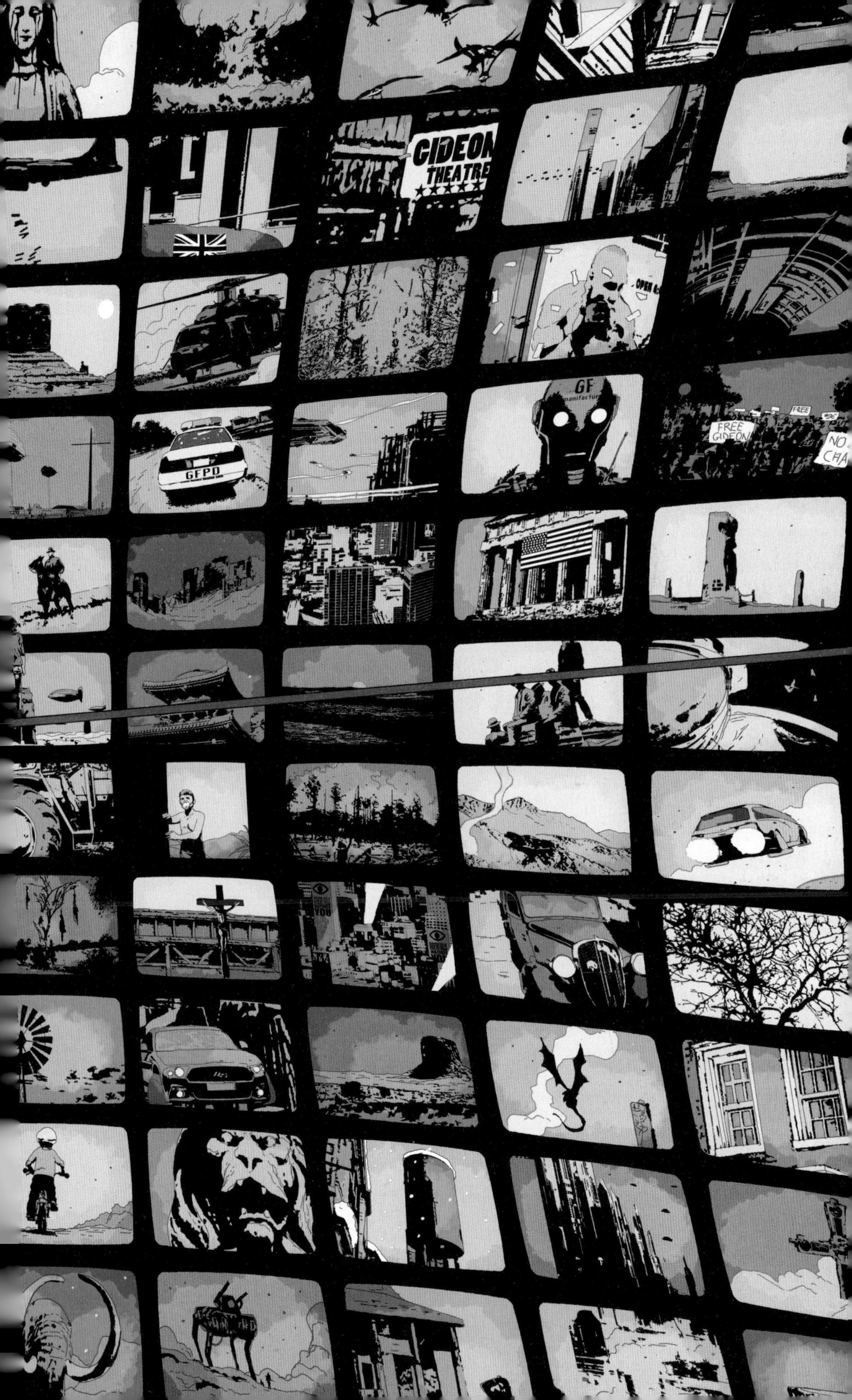

GIDEON
THEATRE
GFPD
GF
FREE GIDEON!

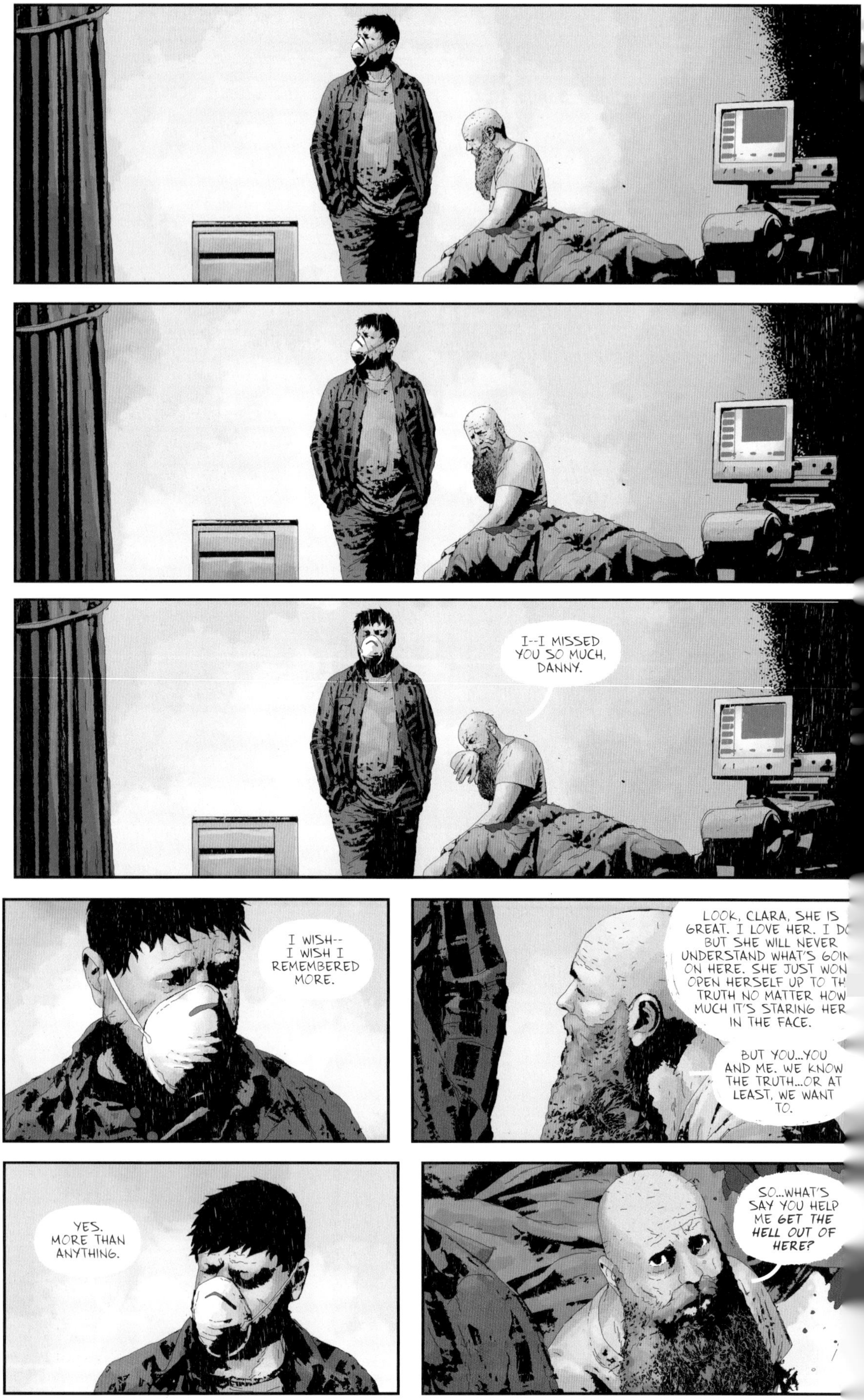
I--I MISSED YOU SO MUCH, DANNY.
I WISH-- I WISH I REMEMBERED MORE.
LOOK, CLARA, SHE IS GREAT. I LOVE HER. I DO BUT SHE WILL NEVER UNDERSTAND WHAT'S GOIN ON HERE. SHE JUST WON OPEN HERSELF UP TO TH TRUTH NO MATTER HOW MUCH IT'S STARING HER IN THE FACE.
BUT YOU...YOU AND ME. WE KNOW THE TRUTH...OR AT LEAST, WE WANT TO.
YES. MORE THAN ANYTHING.
SO...WHAT'S SAY YOU HELP ME ***GET THE HELL OUT OF HERE?***

--WHAT DO YOU HAVE FOR ME?
WELL, I HONESTLY CAN'T MAKE MUCH SENSE OF IT...
OKAY, HERE IS YOUR FATHER'S ROOM RIGHT BEFORE EVERYTHING WENT TO HELL...
C
HERE WE GO...
CAMERA 013
CAMERA 013
HERE! WATCH.
CAM
WHAT THE FUCK WAS THAT?!
KZZZT
CAMERA 013
I HAVE NO IDEA. BUT HERE IT COMES...

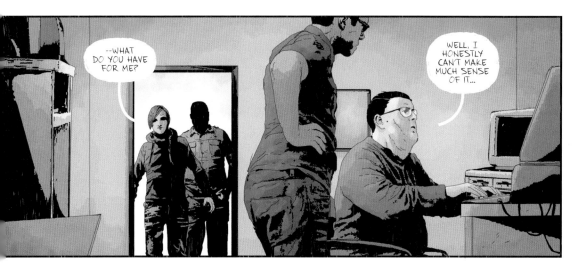

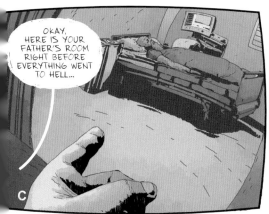

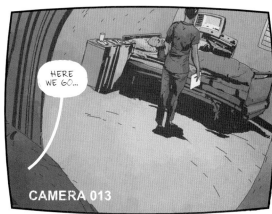

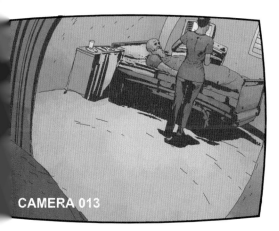

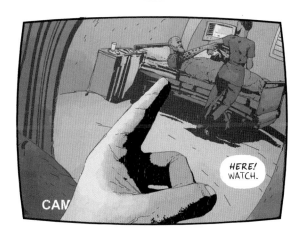

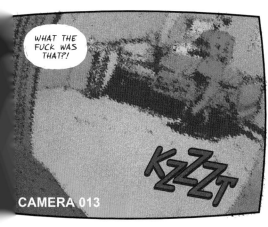

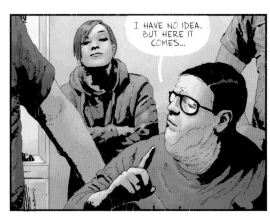

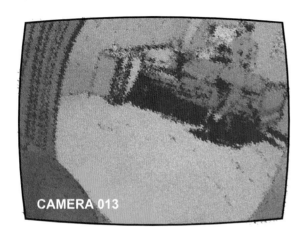

CAMERA 013

CAMERA 013

THE NURSE...

IT--IT WAS *THE* NURSE.

LOOKS THAT WAY. IS IT BAD TO SAY I'M KIND OF RELIEVED?

WHAT?!

WELL... IT WASN'T YOUR DAD, I MEAN.

A MAN *IS DEAD,* BALLARD.

NO, NO, YOU'RE RIGHT. I DIDN'T MEAN--

THE NURSE... WHERE IS SHE NOW?

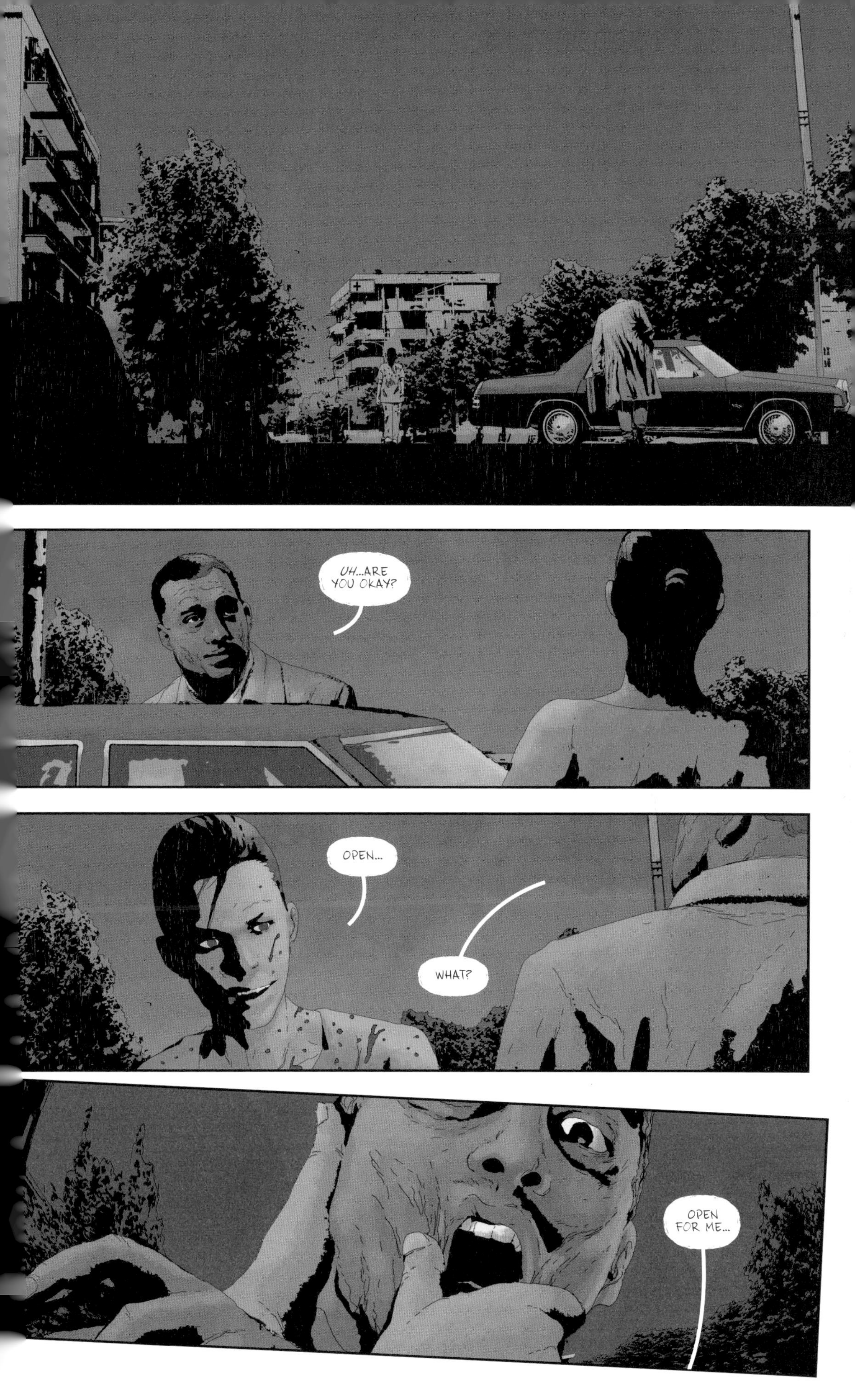
UH...ARE YOU OKAY?
OPEN...
WHAT?
OPEN FOR ME...

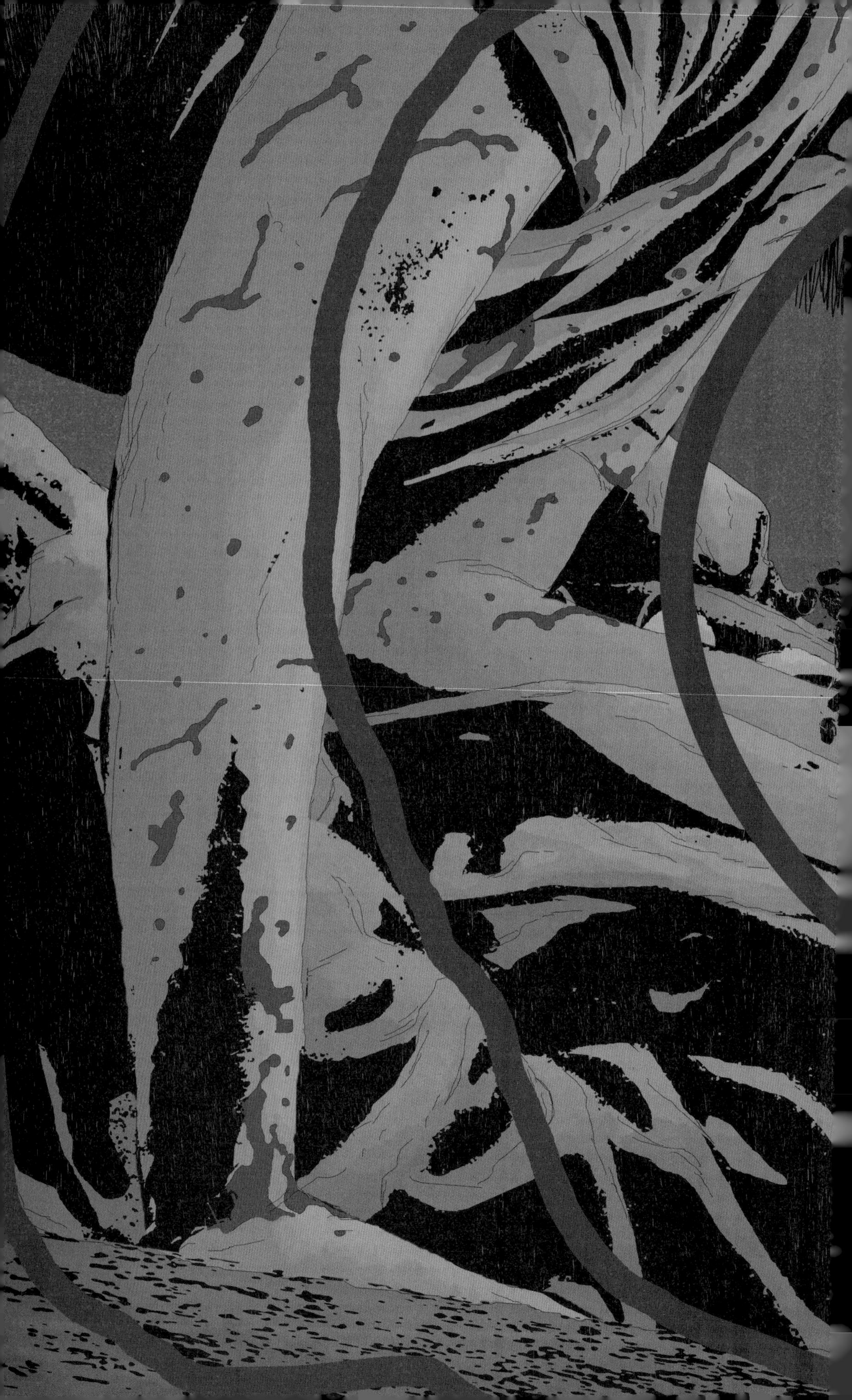

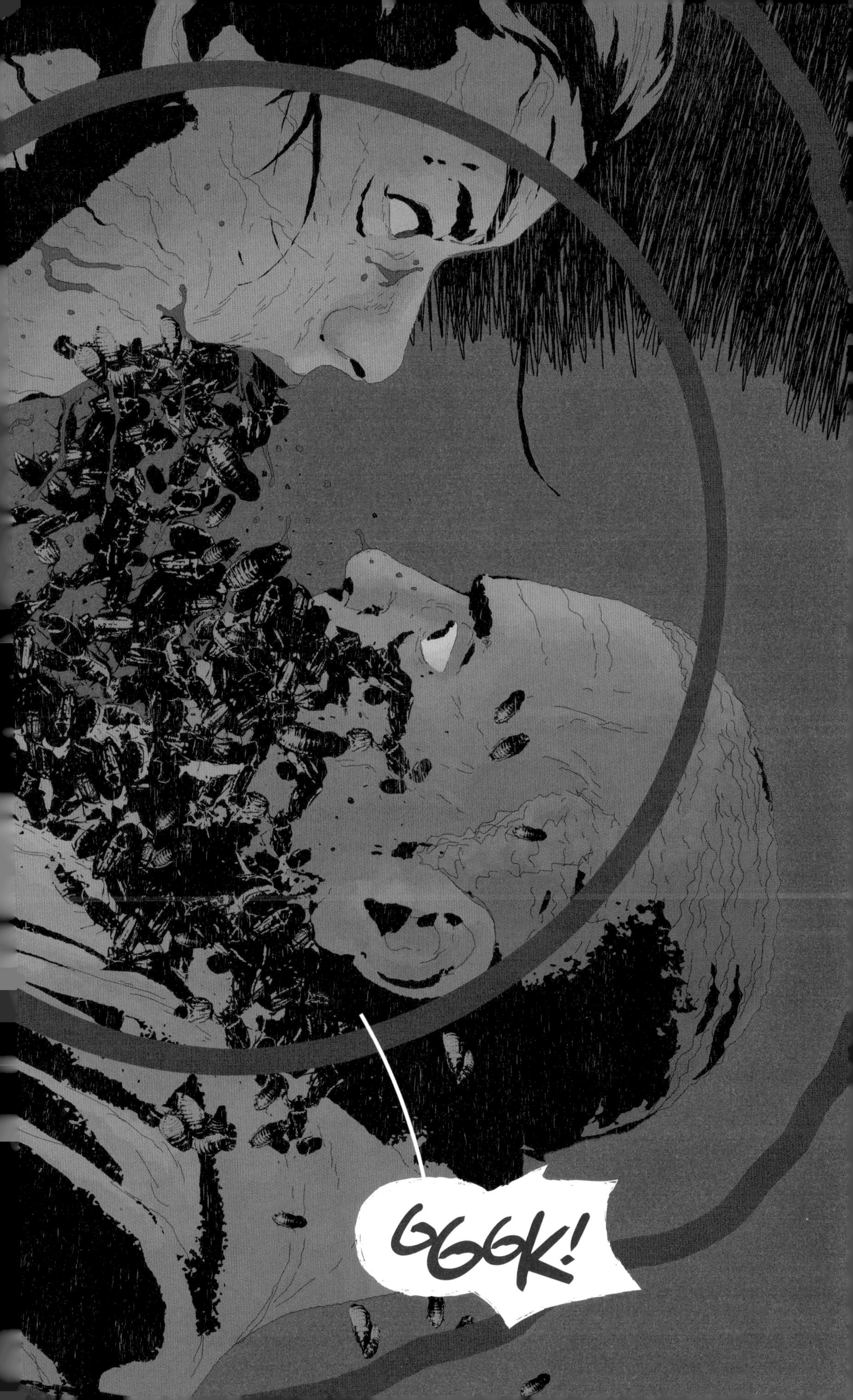
GGGK!

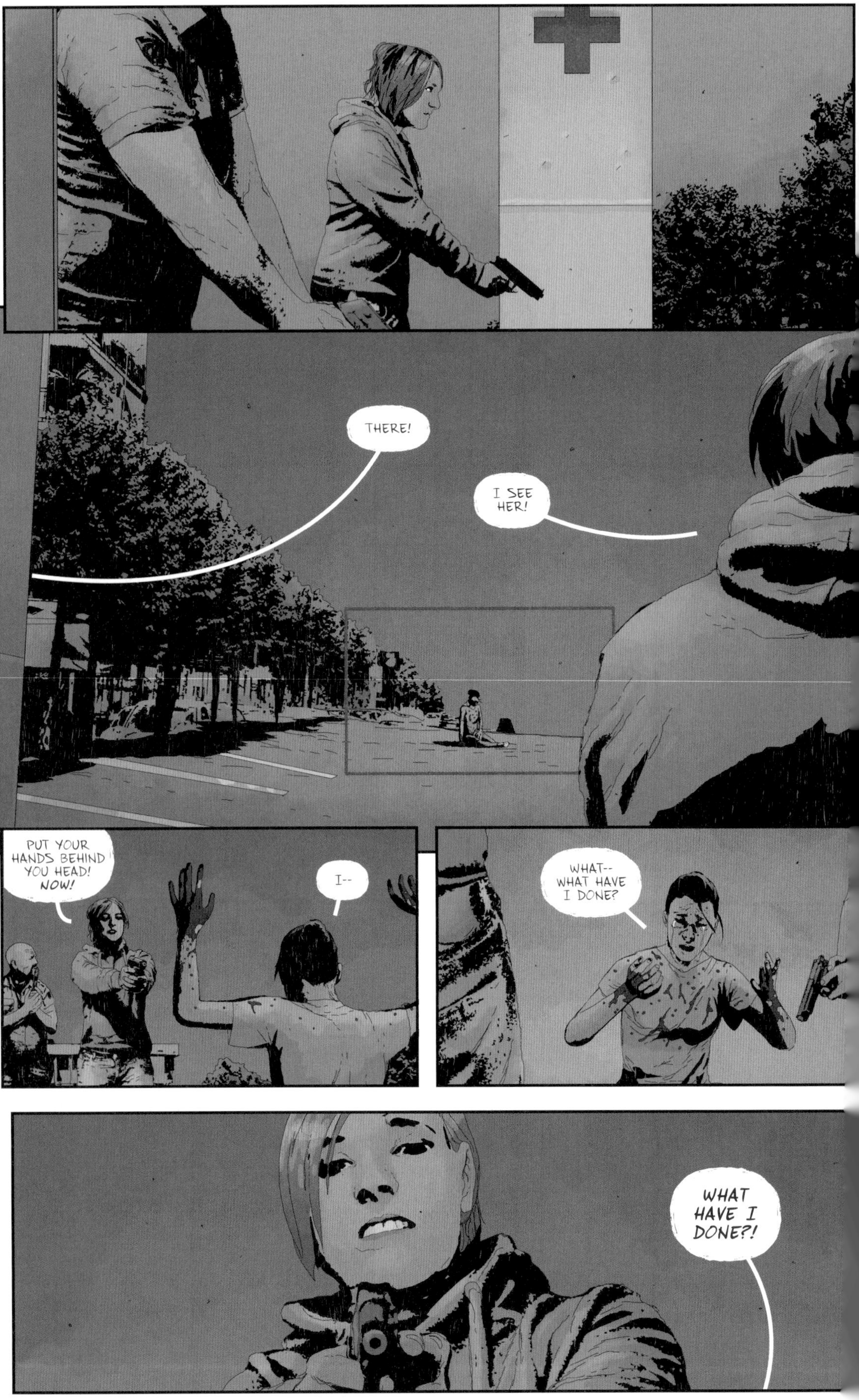
THERE!
I SEE HER!
PUT YOUR HANDS BEHIND YOU HEAD! NOW!
I--
WHAT-- WHAT HAVE I DONE?
WHAT HAVE I DONE?!

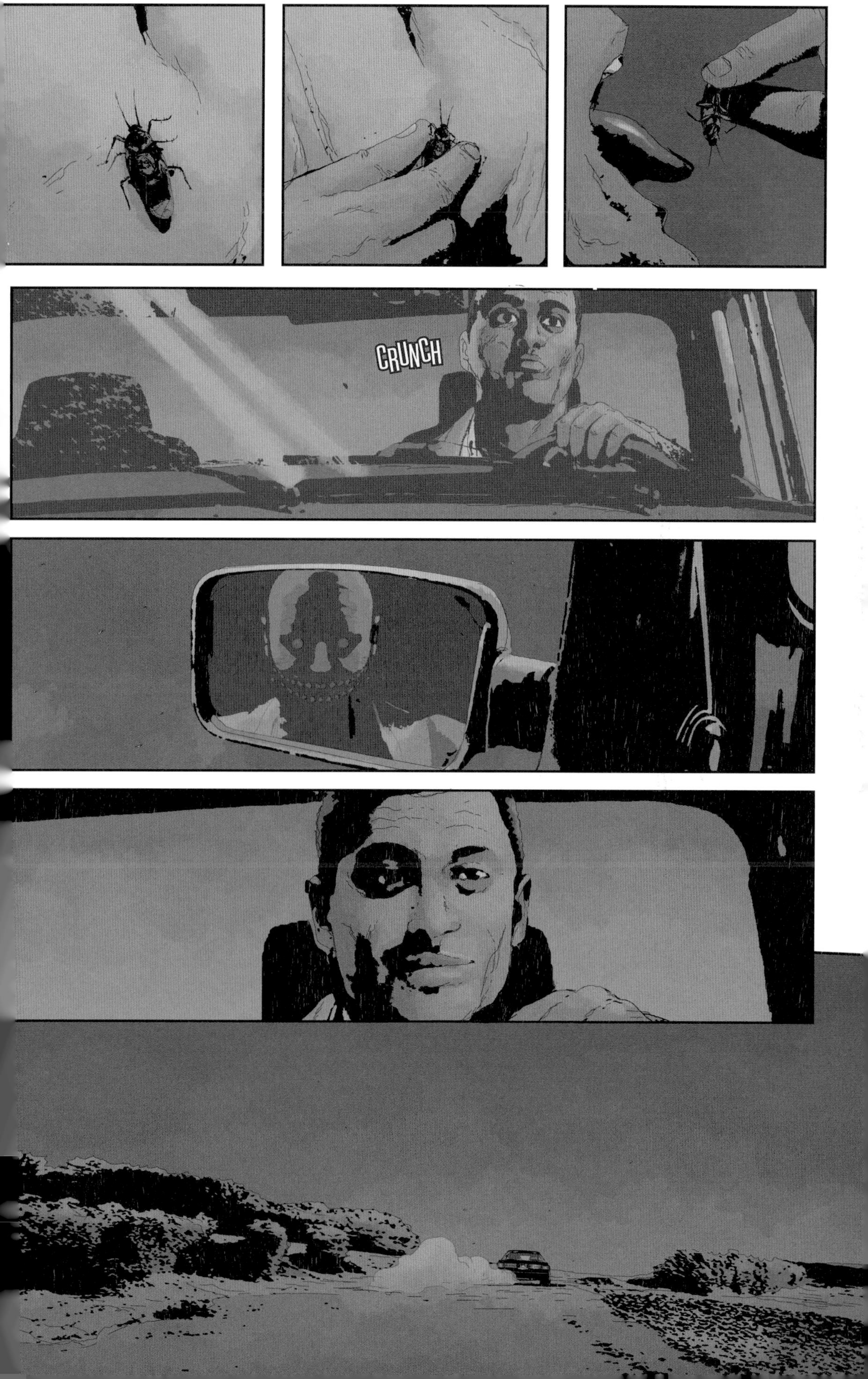
CRUNCH

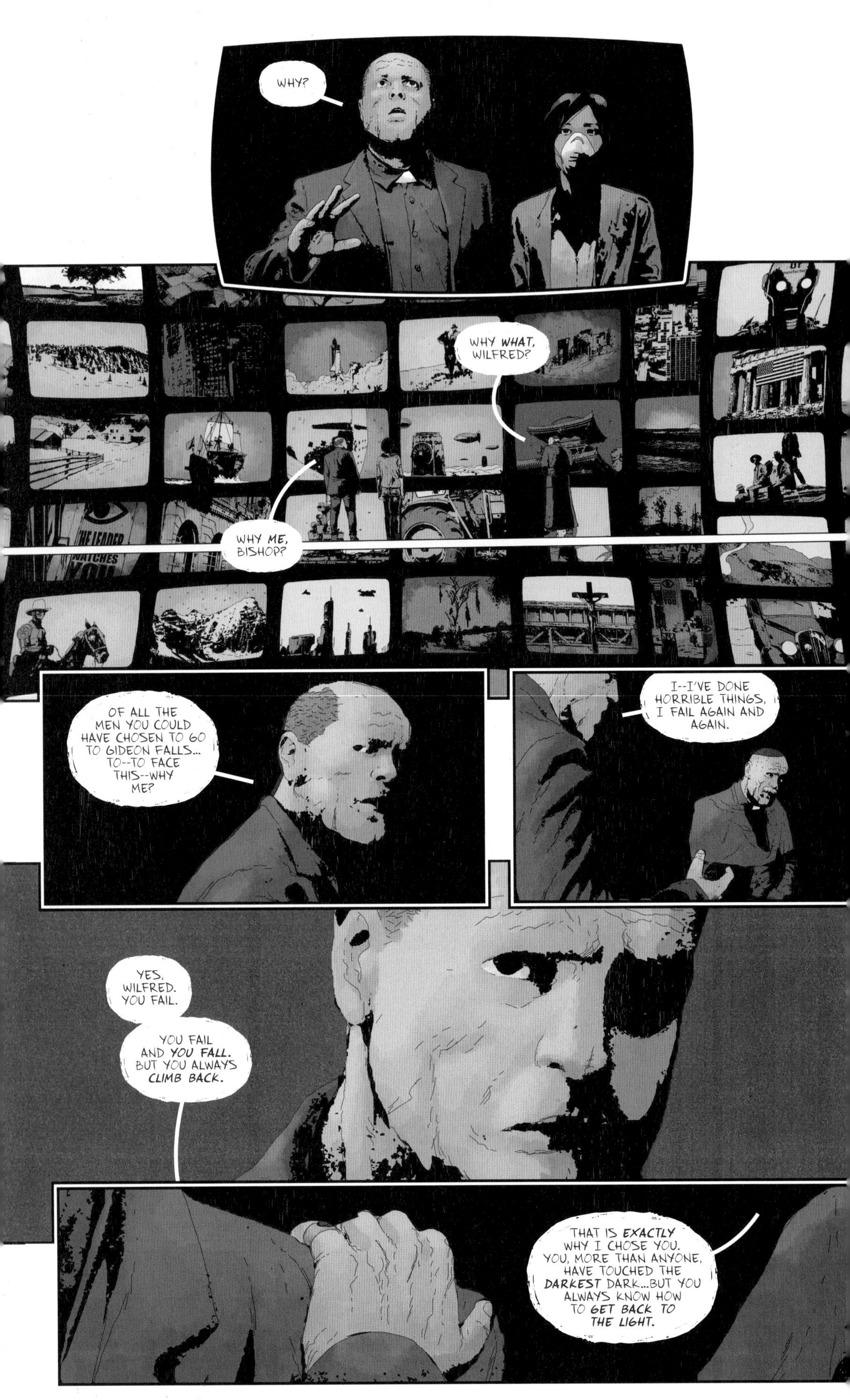
WHY?
WHY WHAT, WILFRED?
WHY ME, BISHOP?
OF ALL THE MEN YOU COULD HAVE CHOSEN TO GO TO GIDEON FALLS... TO--TO FACE THIS--WHY ME?
I--I'VE DONE HORRIBLE THINGS, I FAIL AGAIN AND AGAIN.
YES, WILFRED. YOU FAIL.
YOU FAIL AND YOU FALL. BUT YOU ALWAYS CLIMB BACK.
THAT IS EXACTLY WHY I CHOSE YOU. YOU, MORE THAN ANYONE, HAVE TOUCHED THE DARKEST DARK...BUT YOU ALWAYS KNOW HOW TO GET BACK TO THE LIGHT.

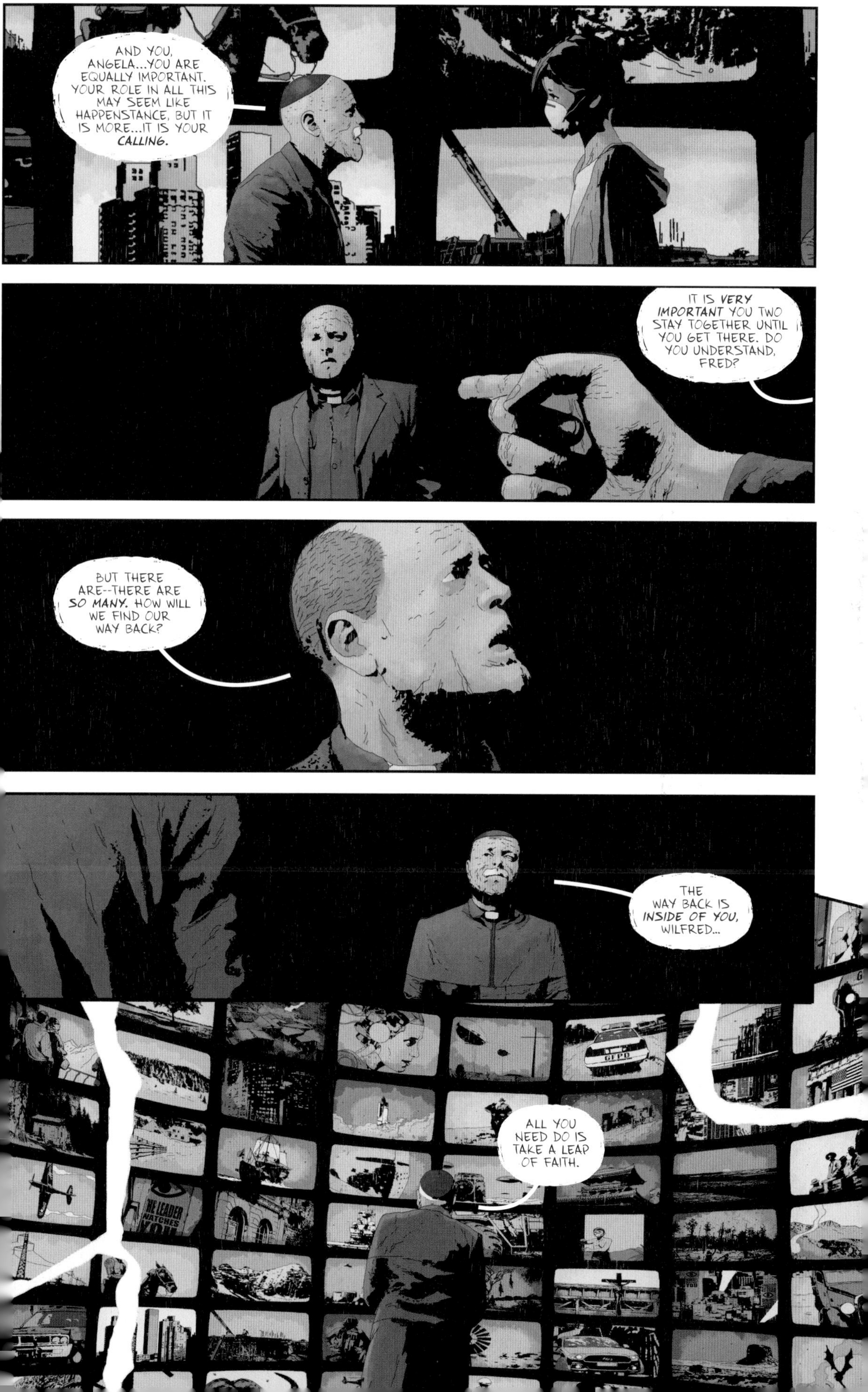
AND YOU, ANGELA...YOU ARE EQUALLY IMPORTANT. YOUR ROLE IN ALL THIS MAY SEEM LIKE HAPPENSTANCE, BUT IT IS MORE...IT IS YOUR **CALLING.**
IT IS ***VERY IMPORTANT*** YOU TWO STAY TOGETHER UNTIL YOU GET THERE. DO YOU UNDERSTAND, FRED?
BUT THERE ARE--THERE ARE ***SO MANY.*** HOW WILL WE FIND OUR WAY BACK?
THE WAY BACK IS ***INSIDE OF YOU,*** WILFRED...
ALL YOU NEED DO IS TAKE A LEAP OF FAITH.

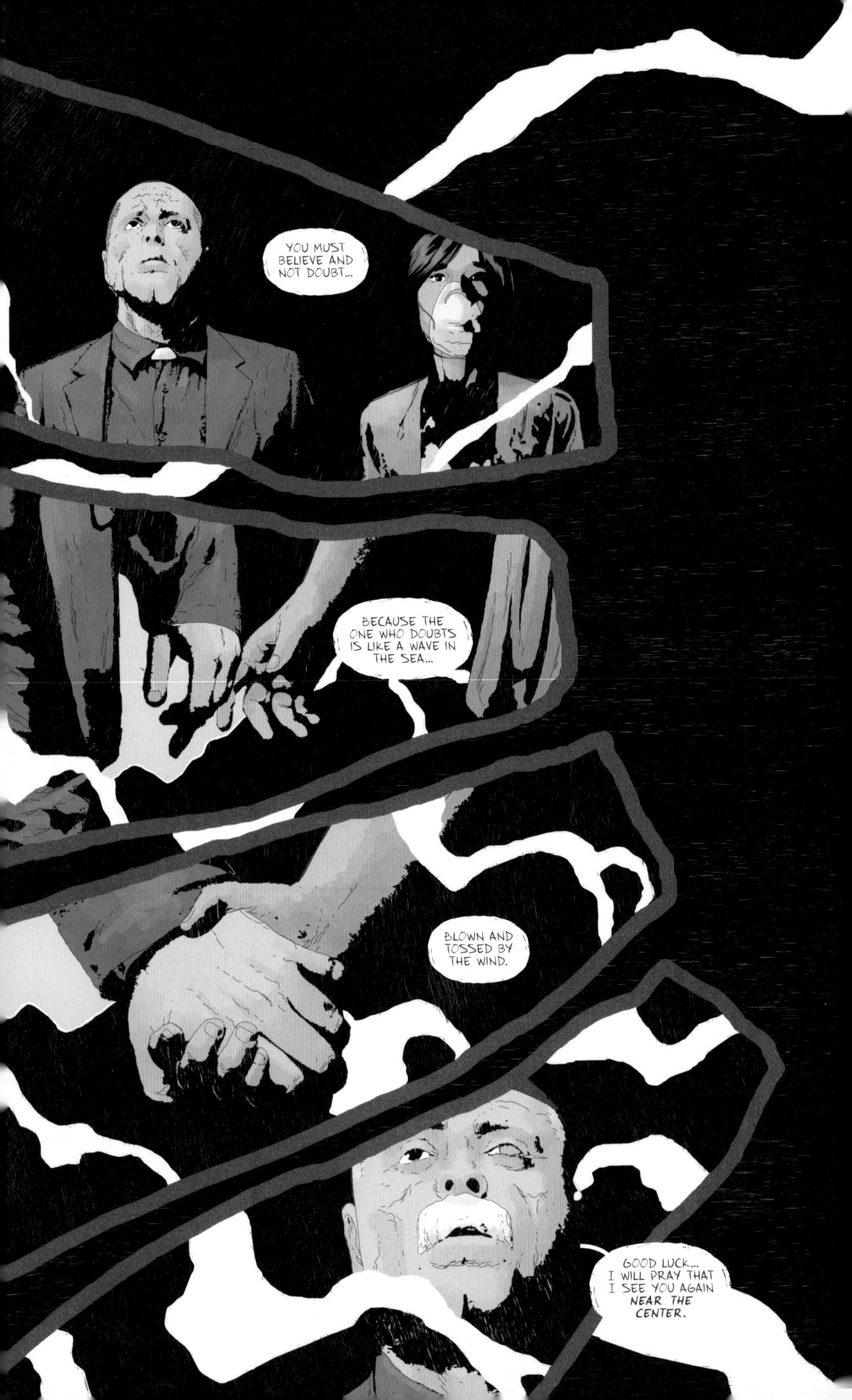
YOU MUST BELIEVE AND NOT DOUBT...
BECAUSE THE ONE WHO DOUBTS IS LIKE A WAVE IN THE SEA...
BLOWN AND TOSSED BY THE WIND.
GOOD LUCK... I WILL PRAY THAT I SEE YOU AGAIN **NEAR THE CENTER.**

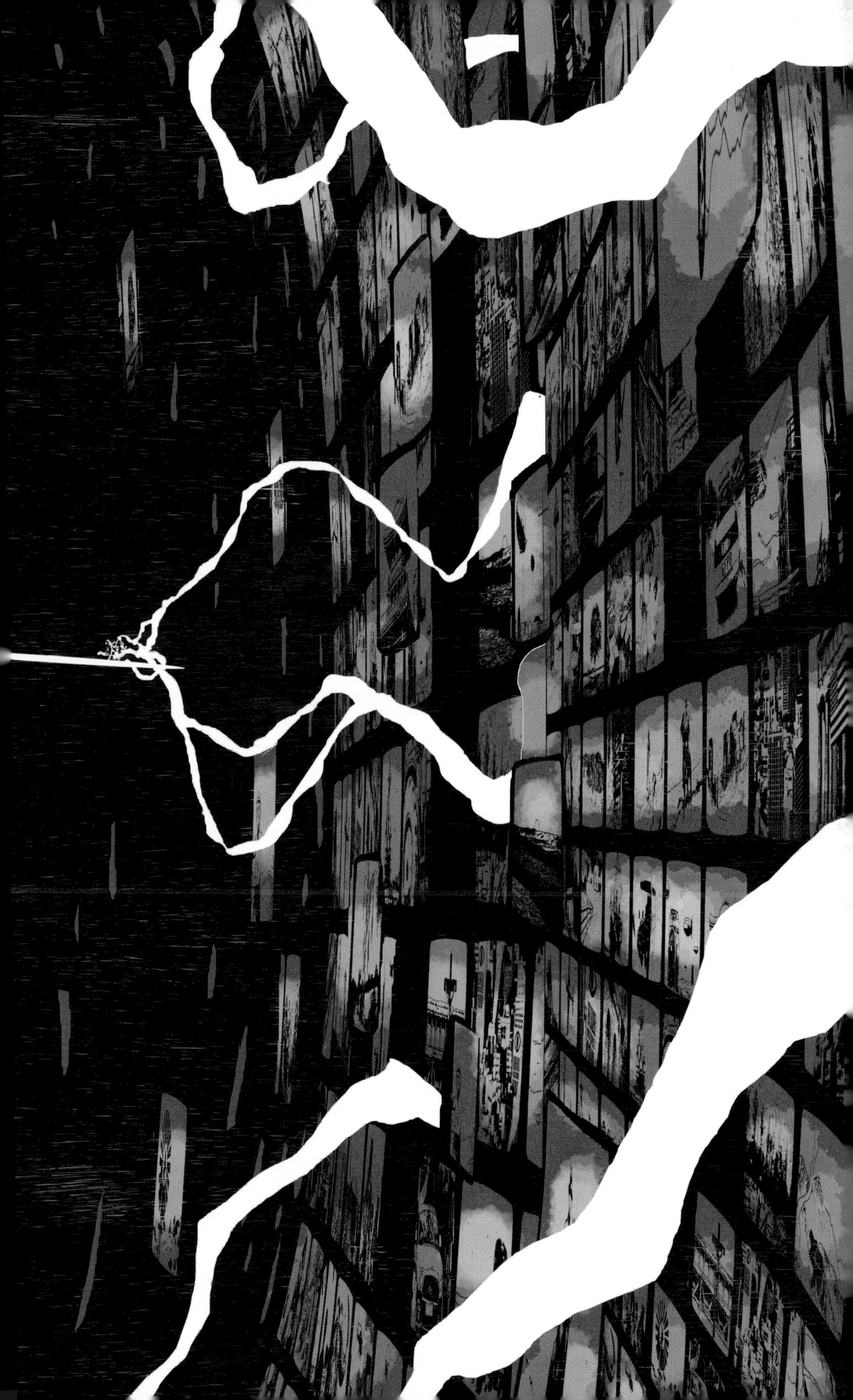

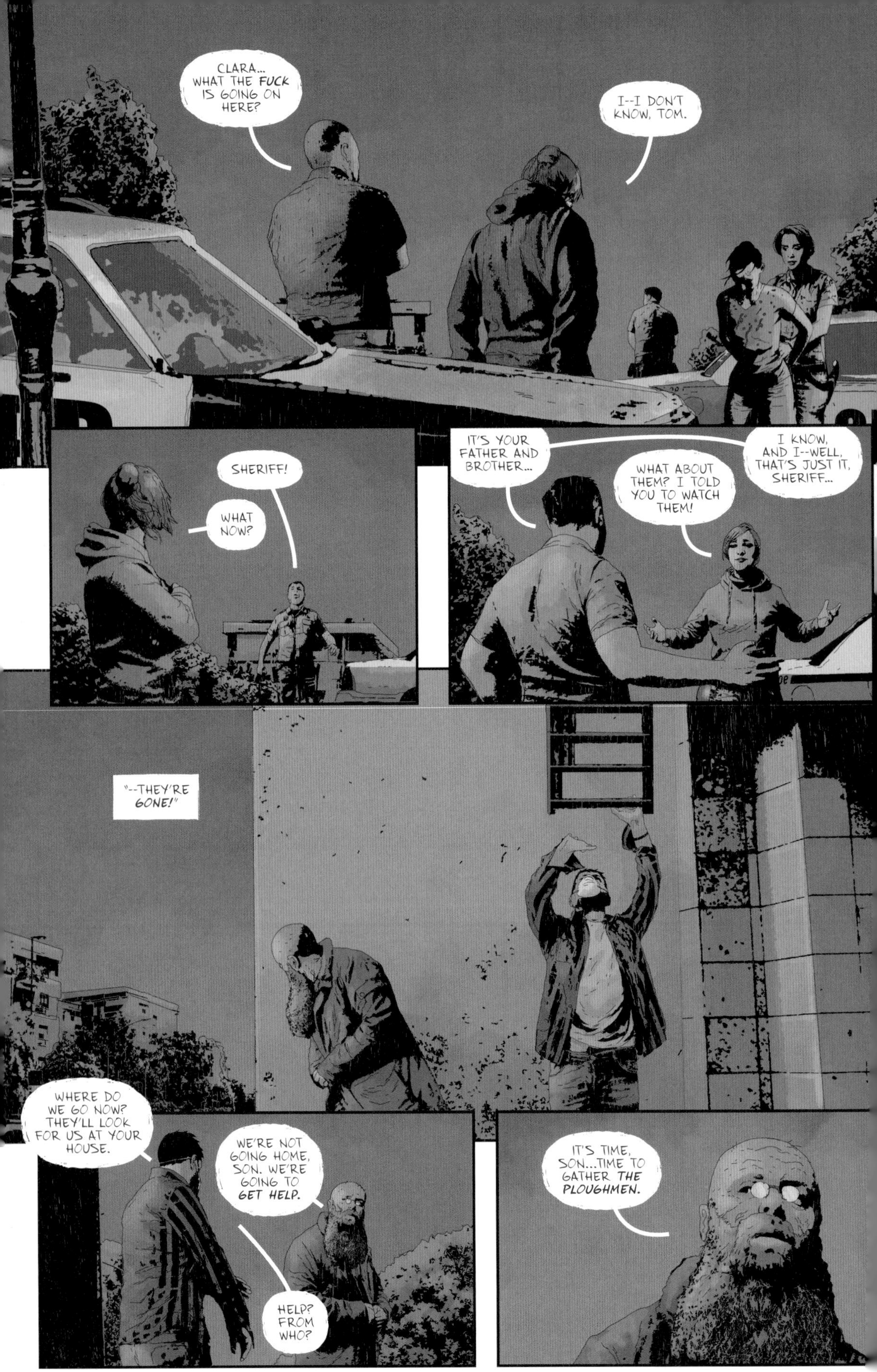
CLARA... WHAT THE FUCK IS GOING ON HERE?
I--I DON'T KNOW, TOM.
SHERIFF!
WHAT NOW?
IT'S YOUR FATHER AND BROTHER...
WHAT ABOUT THEM? I TOLD YOU TO WATCH THEM!
I KNOW, AND I--WELL, THAT'S JUST IT, SHERIFF...
"--THEY'RE GONE!"
WHERE DO WE GO NOW? THEY'LL LOOK FOR US AT YOUR HOUSE.
WE'RE NOT GOING HOME, SON. WE'RE GOING TO GET HELP.
HELP? FROM WHO?
IT'S TIME, SON...TIME TO GATHER THE PLOUGHMEN.

GIDEON
FALLS

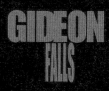

Nineteen

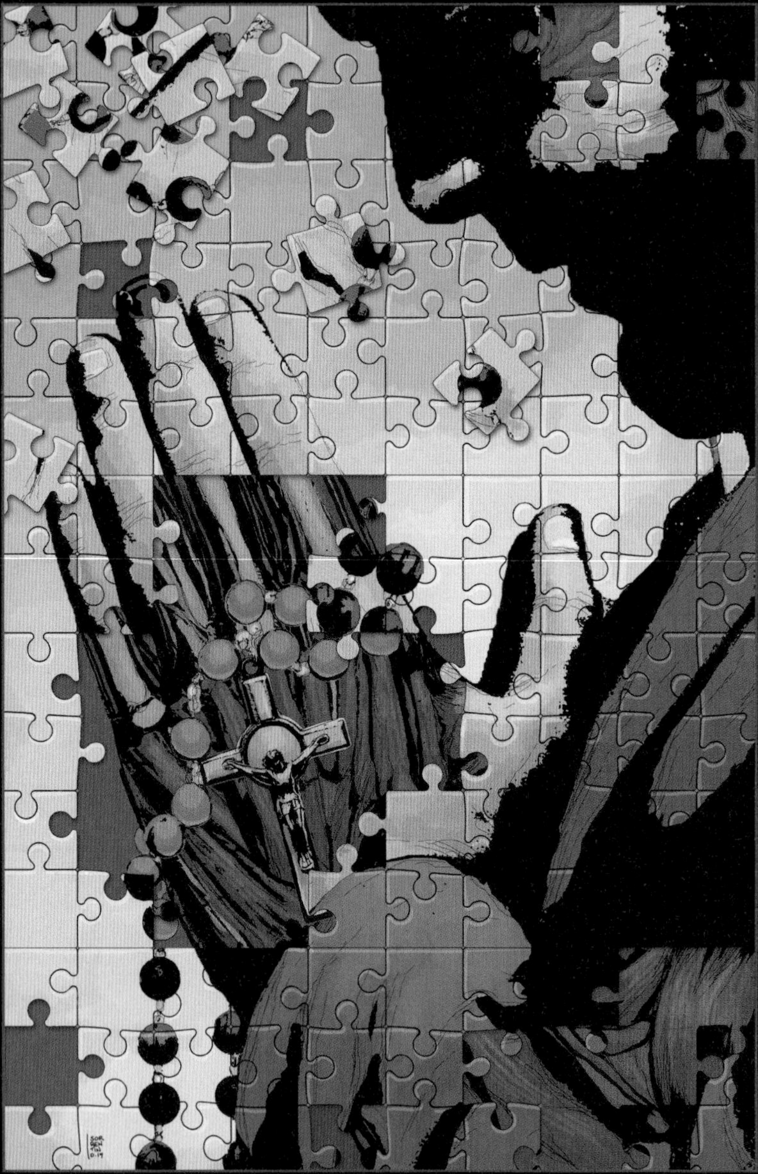

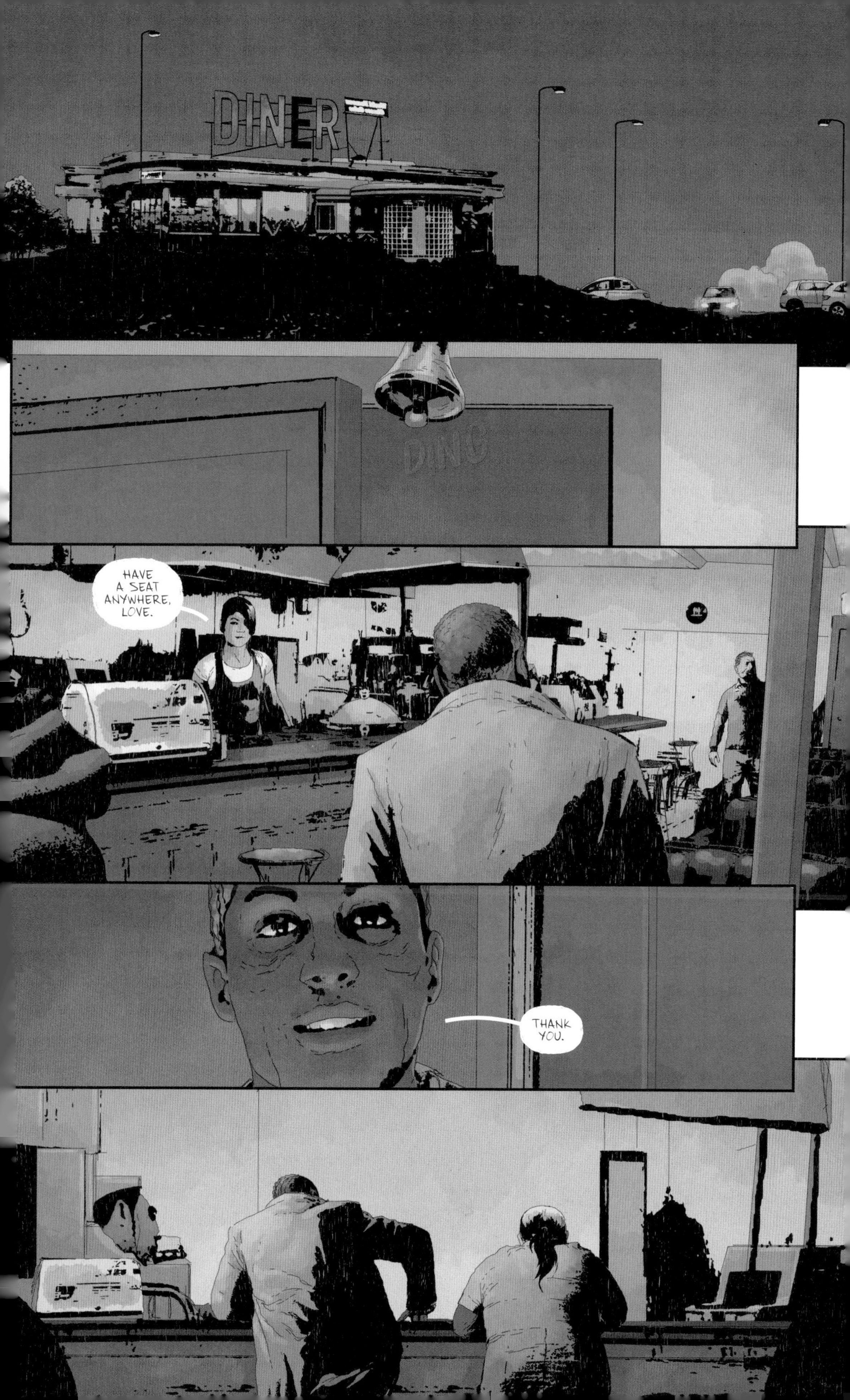
DINER
DING
HAVE A SEAT ANYWHERE, LOVE.
THANK YOU.

THAT LOOKS VERY GOOD.

UH HUH.

I AM HUNGRY...

HEY!

YOU CAN'T-- WHAT THE FUCK, MAN?!

THE HELL IS WRONG WITH YOU?!

SO HUNGRY...

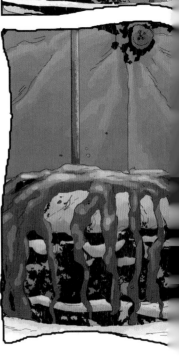

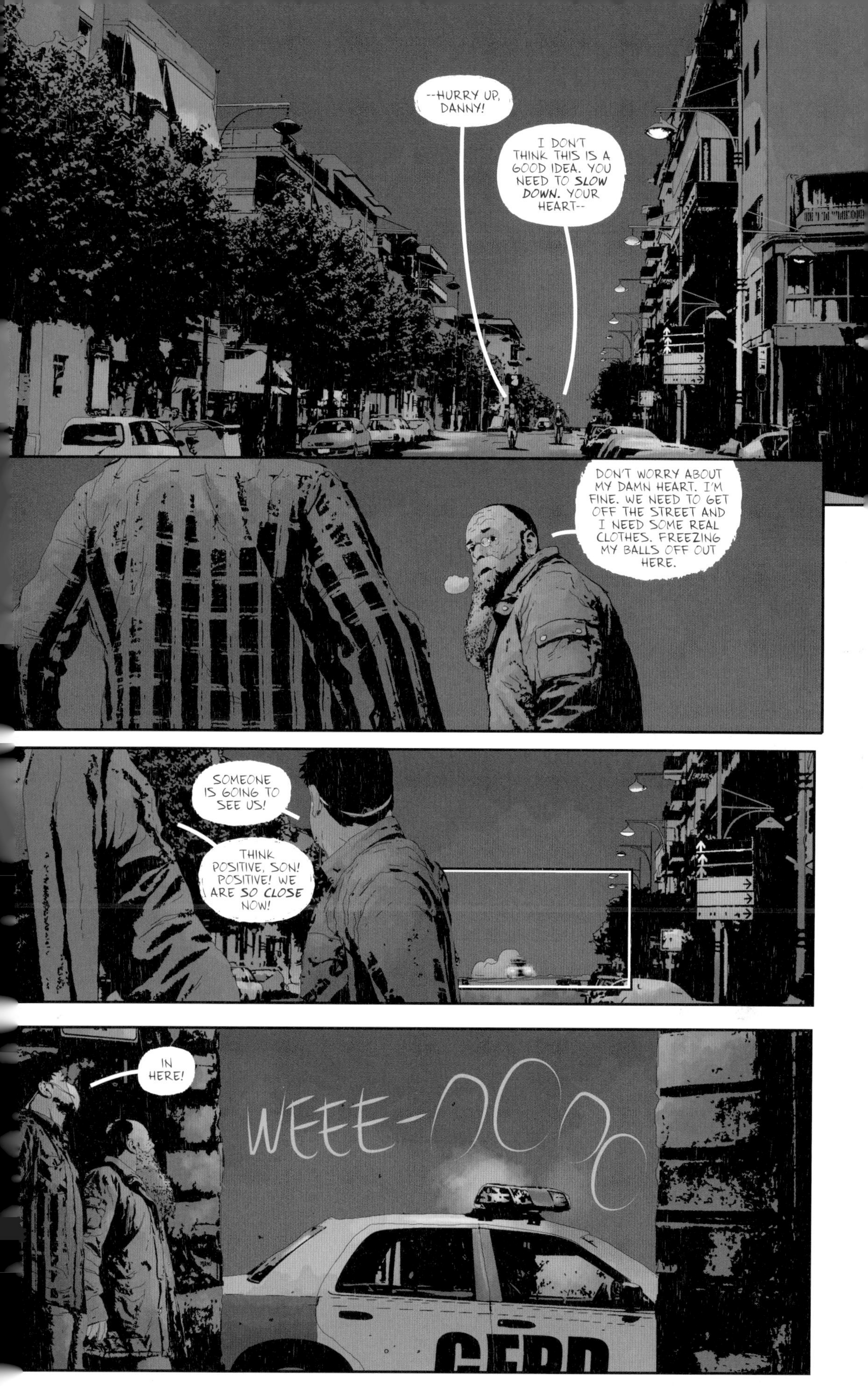
--HURRY UP, DANNY!
I DON'T THINK THIS IS A GOOD IDEA. YOU NEED TO **SLOW DOWN.** YOUR HEART--
DON'T WORRY ABOUT MY DAMN HEART. I'M FINE. WE NEED TO GET OFF THE STREET AND I NEED SOME REAL CLOTHES. FREEZING MY BALLS OFF OUT HERE.
SOMEONE IS GOING TO SEE US!
THINK POSITIVE, SON! POSITIVE! WE ARE **SO CLOSE** NOW!
IN HERE!
WEEE-OOOO

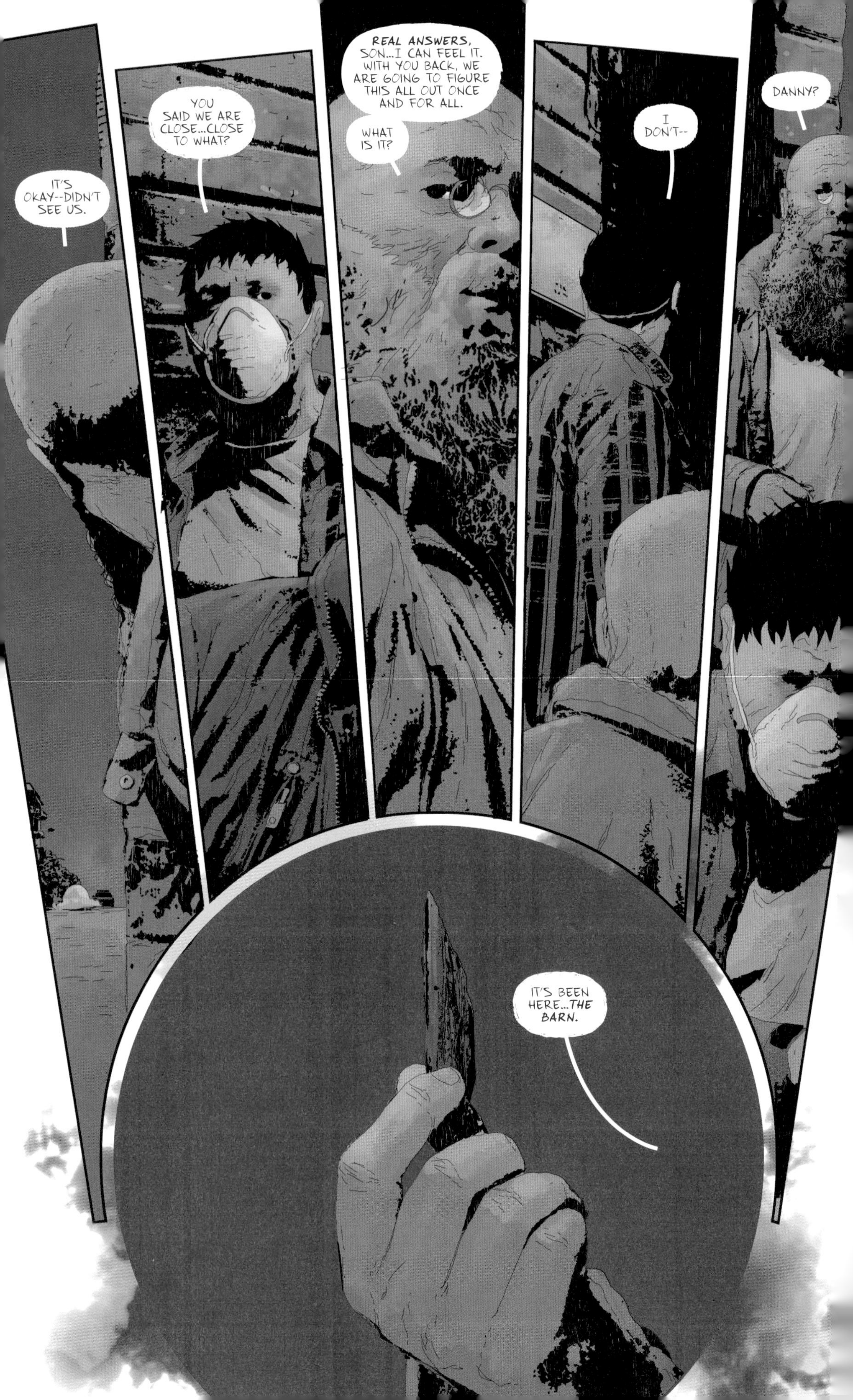

IT'S OKAY--DIDN'T SEE US.
YOU SAID WE ARE CLOSE...CLOSE TO WHAT?
REAL ANSWERS, SON...I CAN FEEL IT. WITH YOU BACK, WE ARE GOING TO FIGURE THIS ALL OUT ONCE AND FOR ALL.
WHAT IS IT?
I DON'T--
DANNY?
IT'S BEEN HERE...THE BARN.

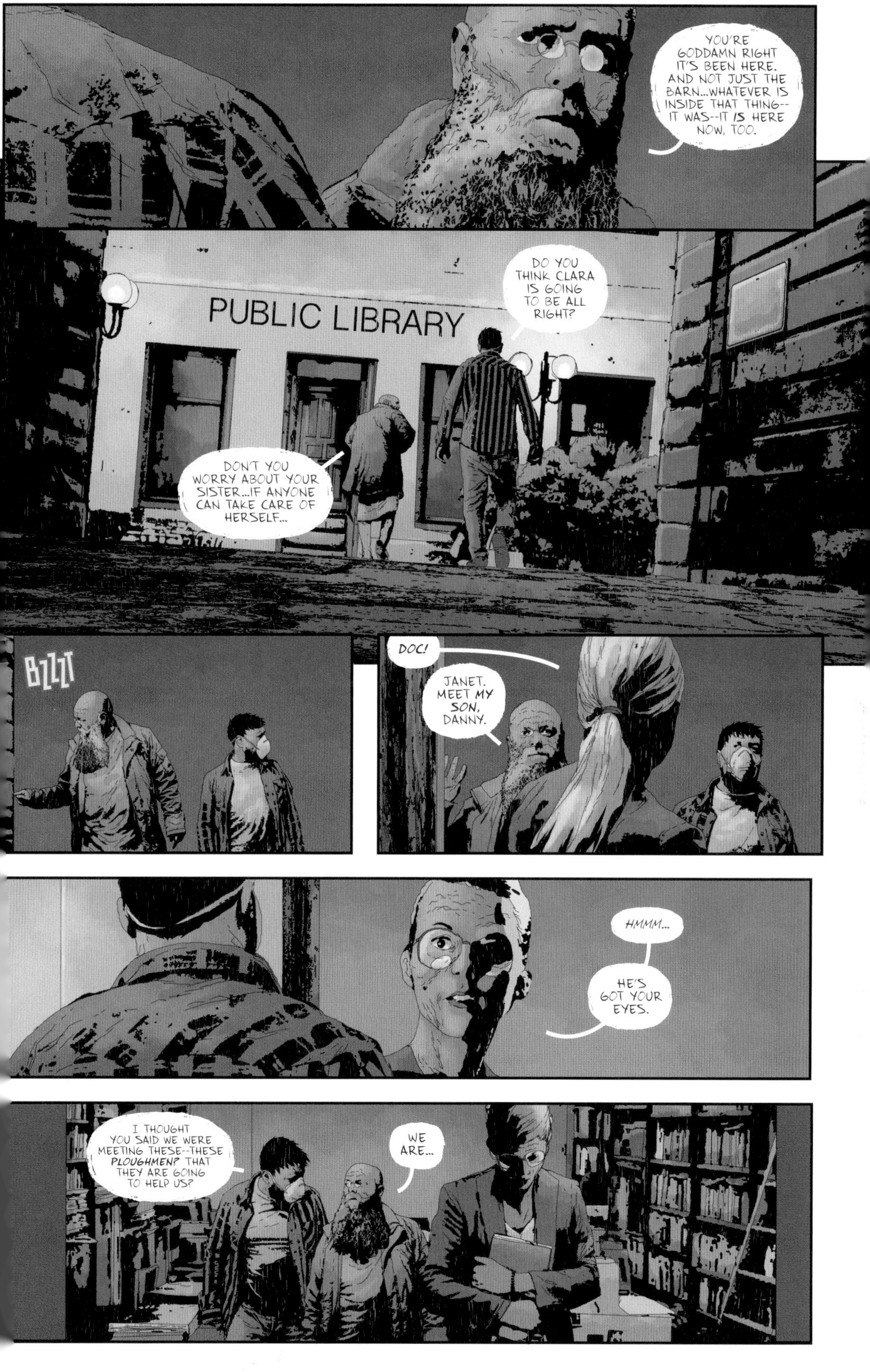
YOU'RE GODDAMN RIGHT IT'S BEEN HERE. AND NOT JUST THE BARN...WHATEVER IS INSIDE THAT THING--IT WAS--IT IS HERE NOW, TOO.
PUBLIC LIBRARY
DO YOU THINK CLARA IS GOING TO BE ALL RIGHT?
DON'T YOU WORRY ABOUT YOUR SISTER...IF ANYONE CAN TAKE CARE OF HERSELF...
BZZZT
DOC!
JANET. MEET MY SON, DANNY.
HMMM...
HE'S GOT YOUR EYES.
I THOUGHT YOU SAID WE WERE MEETING THESE--THESE PLOUGHMEN? THAT THEY ARE GOING TO HELP US?
WE ARE...

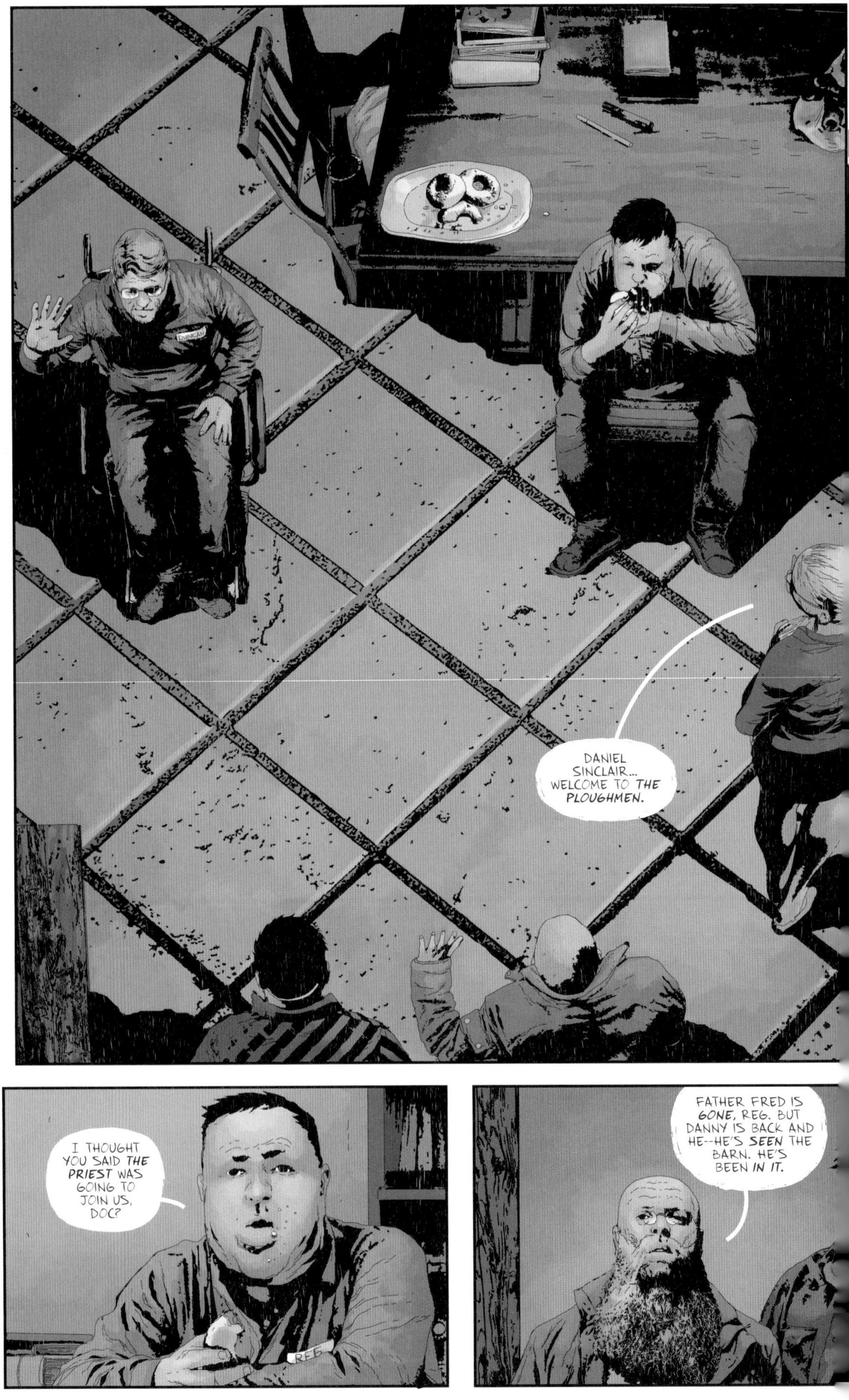
DANIEL SINCLAIR... WELCOME TO THE PLOUGHMEN.
I THOUGHT YOU SAID THE PRIEST WAS GOING TO JOIN US, DOC?
FATHER FRED IS GONE, REG. BUT DANNY IS BACK AND HE--HE'S SEEN THE BARN. HE'S BEEN IN IT.

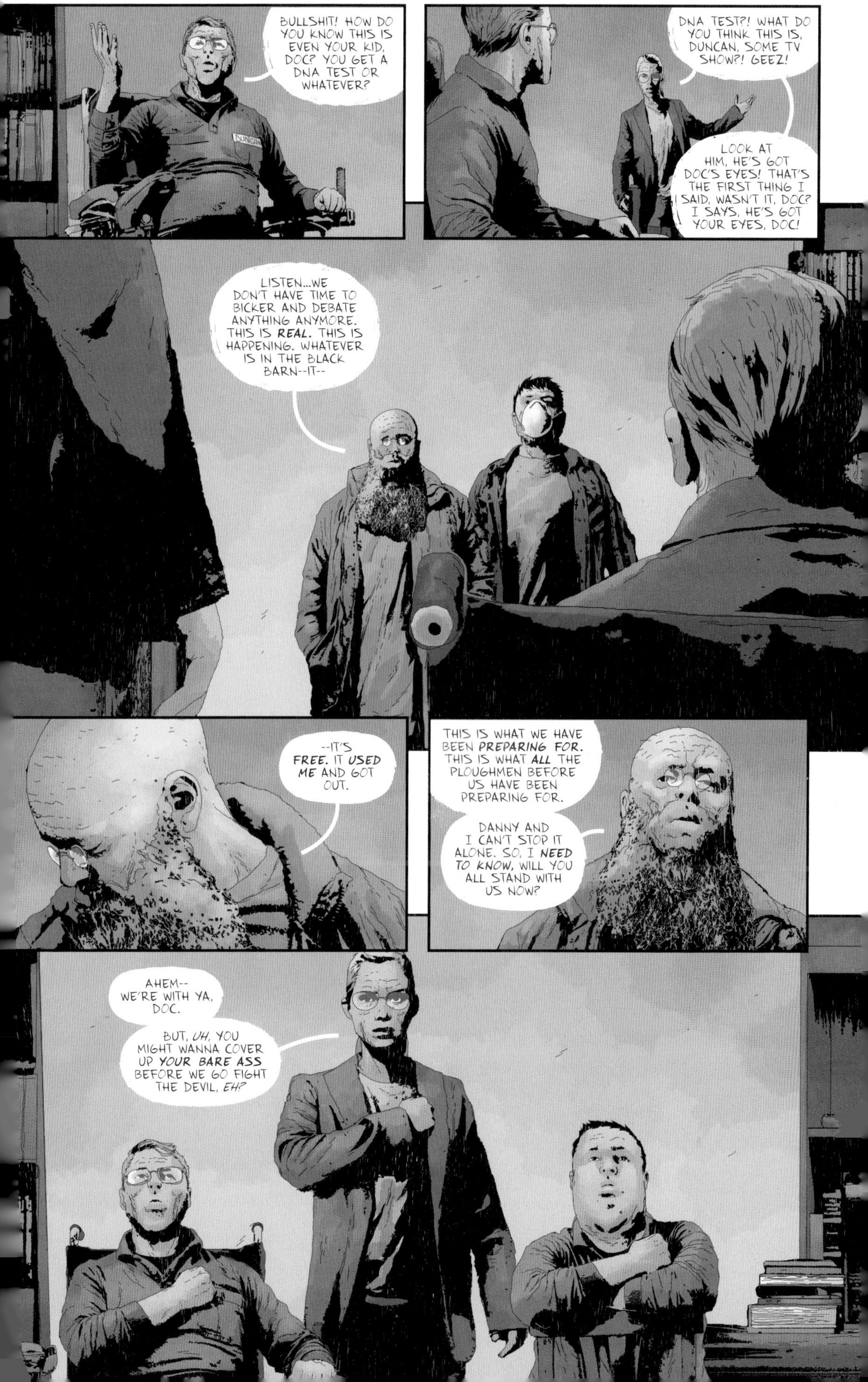
BULLSHIT! HOW DO YOU KNOW THIS IS EVEN YOUR KID, DOC? YOU GET A DNA TEST OR WHATEVER?
DUNCAN
DNA TEST?! WHAT DO YOU THINK THIS IS, DUNCAN, SOME TV SHOW?! GEEZ!
LOOK AT HIM, HE'S GOT DOC'S EYES! THAT'S THE FIRST THING I SAID, WASN'T IT, DOC? I SAYS, HE'S GOT YOUR EYES, DOC!
LISTEN...WE DON'T HAVE TIME TO BICKER AND DEBATE ANYTHING ANYMORE. THIS IS REAL. THIS IS HAPPENING. WHATEVER IS IN THE BLACK BARN--IT--
--IT'S FREE. IT USED ME AND GOT OUT.
THIS IS WHAT WE HAVE BEEN PREPARING FOR. THIS IS WHAT ALL THE PLOUGHMEN BEFORE US HAVE BEEN PREPARING FOR.
DANNY AND I CAN'T STOP IT ALONE. SO, I NEED TO KNOW, WILL YOU ALL STAND WITH US NOW?
AHEM-- WE'RE WITH YA, DOC.
BUT, UH, YOU MIGHT WANNA COVER UP YOUR BARE ASS BEFORE WE GO FIGHT THE DEVIL, EH?

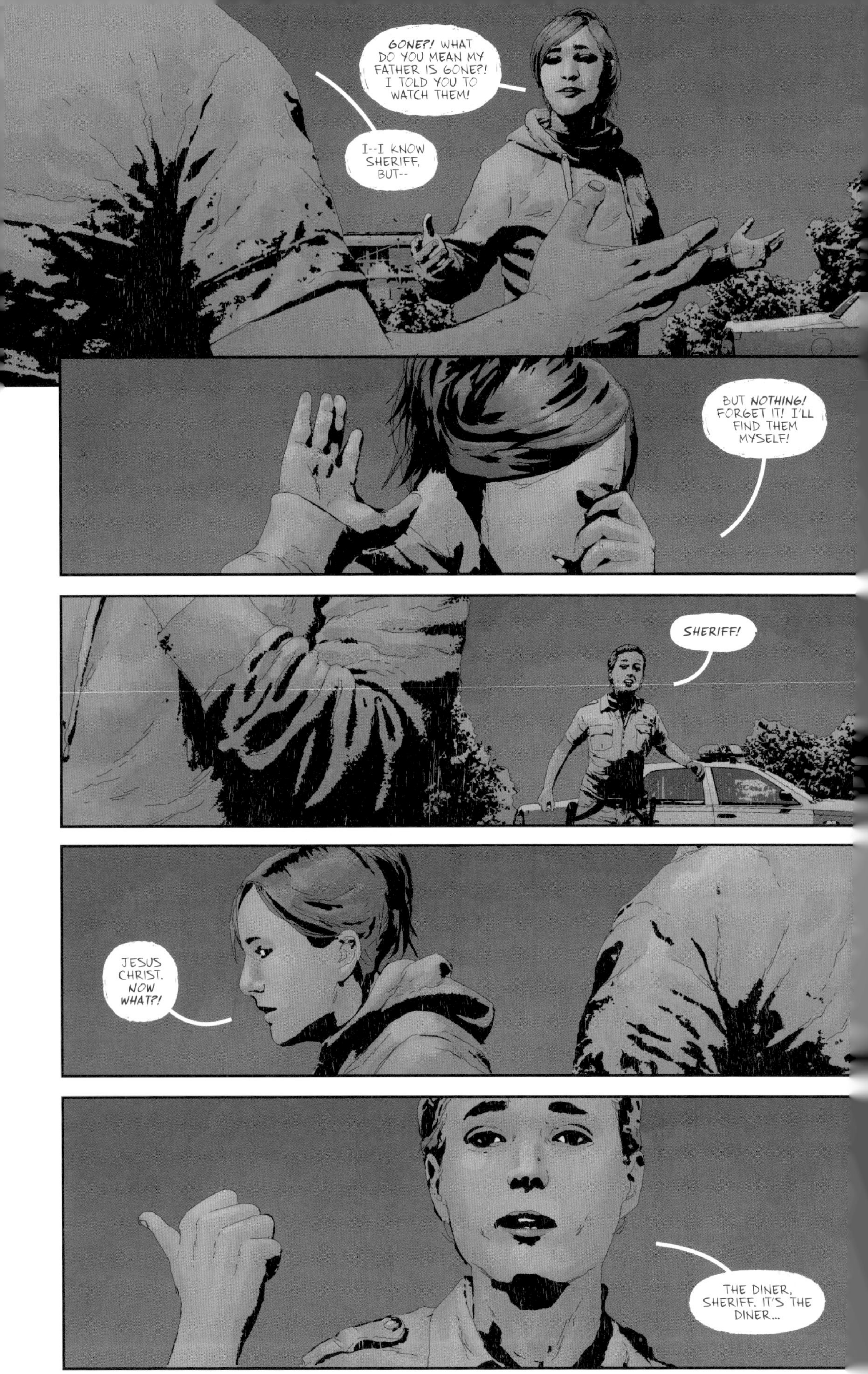
GONE?! WHAT DO YOU MEAN MY FATHER IS GONE?! I TOLD YOU TO WATCH THEM!
I--I KNOW SHERIFF, BUT--
BUT NOTHING! FORGET IT! I'LL FIND THEM MYSELF!
SHERIFF!
JESUS CHRIST. NOW WHAT?!
THE DINER, SHERIFF. IT'S THE DINER...

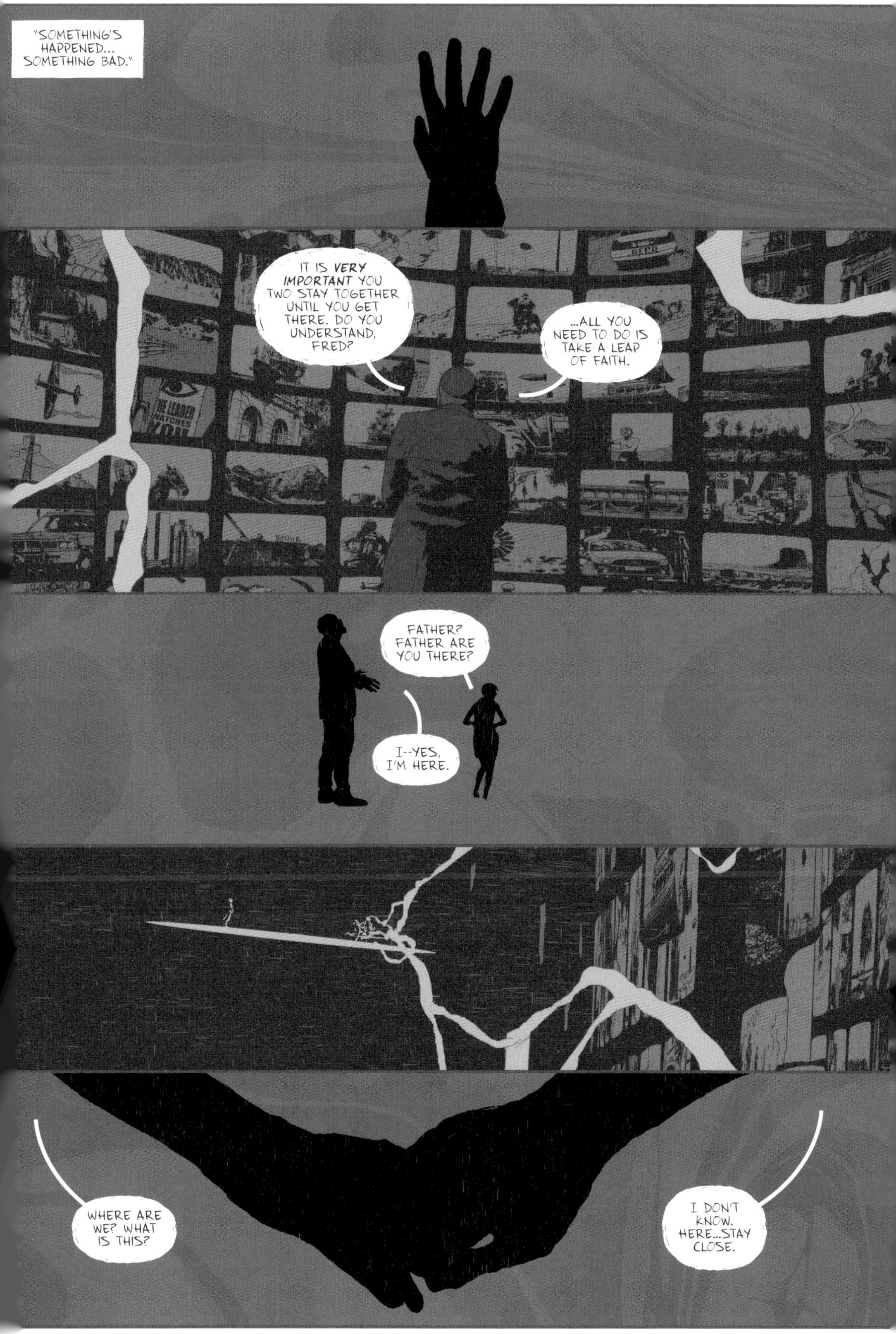
"SOMETHING'S HAPPENED... SOMETHING BAD."
IT IS VERY IMPORTANT YOU TWO STAY TOGETHER UNTIL YOU GET THERE. DO YOU UNDERSTAND, FRED?
...ALL YOU NEED TO DO IS TAKE A LEAP OF FAITH.
FATHER? FATHER ARE YOU THERE?
I--YES, I'M HERE.
WHERE ARE WE? WHAT IS THIS?
I DON'T KNOW. HERE...STAY CLOSE.

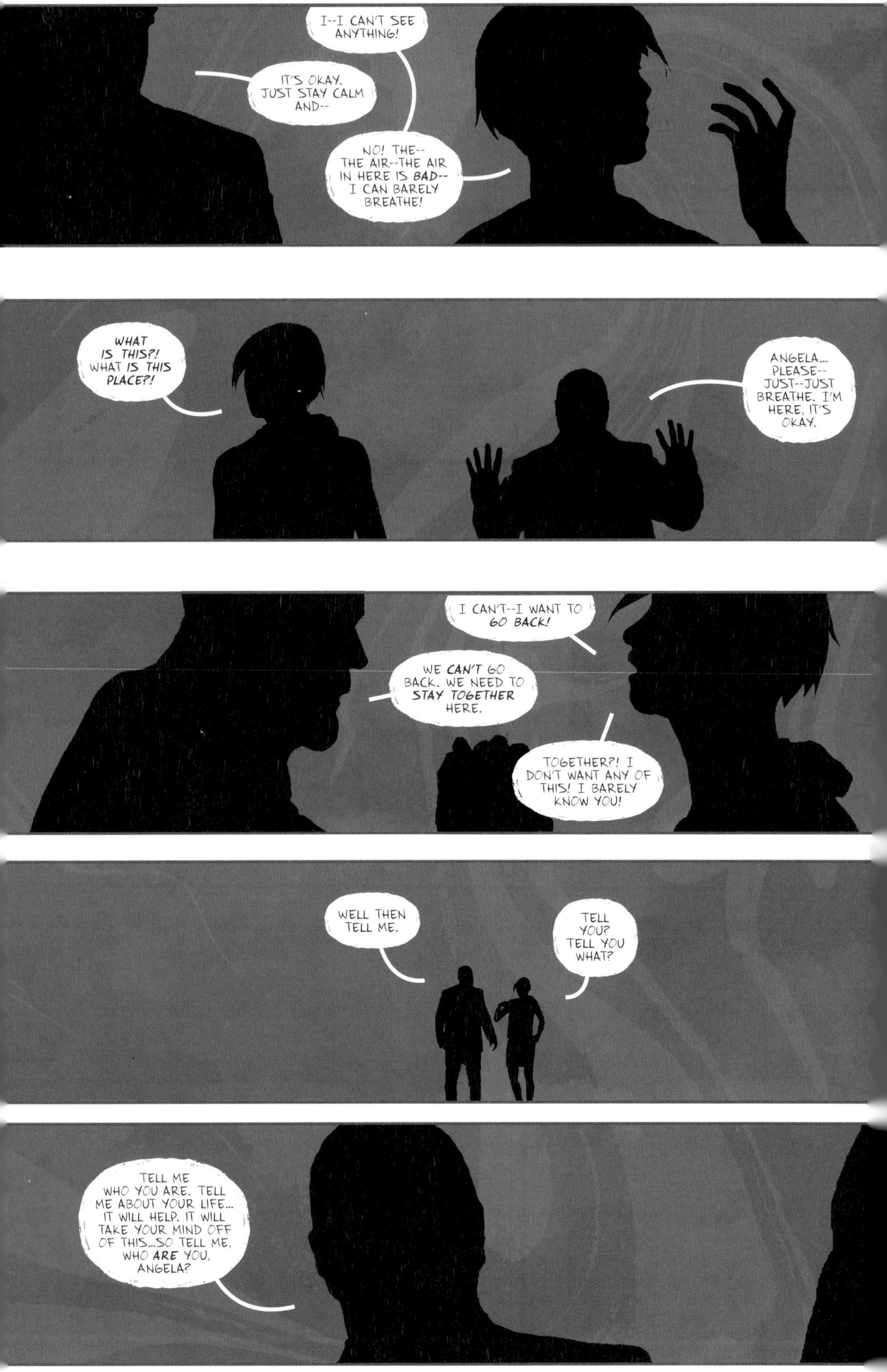
I--I CAN'T SEE ANYTHING!
IT'S OKAY. JUST STAY CALM AND--
NO! THE-- THE AIR--THE AIR IN HERE IS BAD-- I CAN BARELY BREATHE!
WHAT IS THIS?! WHAT IS THIS PLACE?!
ANGELA... PLEASE-- JUST--JUST BREATHE. I'M HERE, IT'S OKAY.
I CAN'T--I WANT TO GO BACK!
WE CAN'T GO BACK. WE NEED TO STAY TOGETHER HERE.
TOGETHER?! I DON'T WANT ANY OF THIS! I BARELY KNOW YOU!
WELL THEN TELL ME.
TELL YOU? TELL YOU WHAT?
TELL ME WHO YOU ARE. TELL ME ABOUT YOUR LIFE... IT WILL HELP. IT WILL TAKE YOUR MIND OFF OF THIS...SO TELL ME, WHO ARE YOU, ANGELA?

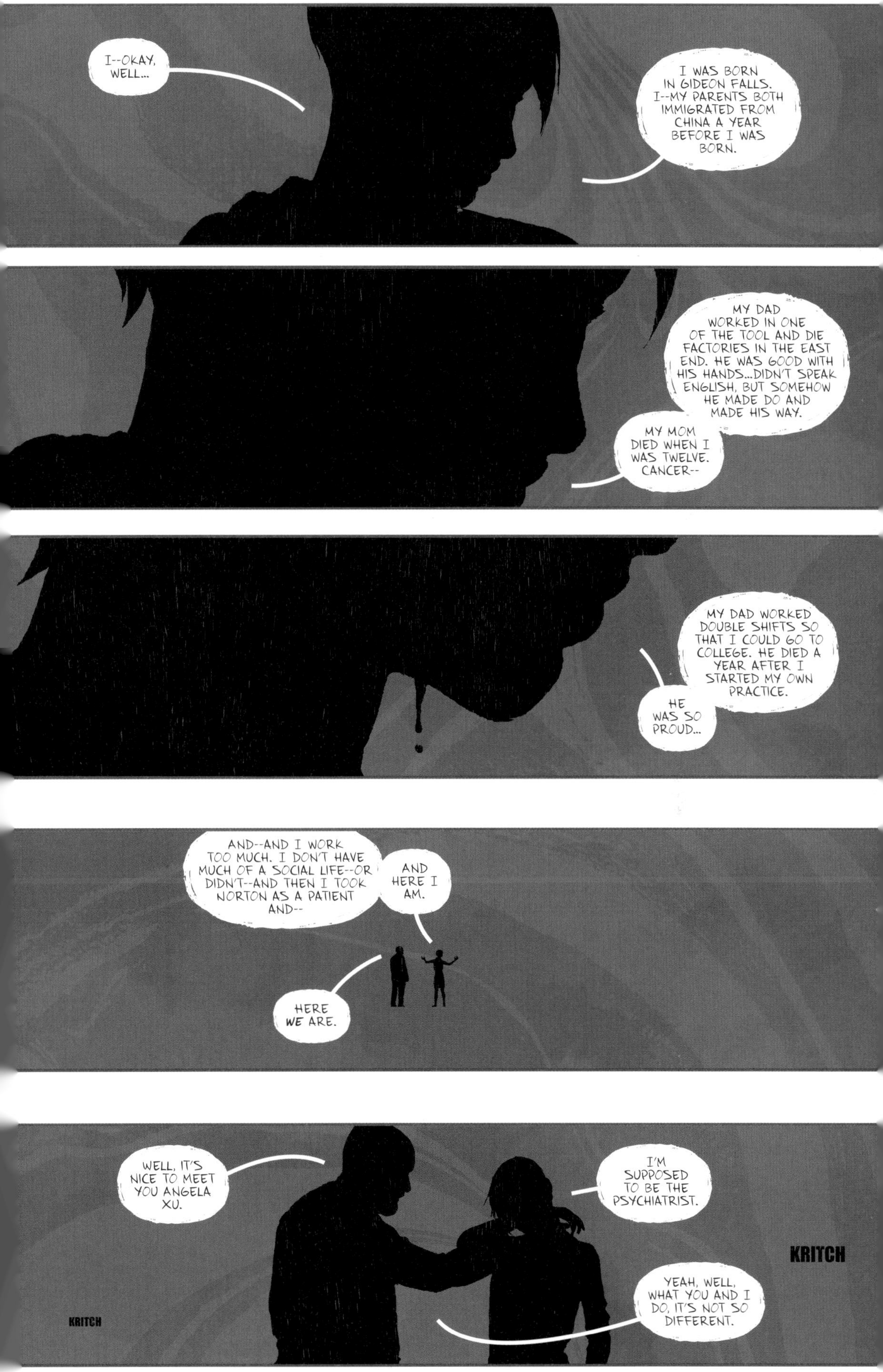
I--OKAY, WELL...
I WAS BORN IN GIDEON FALLS. I--MY PARENTS BOTH IMMIGRATED FROM CHINA A YEAR BEFORE I WAS BORN.
MY DAD WORKED IN ONE OF THE TOOL AND DIE FACTORIES IN THE EAST END. HE WAS GOOD WITH HIS HANDS...DIDN'T SPEAK ENGLISH, BUT SOMEHOW HE MADE DO AND MADE HIS WAY.
MY MOM DIED WHEN I WAS TWELVE. CANCER--
MY DAD WORKED DOUBLE SHIFTS SO THAT I COULD GO TO COLLEGE. HE DIED A YEAR AFTER I STARTED MY OWN PRACTICE.
HE WAS SO PROUD...
AND--AND I WORK TOO MUCH. I DON'T HAVE MUCH OF A SOCIAL LIFE--OR DIDN'T--AND THEN I TOOK NORTON AS A PATIENT AND--
AND HERE I AM.
HERE WE ARE.
WELL, IT'S NICE TO MEET YOU ANGELA XU.
I'M SUPPOSED TO BE THE PSYCHIATRIST.
KRITCH
YEAH, WELL, WHAT YOU AND I DO, IT'S NOT SO DIFFERENT.
KRITCH

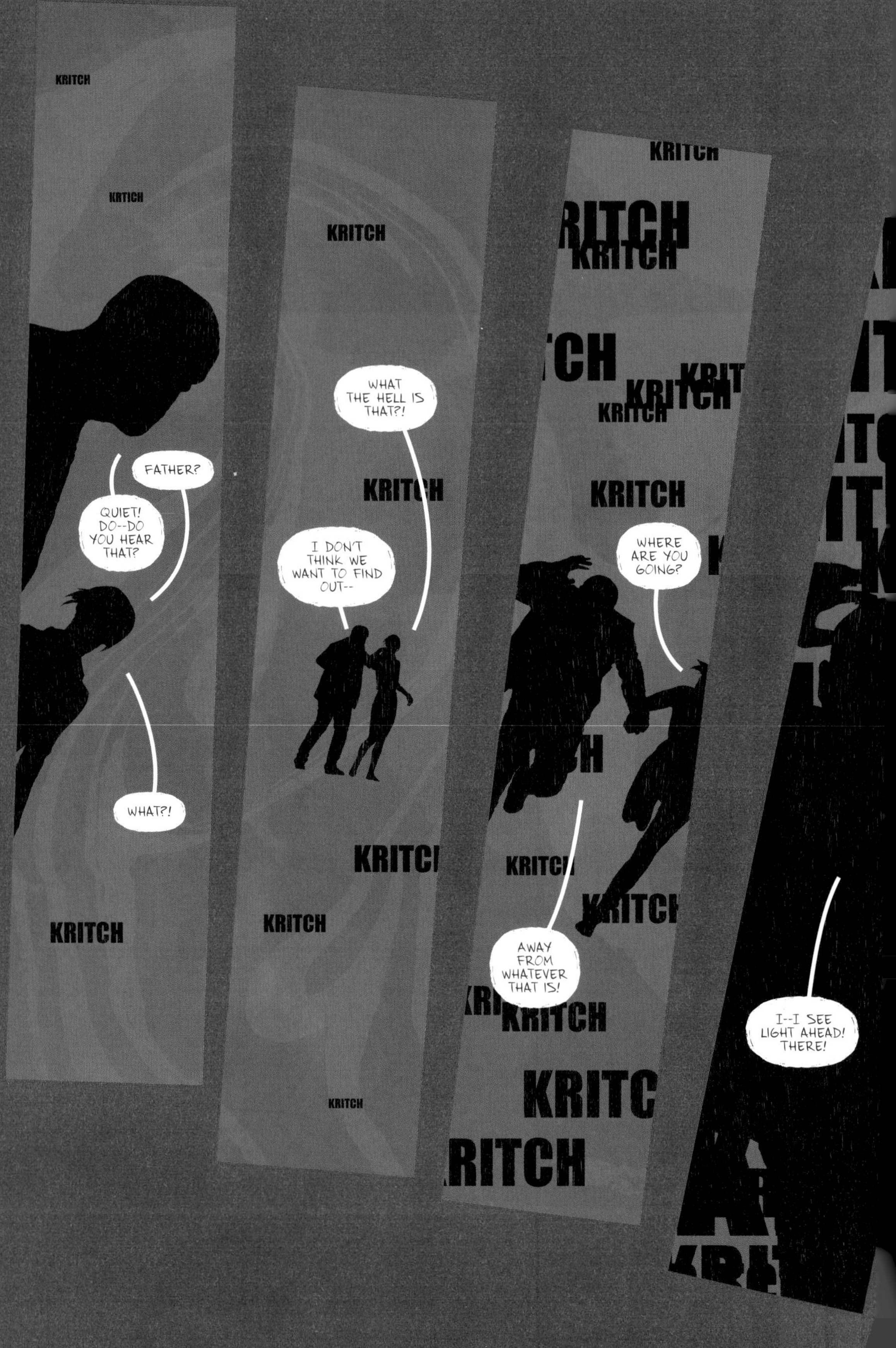
KRITCH
KRTICH
FATHER?
QUIET! DO--DO YOU HEAR THAT?
WHAT?!
KRITCH
KRITCH
WHAT THE HELL IS THAT?!
KRITCH
I DON'T THINK WE WANT TO FIND OUT--
KRITCH
KRITCH
KRITCH
KRITCH
KRITCH
KRITCH
KRITCH
WHERE ARE YOU GOING?
KRITCH
AWAY FROM WHATEVER THAT IS!
KRITCH
I--I SEE LIGHT AHEAD! THERE!

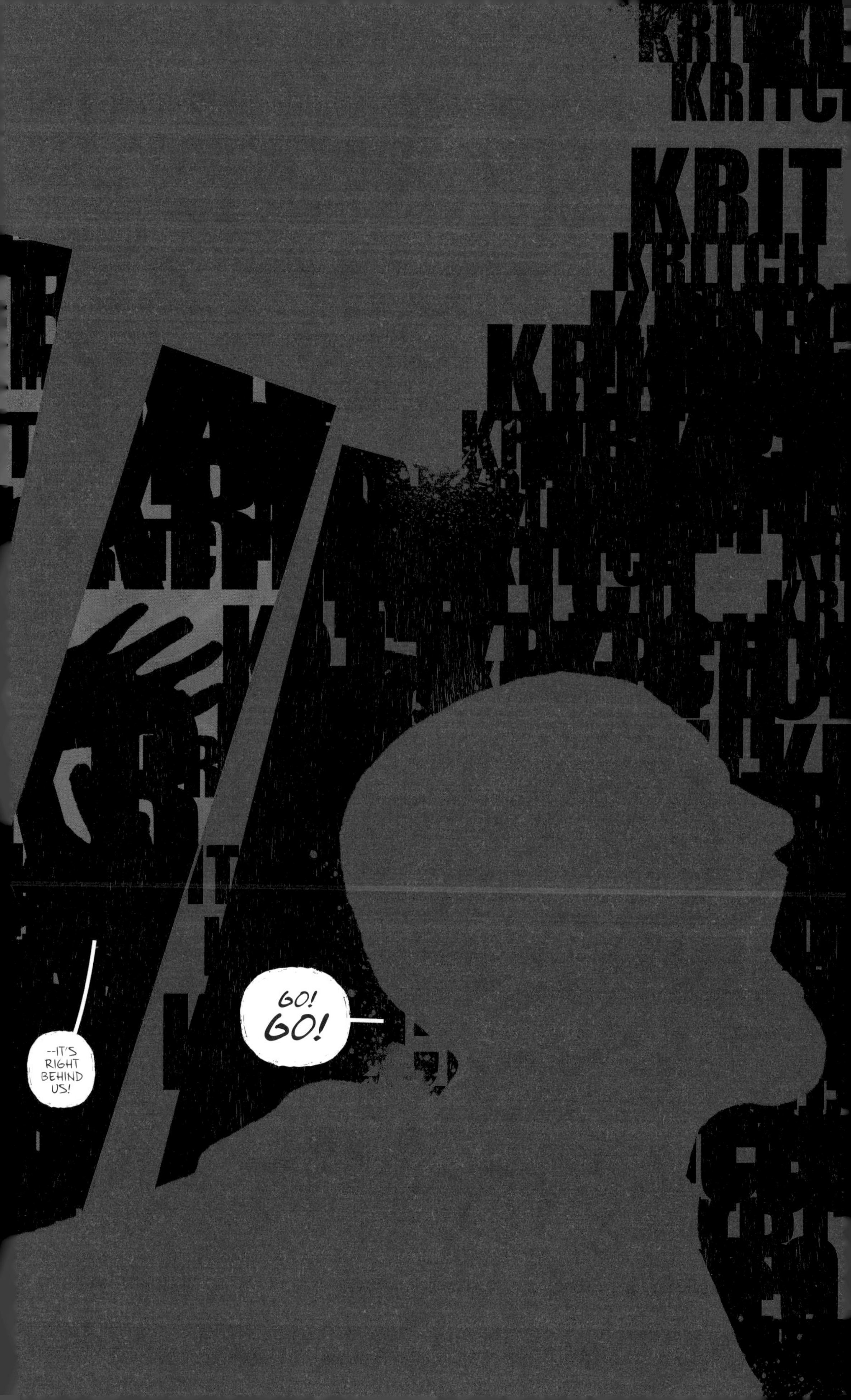
KRITCH
KRIT
--IT'S RIGHT BEHIND US!
GO! GO!

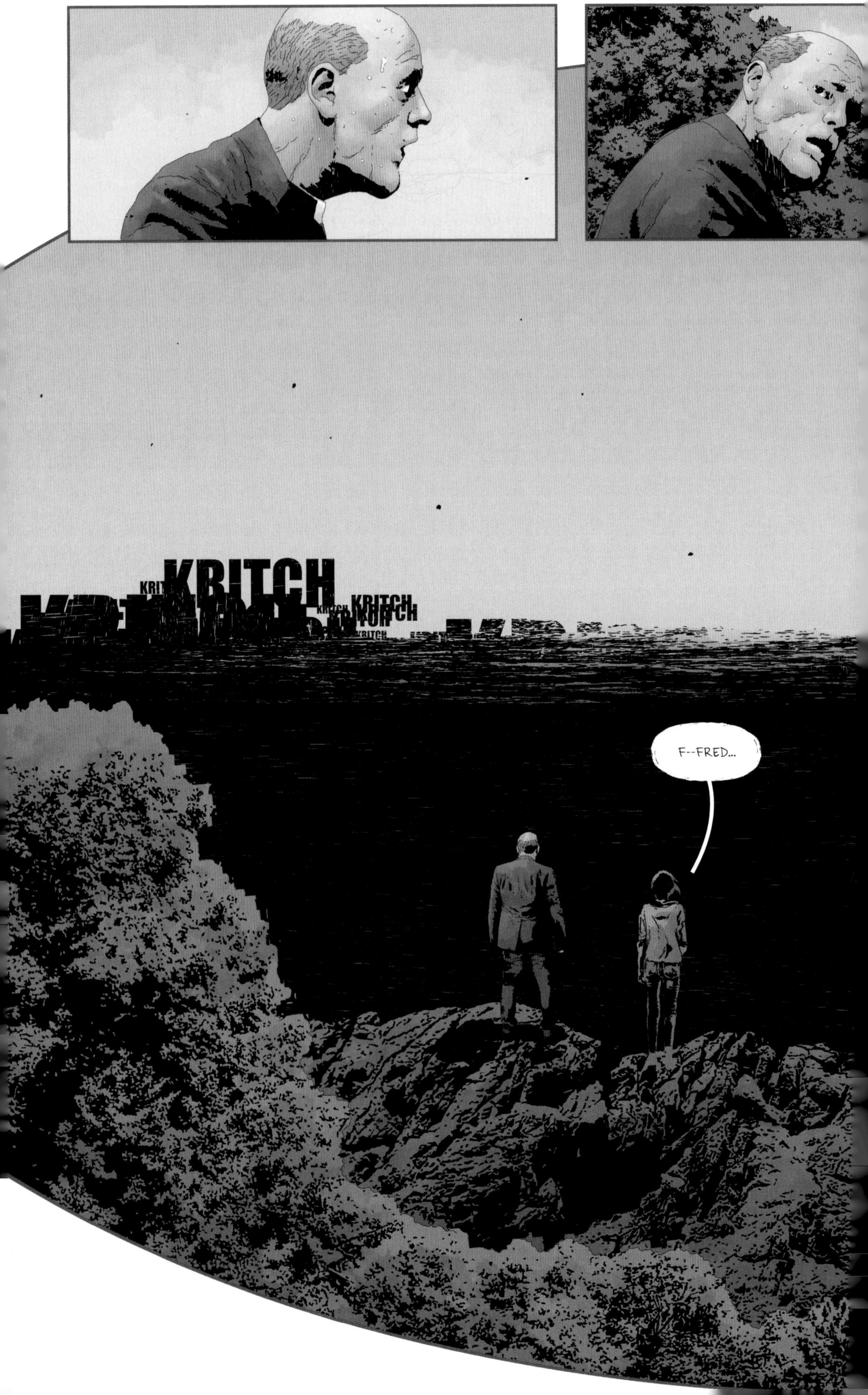
KRIT
KRITCH
KRITCH
F--FRED...

KRITCH
KRITCH
KRITCH
KRITCH
KRITCH
KRITCH
KRITCH
KRITCH
KRITCH
KRITCH
KRITCH
KRITCH
KRIT
KRIT

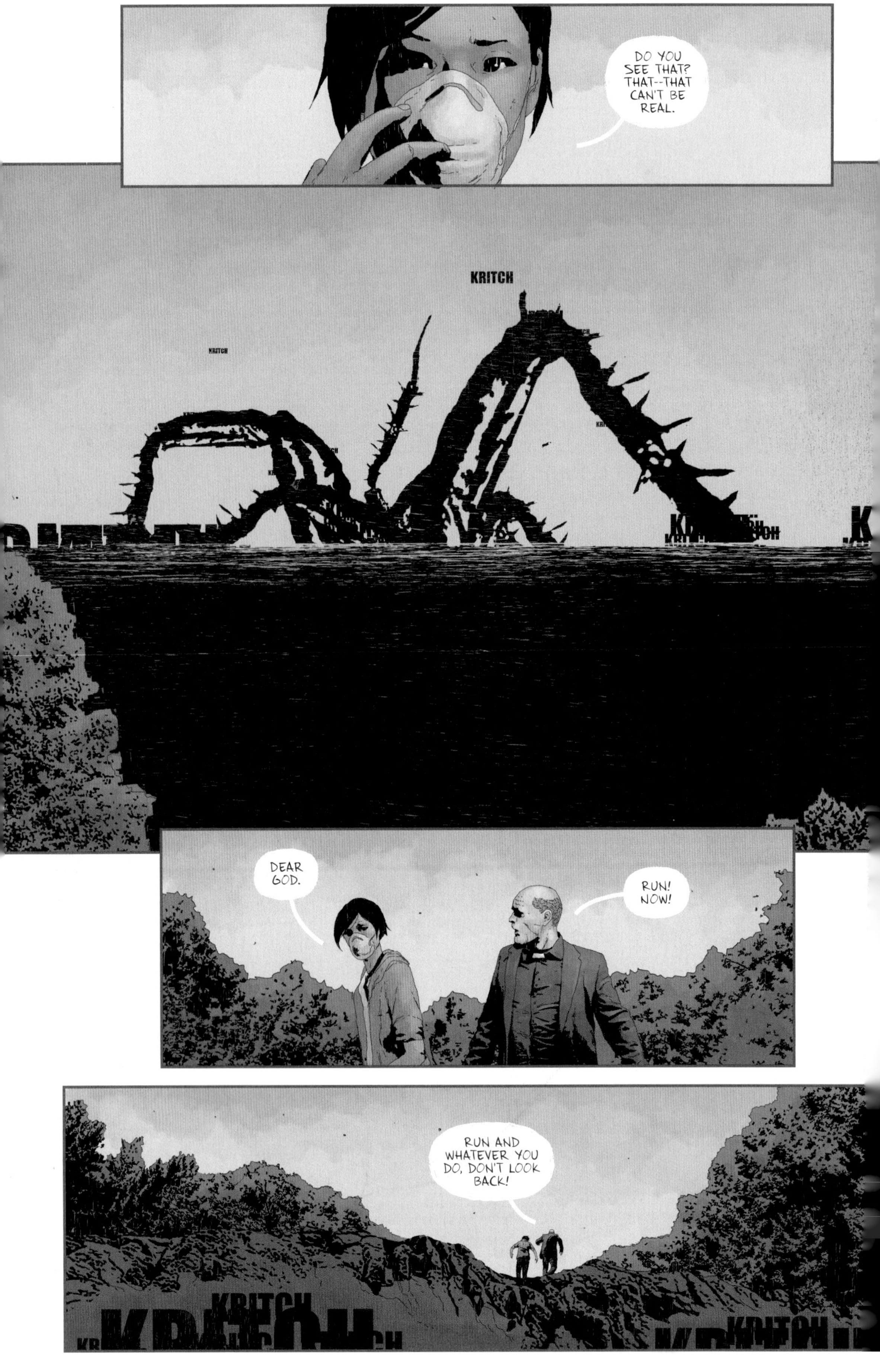
DO YOU SEE THAT? THAT--THAT CAN'T BE REAL.
KRITCH
KRITCH
DEAR GOD.
RUN! NOW!
RUN AND WHATEVER YOU DO, DON'T LOOK BACK!
KRITCH

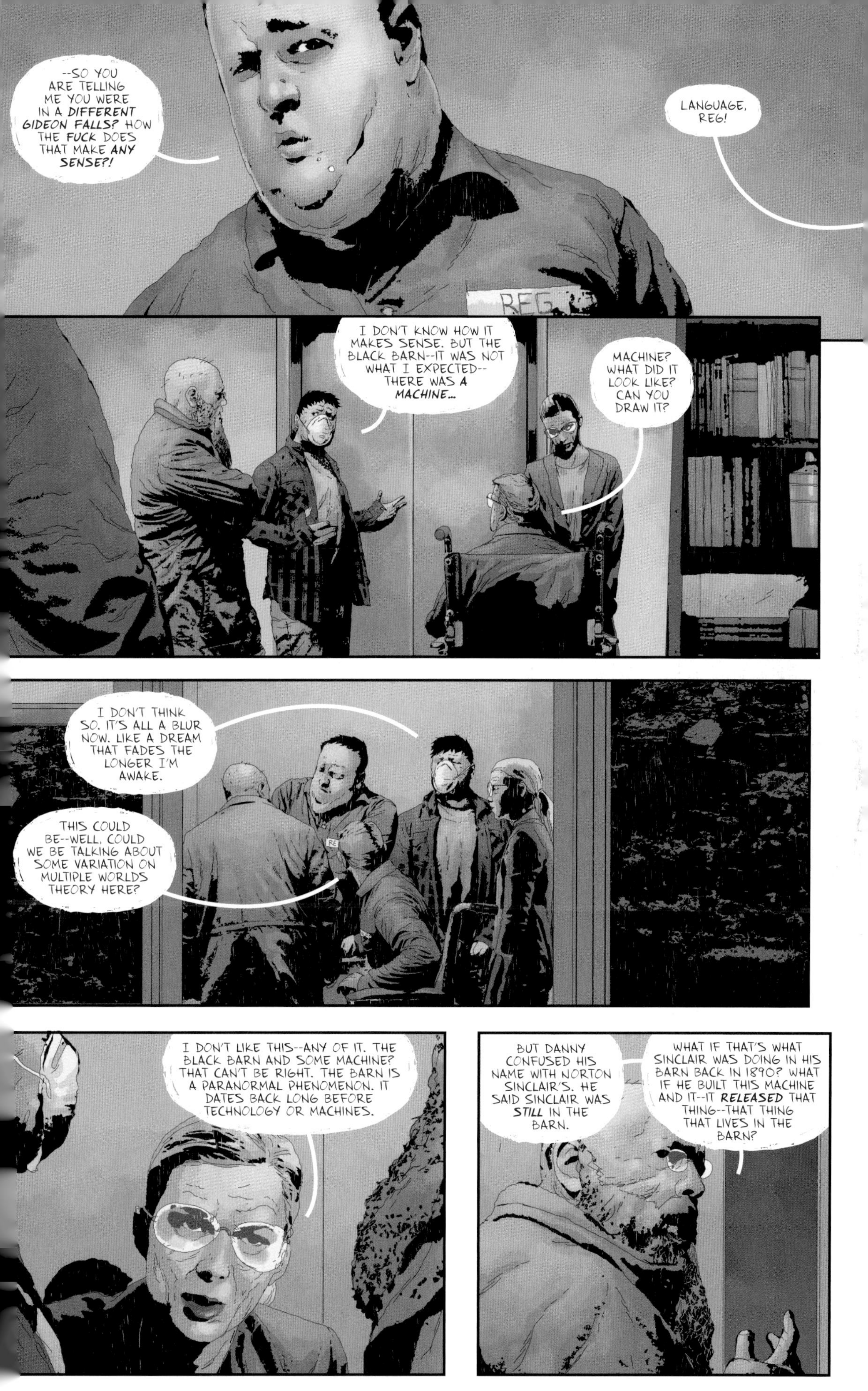
--SO YOU ARE TELLING ME YOU WERE IN A DIFFERENT GIDEON FALLS? HOW THE FUCK DOES THAT MAKE ANY SENSE?!
LANGUAGE, REG!
REG
I DON'T KNOW HOW IT MAKES SENSE. BUT THE BLACK BARN--IT WAS NOT WHAT I EXPECTED--THERE WAS A MACHINE...
MACHINE? WHAT DID IT LOOK LIKE? CAN YOU DRAW IT?
I DON'T THINK SO. IT'S ALL A BLUR NOW. LIKE A DREAM THAT FADES THE LONGER I'M AWAKE.
THIS COULD BE--WELL, COULD WE BE TALKING ABOUT SOME VARIATION ON MULTIPLE WORLDS THEORY HERE?
I DON'T LIKE THIS--ANY OF IT. THE BLACK BARN AND SOME MACHINE? THAT CAN'T BE RIGHT. THE BARN IS A PARANORMAL PHENOMENON. IT DATES BACK LONG BEFORE TECHNOLOGY OR MACHINES.
BUT DANNY CONFUSED HIS NAME WITH NORTON SINCLAIR'S. HE SAID SINCLAIR WAS STILL IN THE BARN.
WHAT IF THAT'S WHAT SINCLAIR WAS DOING IN HIS BARN BACK IN 1890? WHAT IF HE BUILT THIS MACHINE AND IT--IT RELEASED THAT THING--THAT THING THAT LIVES IN THE BARN?

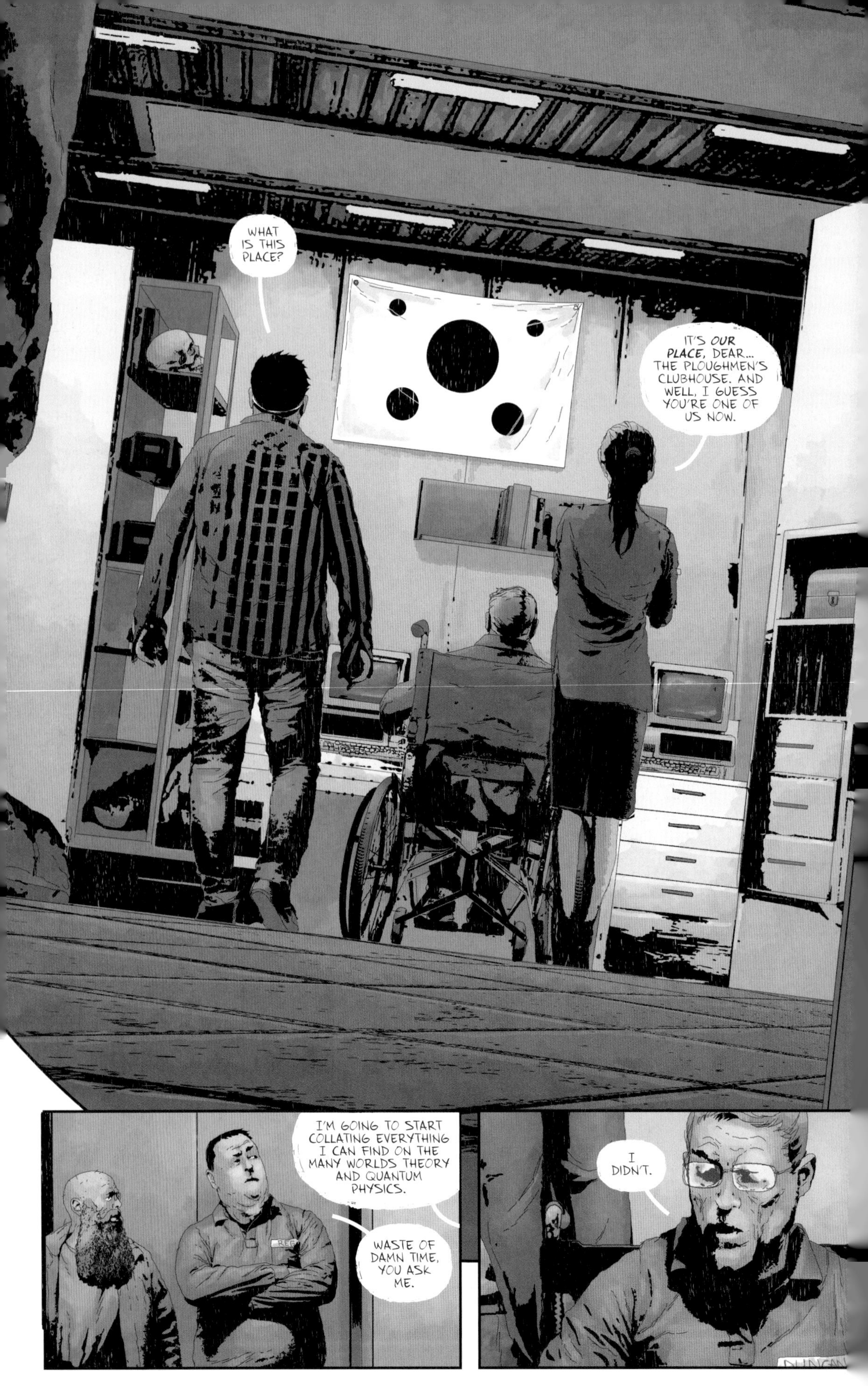
WHAT IS THIS PLACE?
IT'S *OUR PLACE*, DEAR... THE PLOUGHMEN'S CLUBHOUSE. AND WELL, I GUESS YOU'RE ONE OF US NOW.
I'M GOING TO START COLLATING EVERYTHING I CAN FIND ON THE MANY WORLDS THEORY AND QUANTUM PHYSICS.
WASTE OF DAMN TIME, YOU ASK ME.
I DIDN'T.

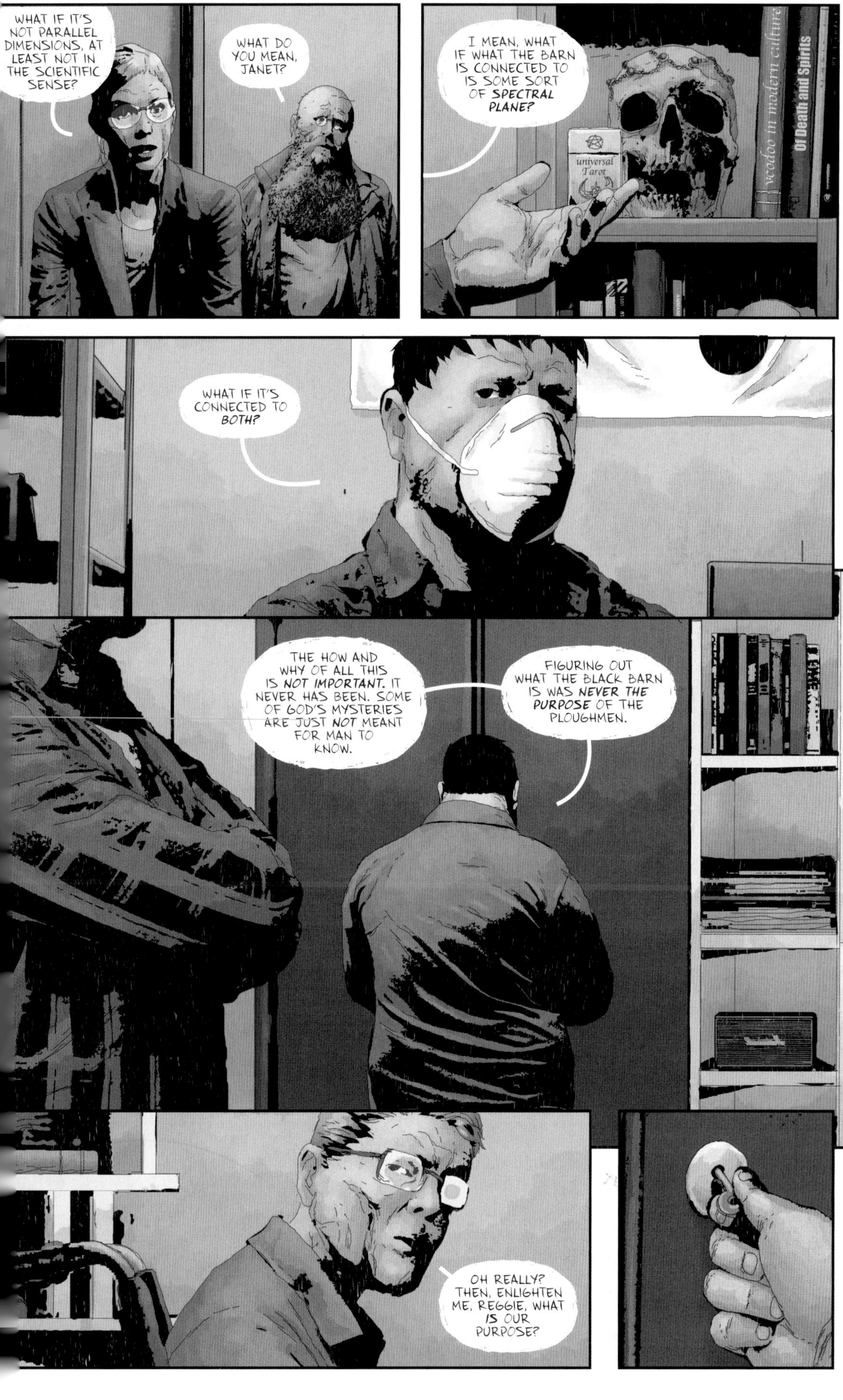
WHAT IF IT'S NOT PARALLEL DIMENSIONS, AT LEAST NOT IN THE SCIENTIFIC SENSE?
WHAT DO YOU MEAN, JANET?
I MEAN, WHAT IF WHAT THE BARN IS CONNECTED TO IS SOME SORT OF SPECTRAL PLANE?
universal Tarot
voodoo in modern culture
Of Death and Spirits
WHAT IF IT'S CONNECTED TO BOTH?
THE HOW AND WHY OF ALL THIS IS NOT IMPORTANT. IT NEVER HAS BEEN. SOME OF GOD'S MYSTERIES ARE JUST NOT MEANT FOR MAN TO KNOW.
FIGURING OUT WHAT THE BLACK BARN IS WAS NEVER THE PURPOSE OF THE PLOUGHMEN.
OH REALLY? THEN, ENLIGHTEN ME, REGGIE, WHAT IS OUR PURPOSE?

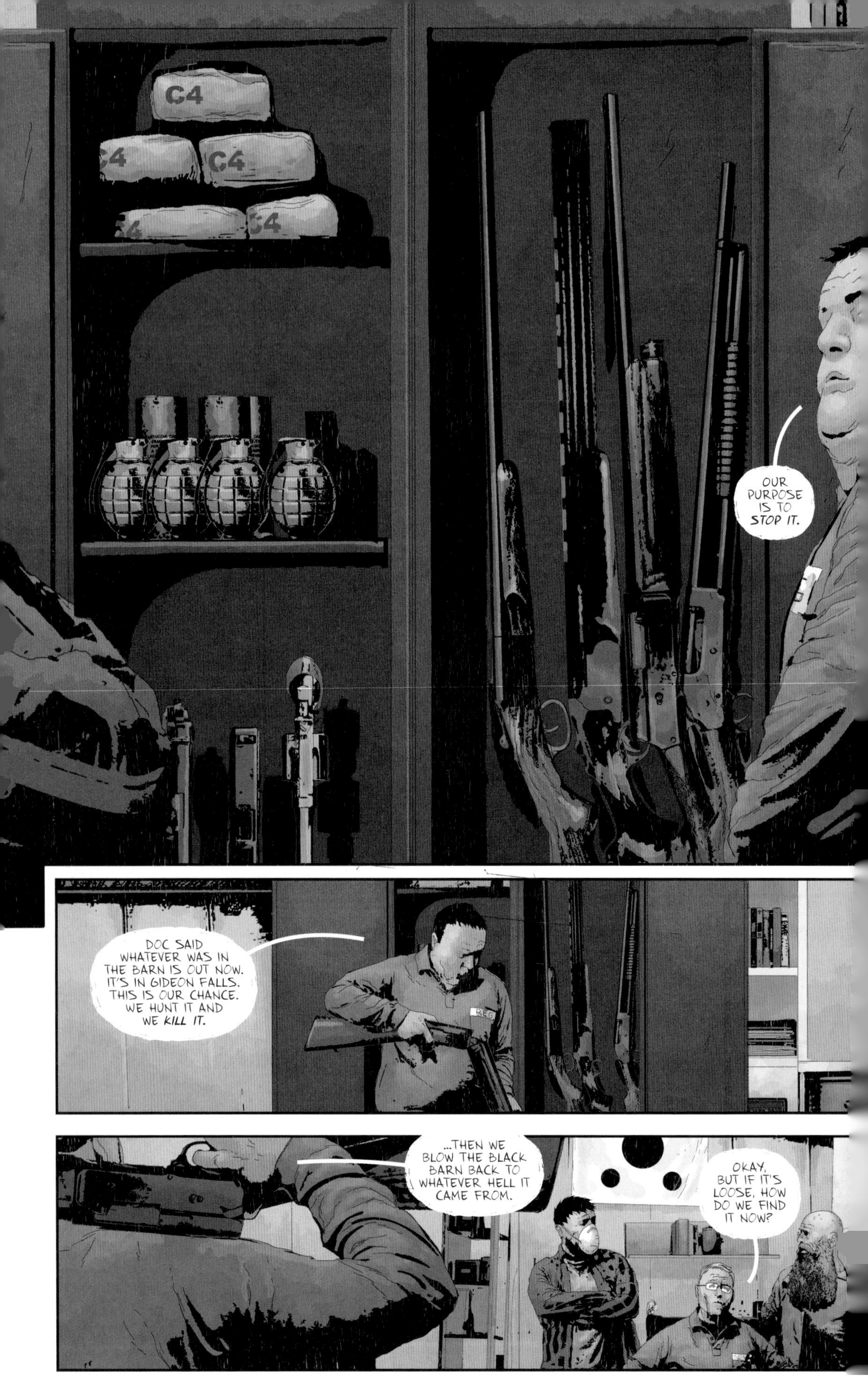
OUR PURPOSE IS TO STOP IT.
DOC SAID WHATEVER WAS IN THE BARN IS OUT NOW. IT'S IN GIDEON FALLS. THIS IS OUR CHANCE. WE HUNT IT AND WE KILL IT.
...THEN WE BLOW THE BLACK BARN BACK TO WHATEVER HELL IT CAME FROM.
OKAY, BUT IF IT'S LOOSE, HOW DO WE FIND IT NOW?

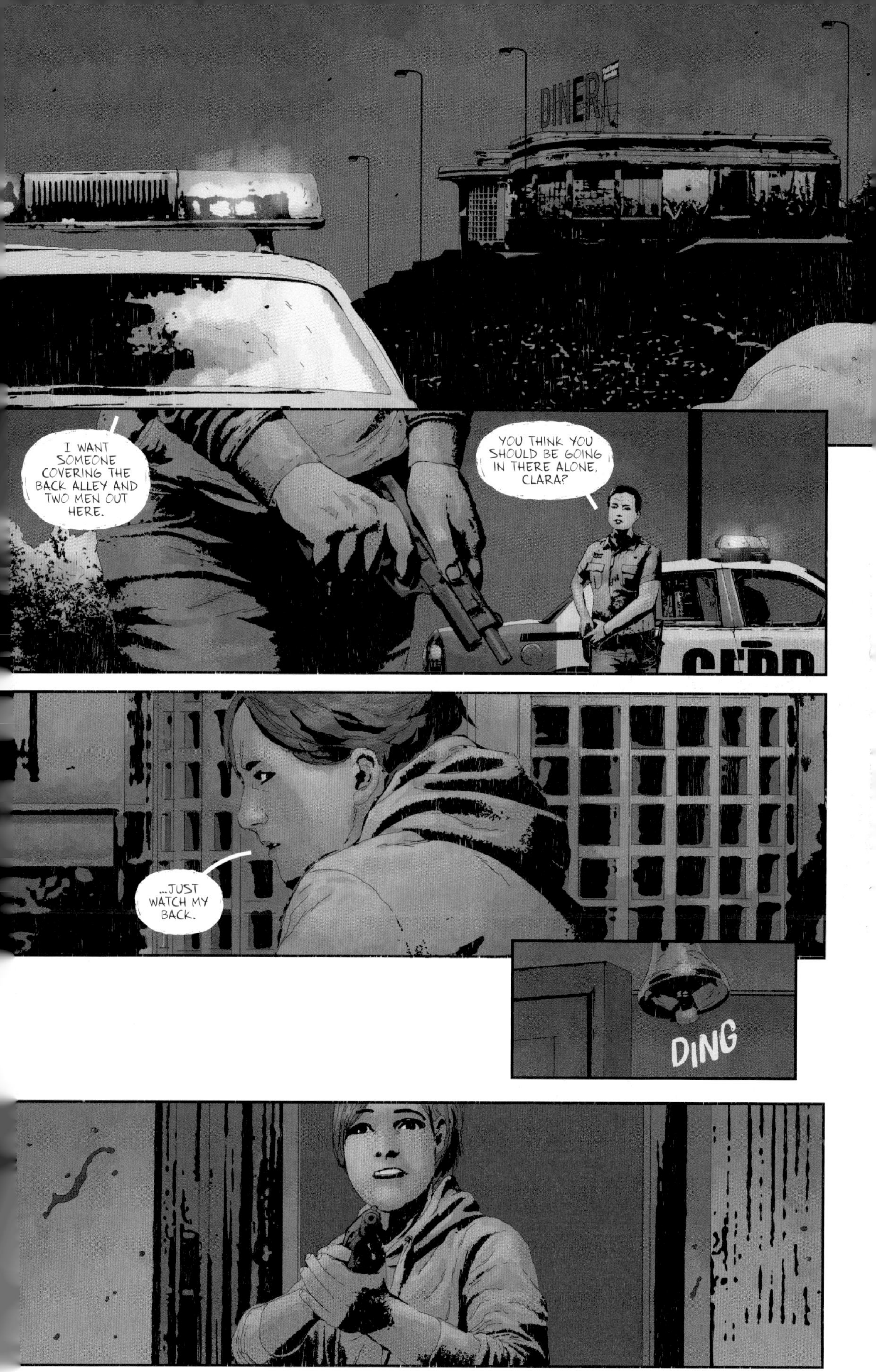
DINER
I WANT SOMEONE COVERING THE BACK ALLEY AND TWO MEN OUT HERE.
YOU THINK YOU SHOULD BE GOING IN THERE ALONE, CLARA?
...JUST WATCH MY BACK.
DING

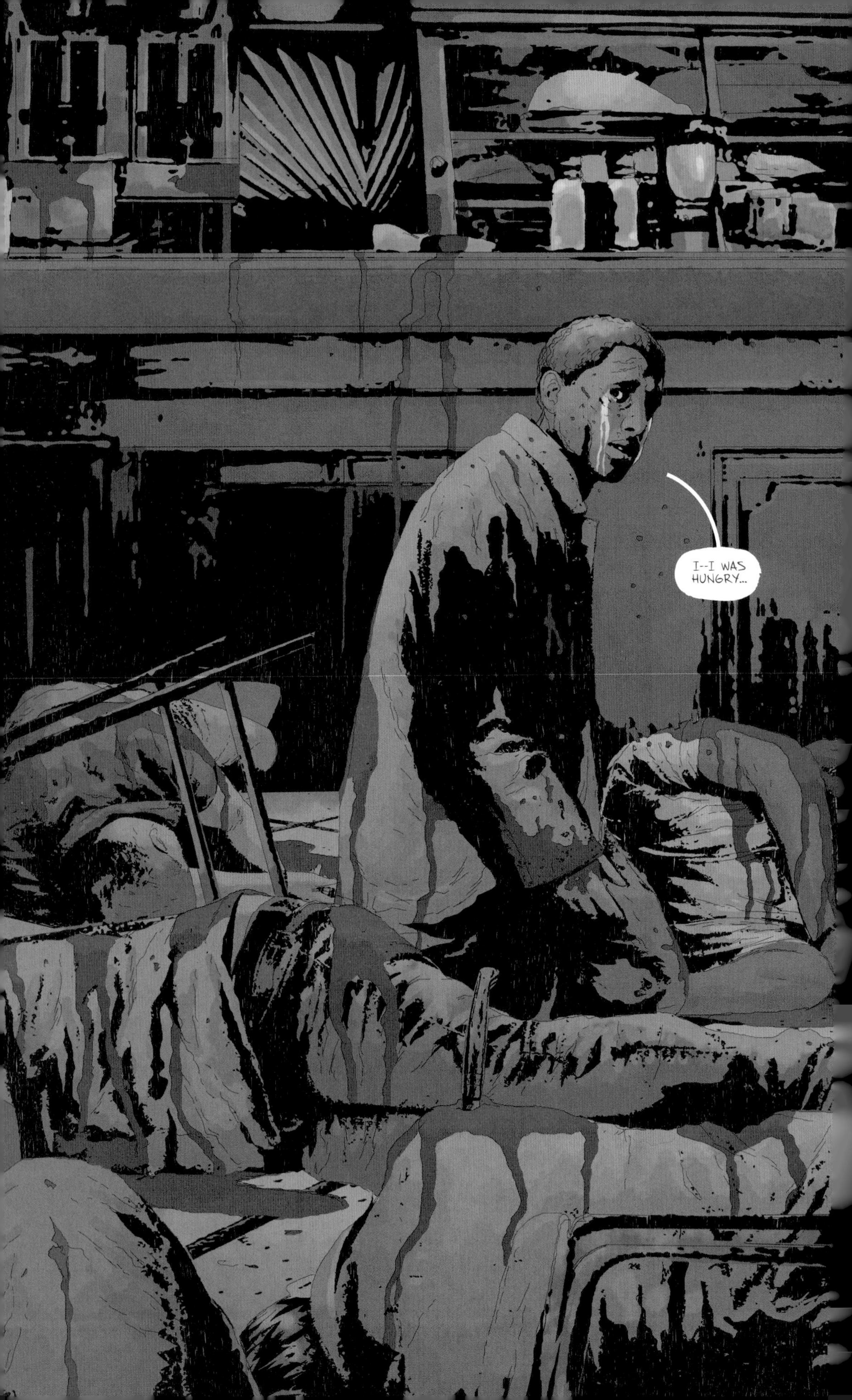
I--I WAS HUNGRY...

GIDEON
FALLS

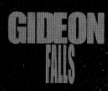

Twenty

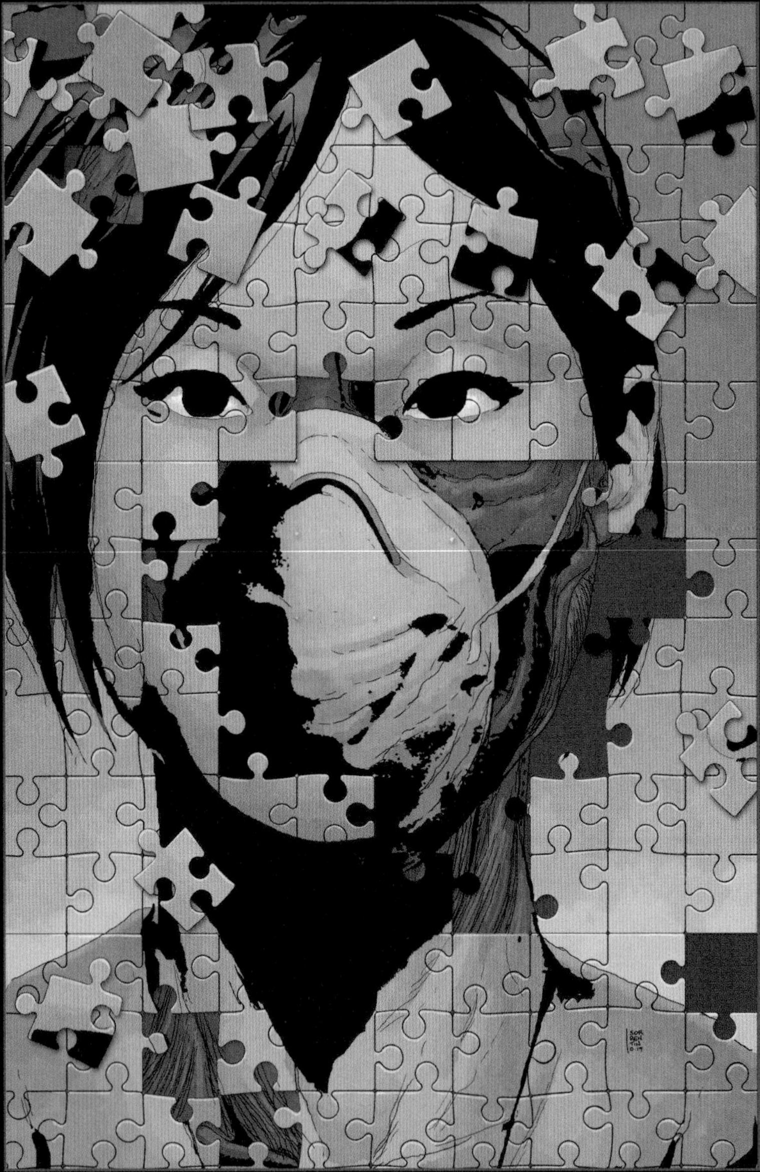

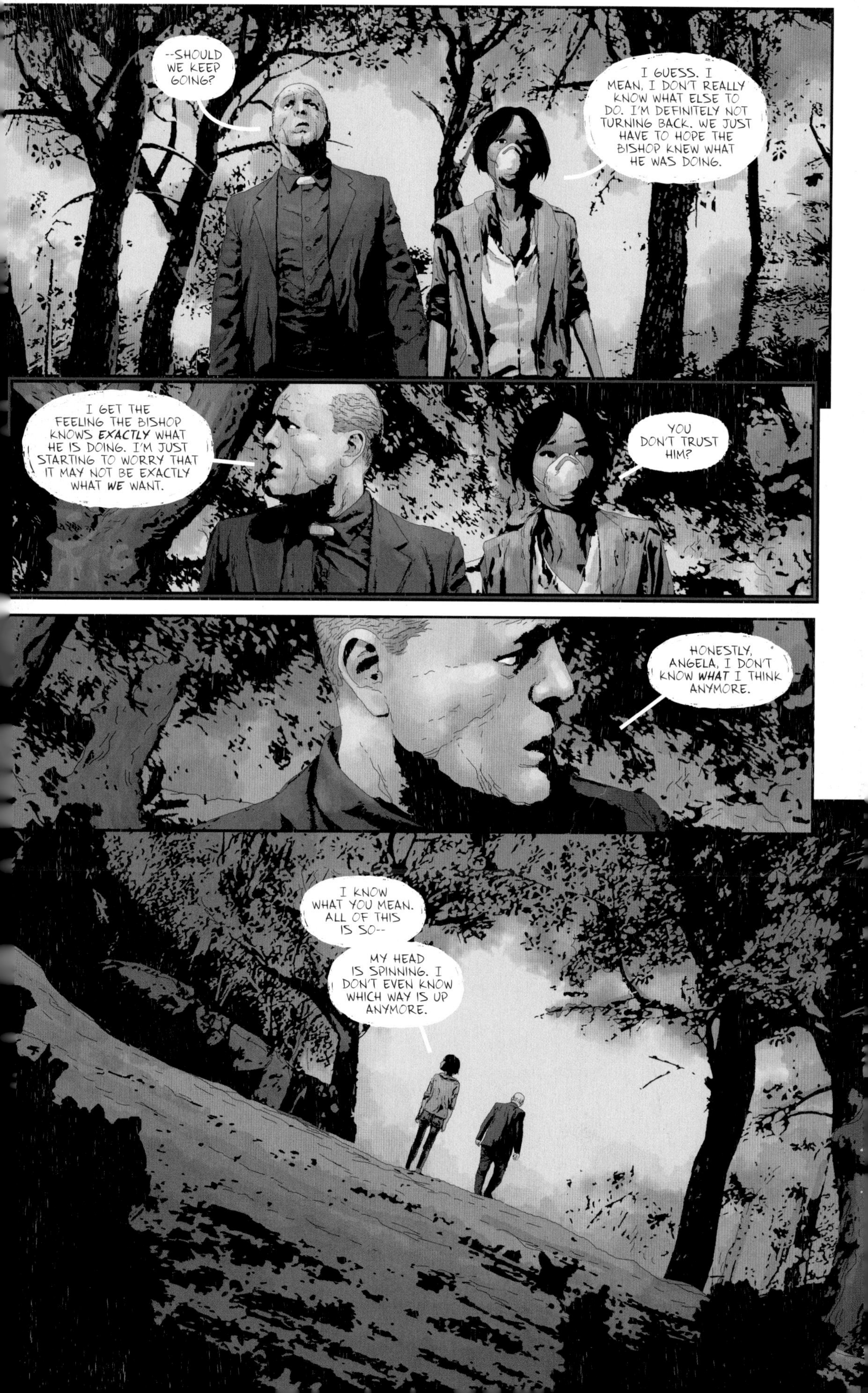

--SHOULD WE KEEP GOING?
I GUESS. I MEAN, I DON'T REALLY KNOW WHAT ELSE TO DO. I'M DEFINITELY NOT TURNING BACK. WE JUST HAVE TO HOPE THE BISHOP KNEW WHAT HE WAS DOING.
I GET THE FEELING THE BISHOP KNOWS EXACTLY WHAT HE IS DOING. I'M JUST STARTING TO WORRY THAT IT MAY NOT BE EXACTLY WHAT WE WANT.
YOU DON'T TRUST HIM?
HONESTLY, ANGELA, I DON'T KNOW WHAT I THINK ANYMORE.
I KNOW WHAT YOU MEAN. ALL OF THIS IS SO--
MY HEAD IS SPINNING. I DON'T EVEN KNOW WHICH WAY IS UP ANYMORE.

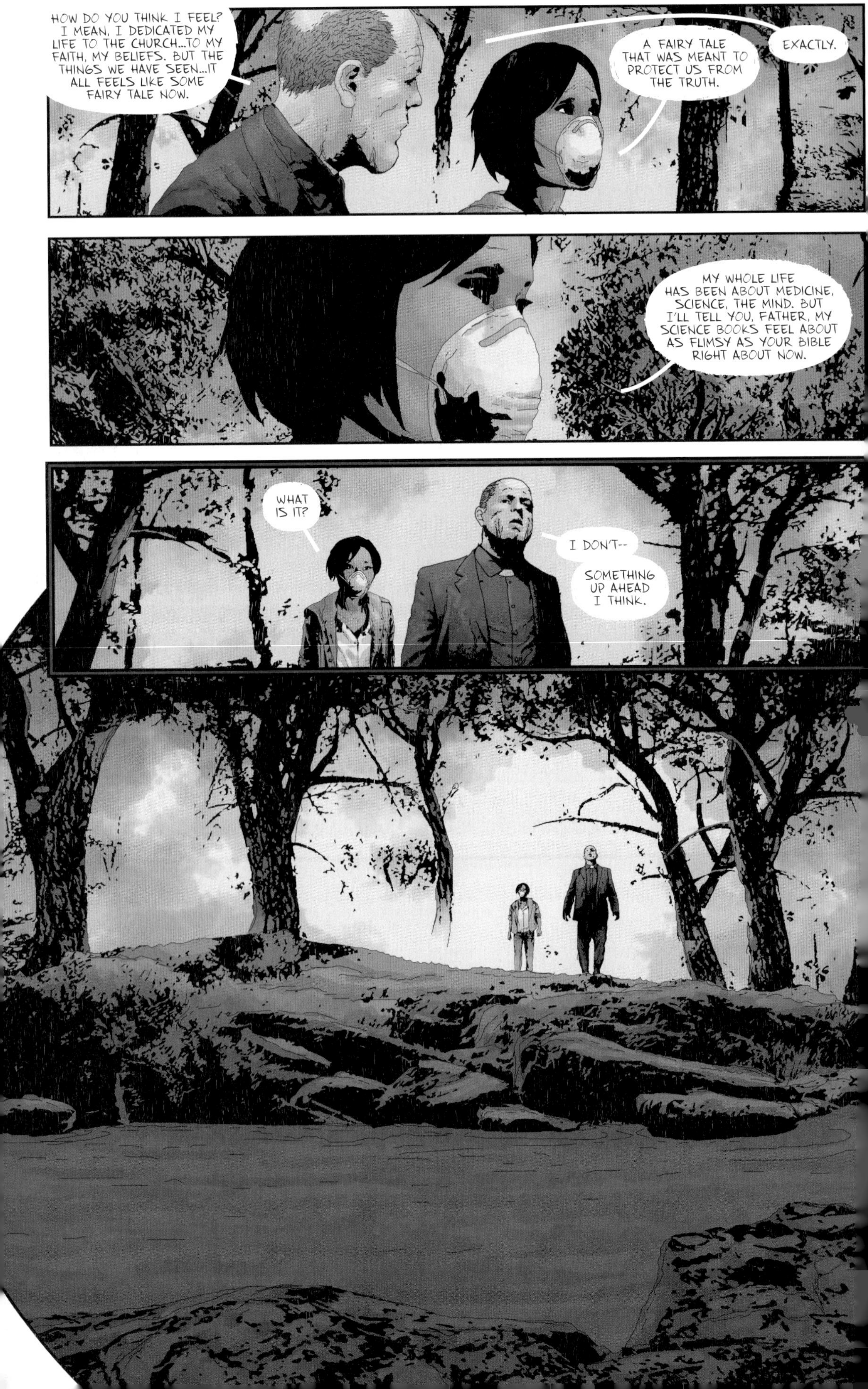
HOW DO YOU THINK I FEEL? I MEAN, I DEDICATED MY LIFE TO THE CHURCH...TO MY FAITH, MY BELIEFS. BUT THE THINGS WE HAVE SEEN...IT ALL FEELS LIKE SOME FAIRY TALE NOW.
A FAIRY TALE THAT WAS MEANT TO PROTECT US FROM THE TRUTH.
EXACTLY.
MY WHOLE LIFE HAS BEEN ABOUT MEDICINE, SCIENCE, THE MIND. BUT I'LL TELL YOU, FATHER, MY SCIENCE BOOKS FEEL ABOUT AS FLIMSY AS YOUR BIBLE RIGHT ABOUT NOW.
WHAT IS IT?
I DON'T--
SOMETHING UP AHEAD I THINK.

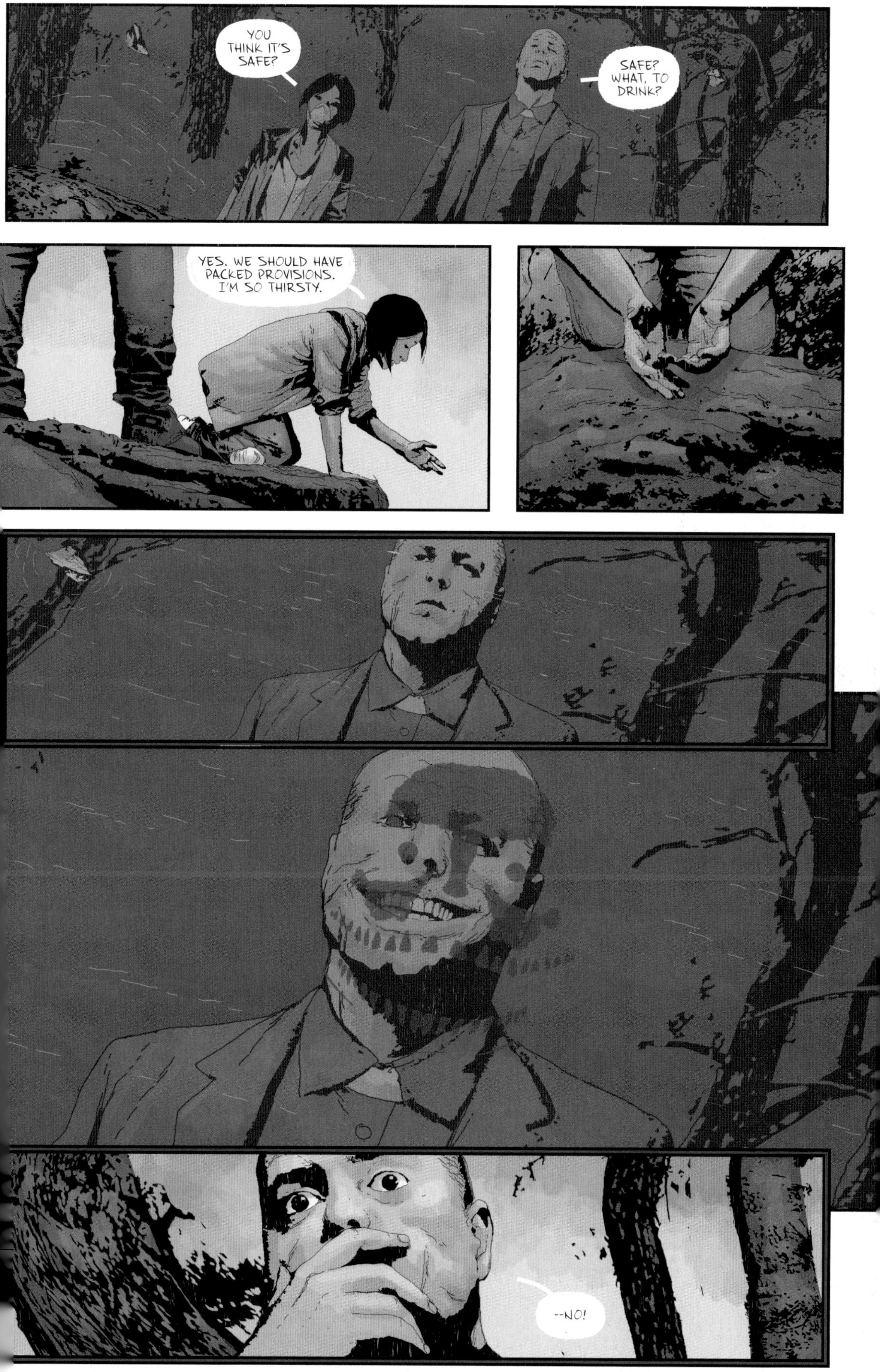
YOU THINK IT'S SAFE?
SAFE? WHAT, TO DRINK?
YES. WE SHOULD HAVE PACKED PROVISIONS. I'M SO THIRSTY.
--NO!

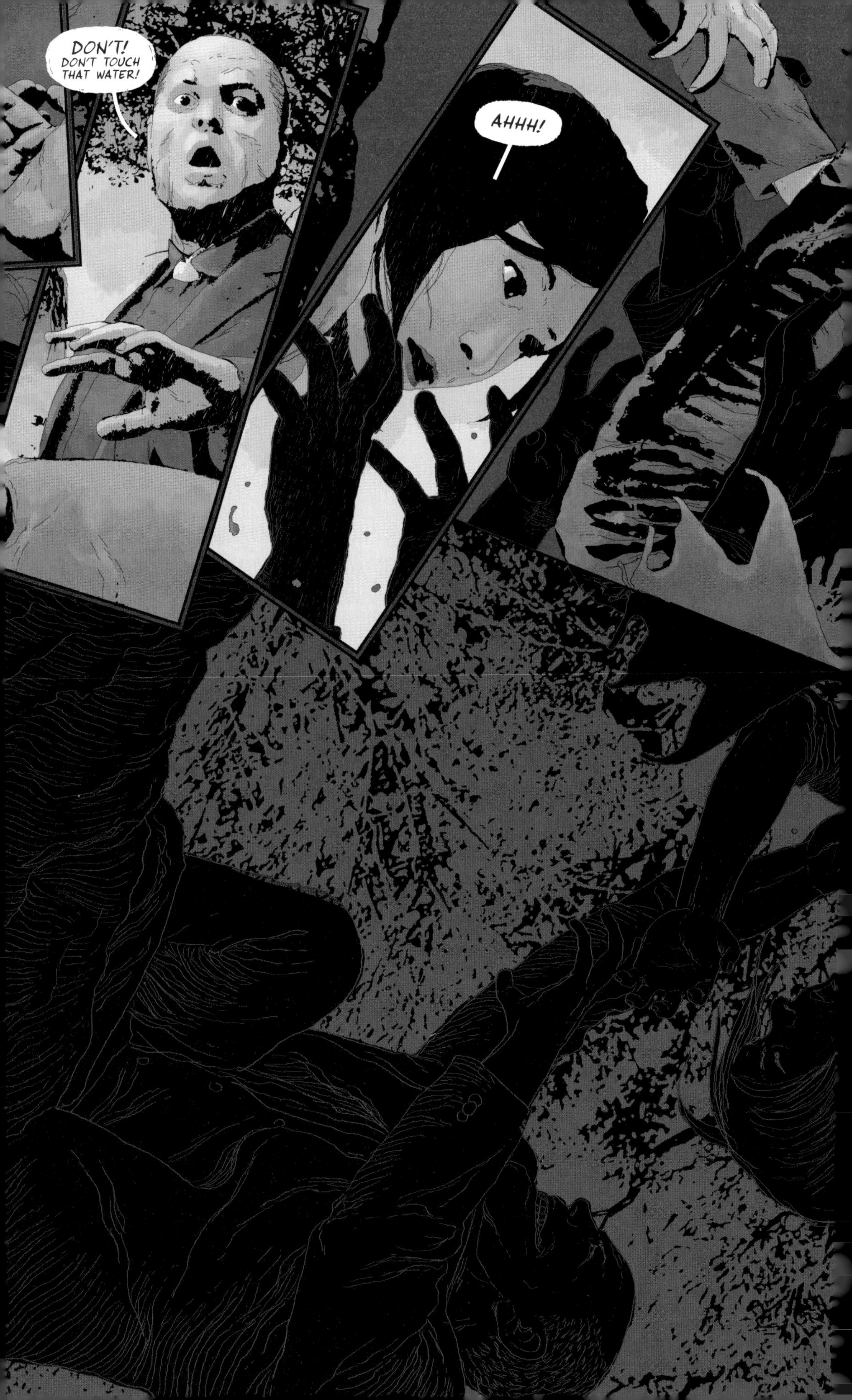
DON'T! DON'T TOUCH THAT WATER!
AHHH!

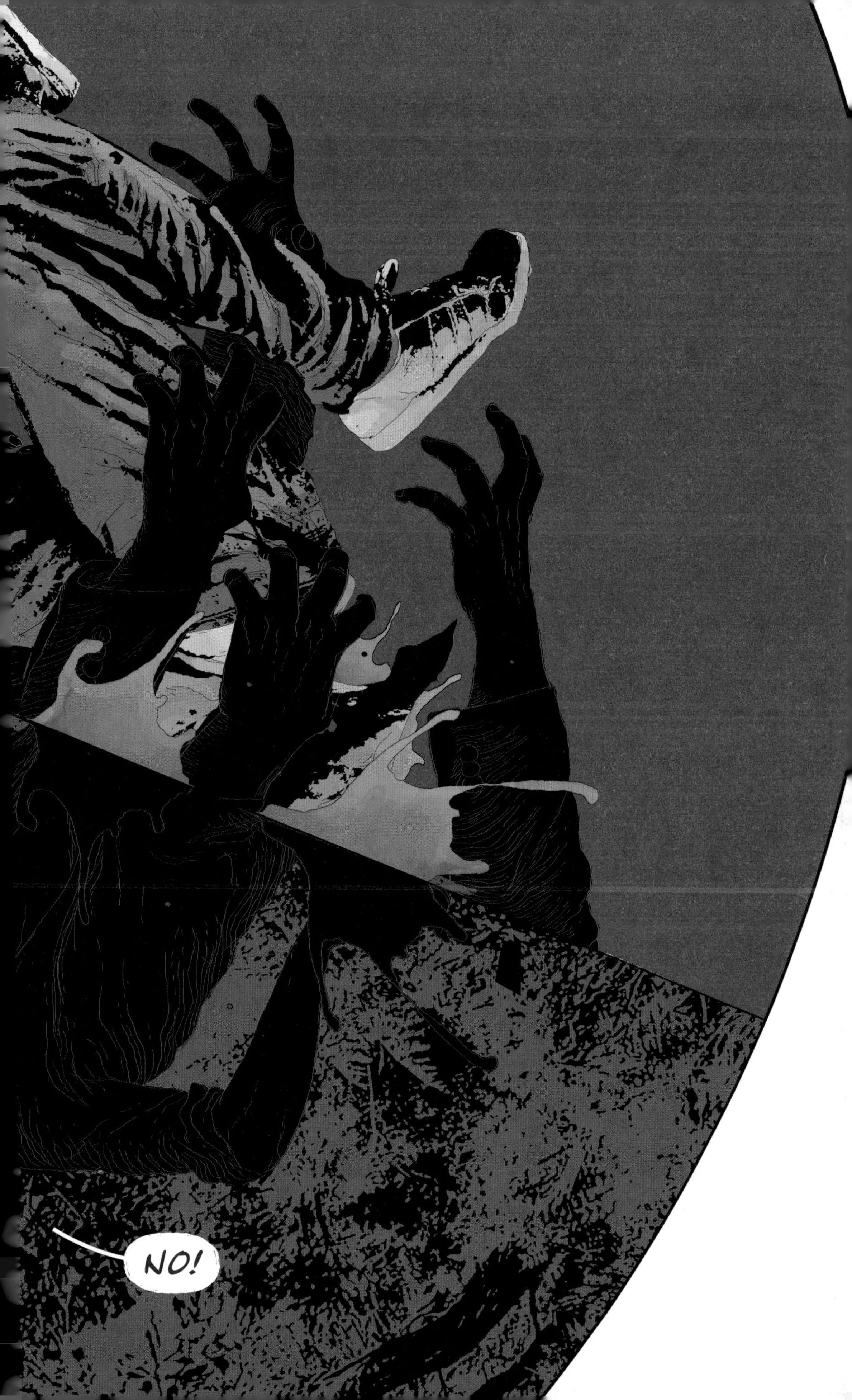
NO!

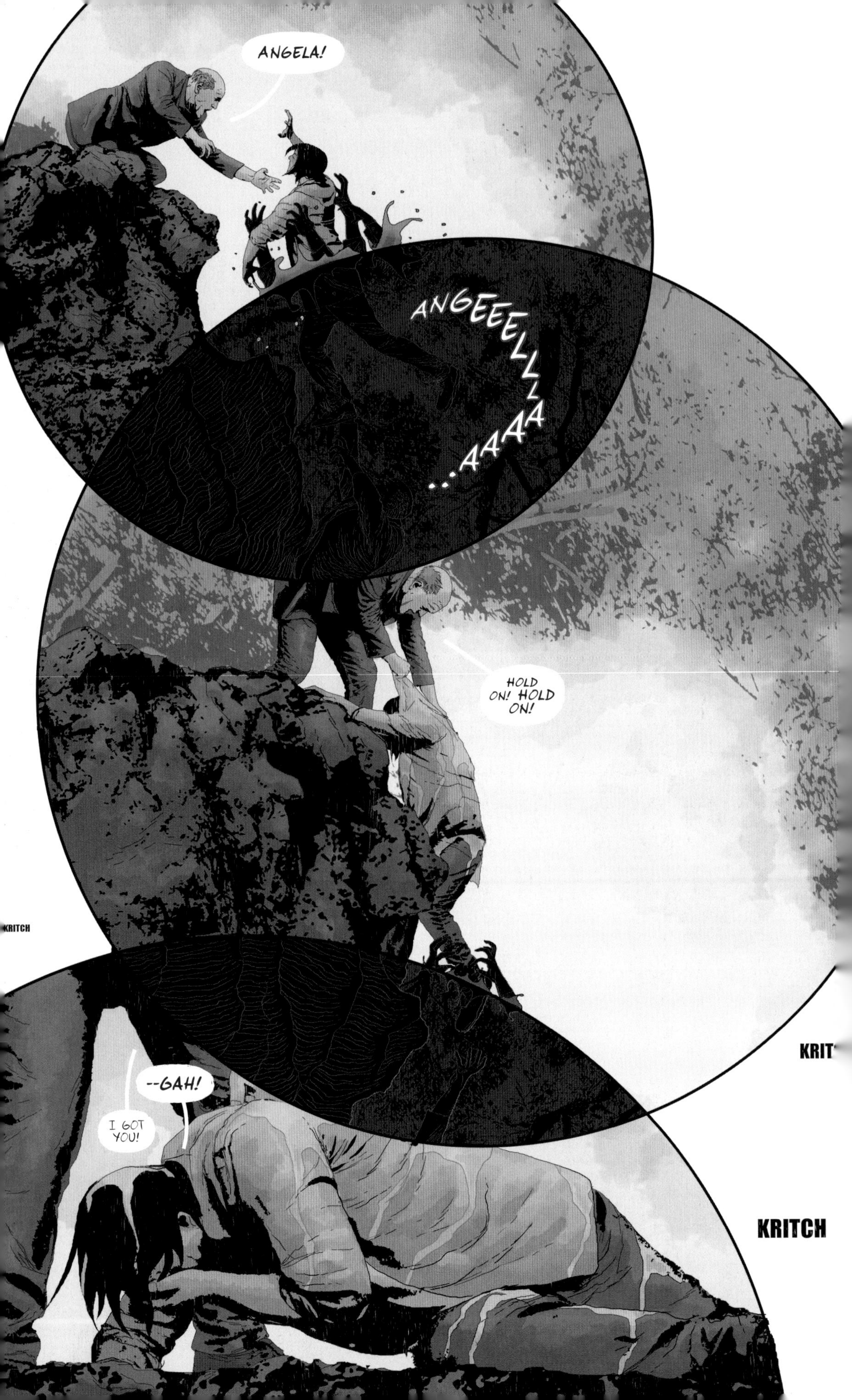
ANGELA!
ANGEEELLLAAAA...AAAA
HOLD ON! HOLD ON!
KRITCH
KRIT
--GAH!
I GOT YOU!
KRITCH

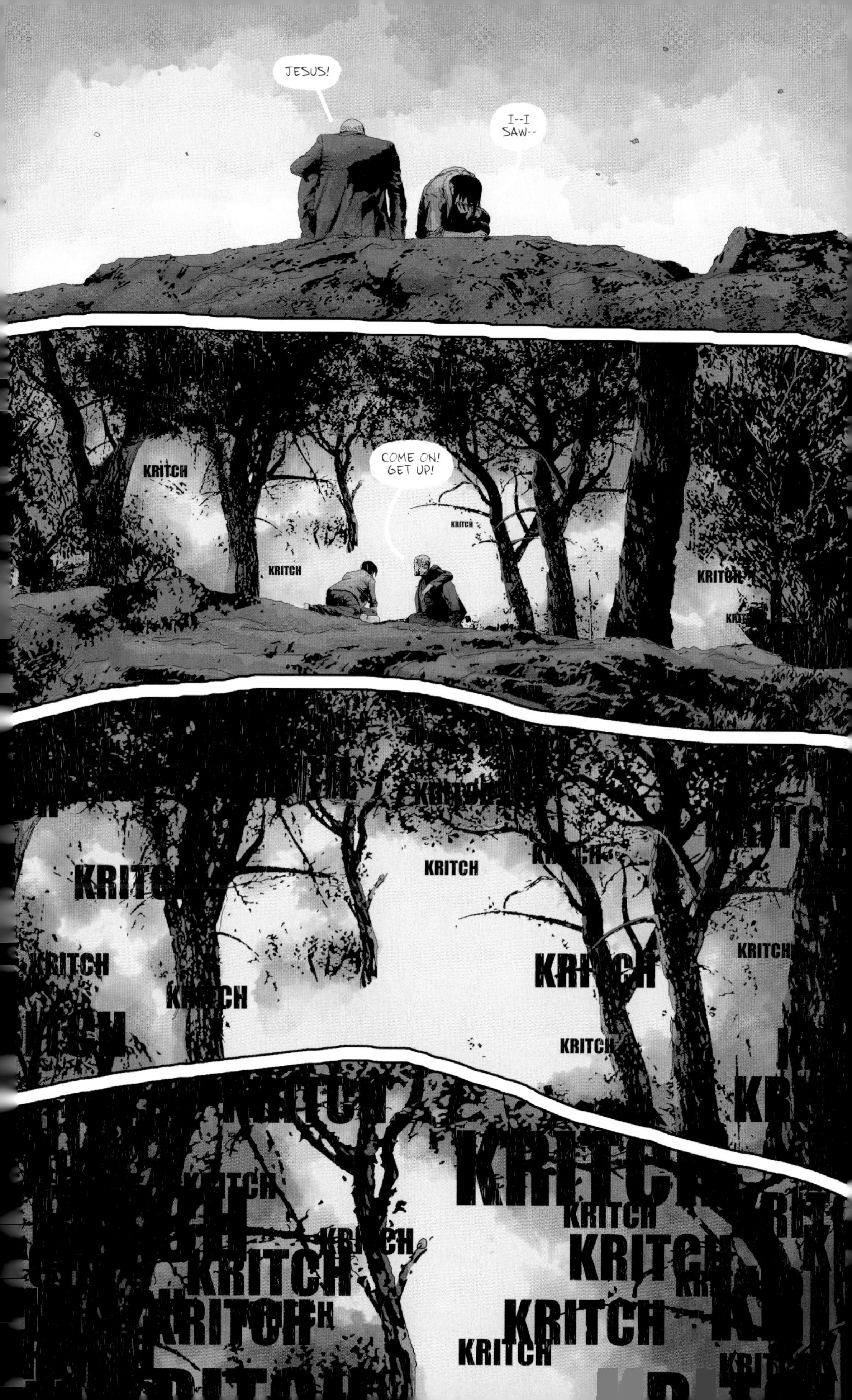
JESUS!
I--I SAW--
COME ON! GET UP!
KRITCH
KRITCH
KRITCH
KRITCH
KRITCH
KRITCH
KRITCH
KRITCH
KRITCH
KRITCH
KRITCH
KRITCH
KRITCH
KRITCH
KRITCH
KRITCH

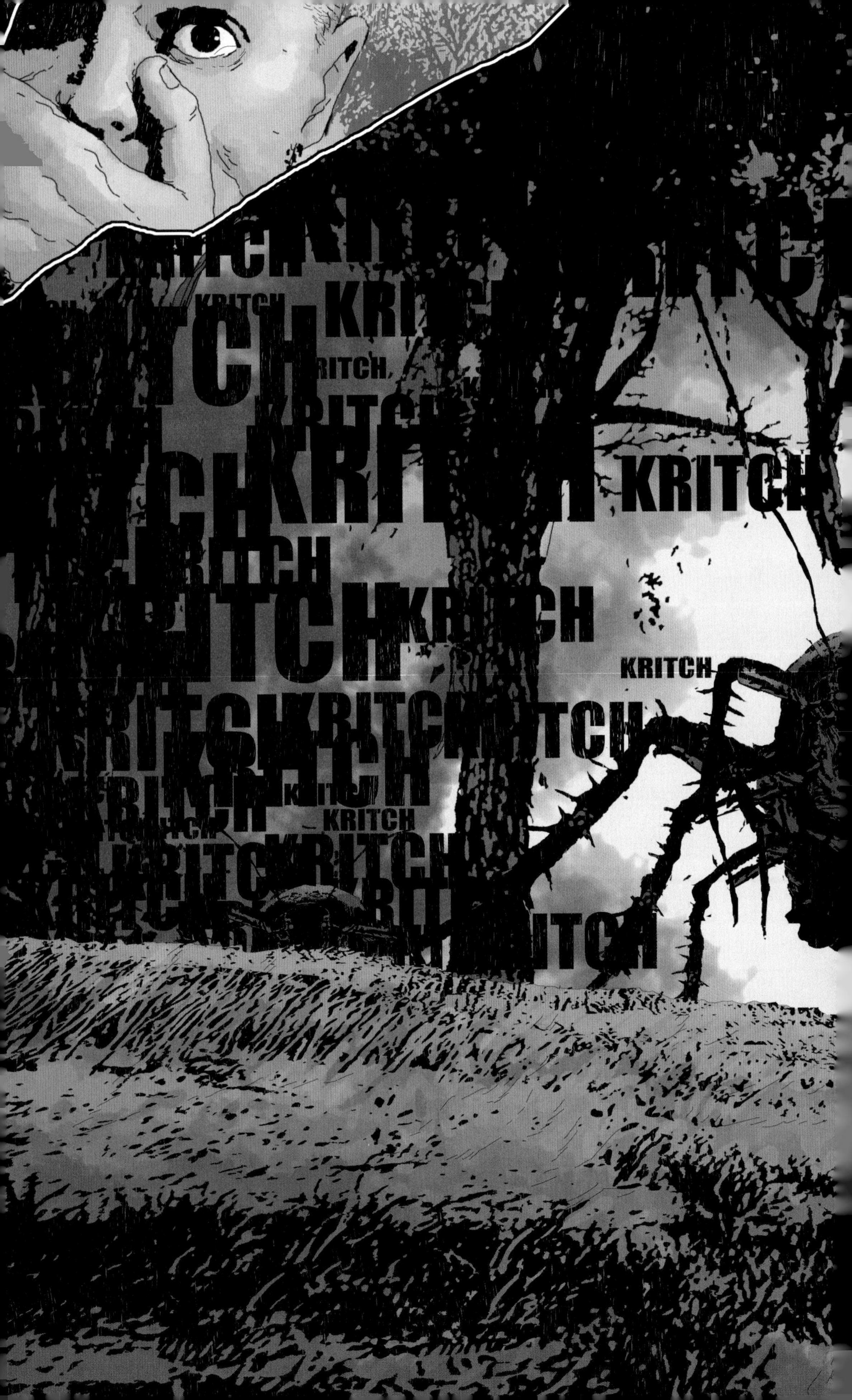
KRITCH
KRITCH
KRITCH
KRITCH

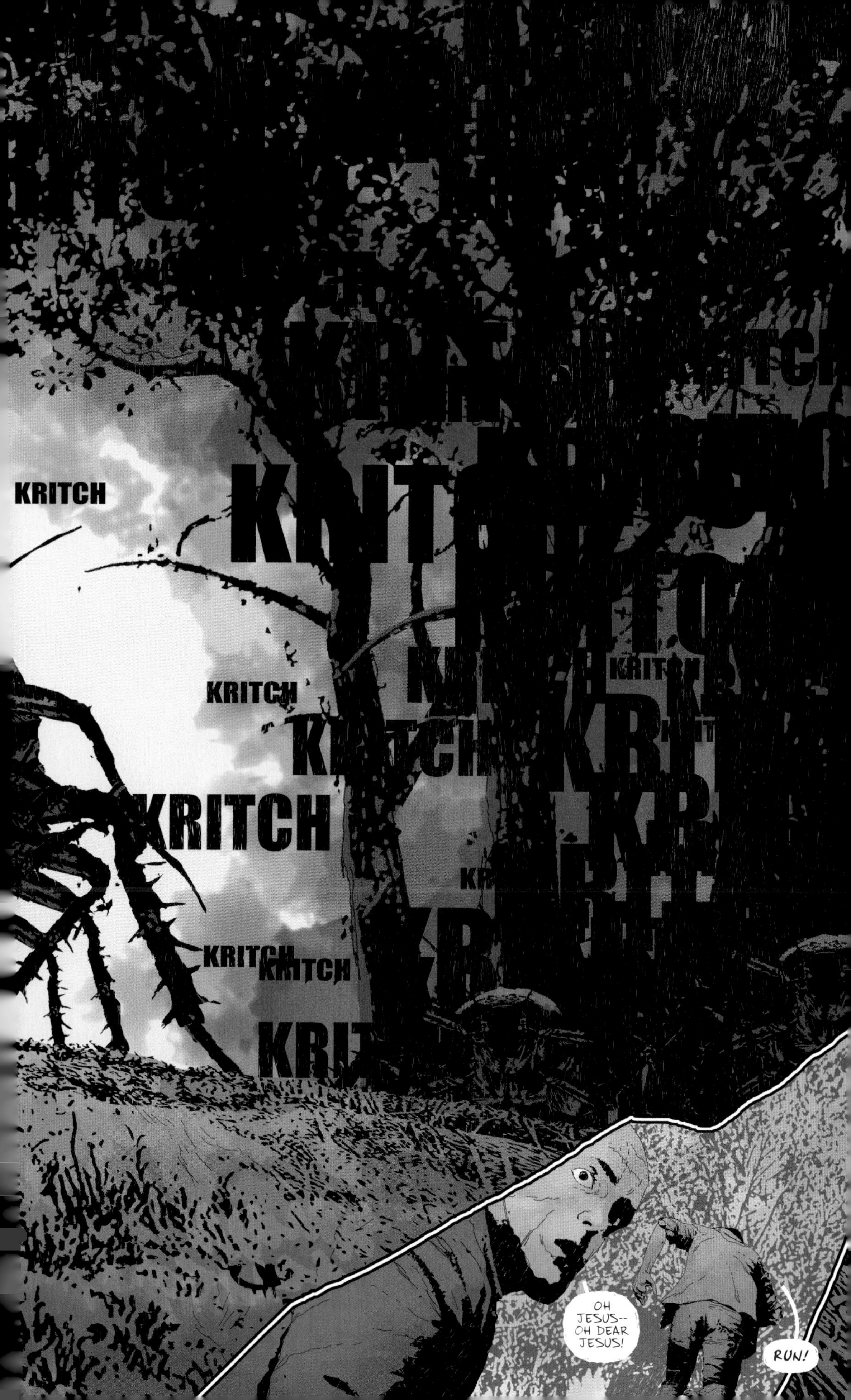

KRITCH
KRITCH
KRITCH
KRITCH
KRITCH
KRITCH
KRITCH
OH JESUS-- OH DEAR JESUS!
RUN!

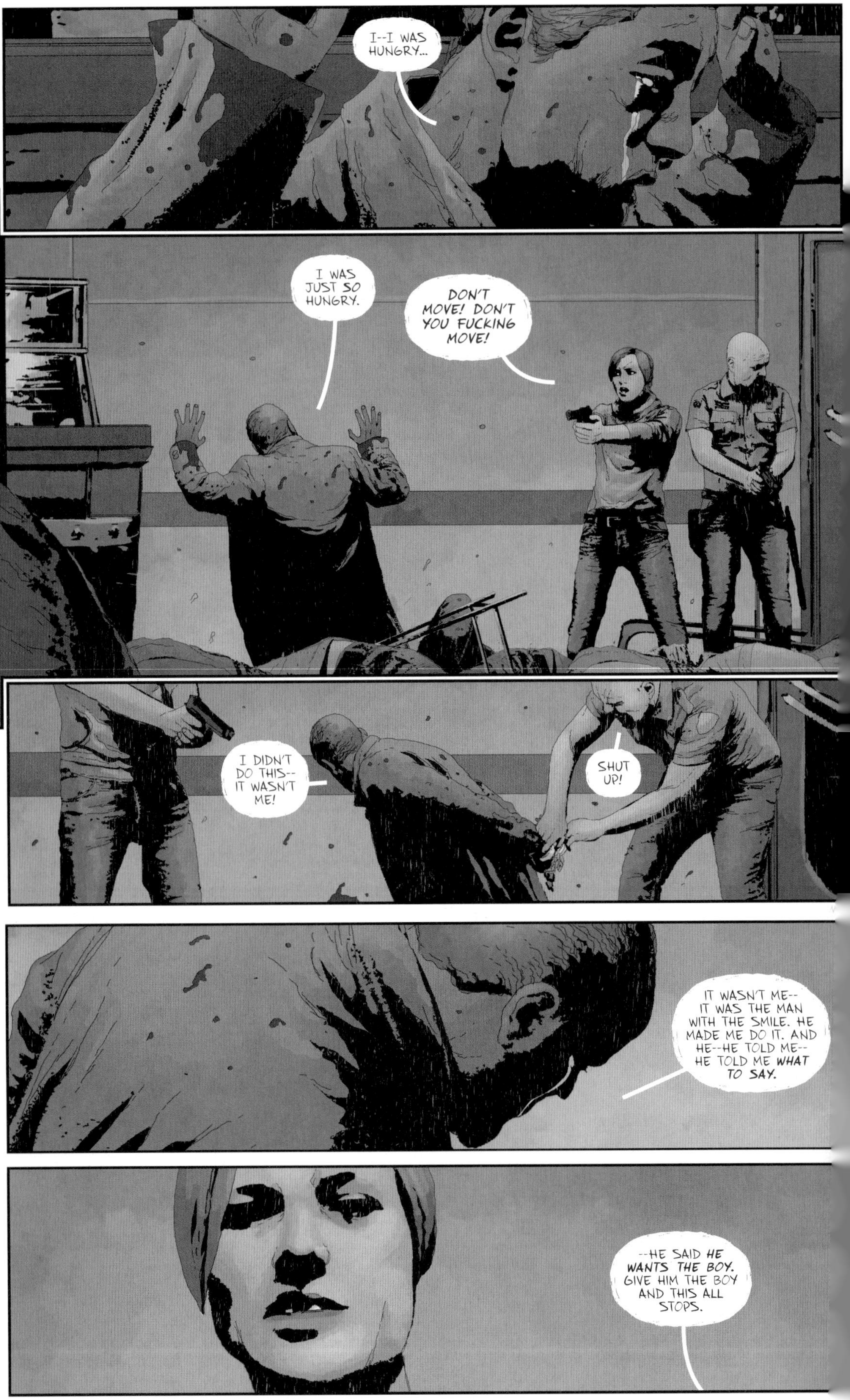
I--I WAS HUNGRY...
I WAS JUST SO HUNGRY.
DON'T MOVE! DON'T YOU FUCKING MOVE!
I DIDN'T DO THIS-- IT WASN'T ME!
SHUT UP!
IT WASN'T ME-- IT WAS THE MAN WITH THE SMILE. HE MADE ME DO IT. AND HE--HE TOLD ME-- HE TOLD ME WHAT TO SAY.
--HE SAID HE WANTS THE BOY. GIVE HIM THE BOY AND THIS ALL STOPS.

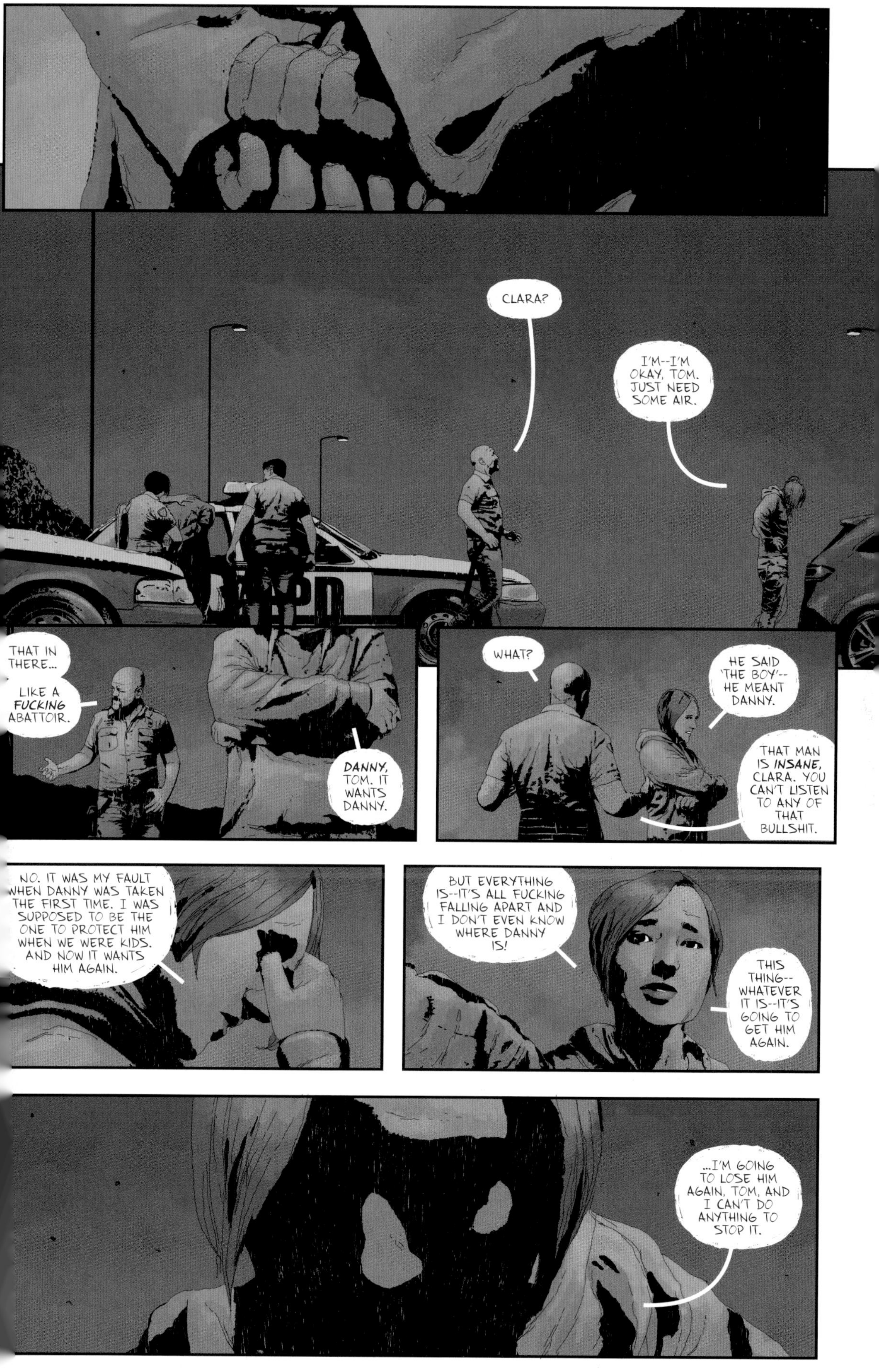
CLARA?
I'M--I'M OKAY, TOM. JUST NEED SOME AIR.
THAT IN THERE...
LIKE A FUCKING ABATTOIR.
DANNY, TOM. IT WANTS DANNY.
WHAT?
HE SAID 'THE BOY'-- HE MEANT DANNY.
THAT MAN IS INSANE, CLARA. YOU CAN'T LISTEN TO ANY OF THAT BULLSHIT.
NO. IT WAS MY FAULT WHEN DANNY WAS TAKEN THE FIRST TIME. I WAS SUPPOSED TO BE THE ONE TO PROTECT HIM WHEN WE WERE KIDS. AND NOW IT WANTS HIM AGAIN.
BUT EVERYTHING IS--IT'S ALL FUCKING FALLING APART AND I DON'T EVEN KNOW WHERE DANNY IS!
THIS THING--WHATEVER IT IS--IT'S GOING TO GET HIM AGAIN.
...I'M GOING TO LOSE HIM AGAIN, TOM, AND I CAN'T DO ANYTHING TO STOP IT.

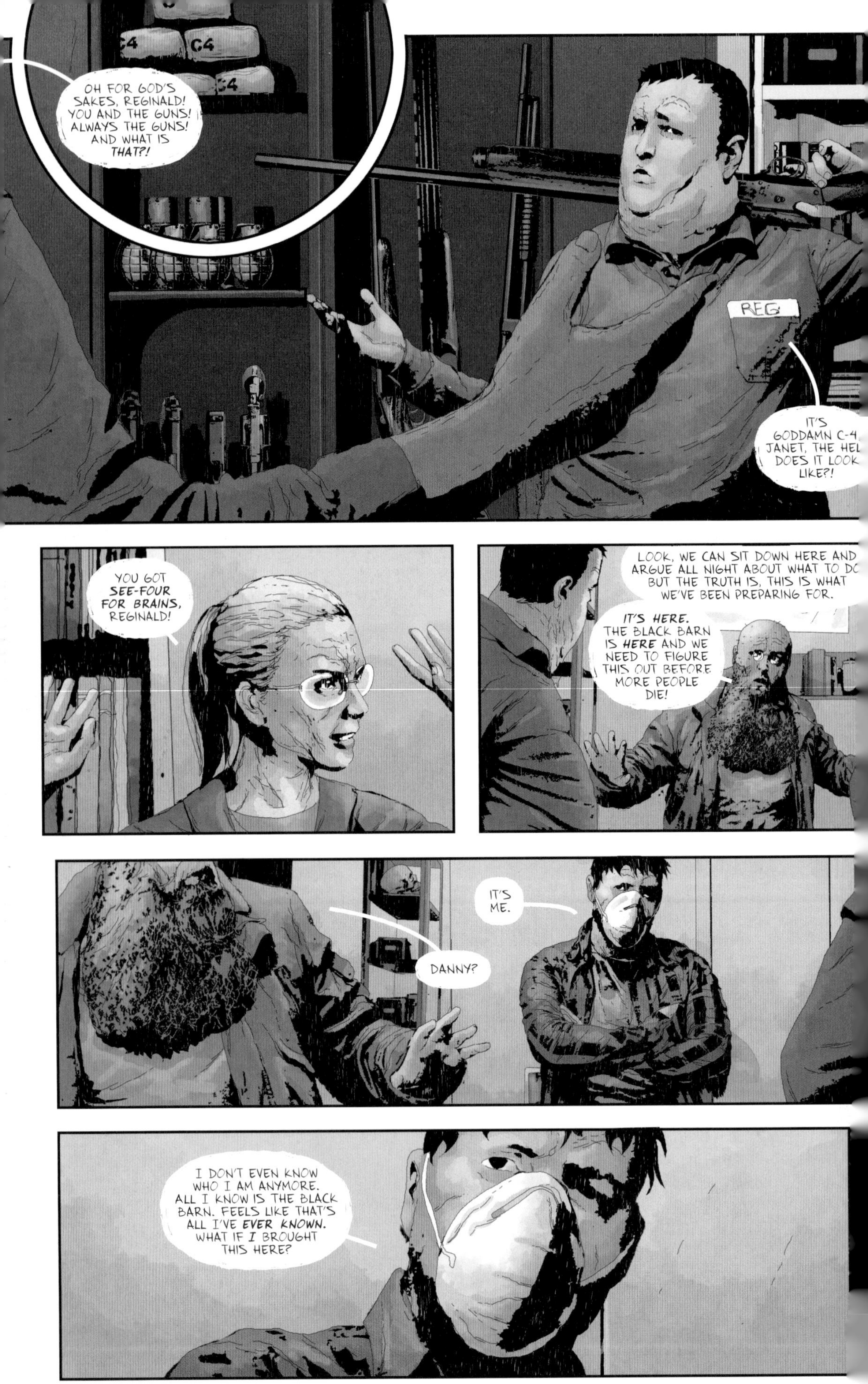
OH FOR GOD'S SAKES, REGINALD! YOU AND THE GUNS! ALWAYS THE GUNS! AND WHAT IS *THAT?!*
IT'S GODDAMN C-4, JANET, THE HEL DOES IT LOOK LIKE?!
YOU GOT **SEE-FOUR FOR BRAINS,** REGINALD!
LOOK, WE CAN SIT DOWN HERE AND ARGUE ALL NIGHT ABOUT WHAT TO DO BUT THE TRUTH IS, THIS IS WHAT WE'VE BEEN PREPARING FOR.
IT'S HERE. THE BLACK BARN IS ***HERE*** AND WE NEED TO FIGURE THIS OUT BEFORE MORE PEOPLE DIE!
IT'S ME.
DANNY?
I DON'T EVEN KNOW WHO I AM ANYMORE. ALL I KNOW IS THE BLACK BARN. FEELS LIKE THAT'S ALL I'VE ***EVER KNOWN.*** WHAT IF *I* BROUGHT THIS HERE?

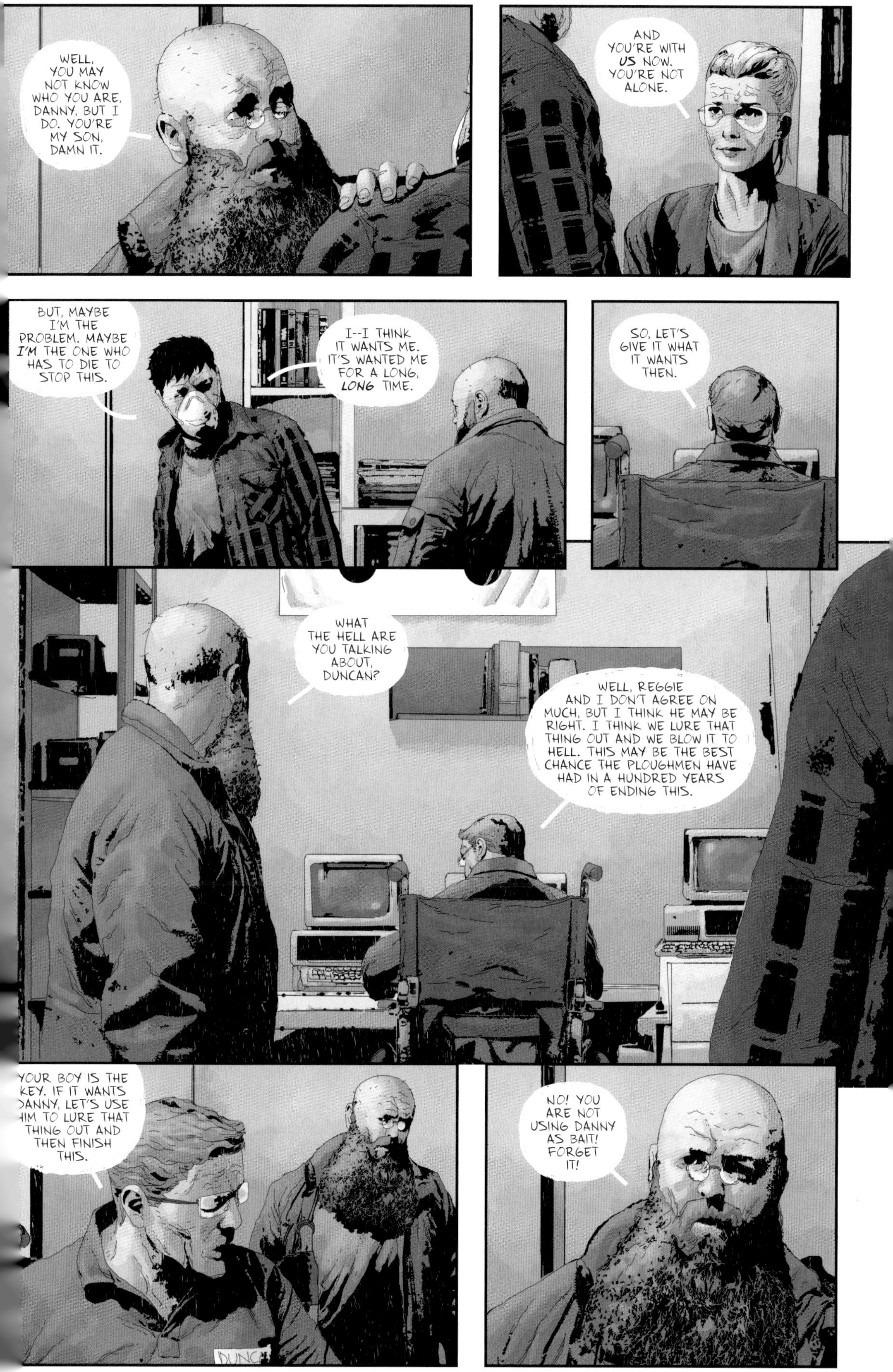
WELL, YOU MAY NOT KNOW WHO YOU ARE, DANNY, BUT I DO. YOU'RE MY SON, DAMN IT.
AND YOU'RE WITH US NOW. YOU'RE NOT ALONE.
BUT, MAYBE I'M THE PROBLEM. MAYBE I'M THE ONE WHO HAS TO DIE TO STOP THIS.
I--I THINK IT WANTS ME. IT'S WANTED ME FOR A LONG, LONG TIME.
SO, LET'S GIVE IT WHAT IT WANTS THEN.
WHAT THE HELL ARE YOU TALKING ABOUT, DUNCAN?
WELL, REGGIE AND I DON'T AGREE ON MUCH, BUT I THINK HE MAY BE RIGHT. I THINK WE LURE THAT THING OUT AND WE BLOW IT TO HELL. THIS MAY BE THE BEST CHANCE THE PLOUGHMEN HAVE HAD IN A HUNDRED YEARS OF ENDING THIS.
YOUR BOY IS THE KEY. IF IT WANTS DANNY, LET'S USE HIM TO LURE THAT THING OUT AND THEN FINISH THIS.
NO! YOU ARE NOT USING DANNY AS BAIT! FORGET IT!

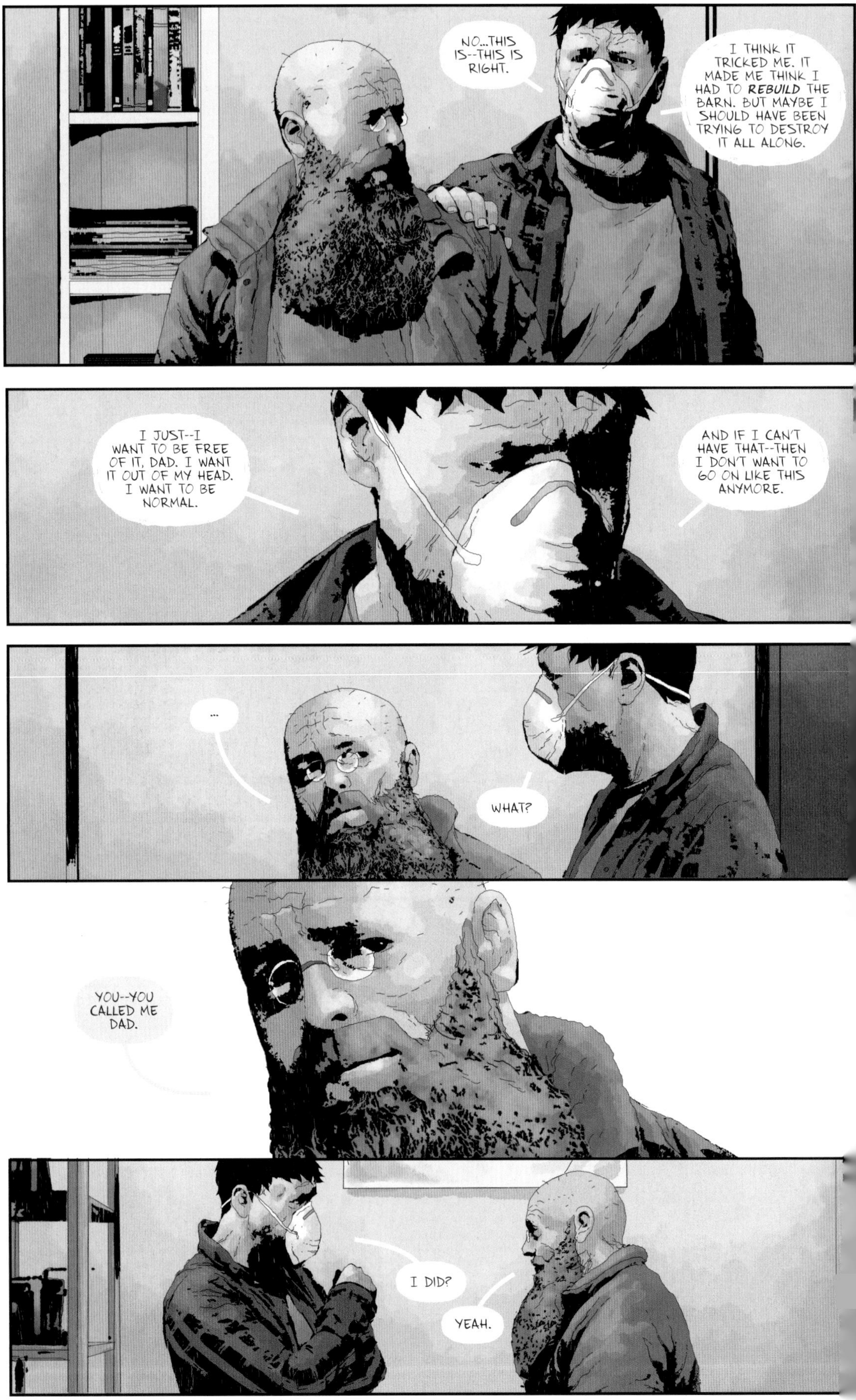
NO...THIS IS--THIS IS RIGHT.
I THINK IT TRICKED ME. IT MADE ME THINK I HAD TO **REBUILD** THE BARN. BUT MAYBE I SHOULD HAVE BEEN TRYING TO DESTROY IT ALL ALONG.
I JUST--I WANT TO BE FREE OF IT, DAD. I WANT IT OUT OF MY HEAD. I WANT TO BE NORMAL.
AND IF I CAN'T HAVE THAT--THEN I DON'T WANT TO GO ON LIKE THIS ANYMORE.
...
WHAT?
YOU--YOU CALLED ME DAD.
I DID?
YEAH.

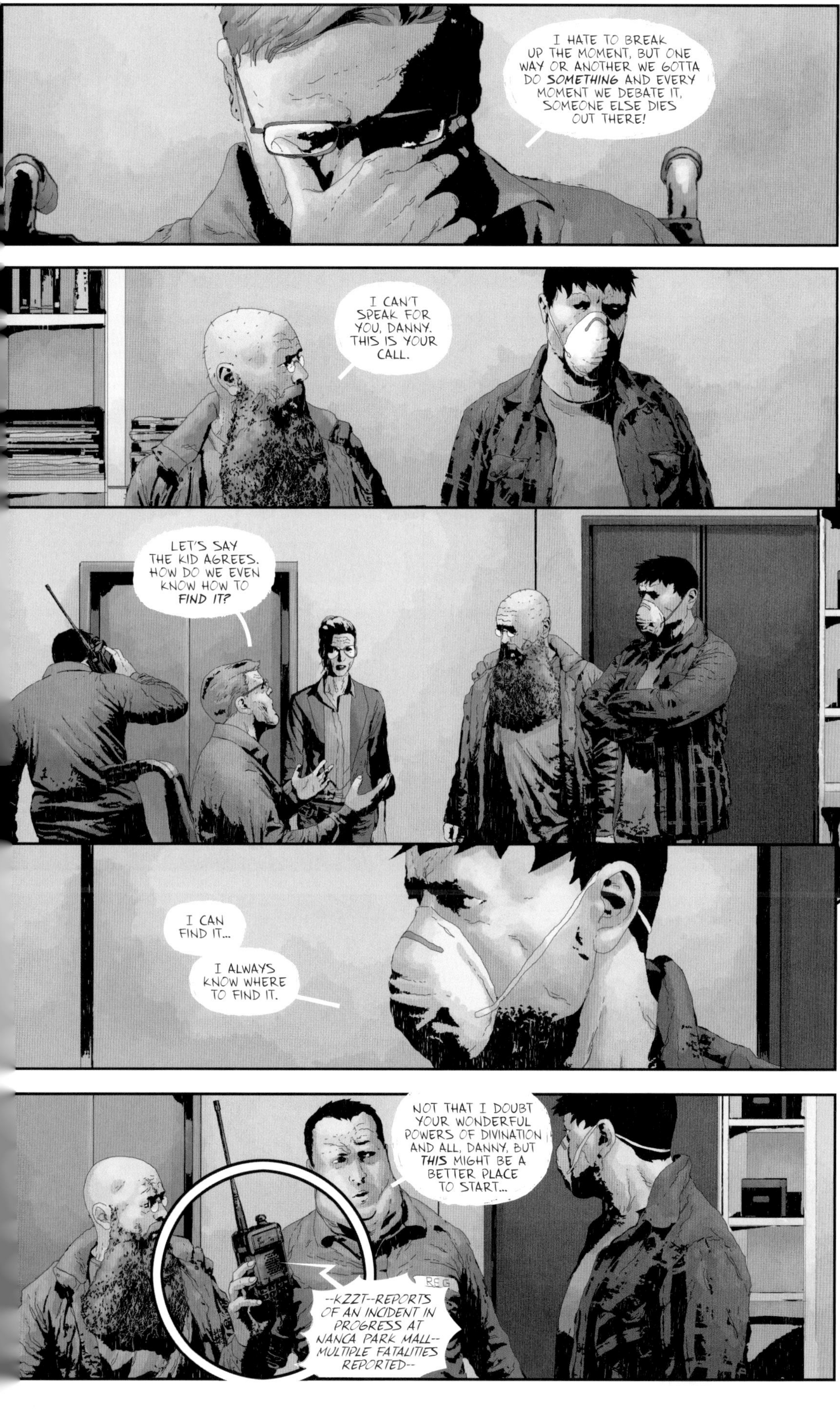
I HATE TO BREAK UP THE MOMENT, BUT ONE WAY OR ANOTHER WE GOTTA DO SOMETHING AND EVERY MOMENT WE DEBATE IT, SOMEONE ELSE DIES OUT THERE!
I CAN'T SPEAK FOR YOU, DANNY. THIS IS YOUR CALL.
LET'S SAY THE KID AGREES. HOW DO WE EVEN KNOW HOW TO FIND IT?
I CAN FIND IT...
I ALWAYS KNOW WHERE TO FIND IT.
NOT THAT I DOUBT YOUR WONDERFUL POWERS OF DIVINATION AND ALL, DANNY, BUT THIS MIGHT BE A BETTER PLACE TO START...
--KZZT--REPORTS OF AN INCIDENT IN PROGRESS AT NANCA PARK MALL--MULTIPLE FATALITIES REPORTED--

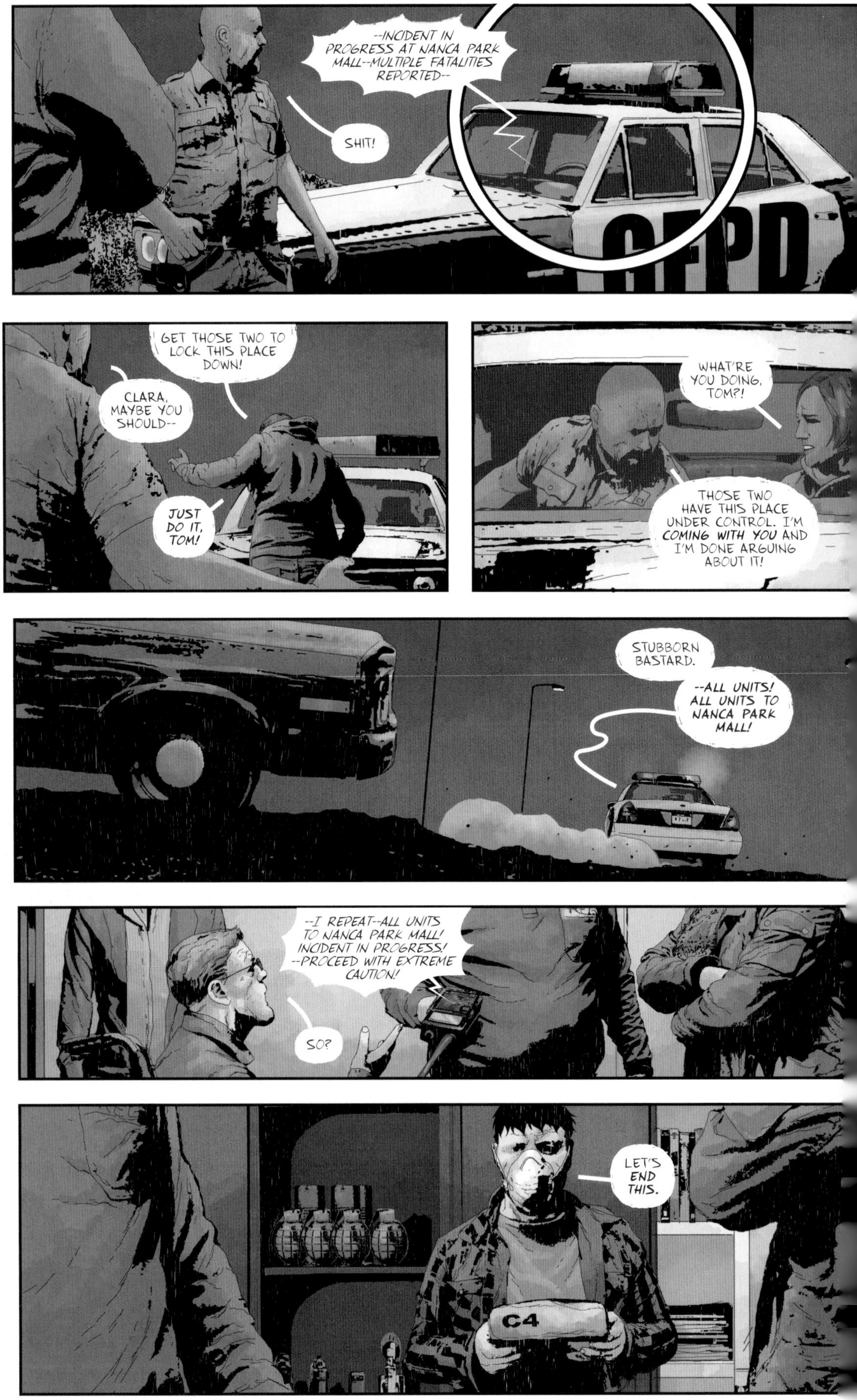
--INCIDENT IN PROGRESS AT NANCA PARK MALL--MULTIPLE FATALITIES REPORTED--
SHIT!
GFPD
GET THOSE TWO TO LOCK THIS PLACE DOWN!
CLARA, MAYBE YOU SHOULD--
JUST DO IT, TOM!
WHAT'RE YOU DOING, TOM?!
THOSE TWO HAVE THIS PLACE UNDER CONTROL. I'M COMING WITH YOU AND I'M DONE ARGUING ABOUT IT!
STUBBORN BASTARD.
--ALL UNITS! ALL UNITS TO NANCA PARK MALL!
--I REPEAT--ALL UNITS TO NANCA PARK MALL! INCIDENT IN PROGRESS! --PROCEED WITH EXTREME CAUTION!
SO?
LET'S END THIS.
C4

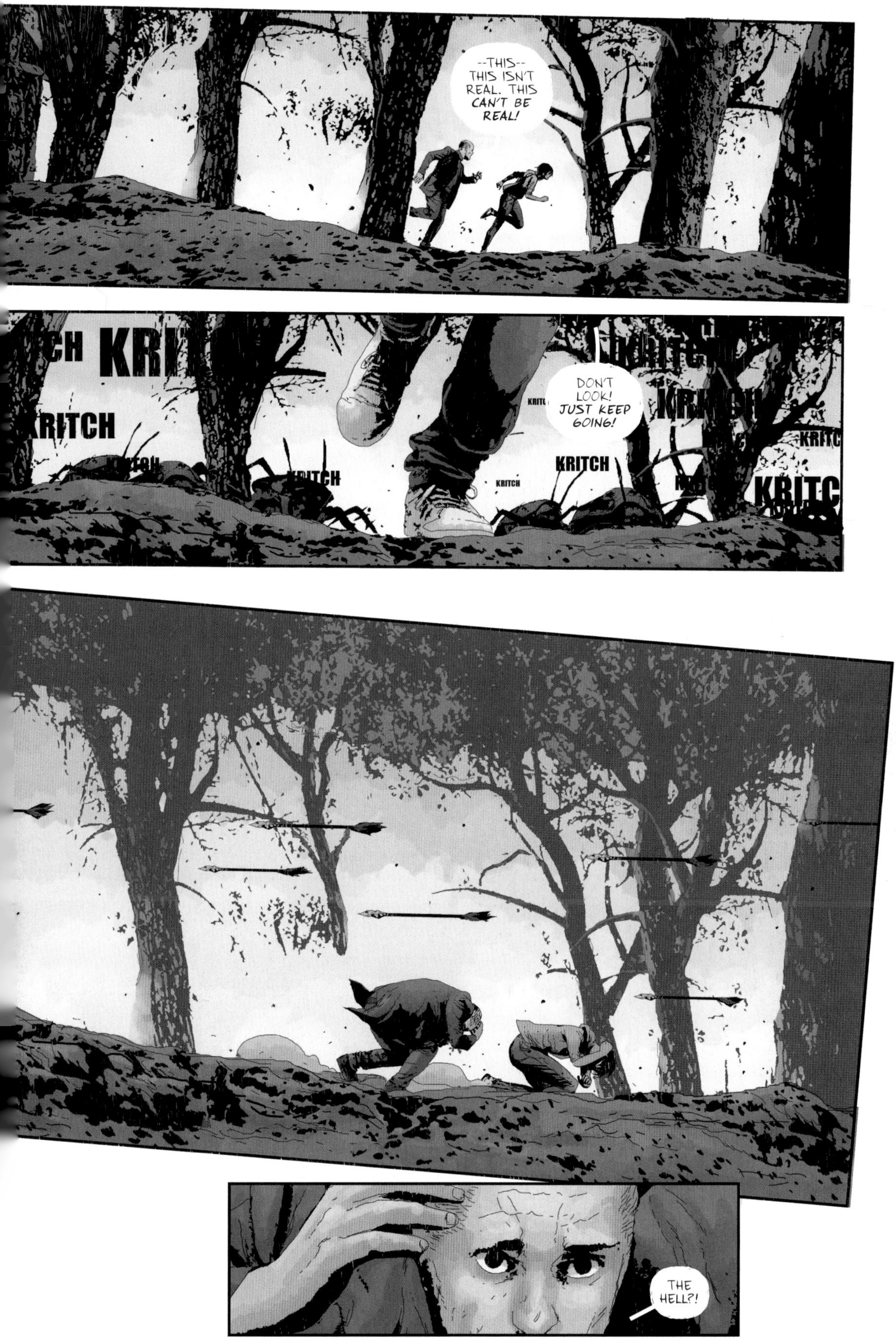
--THIS-- THIS ISN'T REAL. THIS CAN'T BE REAL!
KRITCH
DON'T LOOK! JUST KEEP GOING!
KRITCH
KRITCH
KRITCH
KRITCH
THE HELL?!

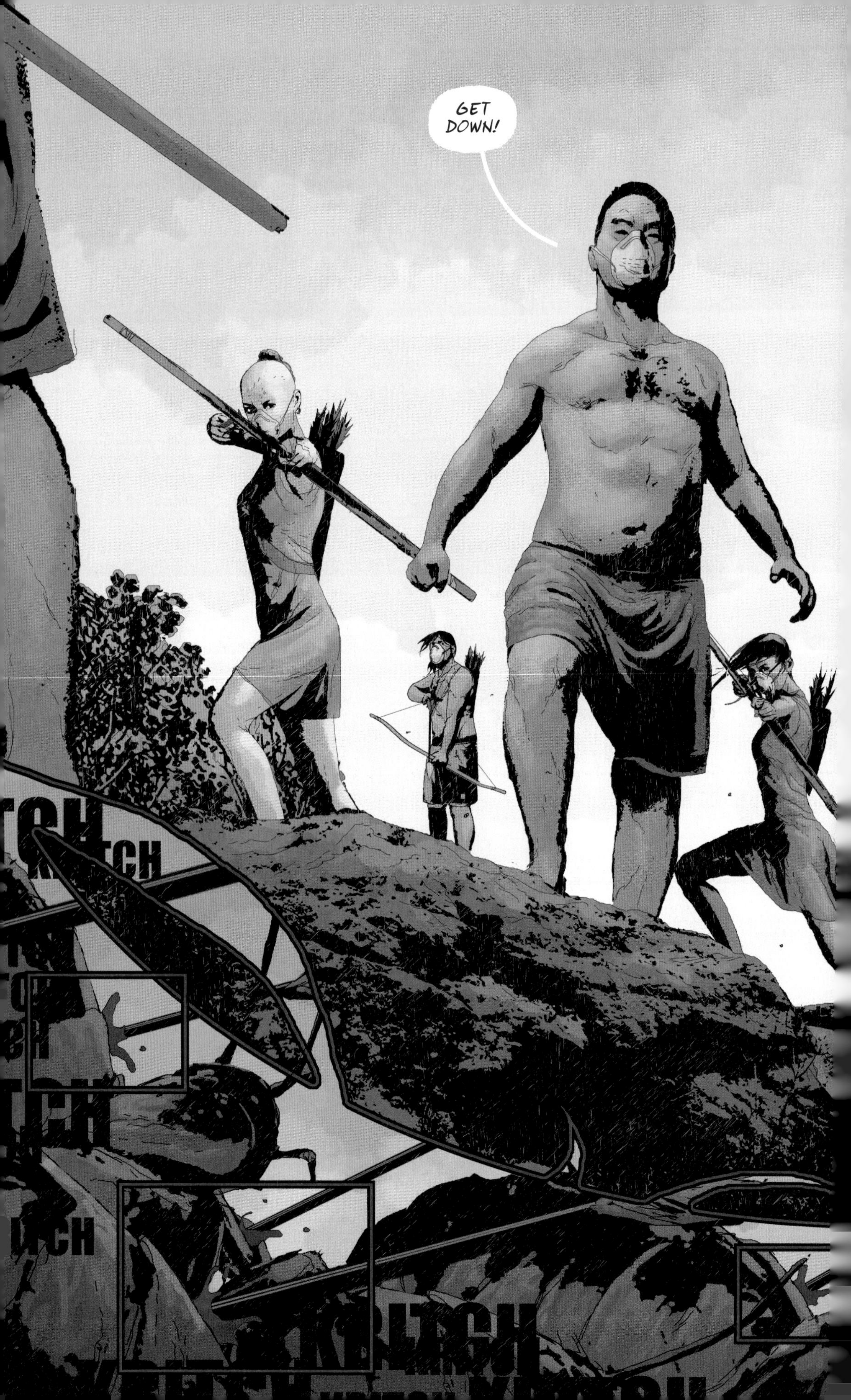
GET DOWN!

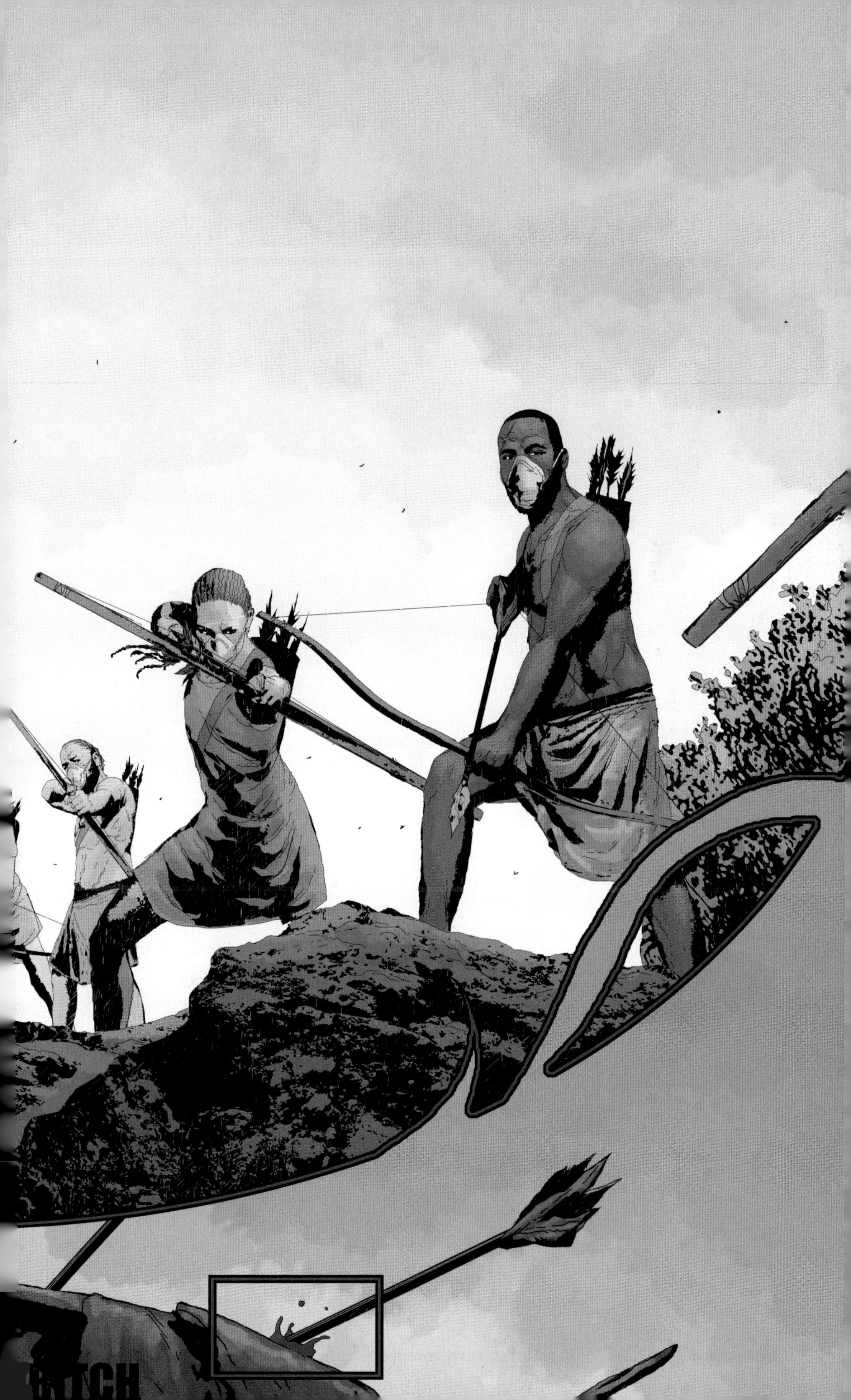

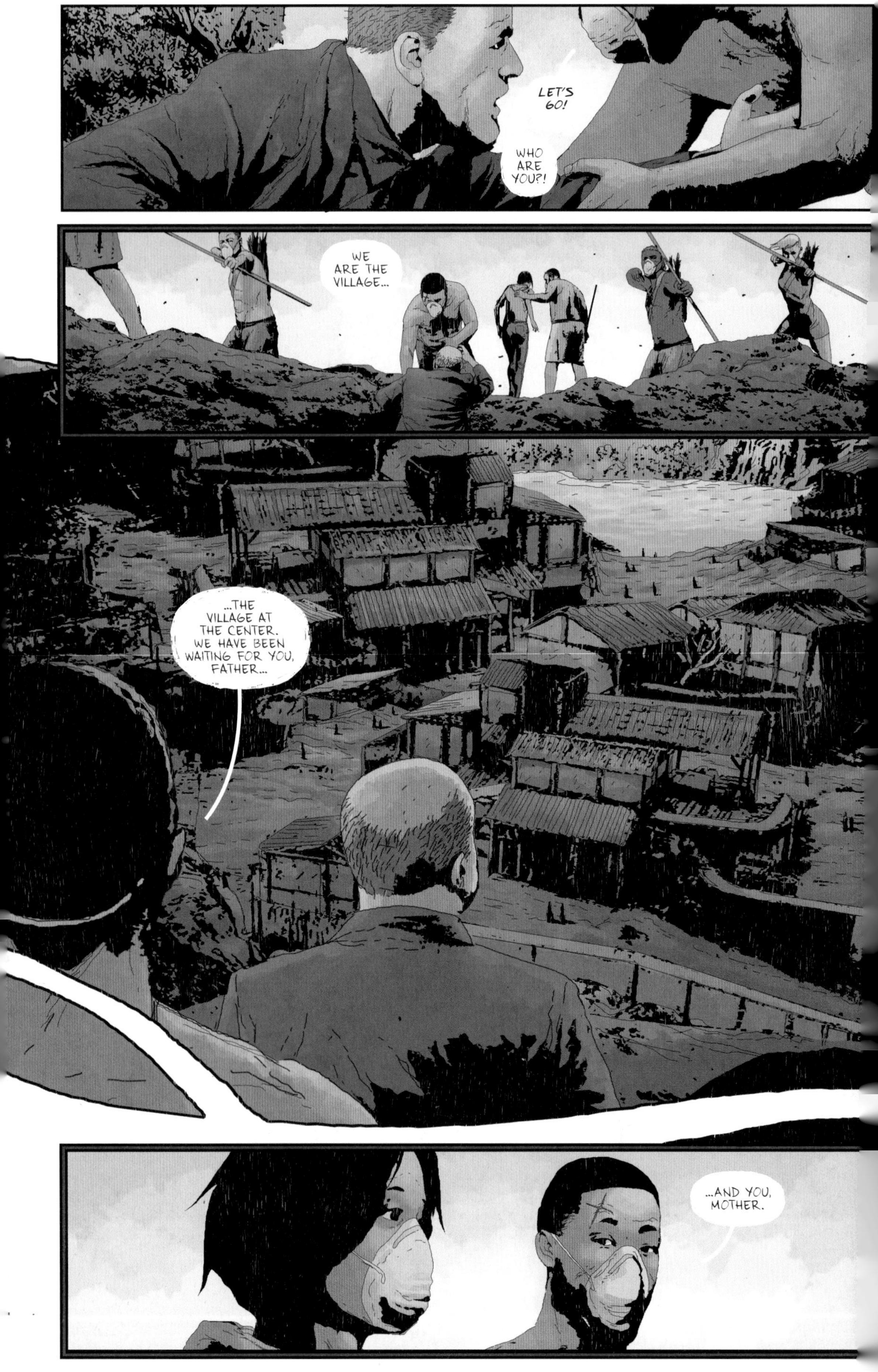
LET'S GO!
WHO ARE YOU?!
WE ARE THE VILLAGE...
...THE VILLAGE AT THE CENTER. WE HAVE BEEN WAITING FOR YOU, FATHER...
...AND YOU, MOTHER.

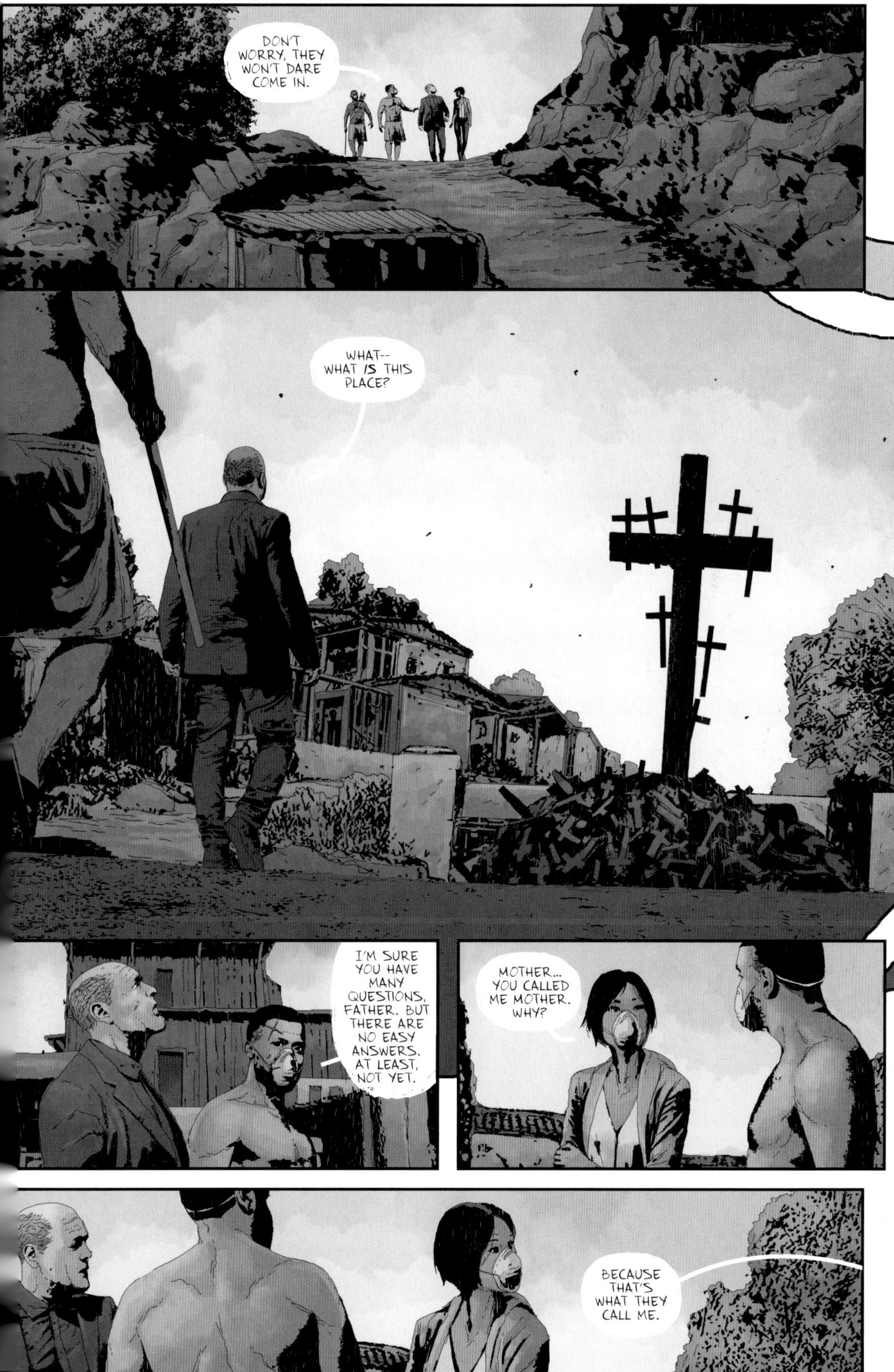
DON'T WORRY, THEY WON'T DARE COME IN.
WHAT-- WHAT IS THIS PLACE?
I'M SURE YOU HAVE MANY QUESTIONS, FATHER. BUT THERE ARE NO EASY ANSWERS. AT LEAST, NOT YET.
MOTHER... YOU CALLED ME MOTHER. WHY?
BECAUSE THAT'S WHAT THEY CALL ME.

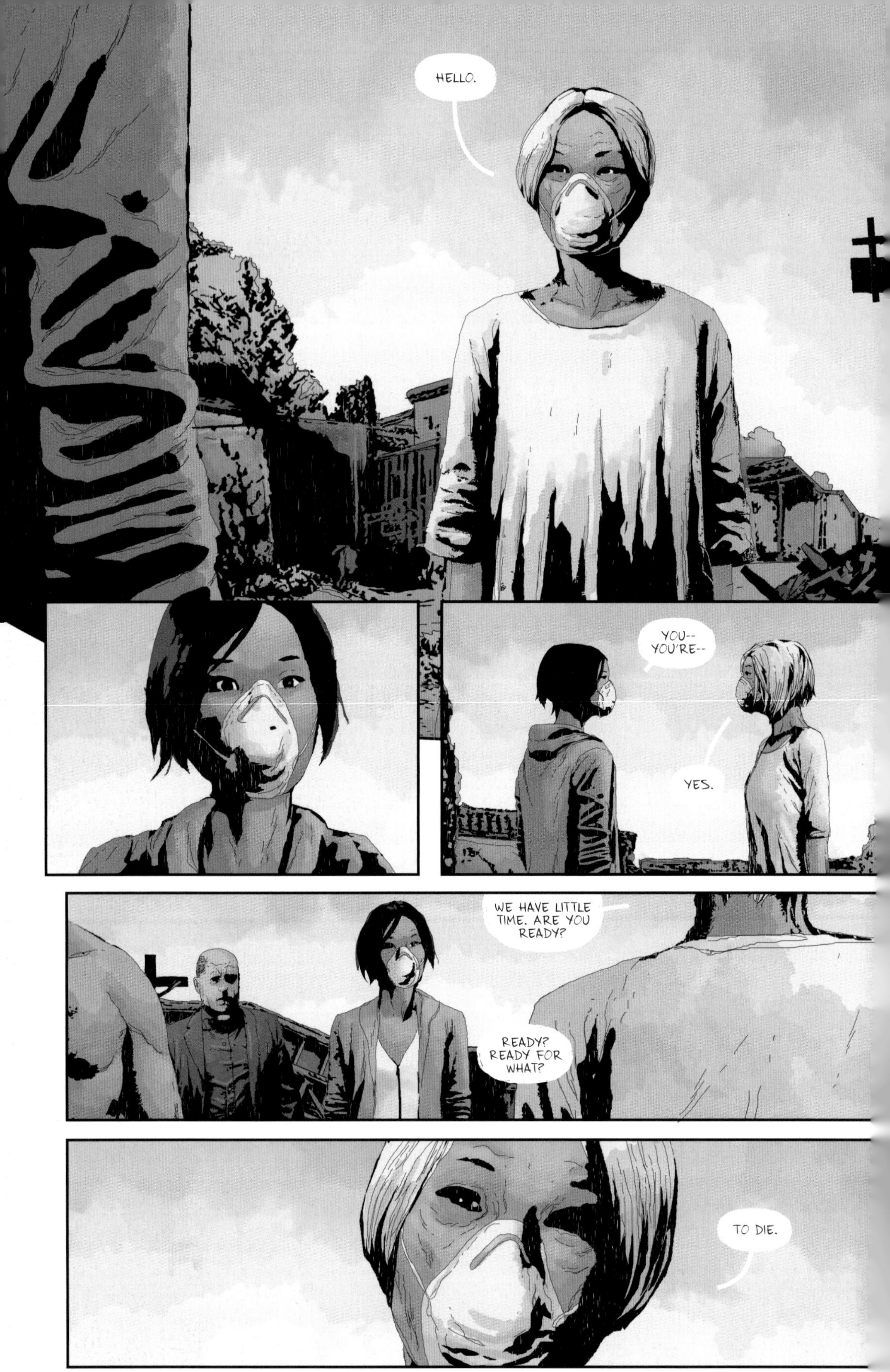
HELLO.
YOU-- YOU'RE--
YES.
WE HAVE LITTLE TIME. ARE YOU READY?
READY? READY FOR WHAT?
TO DIE.

GIDEON
FALLS

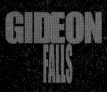

Twenty-One

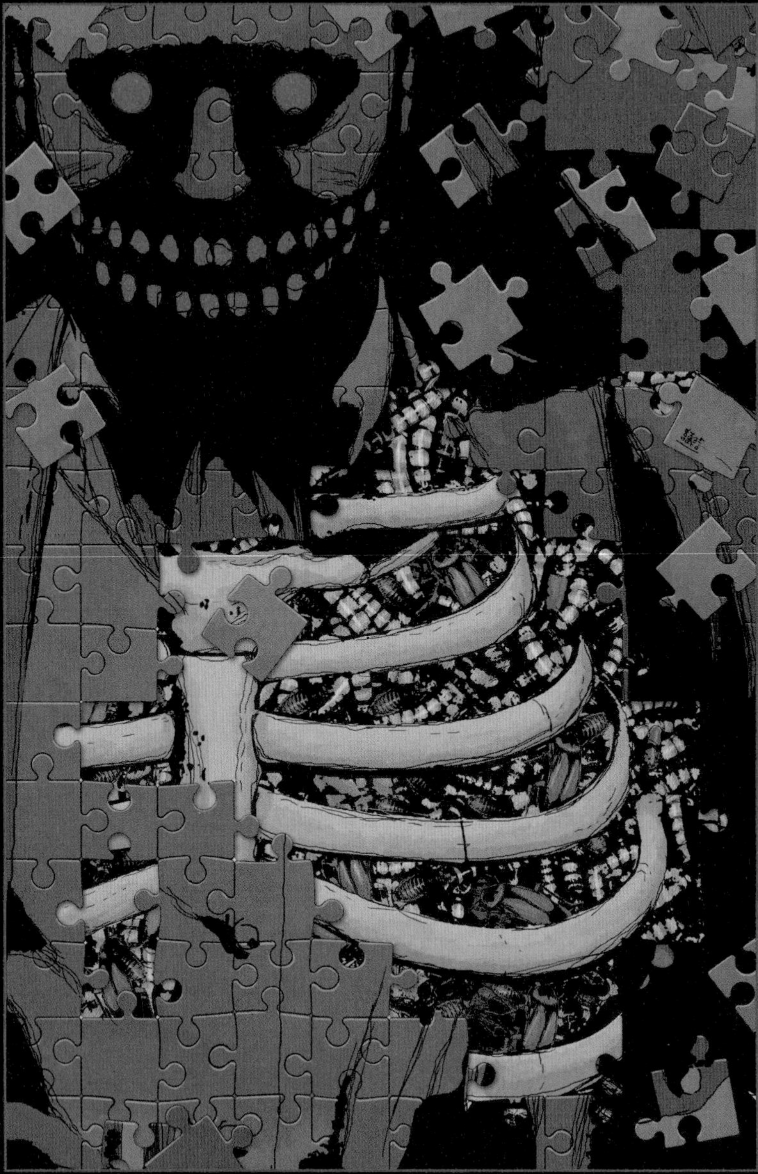

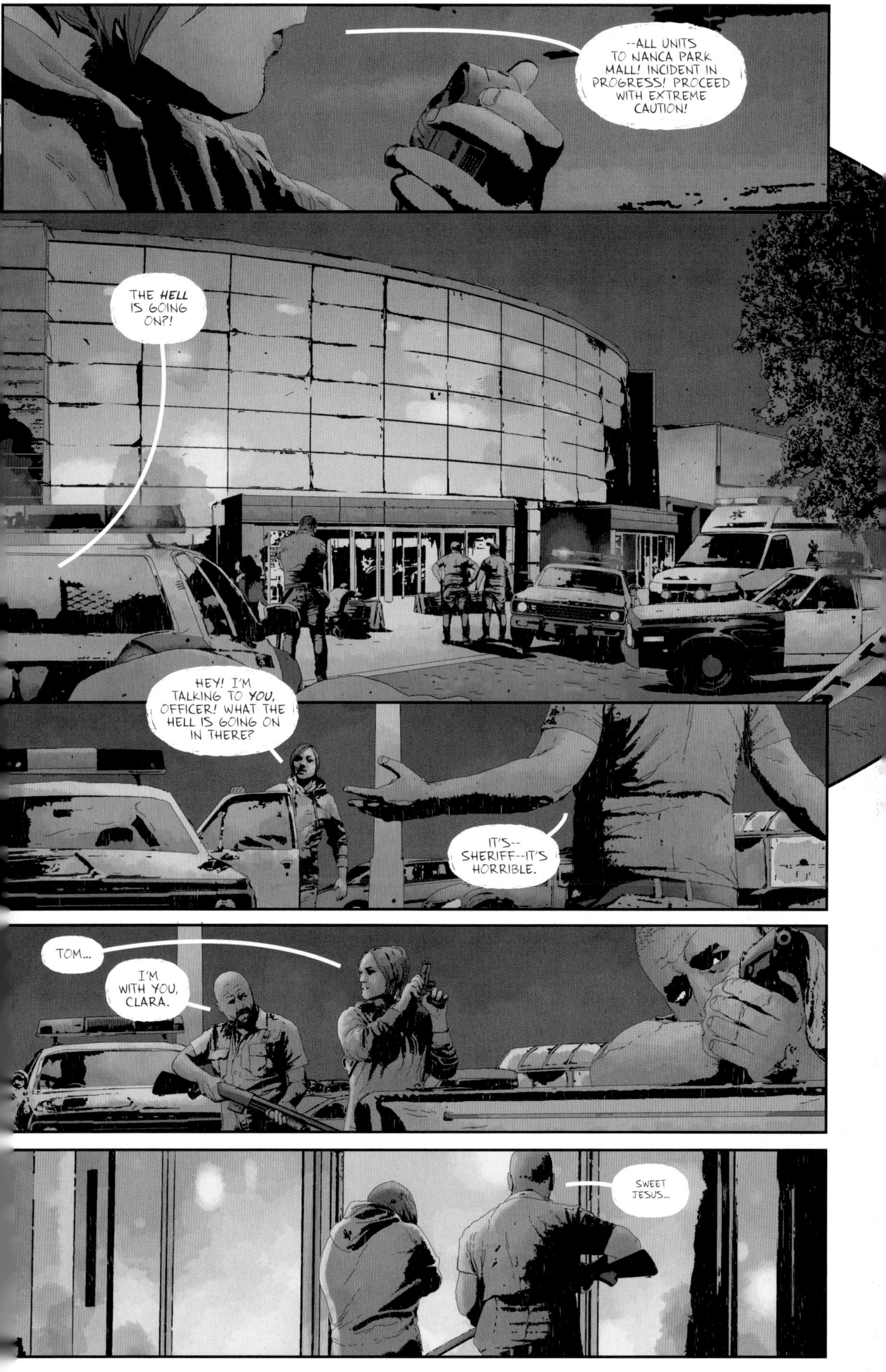
--ALL UNITS TO NANCA PARK MALL! INCIDENT IN PROGRESS! PROCEED WITH EXTREME CAUTION!
THE HELL IS GOING ON?!
HEY! I'M TALKING TO YOU, OFFICER! WHAT THE HELL IS GOING ON IN THERE?
IT'S-- SHERIFF--IT'S HORRIBLE.
TOM...
I'M WITH YOU, CLARA.
SWEET JESUS...

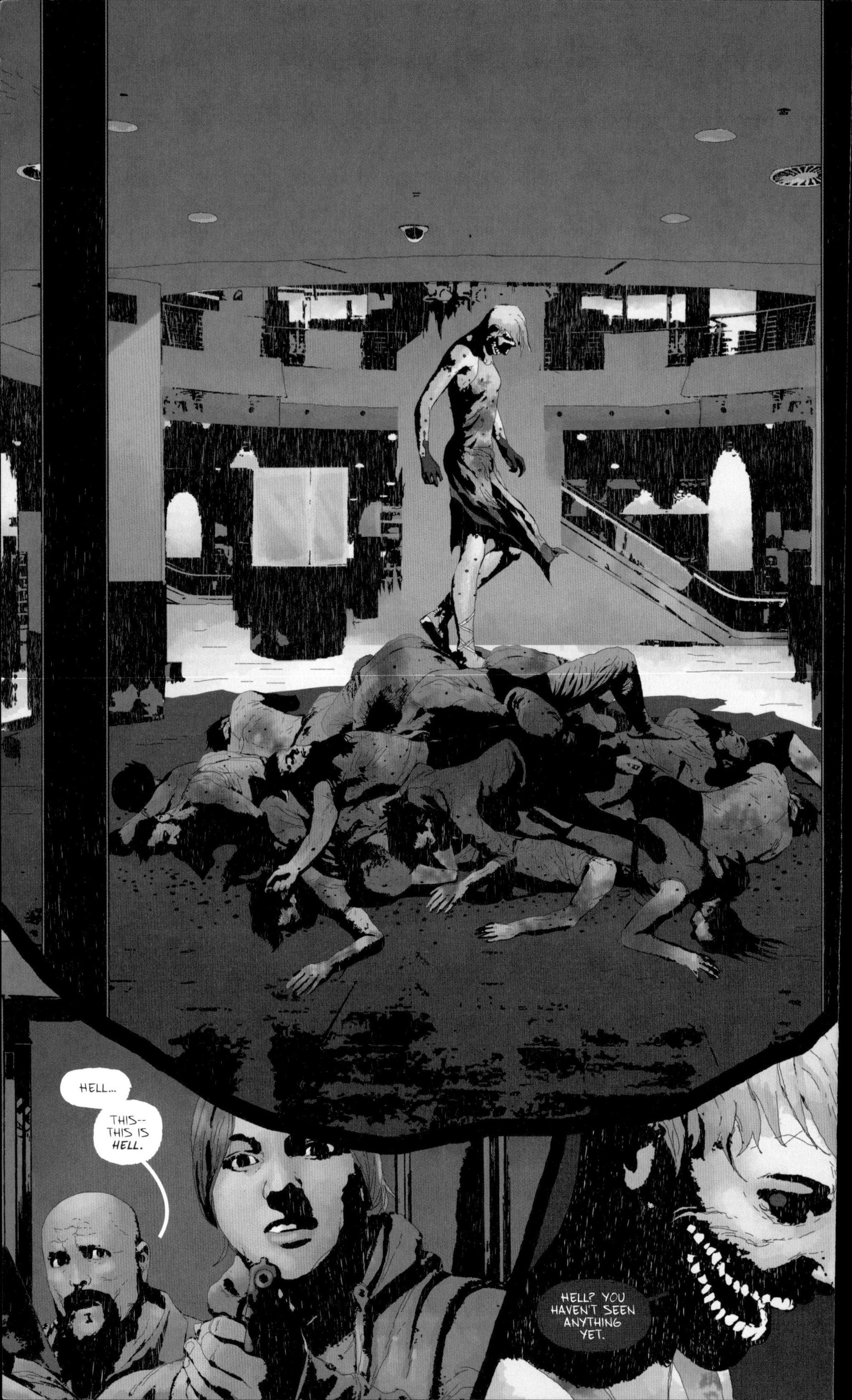
HELL...
THIS-- THIS IS HELL.
HELL? YOU HAVEN'T SEEN ANYTHING YET.

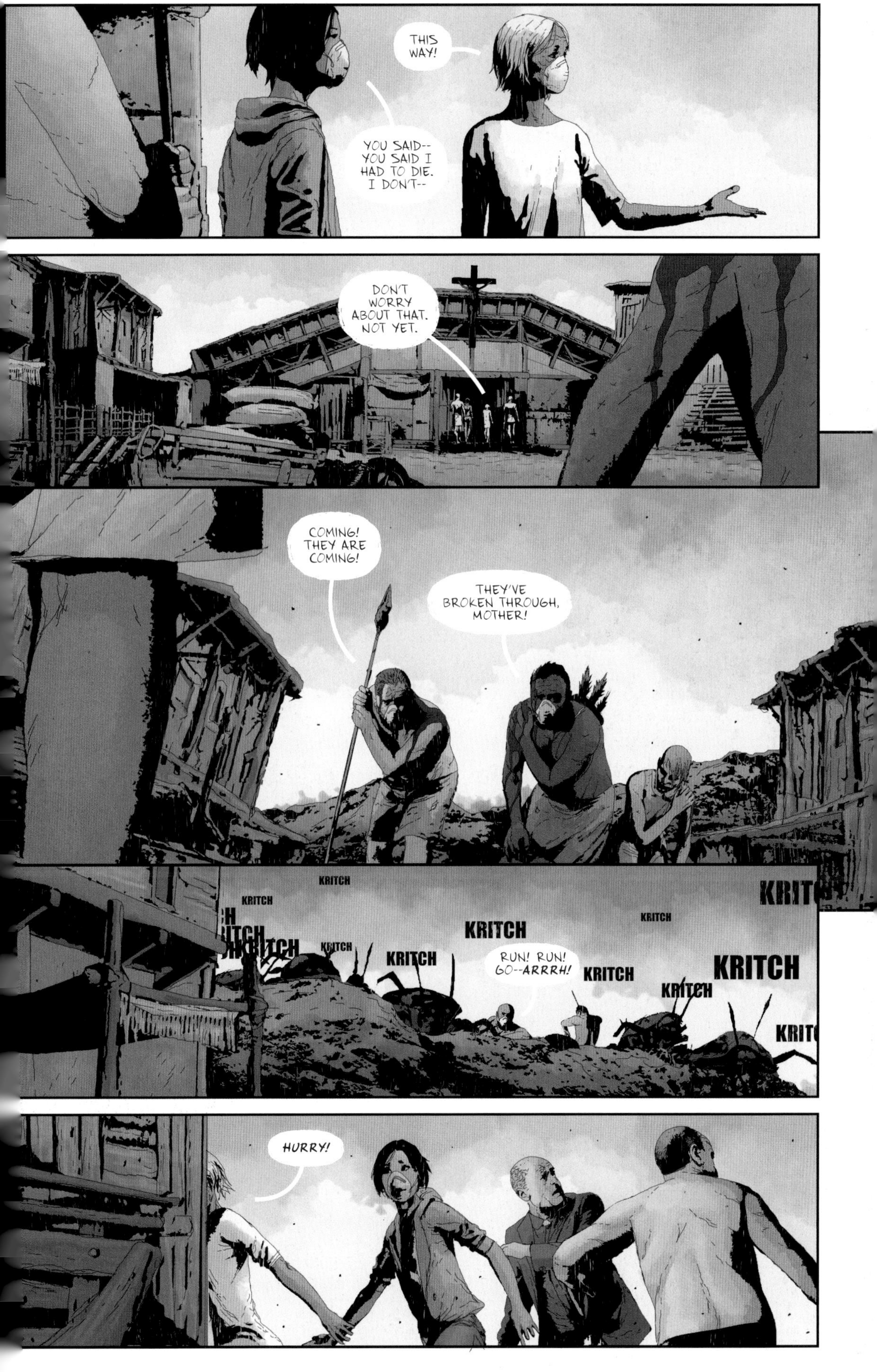
THIS WAY!
YOU SAID-- YOU SAID I HAD TO DIE. I DON'T--
DON'T WORRY ABOUT THAT. NOT YET.
COMING! THEY ARE COMING!
THEY'VE BROKEN THROUGH, MOTHER!
KRITCH
KRITCH
KRITCH
KRITCH
KRITCH
KRITCH
RUN! RUN! GO--ARRRH!
KRITCH
KRITCH
KRITCH
KRITCH
HURRY!

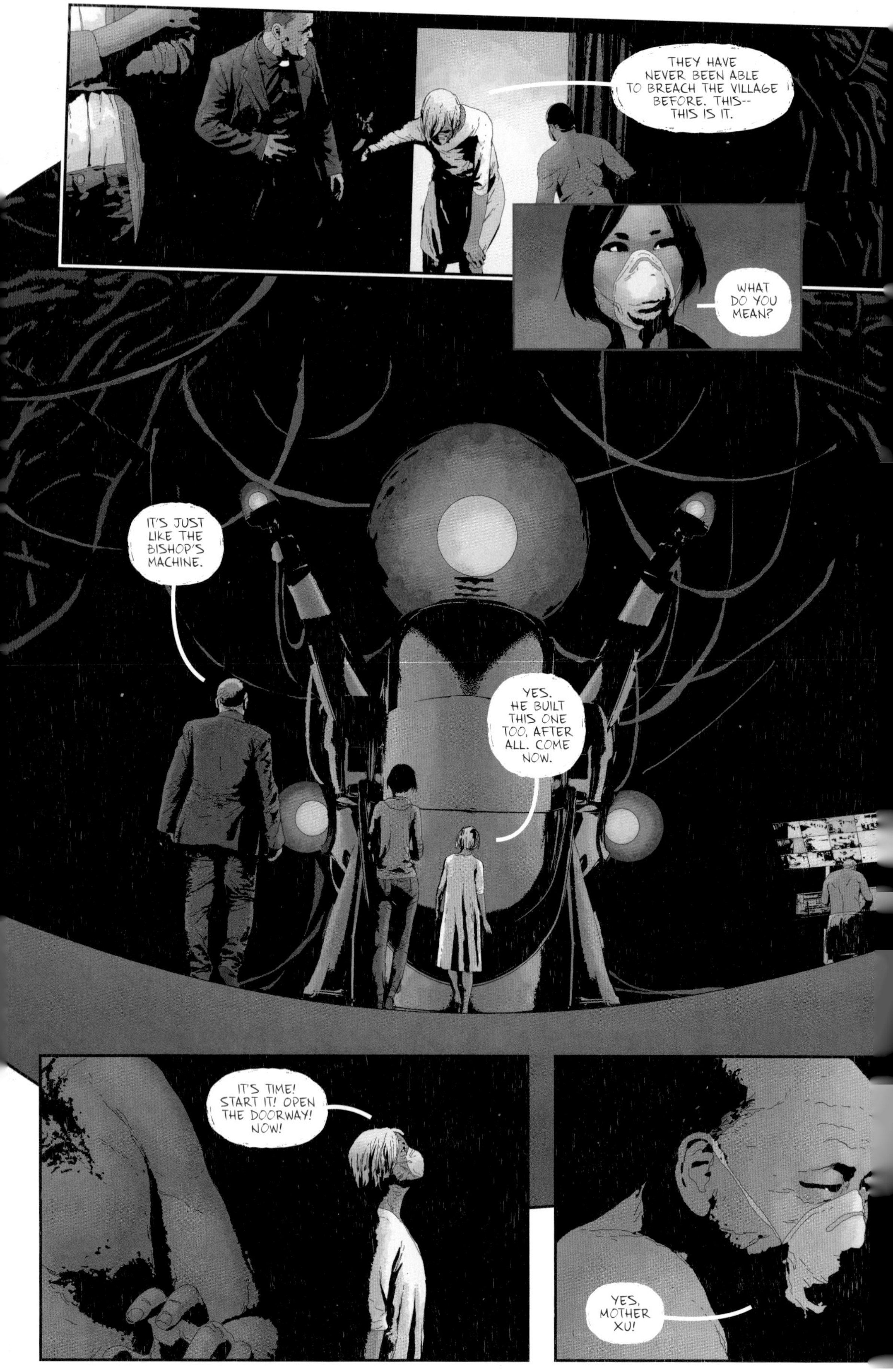
THEY HAVE NEVER BEEN ABLE TO BREACH THE VILLAGE BEFORE. THIS-- THIS IS IT.
WHAT DO YOU MEAN?
IT'S JUST LIKE THE BISHOP'S MACHINE.
YES. HE BUILT THIS ONE TOO, AFTER ALL. COME NOW.
IT'S TIME! START IT! OPEN THE DOORWAY! NOW!
YES, MOTHER XU!

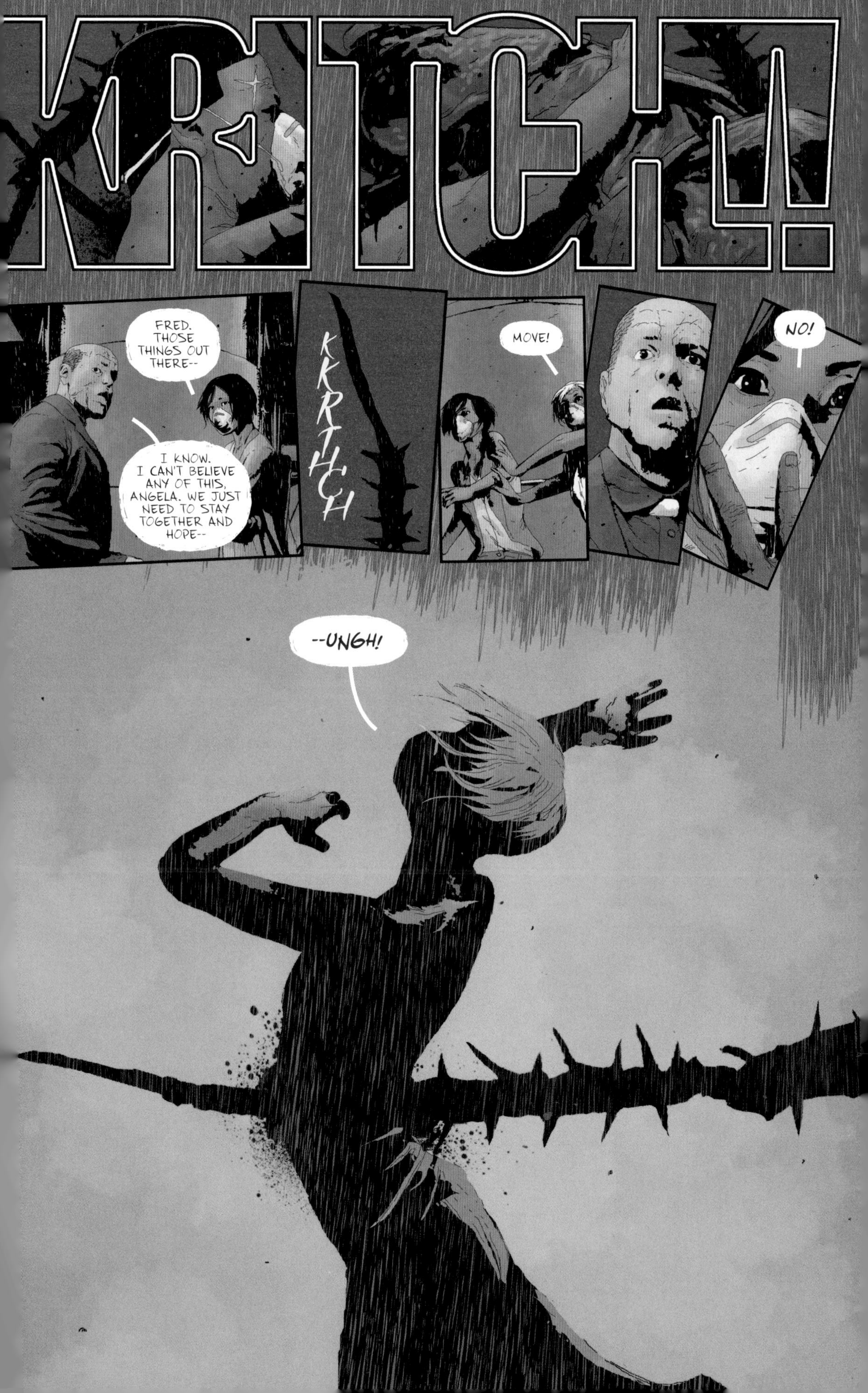
KRITCH!!
FRED. THOSE THINGS OUT THERE--
I KNOW. I CAN'T BELIEVE ANY OF THIS, ANGELA. WE JUST NEED TO STAY TOGETHER AND HOPE--
KKRTHCH
MOVE!
NO!
--UNGH!

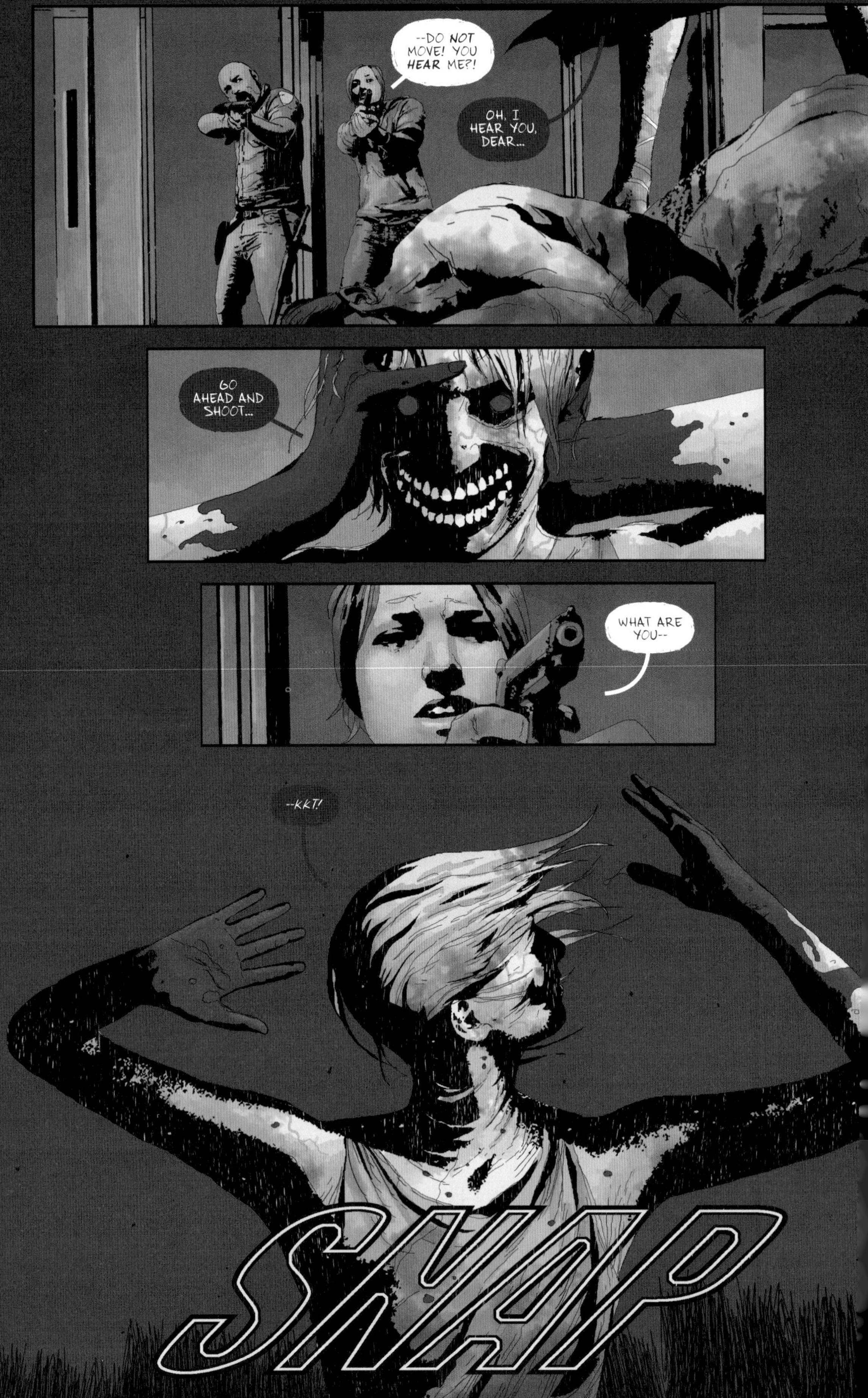
--DO NOT MOVE! YOU HEAR ME?!
OH, I HEAR YOU, DEAR...
GO AHEAD AND SHOOT...
WHAT ARE YOU--
--KKT!
SHNP

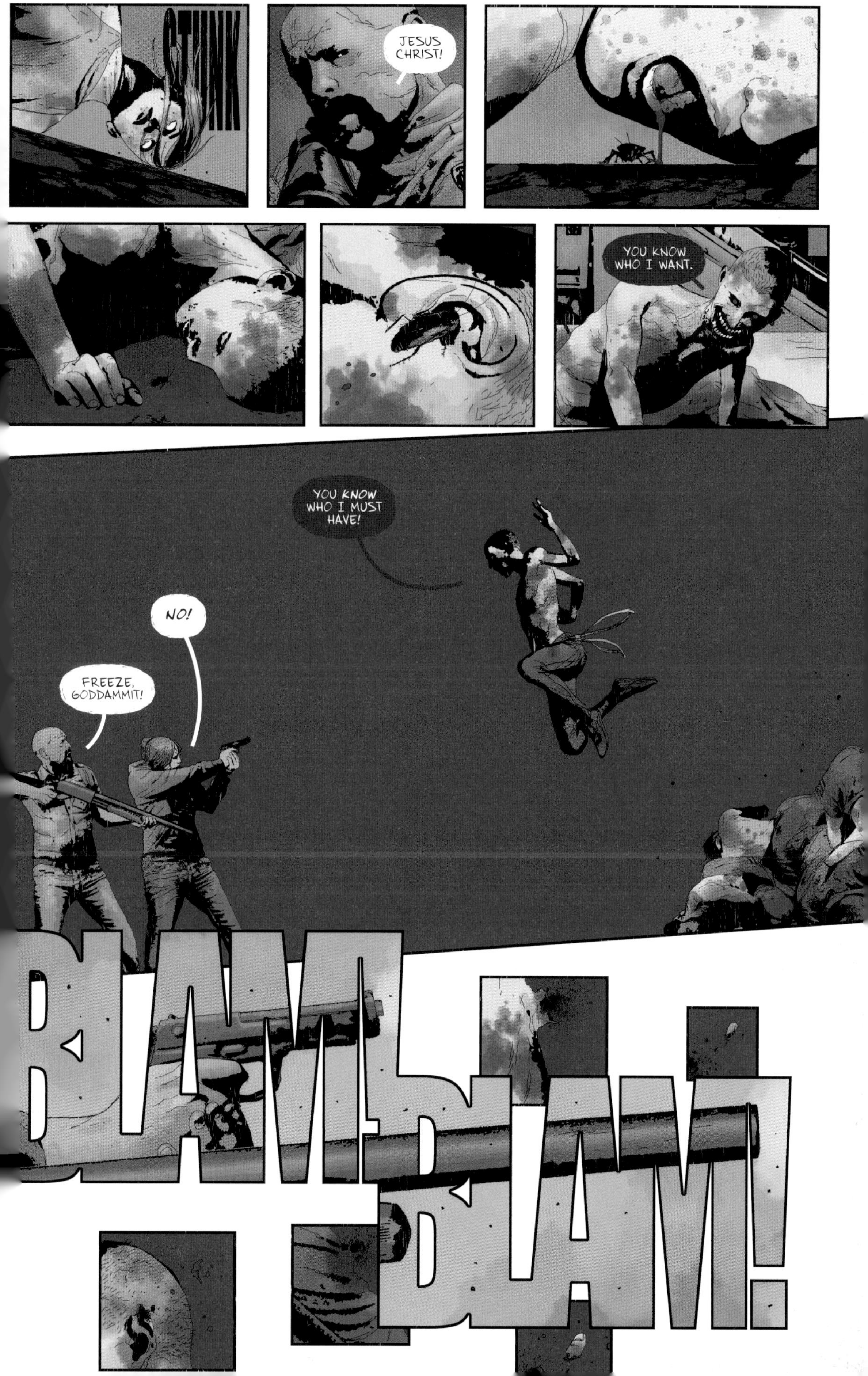
STUNK
JESUS CHRIST!
YOU KNOW WHO I WANT.
YOU KNOW WHO I MUST HAVE!
NO!
FREEZE, GODDAMMIT!
BLAM! BLAM!

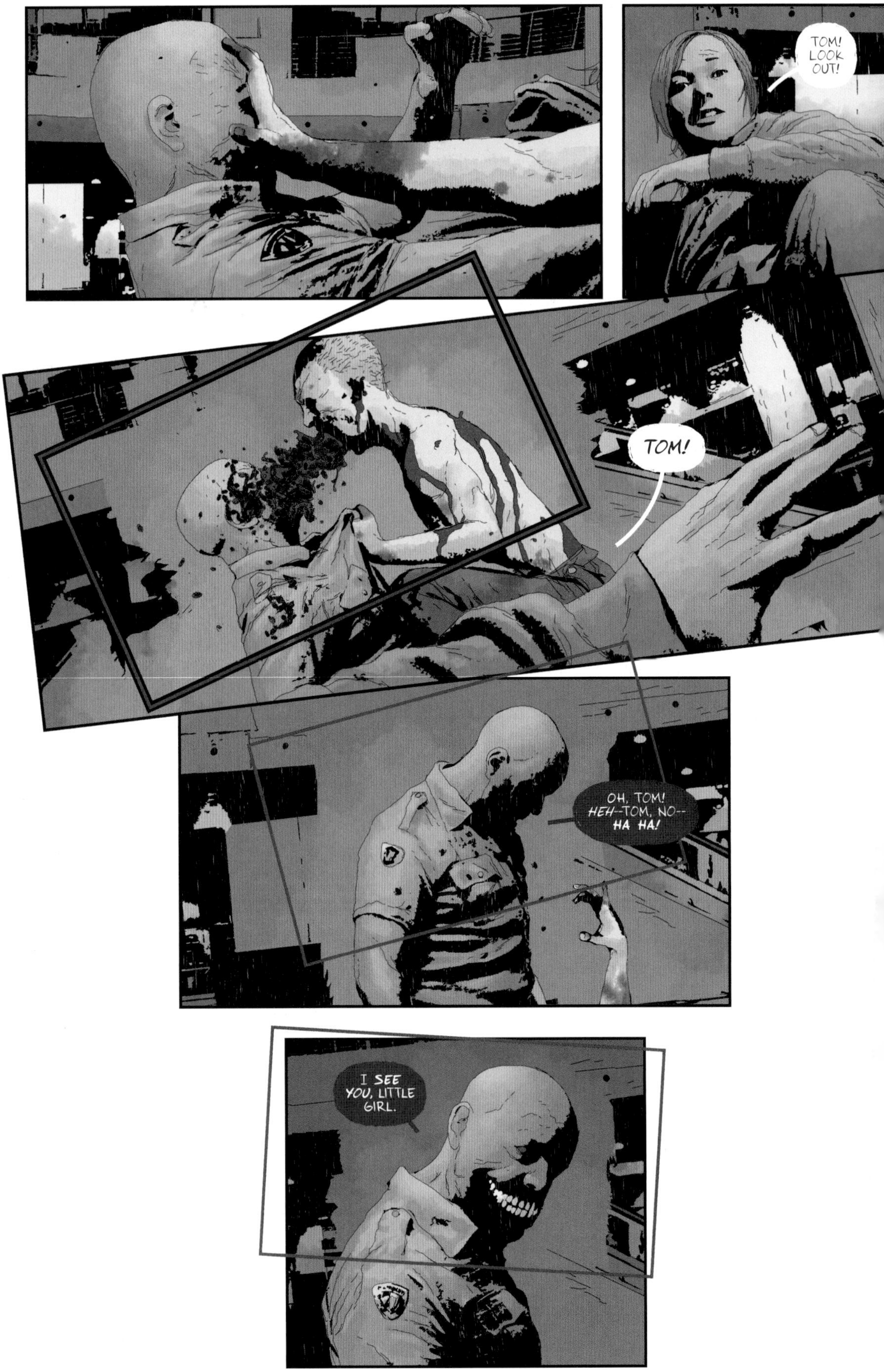
TOM! LOOK OUT!
TOM!
OH, TOM! HEH--TOM, NO-- HA HA!
I SEE YOU, LITTLE GIRL.

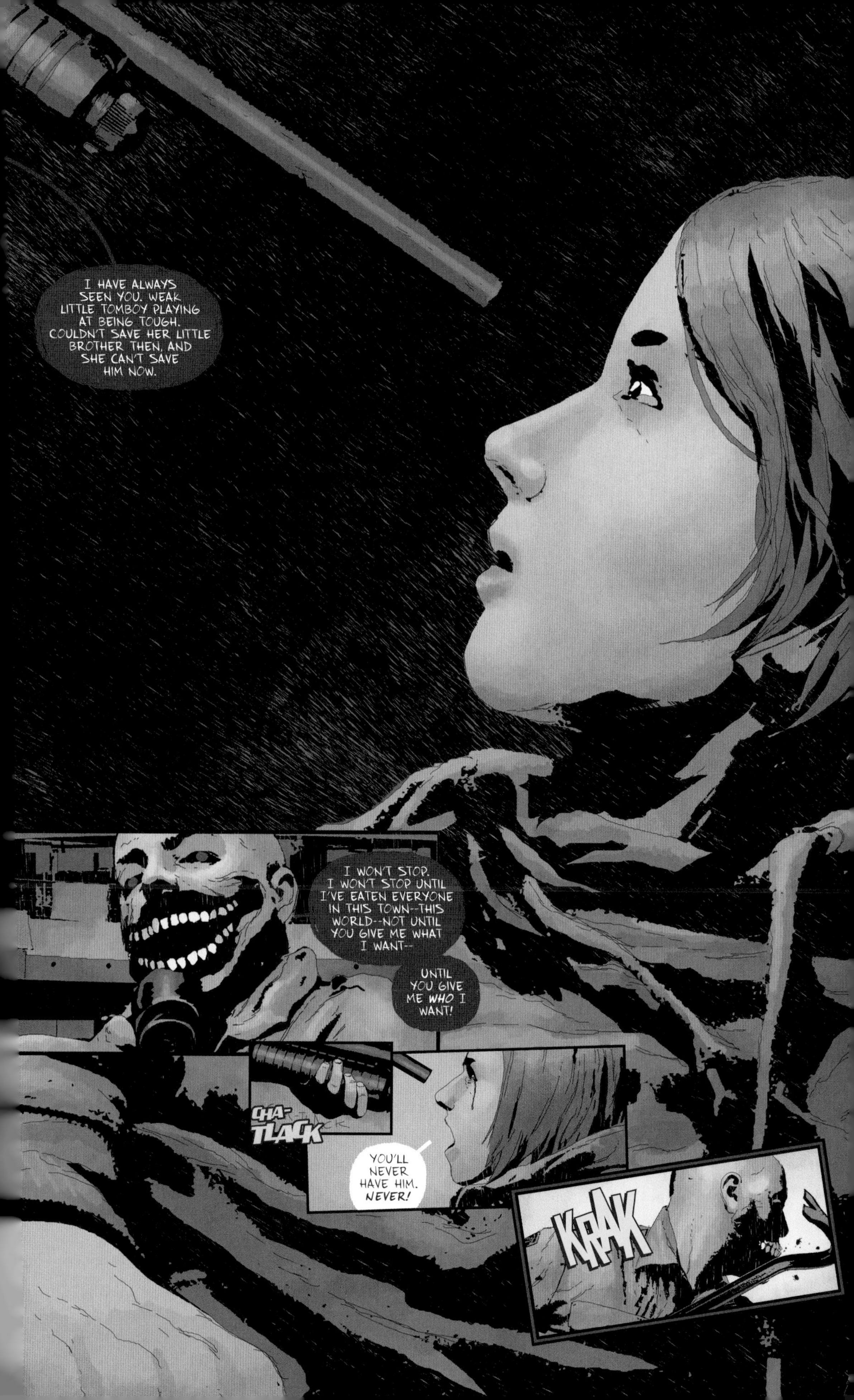
I HAVE ALWAYS SEEN YOU. WEAK LITTLE TOMBOY PLAYING AT BEING TOUGH. COULDN'T SAVE HER LITTLE BROTHER THEN, AND SHE CAN'T SAVE HIM NOW.
I WON'T STOP. I WON'T STOP UNTIL I'VE EATEN EVERYONE IN THIS TOWN--THIS WORLD--NOT UNTIL YOU GIVE ME WHAT I WANT--
UNTIL YOU GIVE ME WHO I WANT!
CHA-TLACK
YOU'LL NEVER HAVE HIM. NEVER!
KRAK

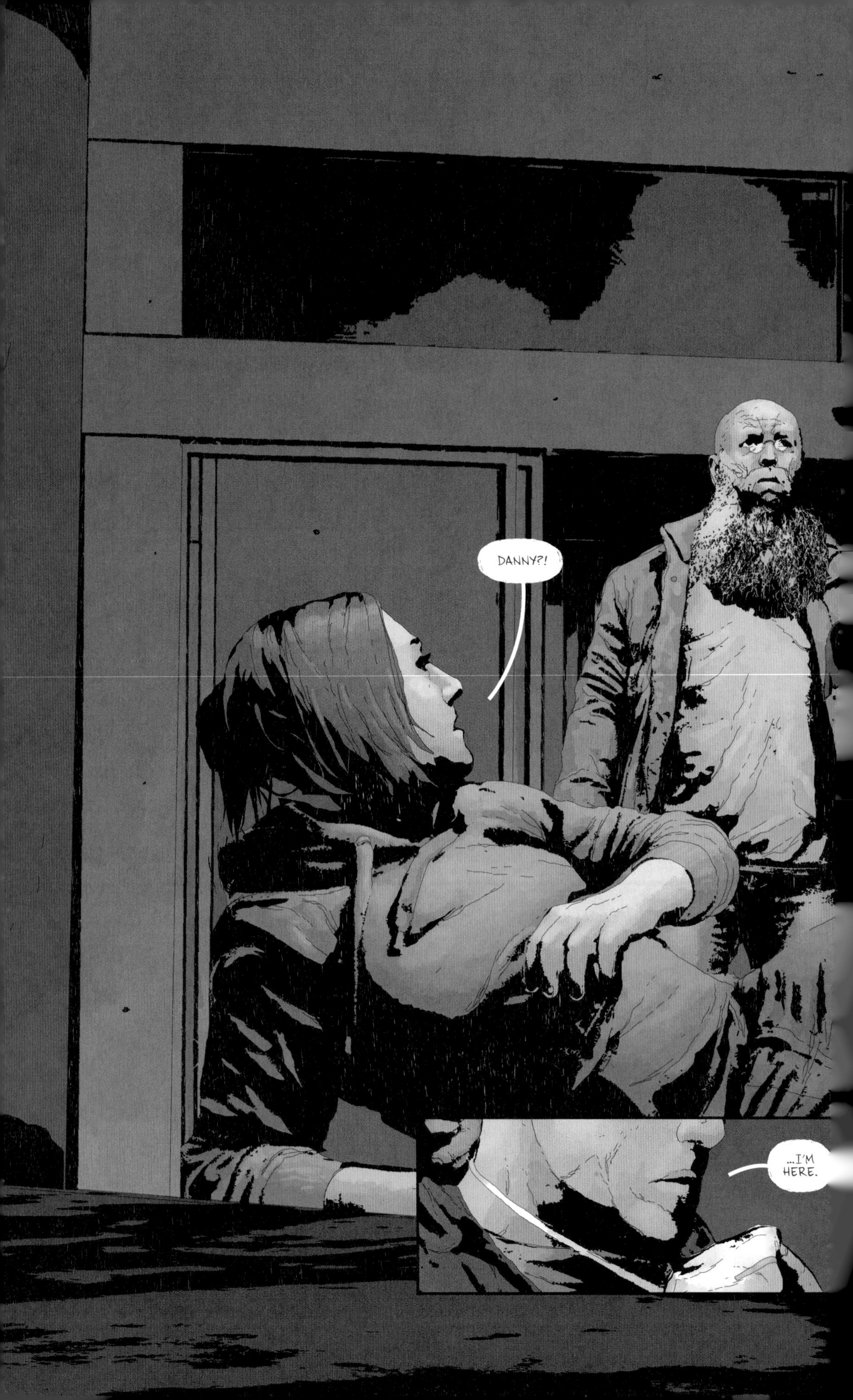
DANNY?!
...I'M HERE.

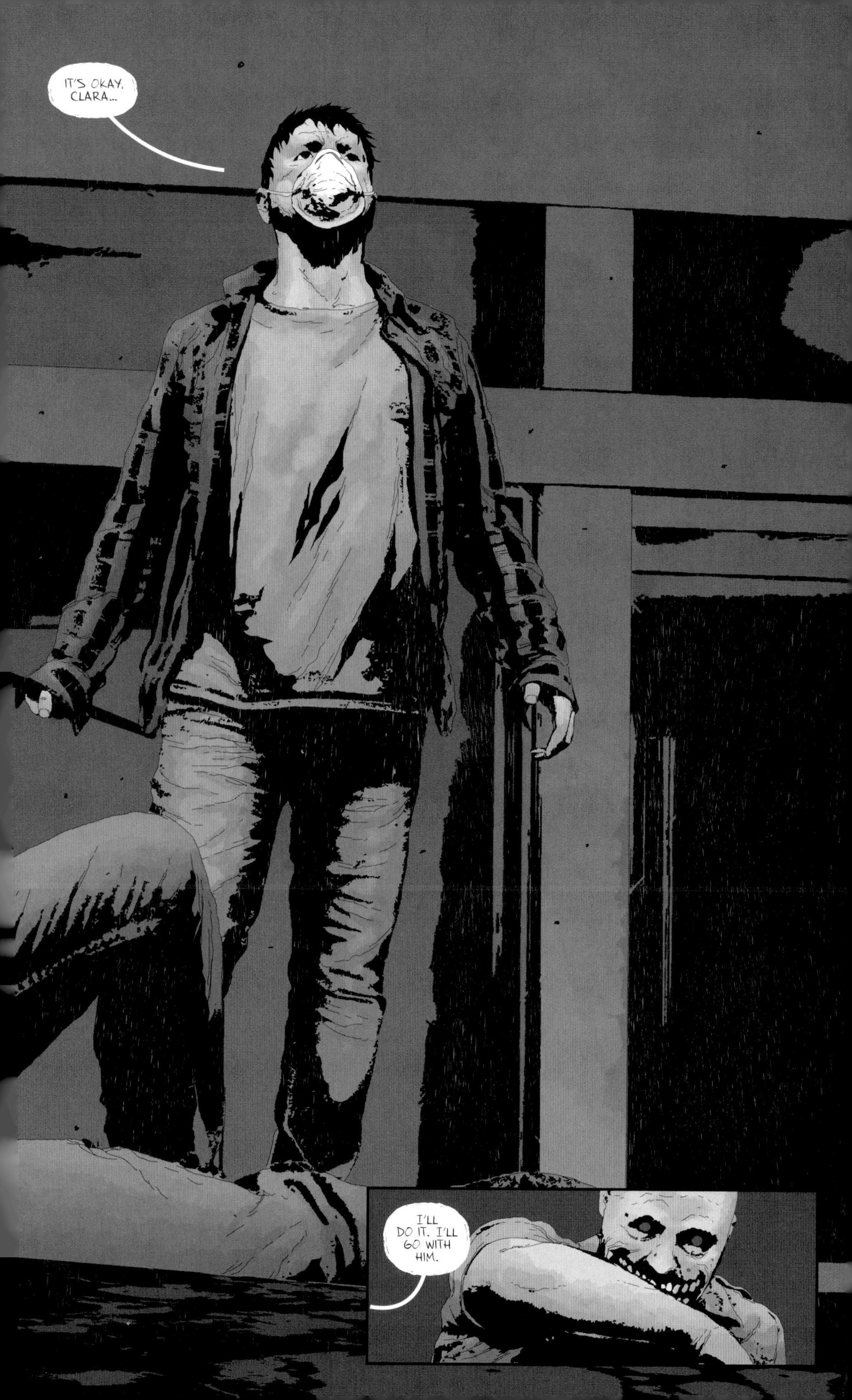
IT'S OKAY, CLARA...
I'LL DO IT. I'LL GO WITH HIM.

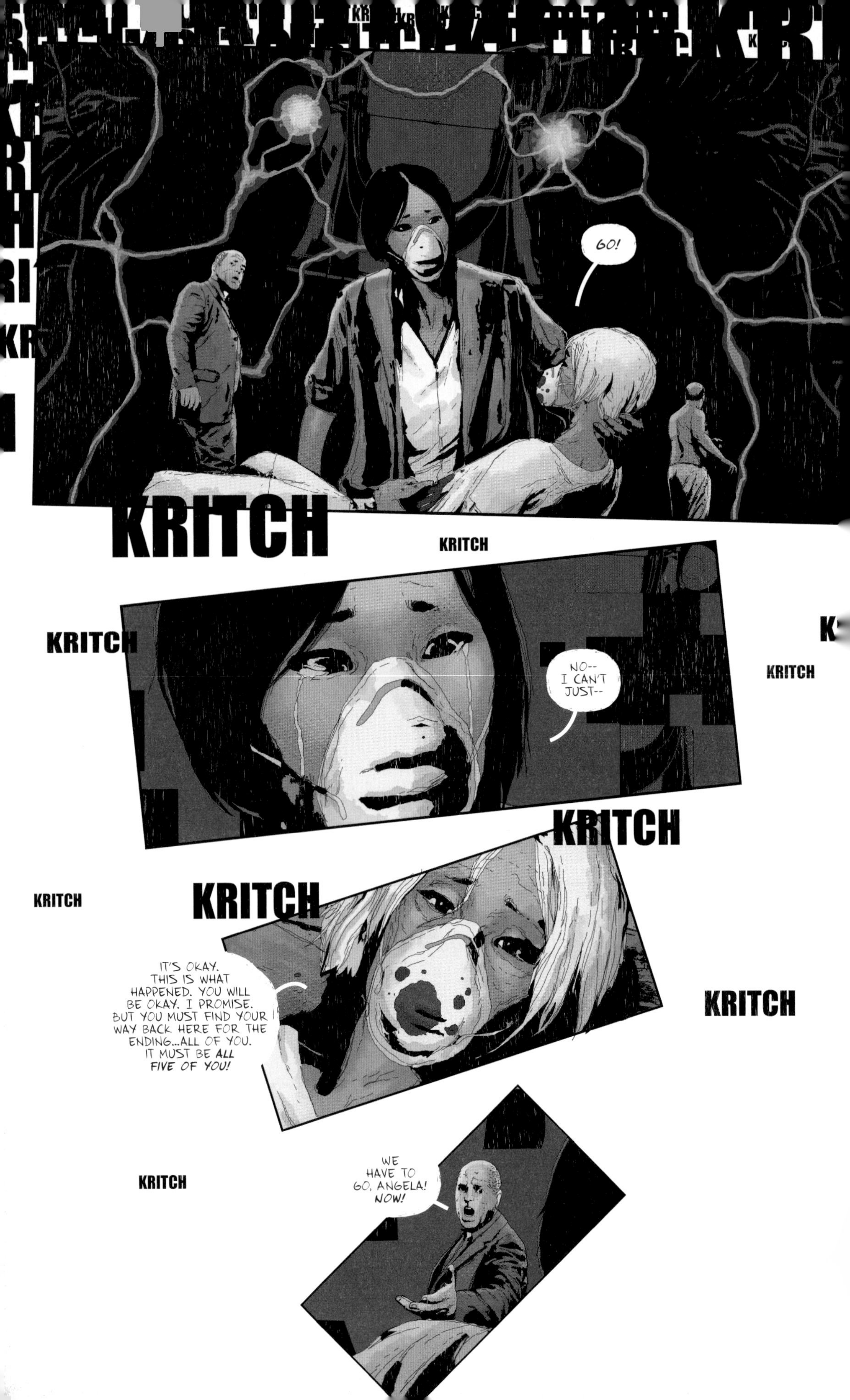
GO!
KRITCH
KRITCH
KRITCH
NO-- I CAN'T JUST--
KRITCH
KRITCH
KRITCH
KRITCH
IT'S OKAY. THIS IS WHAT HAPPENED. YOU WILL BE OKAY. I PROMISE. BUT YOU MUST FIND YOUR WAY BACK HERE FOR THE ENDING...ALL OF YOU. IT MUST BE *ALL FIVE OF YOU!*
KRITCH
KRITCH
WE HAVE TO GO, ANGELA! *NOW!*

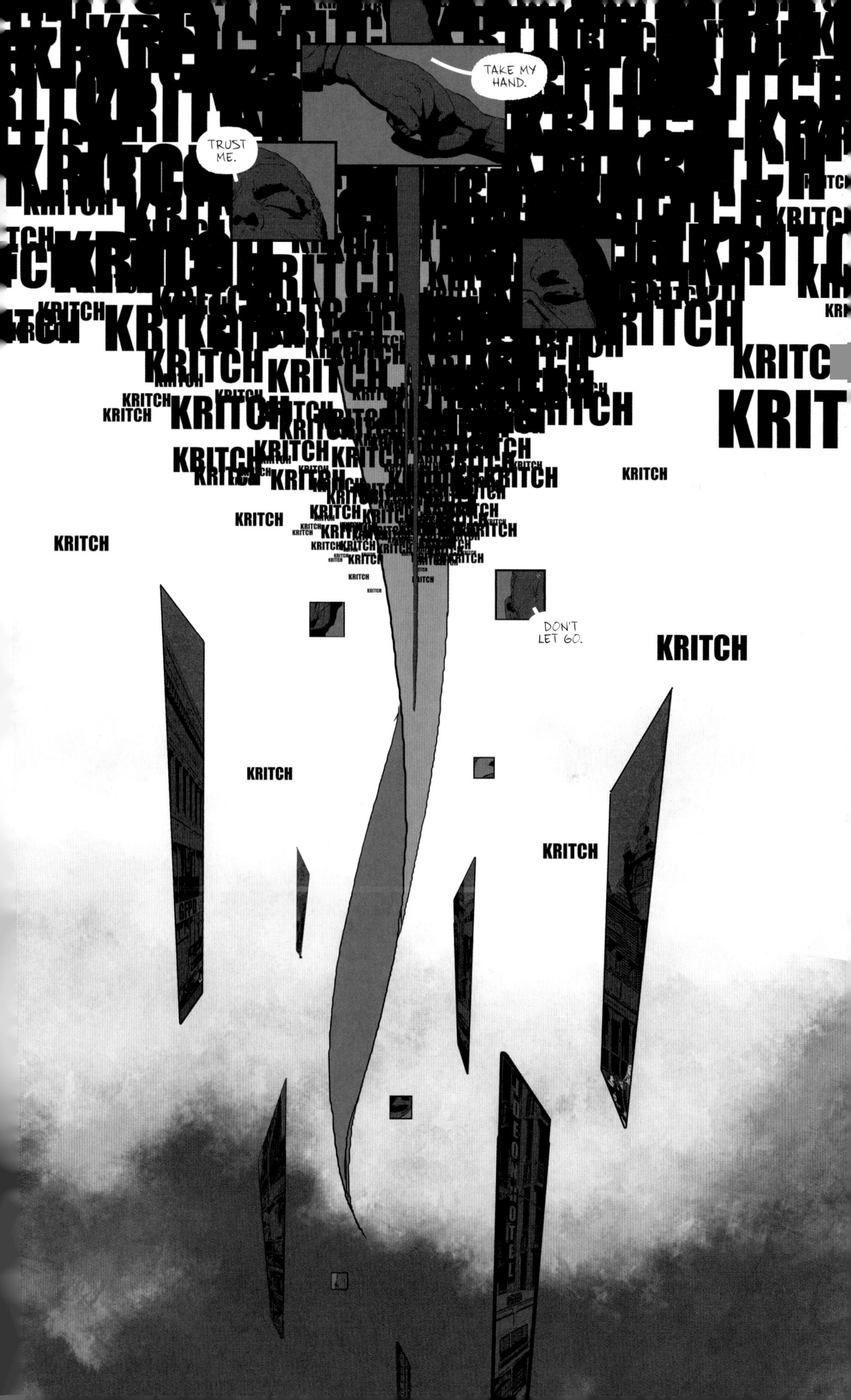
TAKE MY HAND.
TRUST ME.
KRITCH
DON'T LET GO.
KRITCH

DANNY! GET AWAY FROM HERE!

NO, IT'S OKAY. I--I UNDERSTAND NOW. IT WILL STOP IF IT HAS ME.

AH-- MY BOY. MY SPECIAL BOY.

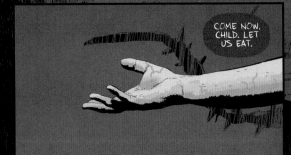

COME NOW, CHILD. LET US EAT.

GET THE FUCK AWAY FROM MY BROTHER!

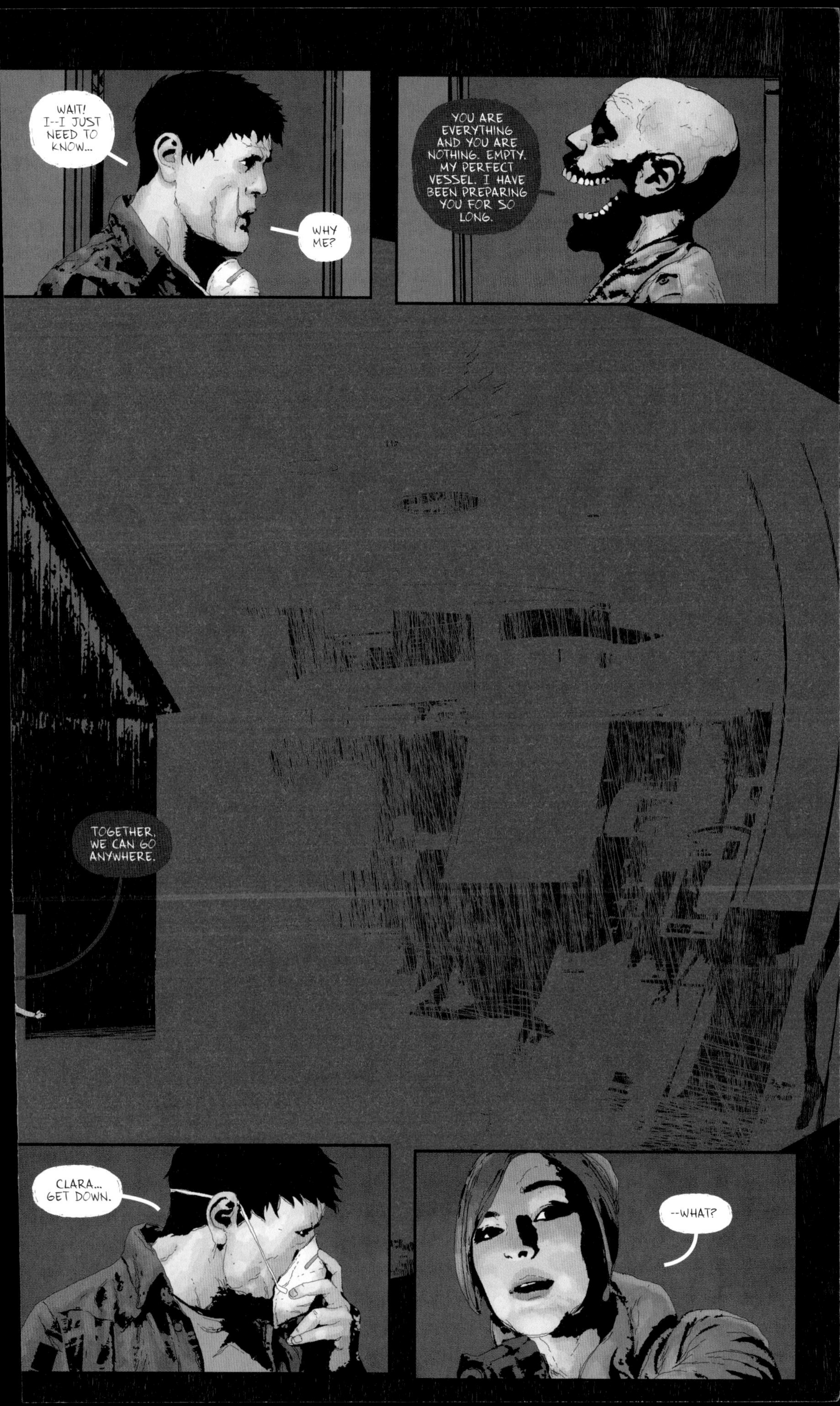
WAIT! I--I JUST NEED TO KNOW...
WHY ME?
YOU ARE EVERYTHING AND YOU ARE NOTHING. EMPTY. MY PERFECT VESSEL. I HAVE BEEN PREPARING YOU FOR SO LONG.
TOGETHER, WE CAN GO ANYWHERE.
CLARA... GET DOWN.
--WHAT?

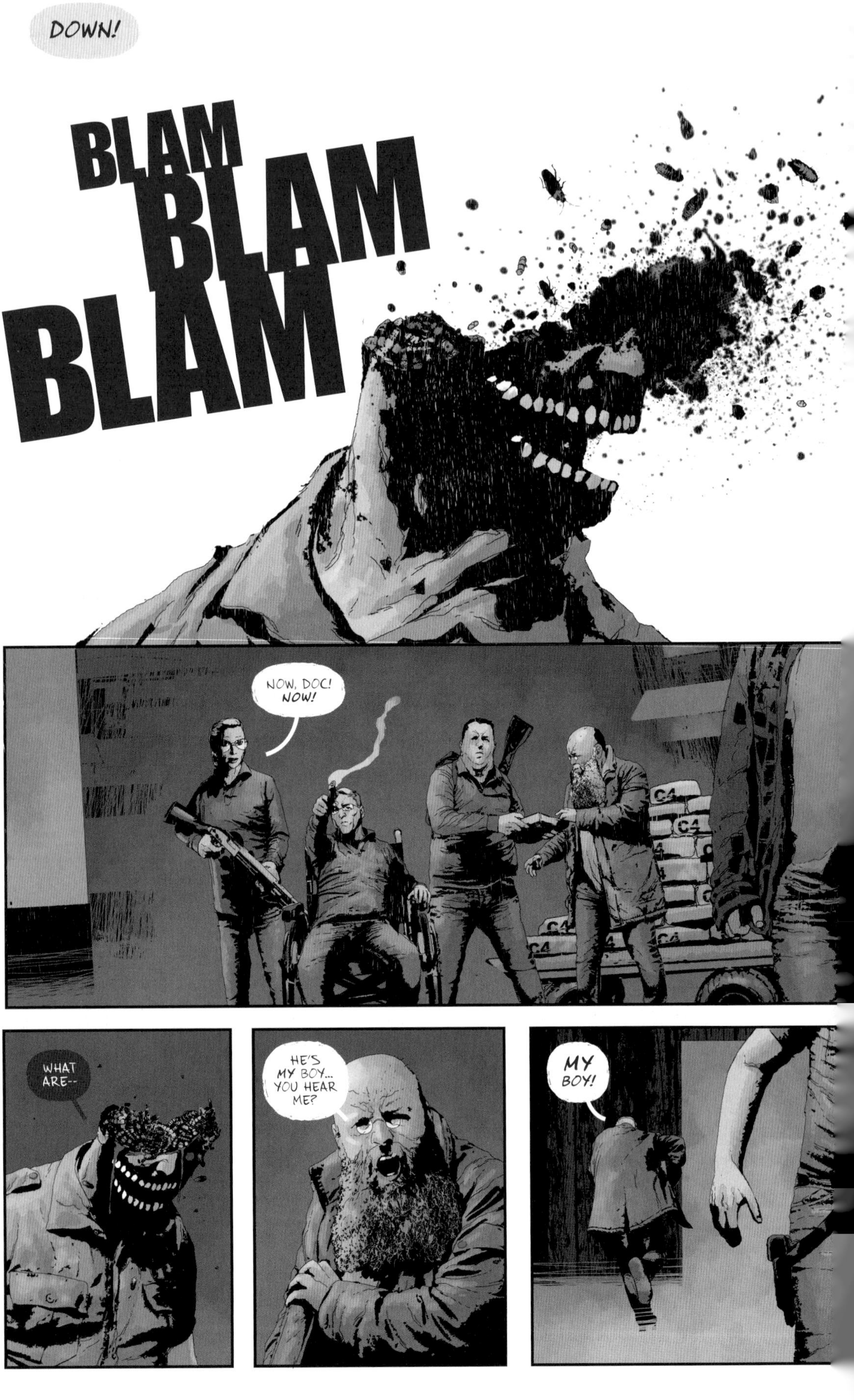
DOWN!
BLAM BLAM BLAM
NOW, DOC! NOW!
WHAT ARE--
HE'S MY BOY... YOU HEAR ME?
MY BOY!

REGGIE! LOOK OUT!
LITTLE THINGS--SILLY LITTLE THINGS.
FRONT TOWARD ENEMY
THIS IS OVER, YOU SON OF A BITCH. OVER!
NOTHING ENDS. NOTHING.
--UNGH!
DAD!
NO!
BLAM

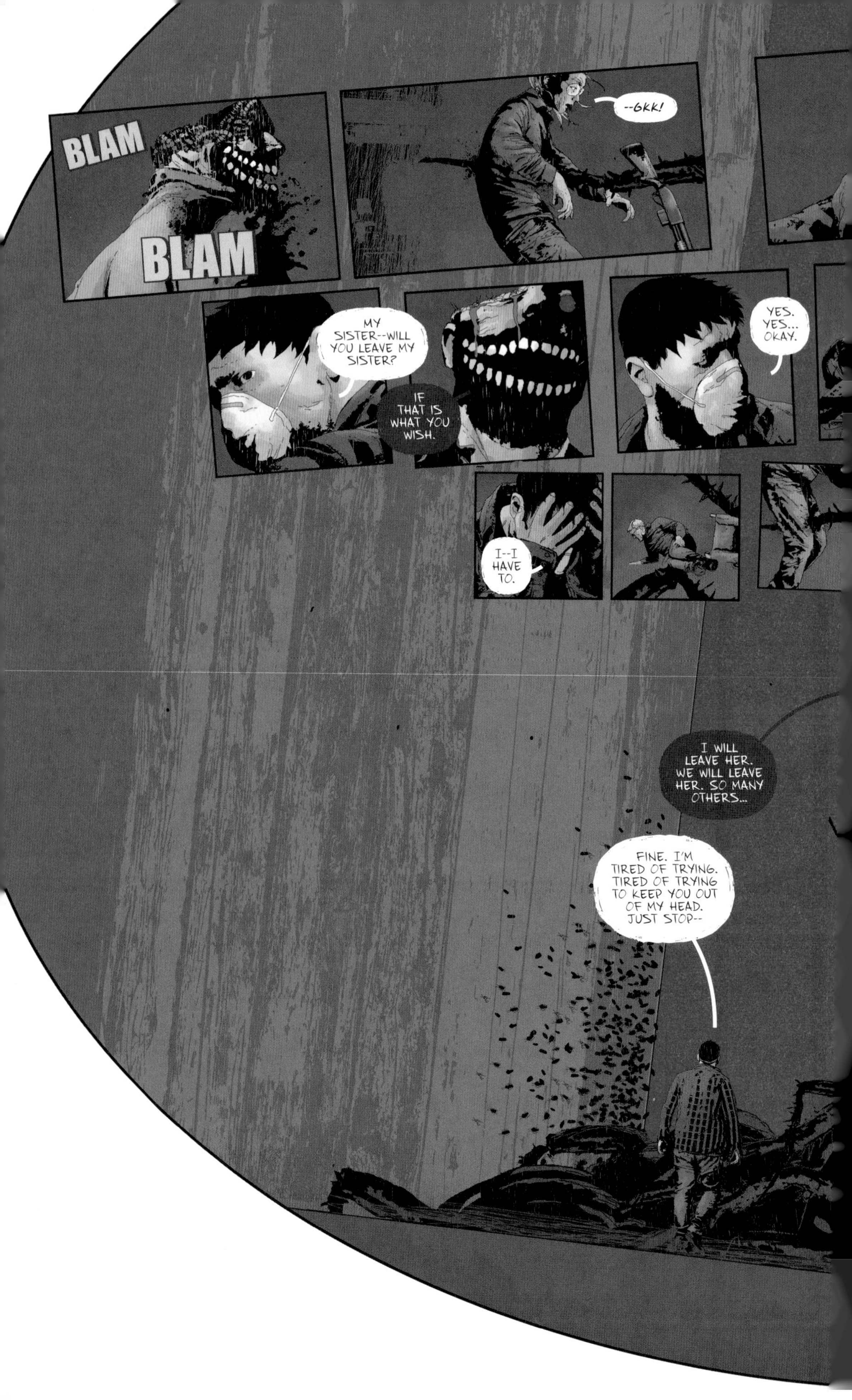
BLAM
BLAM
--GKK!
MY SISTER--WILL YOU LEAVE MY SISTER?
IF THAT IS WHAT YOU WISH.
YES. YES... OKAY.
I--I HAVE TO.
I WILL LEAVE HER. WE WILL LEAVE HER. SO MANY OTHERS...
FINE. I'M TIRED OF TRYING. TIRED OF TRYING TO KEEP YOU OUT OF MY HEAD. JUST STOP--

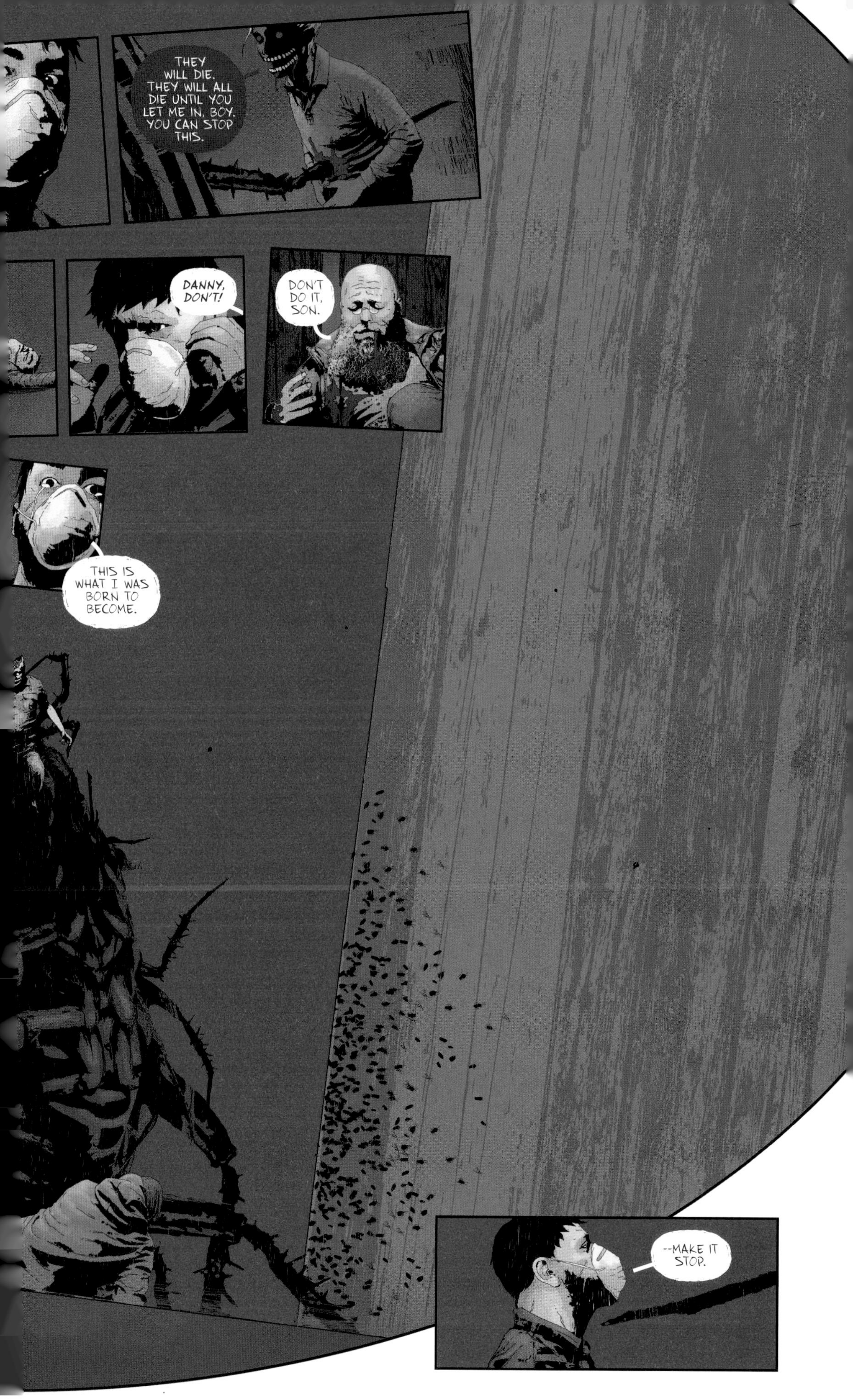
THEY WILL DIE. THEY WILL ALL DIE UNTIL YOU LET ME IN, BOY. YOU CAN STOP THIS.
DANNY, DON'T!
DON'T DO IT, SON.
THIS IS WHAT I WAS BORN TO BECOME.
--MAKE IT STOP.

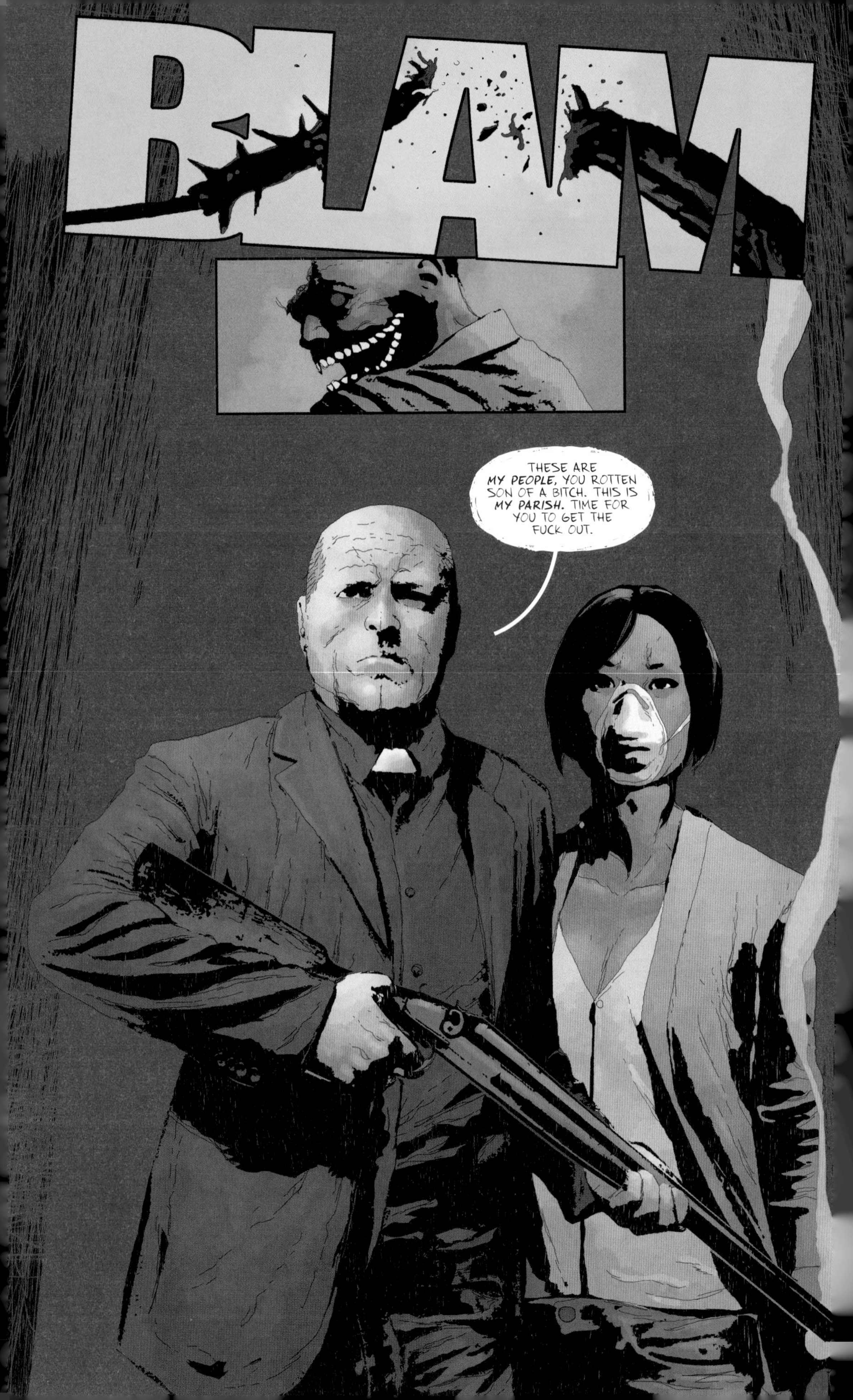
BLAM
THESE ARE MY PEOPLE, YOU ROTTEN SON OF A BITCH. THIS IS MY PARISH. TIME FOR YOU TO GET THE FUCK OUT.

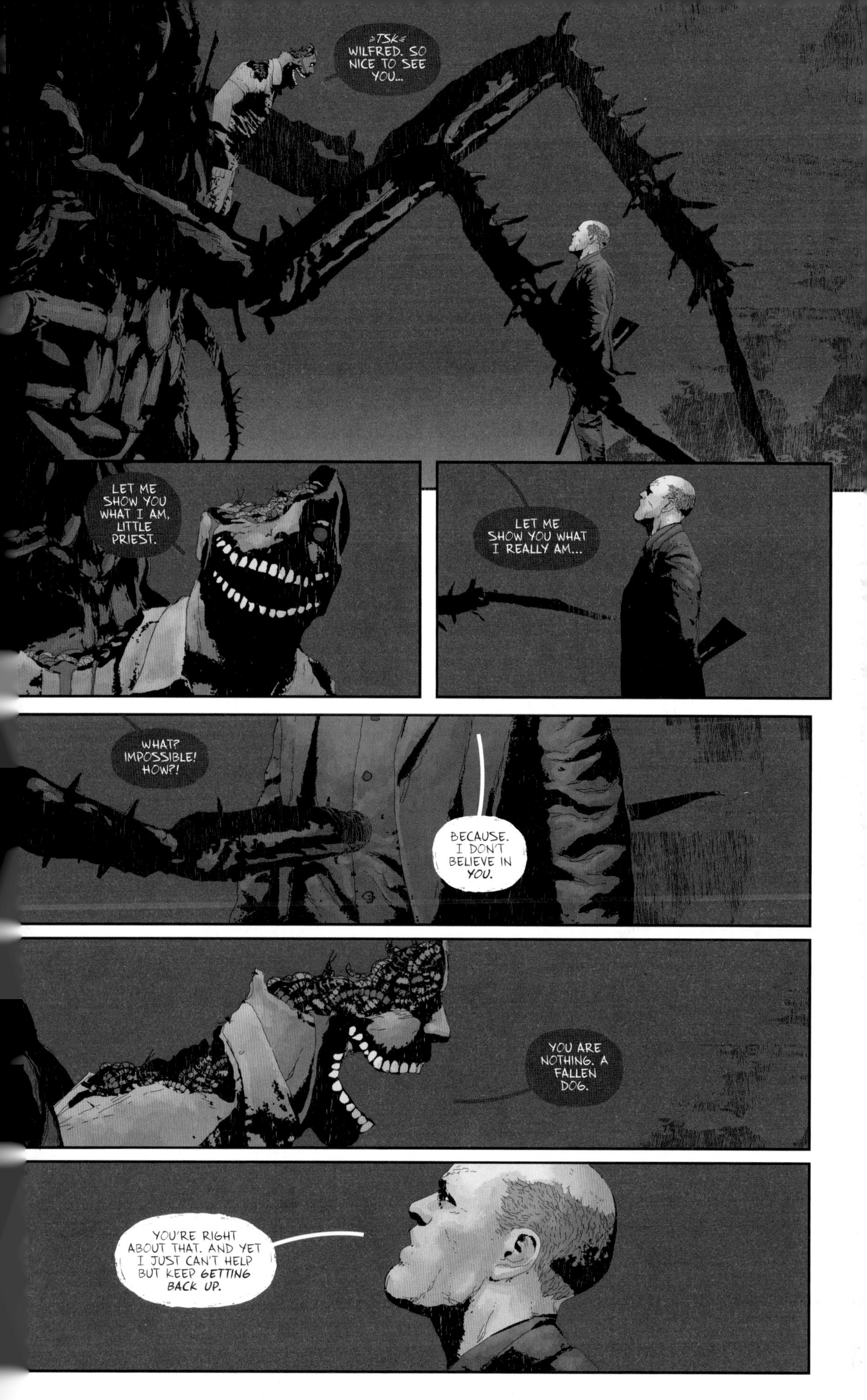

TSK
WILFRED. SO NICE TO SEE YOU...
LET ME SHOW YOU WHAT I AM, LITTLE PRIEST.
LET ME SHOW YOU WHAT I REALLY AM...
WHAT? IMPOSSIBLE! HOW?!
BECAUSE. I DON'T BELIEVE IN *YOU*.
YOU ARE NOTHING. A FALLEN DOG.
YOU'RE RIGHT ABOUT THAT. AND YET I JUST CAN'T HELP BUT KEEP **GETTING BACK UP**.

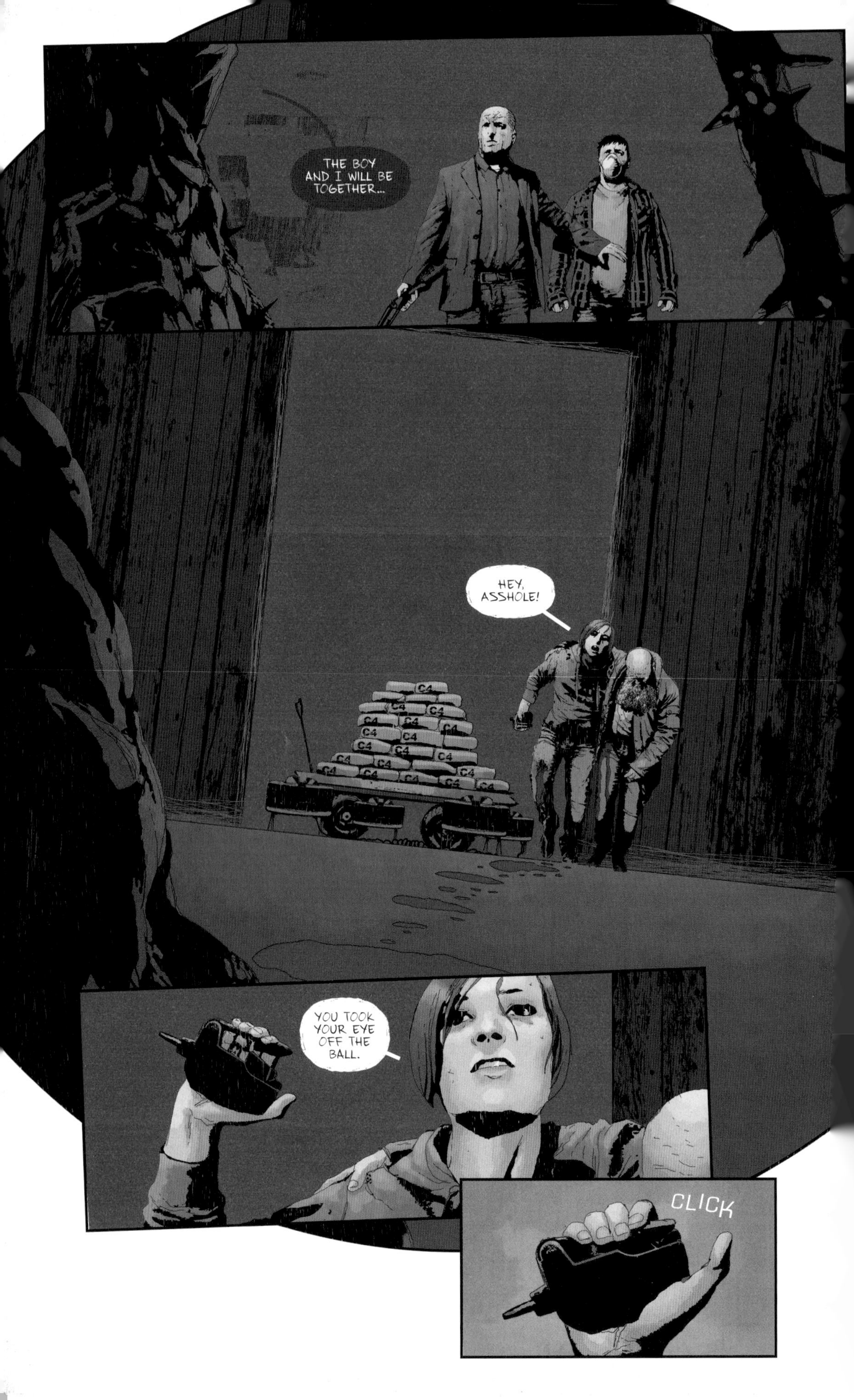
THE BOY AND I WILL BE TOGETHER...
HEY, ASSHOLE!
YOU TOOK YOUR EYE OFF THE BALL.
CLICK

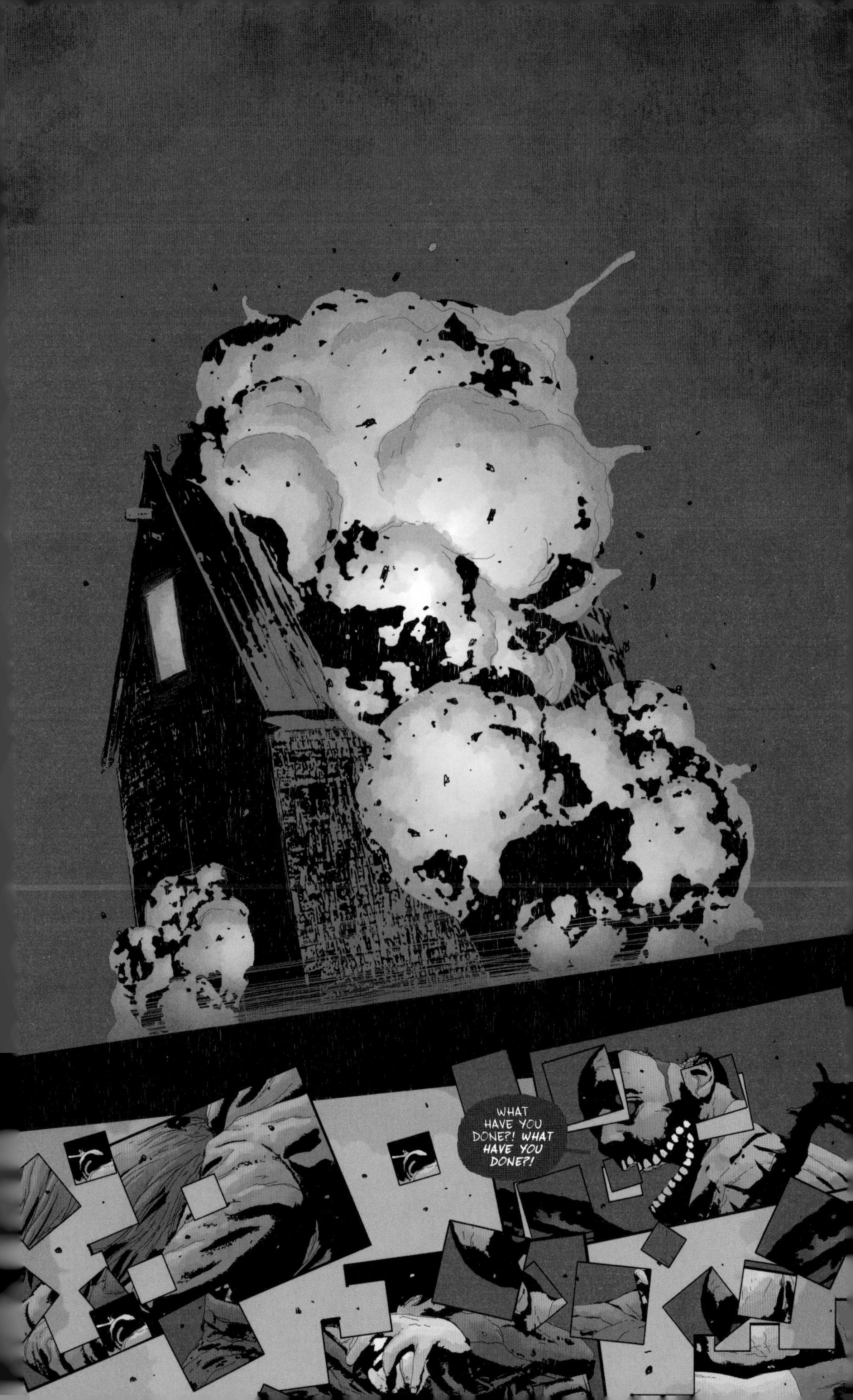
WHAT HAVE YOU DONE?! WHAT HAVE YOU DONE?!

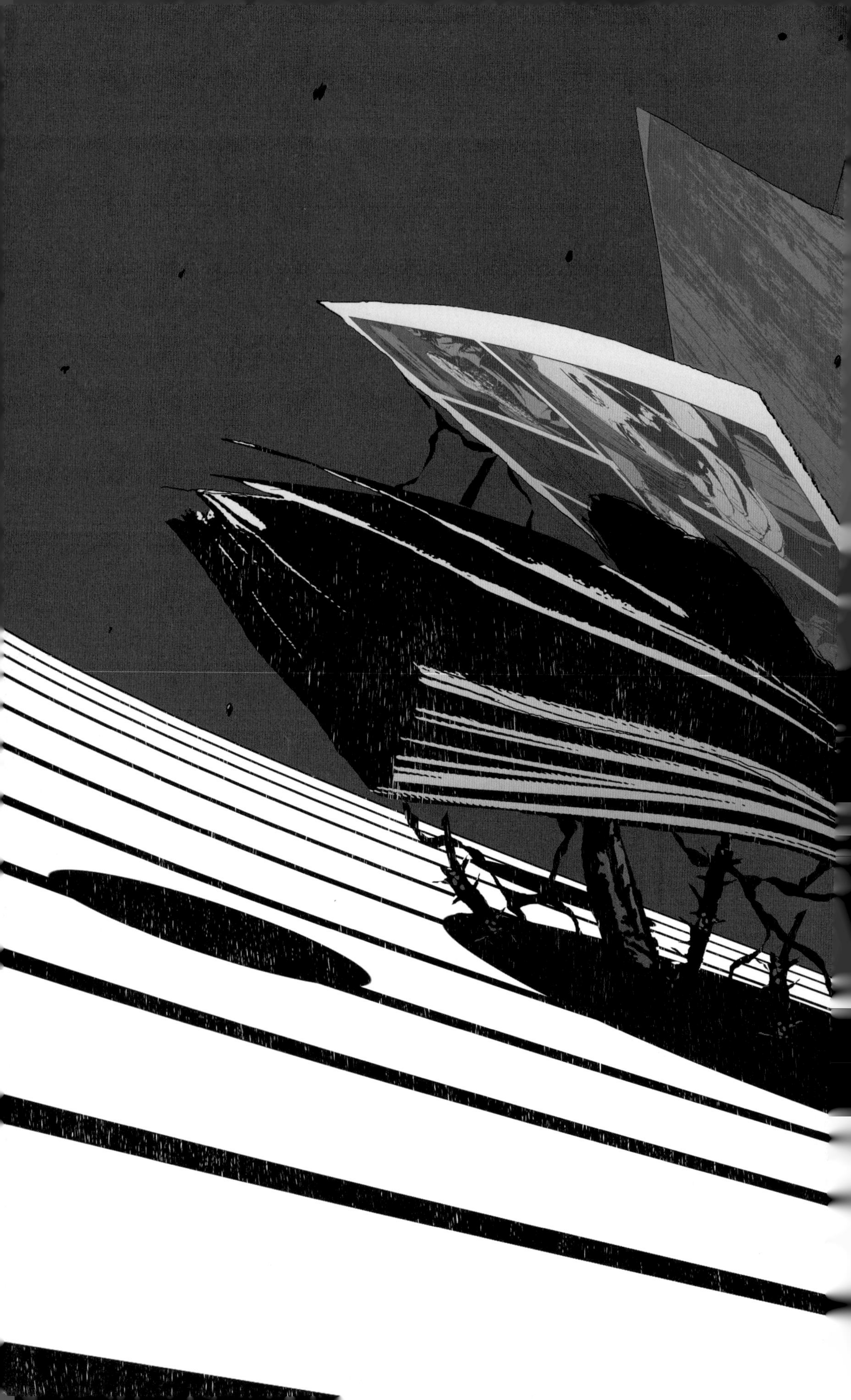

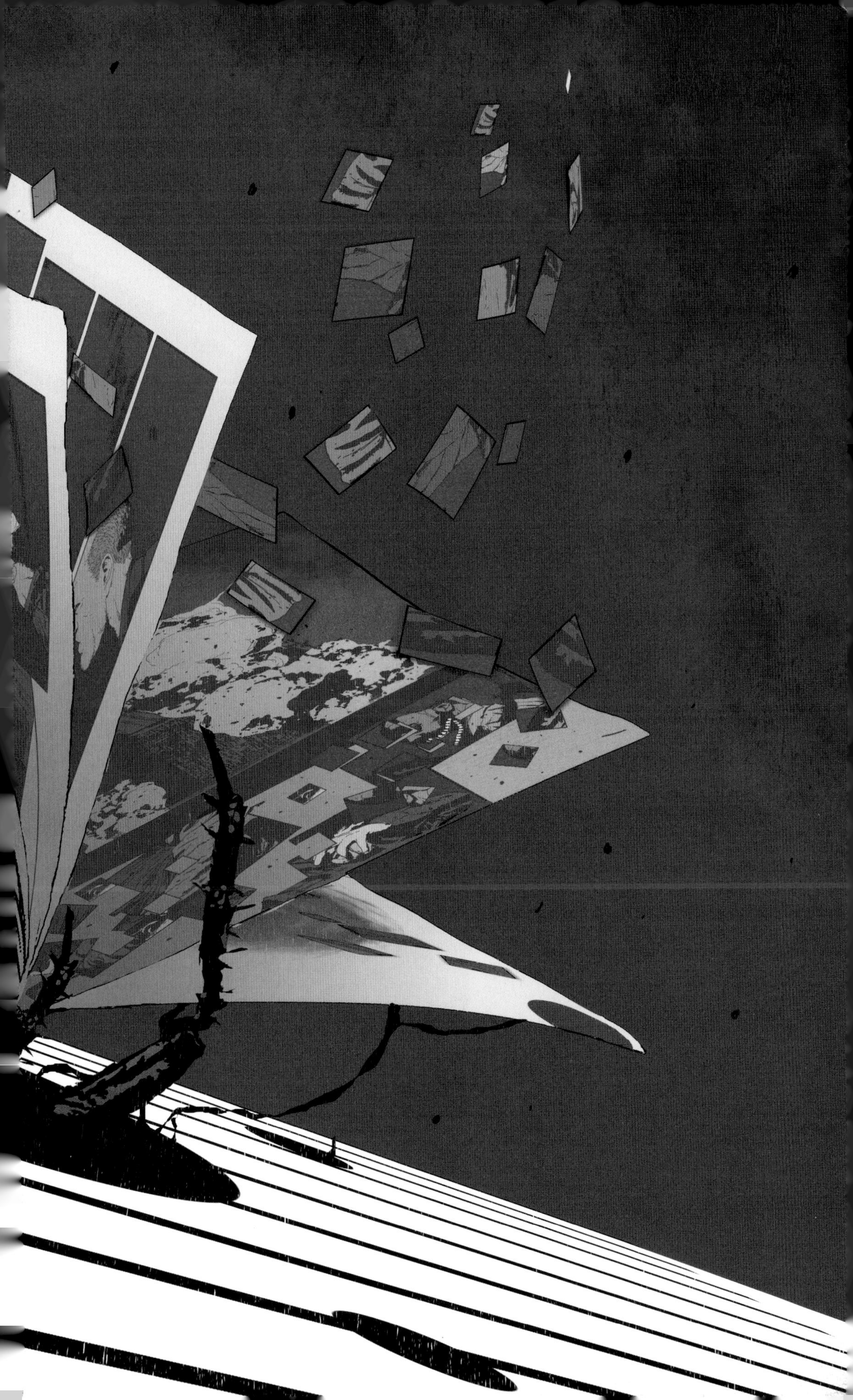

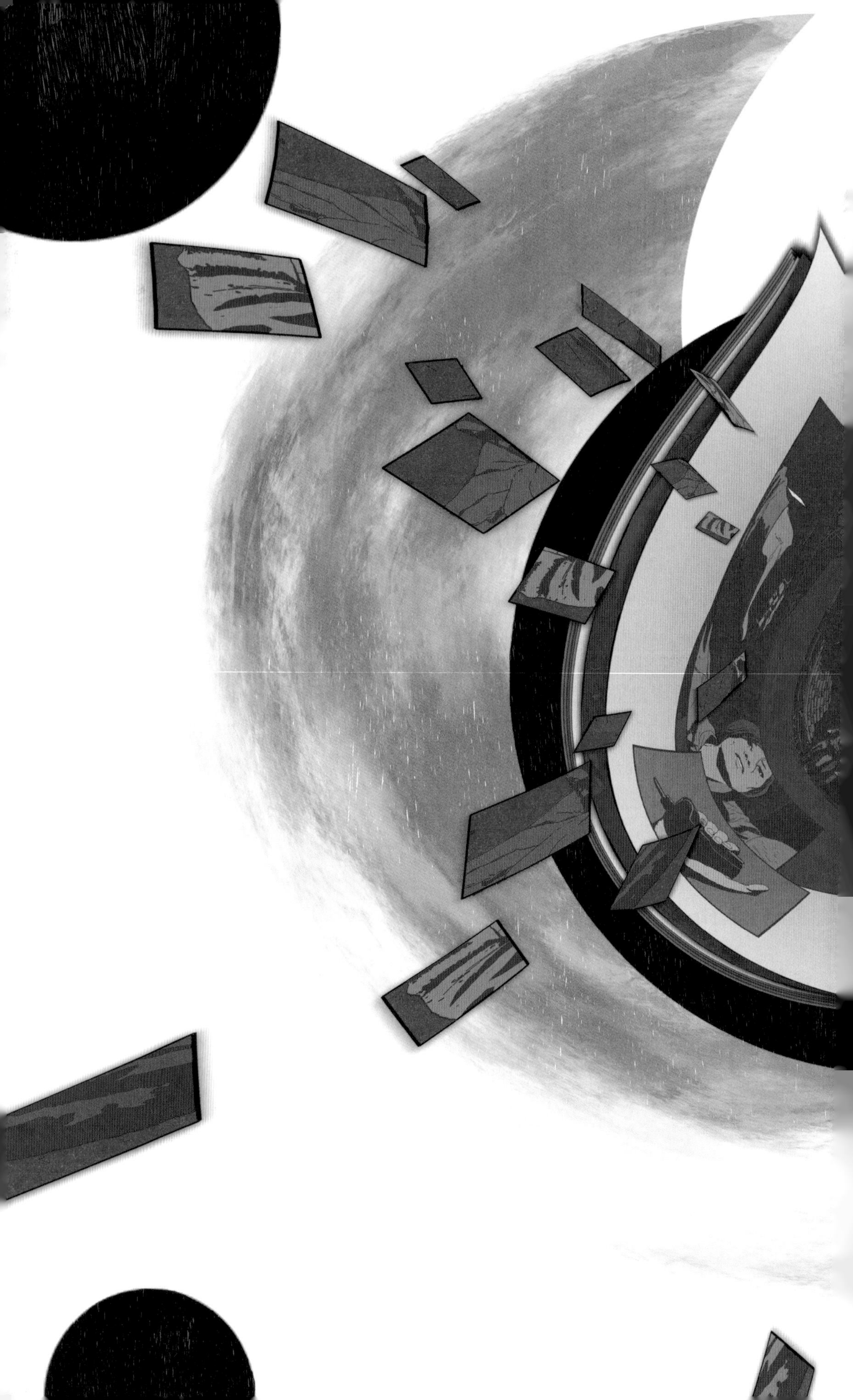

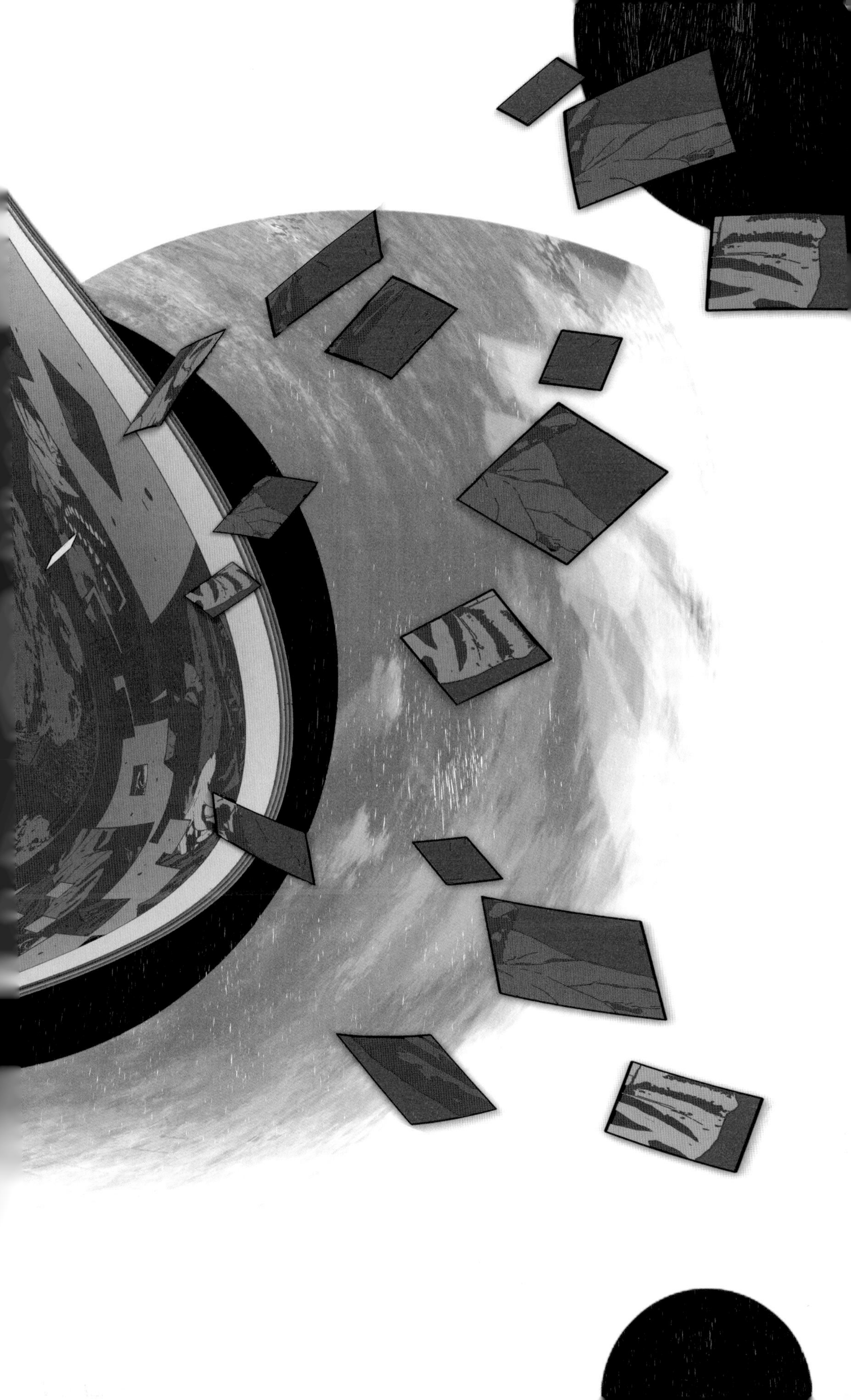

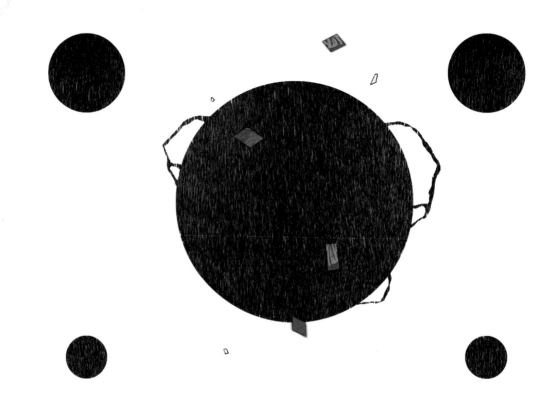

End of book